Toni Cade Bambara
THE SALT EATERS

Toni Cade Bambara is the author of two short story collections *Gorilla My Love* and *Seabirds Are Still Alive*. She has also edited *The Black Woman* and *Tales and Short Stories for Black Folks*. Ms. Bambara's works have appeared in various periodicals and have been translated into several languages. She died in December 1995.

ALSO BY **Toni Cade Bambara**

THE SALT EATERS

THE SALT EATERS

by
Toni Cade Bambara

VINTAGE CONTEMPORARIES

VINTAGE BOOKS

A DIVISION OF RANDOM HOUSE, INC.

NEW YORK

FIRST VINTAGE CONTEMPORARIES EDITION, JULY 1992

Copyright © 1980 by Toni Cade Bambara

Library of Congress Cataloging-in-Publication Data
Bambara, Toni Cade.
    The salt eaters / by Toni Cade Bambara.—1st Vintage
contemporaries ed.
        p.   cm.—(Vintage contemporaries)
    ISBN 0-679-74076-7 (pbk.)
    I. Title.
PS3552.A473S2   1992
813'.54—dc20   91-50902
                        CIP

Manufactured in the United States of America
10   9

Dear Khufu—

The manuscript, assembled finally in the second and third years of the Last Quarter and edited under Leo's double moons, was initially typed by Loretta Hardge and is dedicated to my first friend, teacher, map maker, landscape aide

Mama
Helen Brent Henderson Cade Brehon

who in 1948, having come upon me daydreaming in the middle of the kitchen floor, mopped around me.

Bless the workers and beam on me if you please.

Thank you,
Toni CB
August 27, 1979

THE SALT EATERS

one

"Are you sure, sweetheart, that you want to be well?"

Velma Henry turned stiffly on the stool, the gown ties tight across her back, the knots hard. So taut for so long, she could not swivel. Neck, back, hip joints dry, stiff. Face frozen. She could not glower, suck her teeth, roll her eyes, do any of the Velma-things by way of answering Minnie Ransom, who sat before her humming lazily up and down the scales, making a big to-do of draping her silky shawl, handling it as though it were a cape she'd swirl any minute over Velma's head in a wipe-out veronica, or as though it were a bath towel she was drying her back with in the privacy of her bathroom.

Minnie Ransom herself, the fabled healer of the district, her bright-red flouncy dress drawn in at the waist with two different strips of kenti cloth, up to her elbows in a minor fortune of gold, brass and silver bangles, the silken fringe of the shawl shimmying at her armpits. Her head, wrapped in some juicy hot-pink gelee, was tucked way back into her neck, eyes peering down her nose at Velma as though old-timey spectacles perched there were slipping down.

Velma blinked. Was ole Minnie trying to hypnotize her, mesmerize her? Minnie Ransom, the legendary spinster of Claybourne, Georgia, spinning out a song, drawing *her* of all people up. Velma the swift; Velma the elusive; Velma who had never mastered the kicks, punches and defense blocks, but who had down cold the art of being not there when the blow came. Velma caught, caught up, in the weave of the song Minnie was humming, of the shawl, of the threads, of the silvery tendrils that extended from the healer's neck and hands and disappeared into the sheen of the sunlight. The glistening bangles, the metallic threads, the dancing fringe, the humming like bees. And was the ole swamphag actually sitting there dressed for days, legs crossed, one foot swinging gently against the table where she'd stacked the tapes and records? Sitting there flashing her bridgework and asking some stupid damn question like that, blind to Velma's exasperation, her pain, her humiliation?

Velma could see herself: hair matted and dusty, bandages unraveled and curled at the foot of the stool like a sleeping snake, the hospital gown huge in front, but tied up too tight in back, the breeze from the window billowing out the rough white muslin and widening the opening in the back. She could not focus enough to remember whether she had panties on or not. And Minnie Ransom perched on her stool actually waiting on an answer, drawling out her hummingsong, unconcerned that any minute she might strike the very note that could shatter Velma's bones.

"I like to caution folks, that's all." said Minnie, interrupting her own humming to sigh and say it, the song somehow buzzing right on. "No sense us wasting each other's time, sweetheart." The song running its own course up under the words, up under Velma's hospital gown, notes pressing against her skin and Velma steeling herself against intrusion. "A lot of weight when you're well. Now, you just hold that thought."

Velma didn't know how she was to do that. She could barely manage to hold on to herself, hold on to the stingy stool, be there all of a piece and resist the buzzing bee tune coming at her. Now her whole purpose was surface, to go smooth, be sealed and inviolate.

She tried to withdraw as she'd been doing for weeks and weeks. Withdraw the self to a safe place where husband, lover, teacher, workers, no one could follow, probe. Withdraw her self and prop up a borderguard to negotiate with would-be intruders. She'd been a borderguard all her childhood, so she knew something about it. She was the one sent to the front door to stand off the landlord, the insurance man, the greengrocer, the fishpeddler, to insure Mama Mae one more bit of peace. And at her godmother's, it was Smitty who sent her to the front door to misdirect the posse. No, no one of that name lived here. No, this was not where the note from the principal should be delivered.

She wasn't sure how to move away from Minnie Ransom and from the music, where to throw up the barrier and place the borderguard. She wasn't sure whether she'd been hearing music anyway. Was certain, though, that she didn't know what she was supposed to say or do on that stool. Wasn't even sure whether it was time to breathe in or breathe out. Everything was off, out of whack, the relentless logic she'd lived by sprung. And here she was in Minnie Ransom's hands in the Southwest Community Infirmary. Anything could happen. She could roll off the stool like a ball of wax and melt right through the floor, or sail out of the window, stool and all, and become some new kind of UFO. Anything could happen. And hadn't Ole Minnie been nattering away about just that before the session had begun, before she had wiped down the stools and set them out just so? "In the last quarter, sweetheart, anything can happen. And will," she'd said. Last quarter? Of the moon, of the century, of some damn basketball game? Velma had been, still was, too messed around to figure it out.

"You just hold that thought," Minnie was saying again, leaning forward, the balls of three fingers pressed suddenly, warm and fragrant, against Velma's forehead, the left hand catching her in the back of her head, cupping gently the two stony portions of the temporal bone. And Velma was inhaling in gasps, and exhaling shudderingly. She felt aglow, her eyebrows drawing in toward the touch as if to ward off the invading fingers that were threatening to penetrate her skull. And then the hands went away quickly, and Velma felt she was losing her eyes.

"Hold on now," she heard. It was said the way Mama Mae would say it, leaving her bent in the sink while she went to get a washcloth to wipe the shampoo from her eyes. Velma held on to herself. Her pocketbook on the rungs below, the backless stool in the middle of the room, the hospital gown bunched up now in the back—there was nothing but herself and some dim belief in the reliability of stools to hold on to. But then the old crone had had a few choice words to say about that too, earlier, rearing back on her heels and pressing her knees against the stereo while Velma perched uneasily on the edge of her stool trying to listen, trying to wait patiently for the woman to sit down and get on with it, trying to follow her drift, scrambling to piece together key bits of high school physics, freshman philo, and lessons M'Dear Sophie and Mama Mae had tried to impart. The reliability of stools? Solids, liquids, gases, the dance of atoms, the bounce and race of molecules, ethers, electrical charges. The eyes and habits of illusion. Retinal images, bogus images, traveling to the brain. The pupils trying to tell the truth to the inner eye. The eye of the heart. The eye of the head. The eye of the mind. All seeing differently.

Velma gazed out over the old woman's head and through the window, feeling totally out of it, her eyes cutting easily through panes and panes and panes of glass and other substances, it seemed, until she slammed into the bark of the tree in the Infirmary yard and recoiled, was back on the stool, breathing in and out in almost a regular rhythm, wondering if it was worth it, submitting herself to this ordeal.

It would have been more restful to have simply slept it off; said no when the nurse had wakened her, no she didn't want to see Miz Minnie; no she didn't want to be bothered right now, but could someone call her husband, her sister, her godmother, somebody, anybody to come sign her out in the morning. But what a rough shock it would have been for the family to see her like that. Obie, Palma, M'Dear Sophie or her son Lil James. Rougher still to be seen. She wasn't meant for these scenes, wasn't meant to be sitting up there in the Southwest Community Infirmary with her ass out, in the middle of the day, and strangers cluttering up the treatment room, ogling her in her misery. She wasn't meant for any of it. But then M'Dear Sophie always said, "Find meaning where you're put, Vee." So she exhaled deeply and tried to relax and stick it out and pay attention.

Rumor was these sessions never lasted more than ten or fifteen minutes anyway. It wouldn't kill her to go along with the thing. Wouldn't kill her. She almost laughed. She might have died. *I might have died.* It was an incredible thought now. She sat there holding on to *that* thought, waiting for Minnie Ransom to quit playing to the gallery and get on with it. Sat there, every cell flooded with the light of that idea, with the rhythm of her own breathing, with the sensation of having not died at all at any time, not on the attic stairs, not at the kitchen drawer, not in the ambulance, not on the operating table, not in that other place where the mud mothers were painting the walls of the cave and calling to her, not in the sheets she thrashed out in strangling her legs, her rib cage, fighting off the woman with snakes in her hair, the crowds that moved in and out of each other around the bed trying to tell her about the difference between snakes and serpents, the difference between eating salt as an antidote to snakebite and turning into salt, succumbing to the serpent.

"Folks come in here," Minnie Ransom was saying, "moaning and carrying on and *say* they wanna be well. Don't know what in heaven and hell they want." She had uncrossed her legs, had spread her legs out and was resting on the heels of her T-strap, beige suedes, the black soles up and visible. And she was leaning forward toward Velma, poking yards of dress down between her knees. She looked like a farmer in a Halston, a snuff dipper in a Givenchy.

"Just this morning, fore they rolled you in with your veins open and your face bloated, this great big overgrown woman came in here tearing at her clothes, clawing at her hair, wailing to beat the band, asking for some pills. Wanted a pill cause she was in pain, felt bad, wanted to feel good. You ready?"

Velma studied the woman's posture, the rope veins in the back of her hands, the purple shadows in the folds of her dress spilling over the stool edge, draping down toward the floor. Velma tried not to get lost in the reds and purples. She understood she was being invited to play straight man in a routine she hadn't rehearsed.

"So I say, 'Sweetheart, what's the matter?' And she says 'My mama died and I feel so bad, I can't go on' and dah dah dah. Her mama died, she's *supposed* to feel bad. Expect to feel good when ya mama's gone! Climbed right into my lap," she was nudging Velma to check out the skimp of her lap. "Two hundred pounds of grief and heft if she was one-fifty. Bless her heart, just a babe of the times. Wants to be smiling and feeling good all the time. Smooth sailing as they lower the mama into the ground. Then there's you. What's your story?"

Velma clutched the sides of the stool and wondered what she was supposed to say at this point. What she wanted to do was go away, be somewhere, anywhere, else. But where was there to go? Far as most folks knew, she was at work or out of town.

"As I said, folks come in here moaning and carrying on and *say* they want to be healed. But like the wisdom warns, 'Doan letcha mouf gitcha in what ya backbone caint stand.' " This the old woman said loud enough for the others to hear.

The Infirmary staff, lounging in the rear of the treatment room, leaned away from the walls to grunt approval, though many privately thought this was one helluva way to conduct a healing. Others, who had witnessed the miracle of Minnie Ransom's laying on the hands over the years, were worried. It wasn't like her to be talking on and on, taking so long a time to get started. But then the whole day's program that Doc Serge had arranged for the visitors had been slapdash and sloppy.

The visiting interns, nurses and technicians stood by in crisp white jackets and listened, some in disbelief, others with amusement. Others scratched around in their starchy pockets skeptical, most shifted from foot to foot embarrassed just to be there. And it looked as though the session would run overtime at the rate things were going. There'd never be enough time to get through the day's itinerary. And the bus wasn't going to wait. The driver had made that quite plain. He would be pulling in at 3:08 from his regular run, taking a dinner break, then pulling out sharply with the charter bus at 5:30. That too had been printed up on the itinerary, but the Infirmary hosts did not seem to be alert to the demands of time.

The staff, asprawl behind the visitors on chairs, carts, table corners, swinging their legs and doing manicures with the edges of matchbooks, seemed to be content to watch the show for hours. But less than fifteen minutes ago they'd actually been on the front steps making bets, actually making cash bets with patients and various passers-by, that the healing session would take no more than five or ten minutes. And here it was already going on 3:00 with what could hardly be called an auspicious beginning. The administrator, Dr. Serge, had strolled out, various and sundry folk had come strolling in. The healer had sat there for the longest time playing with her bottom lip, jangling her bracelets, fiddling with the straps of the patient's gown. And now she was goofing around, deliberately, it seemed, exasperating the patient. There seemed to be, many of the visitors concluded, a blatant lack of discipline at the Southwest Community Infirmary that made suspect the reputation it enjoyed in radical medical circles.

"Just so's you're sure, sweetheart, and ready to be healed, cause wholeness is no trifling matter. A lot of weight when you're well."

"That's the truth," muttered one of the "old-timers," as all old folks around the Infirmary were called. "Don't I know the truth of that?" the little woman continued, pushing up the sleeves of her bulky sweater as if home, as if readying up to haul her mother-in-law from wheelchair to toilet, or grab up the mop or tackle the laundry. She would have had more to say about the burdens of the healthy had she not been silenced by an elbow in her side pocket and noticed folks were cutting their eyes at her. Cora Rider hunched her shoulders sharply and tucked her head deep into the turtleneck by way of begging pardon from those around her, many of whom still held their clinic cards and appointment slips in their hands as if passing through the room merely, with no intention of staying for the whole of it.

"Thank you, Spirit" drifted toward her. She searched the faces of the circle of twelve that ringed the two women in the center of the room, wondering whether God was being thanked for giving Miz Minnie the gift or for shutting Cora up. The twelve, or The Master's Mind as some folks called them, stood with heads bowed and hands clasped. Yellow seemed to predominate, yellow and white. Shirts, dresses, smocks, slacks—yellow and white were as much an announcement that a healing session had been scheduled as the notice on the board. The bobbing roses, pink and yellow chiffon flowerettes on Mrs. Sophie Heywood's hat, seemed to suggest that she was the one who'd praised God. Though the gent humming in long meter, his striped tie looking suspiciously like a remnant from a lemonade-stand awning, could just as well have been the one, Cora Rider thought. Though what Mr. Daniels had to be so grateful for all the time was a mystery to her, what with an alcoholic wife, a fast and loose bunch of daughters, and a bedraggled shoeshine parlor.

Cora Rider shrugged and bowed her head in prayer, or at least in imitation of the circle folks, who seemed, as usual, lost in thought until several members looked up, suddenly aware that one of their number was inching away from the group. Cora looked up too, and like the old-timers and staffers who noticed, was astounded. For surely Sophie Heywood of all people, godmother of Velma Henry, co-convener of The Master's Mind, could not actually be leaving.

Sophie Heywood had been in attendance at every other major event in Velma Henry's life. No one could say for sure if Sophie had been there when Velma had tried to do herself in, that part of the girl's story hadn't been put together yet. But she'd been there at the beginning with her baby-catching hands. There again urging "pretty please" on Velma's behalf while Mama Mae, the blood mother, plaited peach switches to tear up some behind. Calling herself running away to China to seek her fortune like some character she'd read about in a book, young Velma had dug a hole in the landfill, then tunneled her way through a drainpipe that led to the highway connector past the marshes before her sister Palma could catch up with her and bring her back.

All those years Sophie had been turning a warm eye on the child's triumphs, a glass eye on everything else, which was a lot, to hear the old folks tell it, as the girl, breaking her bonds and casting away the cord, was steady making her bed hard. For those old-timers, though, that walked the chalk, why a woman such as Sophie Heywood, chapter president of the Women's Auxiliary of the Sleeping Car Porters for two decades running, would even cross the street for the likes of Velma Henry was a mystery anyway. But there it was, so must it be—the godmother ever ready to turn the lamp down low on the godchild's indiscretions.

The prayer group moved closer to repair the circle, searching Sophie's face for a clue to the break and the odd leavetaking. But the woman's eyes were as still as water in the baptismal pit, reminding them that she had been there too the day the congregation had stood by waiting for a moving of the water, had shouted when Velma had come through religion, had cheered when she walked across the stage of Douglass High to get her diploma, had stood up at her first wedding, hasty as you please and in a night club too, and worn white to the railroad station as the rites of good riddance had been performed. And when Velma had swapped that out-of-town-who's-his-people-anyway husband for a good home boy whose goodness could maybe lay her wildness down and urge her through college, there was Sophie in her best threads following the child down the aisle, her needle still working in the hem of the gown.

And here she was now, Sophie Heywood, not only walking away from her godchild, but removing Scorpio from the Mind. Heads turned round as she reached the door and stood there gazing up, they thought, at the ceiling, drawing other heads up too to study the ceiling's luster, the gleam of the fluorescent rods. And study they did, for Sophie was forever reading signs before they were even so.

"Every event is preceded by a sign," she always instructed her students, or anyone else in her orbit who'd listen. "We're all clairvoyant if we'd only know it." The lesson was not lost on Cora Rider, whose bed, kitchen table and porch swing were forever cluttered with *Three Wise Men, Red Devil, Lucky Seven, Black Cat, Three Witches, Aunt Dinah's Dream Book*, and other incense-fragrant softback books that sometimes resulted in a hit. Now, though, like some others, Cora studied the pockmarks in the plaster, the dance of light overhead, searching not so much for a number to box as for a clue to Sophie Heywood's exit.

Buster and Nadeen, the couple from the Teenage Parent Clinic, studied the ceiling too, recalling the counsel of Mrs. Heywood. Close enough to hear each other's breathing, his arm around her, palm resting on the side of her bulging belly, he reviewed the way "sign reading" had been applied by the political theorists at the Academy of the 7 Arts, while she, palms resting on the rise of her stomach, remained attentive to the movement beneath her hands.

What anyone made of the shadows on the ceiling or of the fissures in the plaster overhead was not well telegraphed around the room, though many were visibly intent on decoding the flickering touch of mind on mind and looking about for someone to head Sophie Heywood off at the pass. What did bounce around the circle of eleven was the opinion that Sophie should return and restore the group intact. But what jumped the circle to pass through bone, white jackets, wood chairs and air for Sophie to contemplate, did not bounce back. The only answer was the high-pitch wail of birds overhead like whistling knives in the sky.

Sophie opened the door without a backward glance at the group or at the godchild huddled on the stool so mournful and forlorn. The child Sophie grieved for took another form altogether. So stepping over the threshold into the hall she was stepping over that sack of work tools by his bedroom door again, a heavy gray canvas sack spilling out before enemy eyes —screwdriver, syringe, clockworks, dynamite. She looked out into the hall of the Southwest Community Infirmary, fresh white paint dizzying her, temples buzzing, eyes stinging. Smitty.

Smitty climbing the leg of the statue. The other students running down the street waving banners made from sheets. Mrs. Taylor watching from the window, leaning on pillows she'd made from rally banners. Smitty on the arm of the war hero chanting "Hell, no, we won't go." Sirens scattering the marchers. TV cameras and trucks shoving through the crowd. Mrs. Taylor screaming in the window. A boy face down in the street, his book bag flattened. The police rushing the statue like a tank. The package up under Smitty's arm. The other flung across the hind of the first brass horse. The blow that caught him in the shins.

Sophie face down in the jailhouse bed springs. Portland Edgers, her neighbor, handed a billy club. The sheriff threatening.

Mrs. Taylor moaning in the window. The boy gagging on his own blood face down in the street, the cameras on him. Smitty with a bull horn. A Black TV announcer misnumbering the crowd, mixmatching the facts, lost to the community.

14

Smitty. The blow that caught him in the groin.

The blow that caught her in the kidney. Someone howling in the next cell. A delegation from the church out front talking reasonably. Sophie face down on the jailhouse bed springs, the rusty metal cutting biscuits out of her cheeks.

Smitty kicking at the clubs, the hands. Smitty jammed between the second brass horse and the flagpole. The package balanced in the crook of the bayonet. The blow that caught him from behind.

Portland Edgers turning on the sheriff and wrestled down on her back and beaten. Sophie mashed into the springs. Portland Edgers screaming into her neck.

Smitty pulled down against the cement pedestal, slammed against the horses' hooves, dragged on his stomach to the van. A boot in his neck. Child. Four knees in his back. Son. The package ripped from his grip. The policeman racing on his own path and none other's. The man, the statue going up Pegasus. Manes, hooves, hinds, the brass head of some dead soldier and a limb of one once-live officer airborne over city hall. A flagpole buckling at the knees.

And a tall building tottering trembling falling down inside her face down in the jailhouse bed springs teeth splintering and soul groaning. Smitty. Edgers. Reverend Michaels in the corridor being reasonable.

Sophie Heywood closed the door of the treatment room. And there was something in the click of it that made many of the old-timers, veterans of the incessant war—Garveyites, Southern Tenant Associates, trade unionists, Party members, Pan-Africanists—remembering night riders and day traitors and the cocking of guns, shudder.

"Are you sure, sweetheart? I'm just asking is all," Minnie Ransom was saying, playfully pulling at her lower lip till three

15

different shades of purple showed. "Take away the miseries and you take away some folks' reason for living. Their conversation piece anyway."

"I been there," Cora Rider testified, wagging both hands by the wrists overhead. "I know exactly what the good woman means," she assured all around her.

"We all been there, one way or t'other," the old gent with the lemonade tie said, hummed, chanted and was echoed by his twin from the other side of the circle, singing in common meter just like it was church.

Minnie Ransom's hands went out at last, and the visitors, noting the way several people around them checked their watches, concluded that this was either the official beginning of the healing or the end, it was hard to tell.

"I can feel, sweetheart, that you're not quite ready to dump the shit," Minnie Ransom said, her next few words drowned out by the gasps, the rib nudges against starchy jackets, and shuffling of feet. ". . . got to give it all up, the pain, the hurt, the anger and make room for lovely things to rush in and fill you full. Nature abhors a so-called vacuum, don't you know?" She waited till she got a nod out of Velma. "But you want to stomp around a little more in the mud puddle, I see, like a little kid fore you come into the warm and be done with mud. Nothing wrong with that," she said pleasantly, moving her hands back to her own lap, not that they had made contact with Velma, but stopped some two or three inches away from the patient and moved around as if trying to memorize the contours for a full-length portrait to be done later without the model.

Several old-timers at this point craned their necks round to check with the veteran staff in the rear. It was all very strange, this behavior of Miz Minnie. Maybe she was finally into her dotage. "A hundred, if she's a day," murmured Cora.

"I can wait," Minnie said, as though it were a matter of

handing Jake Daniels her shoes and sitting in the booth in stocking feet to flip through a magazine while her lifts were replaced. She crossed her legs again, leaned forward onto the high knee, dropped her chin into that palm, then slapped her other arm and a length of silk around her waist and closed her eyes. She could've been modeling new fashions for the golden age set or waiting for a bus.

"Looking more like a monkey every day," Cora thought she was thinking to herself till someone jostled her elbow from behind and scorched the back of her neck with a frown.

"Far out," one of the visitors was heard to mumble. "Far fucking out. So whadda we supposed to do, stand here for this comedy?"

"Shush."

"Look, lady," tapping on his watch, "We—"

"I said to shush, so shush."

The visitor turned red when the giggles from the rear and side drifted his way. And the woman who had shushed him, a retired schoolteacher from the back district, shifted her position so that she no longer faced the two women but was standing kitty-corner, her arms folded across her chest, keeping one eye on her former student in the gown with her behind out and the other on the redbone who seemed to have more to say but not if she had anything to do with it.

Velma Henry clutched the stool. She felt faint, too faint to ask for a decent chair to sit in. She felt like she was in the back room of some precinct, or in the interrogation room of terrorist kidnappers, or in the walnut-paneled office of Transchemical being asked about an error. She cut that short. She hadn't the strength. She felt her eyes rolling away. Once before she'd had that feeling. The preacher in hip boots spreading his white satin wings as she stepped toward him and was plunged under and everything went white.

She closed her eyes and they rolled back into her head, rolled back to the edge of the table in her kitchen, to the edge of the sheen—to cling there like globules of furniture oil, cling there over the drop, then hiding into the wood, cringing into the grain as the woman who was her moved from sink to stove to countertop turning things on, turning the radio up. Opening drawers, opening things up. Her life line lying for an instant in the cradle of the scissors' X, the radio's song going on and on and no stop-notes as she leaned into the oven. The melody thickening as she was sucked into the carbon walls of the cave, then the song blending with the song of the gas.

"Release, sweetheart. Give it all up. Forgive everyone every-thing. Free them. Free self."

Velma tried to pry her eyelids up to see if the woman was actually speaking. She was certain Mrs. Ransom had not spoken, just as she was sure she'd heard what she heard. She tried to summon her eyes back, to cut the connection. She was seeing more than she wished to remember in that kitchen. But there she was in a telepathic visit with her former self, who seemed to be still there in the kitchen reenacting the scene like time counted for nothing. She tried to move from that place to this, to see this yellow room, this stool, this white tile, this window where the path to the woods began, this Ransom woman who was calling her back. But the journey back from the kitchen was like the journey in the woods to gather. And gathering is a particular thing where the eyes are concerned, M'Dear Sophie taught. You see nothing but what you're look-ing for. After sassafras, you see only the reddish-brown barkish things of the woods. Or after searching out eucalyptus, the eyes stay tuned within a given range of blue-green-gray and cancel out the rest of the world. And never mind that it's late, that the basket is full, that you got what you came for, that you are ready to catch the bus back to town, are leisurely walking now on the lookout for flowers or berries or a little holding stone to keep you company. The gathering's demands stay with you, lock you in to particular sights. The eyes will not let you let it go.

All Velma could summon now before her eyes were the things of her kitchen, those things she'd sought while hunting for the end. Leaves, grasses, buds dry but alive and still in jars stuffed with cork, alive but inert on the shelf of oak, alive but arrested over the stove next to the matchbox she'd reached toward out of habit, forgetting she did not want the fire, she only wanted the gas. Leaning against the stove then as the performer leaned now, looking at the glass jars thinking who-knew-what then, her mind taken over, thinking, now, that in the jars was no air, therefore no sound, for sound waves weren't all that self-sufficient, needed a material medium to transmit. But light waves need nothing to carry pictures in, to travel in, can go anywhere in the universe with their independent pictures. So there'd be things to see in the jars, were she in there sealed and unavailable to sounds, voices, cries. So she would be light. Would go back to her beginnings in the stars and be star light, over and done with, but the flame traveling wherever it pleased. And the pictures would follow her, haunt her. Be vivid and sharp in a vacuum. To haunt her. Pictures, sounds and bounce were everywhere, no matter what you did or where you went. Sound broke glass. Light could cut through even steel. There was no escaping the calling, the caves, the mud mothers, the others. No escape.

She'd been in a stupor, her gaze gliding greasily over the jars on the shelf till she fastened onto the egg timer, a little hour-glass affair. To be that sealed—sound, taste, air, nothing seeping in. To be that unavailable at last, sealed in and the noise of the world, the garbage, locked out. To pour herself grain by grain into the top globe and sift silently down to a heap in the bottom one. That was the sight she'd been on the hunt for. To lie coiled on the floor of the thing and then to bunch up with all her strength and push off from the bottom and squeeze through the waistline of the thing and tip time over for one last sandstorm and then be still, finally be still. Her grandmother would be pleased, her godmother Sophie too. "Girl, be still," they'd been telling her for years, meaning different things.

And she'd be still in the globes, in the glass jars, sealed from time and life. All that was so indelible on her retina that the treatment room and all its clutter and mutterings were canceled out. Her kitchen, that woman moving about in obsessive repetition, the things on the shelf, the search, the demand would not let her eyes, let her, come back to the healer's hands that were on her now.

"A grown woman won't mess around in mud puddles too long before she releases. It's warmer inside," she thought she was hearing. "Release, sweetheart. Let it go. Let the healing power flow."

She had had on a velour blouse, brown, crocheted. She felt good in it, moving about the booth in it, the cush, the plush soft against her breasts. The kind of blouse that years ago she would have worn to put James Lee Henry, called Obie now, under her spell. She moved about in the booth, the leather sticky under her knees, but the velour comforting against her skin. He no longer thought she was a prize to win. But the blouse was surely doing something to him, she was certain. But certain too that she was, even sitting right there, just a quaint memory for him, like a lucky marble or a coin caught from the Mardi Gras parade. She didn't want to think too much on that. She was losing the thread of her story. She had been telling him about those Chinese pajamas and the silver buckets but had lost her way.

But it wasn't the blouse feeling good or the memories of

their courting days that was distracting her. James Lee had begun moving the dishes aside, disrupting her meal. Her salad bowl no longer up under her right wrist where she could get at it between chunks of steak and mouthfuls of potatoes but shoved up against the wall next to the napkin rack. Her sweet potato pie totally out of reach. And now he moved her teacup toward the hot sauce bottle. He was interrupting her story, breaking right in just as she was about to get to the good part, to tell her to put her fork down and listen. She was seriously considering jabbing his hand with the fork as he reached to grasp her hands, his tie falling into her plate, covering the last two pieces cut from near the bone that she'd been saving to relish after she finished talking.

"Baby, I wish you were as courageous emotionally as you are . . ."

She missed hearing it somehow. Close as his face was to hers, plainly as he was speaking, attentive as she tried to be, she just couldn't hear what the hell he was saying. She couldn't blame it on the waiters. Usually rattling trays and slinging silverware into the washer, most of them were at the busboy table drinking ice tea and murmuring low. No diners were laughing or talking loud, only a few men sat about alone reading the Sunday papers and sipping coffee. The winos who usually parked by the coatrack to bug the diners lining up for the cashier were outside, sitting on the curb. It was quiet. But she still couldn't quite seem to make out what he was jabbering about all up in her face.

"Let me help you, Velma. Whatever it is we . . . wherever we're at now . . . I can help you break that habit . . . learn to let go of past pain . . . like you got me to stop smoking. We could . . ."

She heard some of it. He was making an appeal, a reconciliation of some sort, conditions, limits, an agenda, help. Something about emotional caring or daring or sharing. James Lee could be tiresome in these moods. She pulled her hand away and reached for her bag. If things were going to get heavy, she needed a cigarette. But he caught her hands again. Rising up out of the booth and damn near coming across the table, he pulled her hands away from her lighter and held them, then resumed his seat and went right on talking, talking.

"Dammit, James. Obie. Let go. I haven't finished my—"

"Let me finish. What I want to say . . ." He paused and wagged his head like it was a sorrowful thing he had to tell her. She snorted. There was a shred of spinach clinging between his front teeth like a fang, which made it all ridiculous. "Do you have any idea, Velma, how you look when you launch into one of your anecdotes? It's got to be costing you something to hang on to old pains. Just look at you. Your eyes slit, the cords jump out of your neck, your voice trembles, I expect fire to come blasting out of your nostrils any minute. It takes something out of you, Velma, to keep all them dead moments alive. Why can't you just . . . forget . . . forgive . . . and always it's some situation that was over and done with ten, fifteen years ago. But here you are still all fired up about it, still plotting, up to your jaws in ancient shit."

"Up to my jaws in ancient shit. Nice line."

"Like what you were going on and on about this afternoon. The time your mother wouldn't let you go to the Freeman birthday party because Palma hadn't been invited too. Hell, that was twenty years ago, Vee. And for the hundredth time you got to sink your teeth all in it. The invitation with the little elephant and the party hat and how—"

"So why are you giving me the details of it? We taping this session? If I've gone over it a hundred times, surely I've got it down pat. You seem to. And get your tie out of my plate, James. Obie."

"All I want to know is how long are you going to overload your circuits with—"

"Until I get my pint of blood," she said, shaking one hand free and pulling her plate toward her.

"Mixed metaphor, kiddo."

She stretched her face into a grin that ended in a sneer. If he could only see himself, she thought, the shred of spinach reducing him.

"We're different people, James. Obie. Somebody shit all over you, you forgive and forget. You start talking about how we're all damaged and colonialism and the underdeveloped blah blah. That's why everybody walks all over you."

"You're the only one to ever try to walk over me, Vee."

"That's why I just can't stay with you. I don't respect—"

"That's not why, Vee.

"What?"

"Scared. Anytime you're not in absolute control, you panic."

"Scared?" She chewed with her mouth open, certain the sight would make him shut up or at least turn away. "Shit. Scared of you? Sheeeeet. Obie."

"Intimacy. Love. Taking a chance when the issue of control just isn't—"

She cut him off with a snort when he seemed to be speaking in imitation of her chewing. People trying to be earnest, serious or supercilious with their fly open or a button dangling from their blouse always cracked her up, made her feel sneery and sympathetic at the same time. She wasn't sure which she felt. Mama Mae in the doorway doing her mother act while the safety pin in her bra worked itself loose was usually an object of pity. Or Lil James spreading the peanut butter thick and going on and on about the basketball game and how he'd had to sit it out on the bench when the coach knew full well he could save the day, a bugga hanging from his nose, always triggered a wave of compassion that made her move to hug him, though these days he shied away from her sudden bursts of affection.

She wiped her fingers on the napkin and made her hand available, but her husband did not take it, kept talking, the green leaf waving, mocking. The two hands lay there side by side on the table like a still life. She rubbed his hand and he did not pull it away exactly, just sort of. She rubbed the ridges in his thumbnail and tried to listen to what he was saying now about the atmosphere she set up in the house, what her emotional something or other was doing to the kid, to him, mostly to her. She heard bits of it while floating in and out of the scene, thinking on that first day when she fell in love with his hands or called it love and called it, smirking, falling.

"Nice statement. Strong," he had said, easing up on her right side when the curator had stepped away to mount another painting. "I like her work." His head was cocked sideways and his hands were out framing a particular section of Palma's collage less than three feet away.

"And I find you attractive too," Velma'd said, looking into his face as he turned toward her grinning, stunned, intrigued. And she'd slid her gaze from his face to his hands and knew in that instant that he considered these hands his best feature, his soul, and so she openly admired them and he was captured, under her spell, drawn to her, as though he'd been waiting all his life for just this sign, just this woman, a woman who could get past his clothes, his face, his rap, and recognize that who he was was his hands.

"Ahh," she'd said, reaching out and clasping them together in hers, "these are some very special hands," as though she were entranced, as though usually shy, reserved, ultra cool, she'd simply been overcome by the sight of them, taken outside of herself by the fact of them, moved. She'd let go suddenly as though remembering herself and had smiled inside—"it's all over, buddy"—standing there holding herself out, a promise of possession, a prize.

"Can't we, Vee? Push all the past aside, dump all of it." His hands were churning the air and the spinach thread was wiggling. "Create a vacuum for good things to rush in. Good things."

Like work and no let up and tears in the night. Like being rolled to the edge of the bed, to extremes, clutching a stingy share of the covers and about to drop over the side, like getting up and walking, bare feet on cold floor, round to the other side and climbing in and too mad to snuggle for warmth, freeze. Like going to jail and being forgotten, forgotten, or at least deprioritized cause bail was not as pressing as the printer's bill. Like raising funds and selling some fool to the community with his heart set on running for public office. Like being called in on five-minute notice after all the interesting decisions had been made, called in out of personal loyalty and expected to break her hump pulling off what the men had decided was crucial for the community good. She could feel his eyes on her. He was looking at her attempts to get settled with such compassion, she wondered if maybe she had bird shit on her shoulder. But she wanted to get it said about those Chinese pajamas. The men. The women. The meeting he'd begrudgingly driven her to at the Patterson Professional Building . . .

Once again the women of the ad hoc committee sat down in the Patterson suite. This time not to hear the agenda but to capture it. And the sooner the better, Palma made clear, drumming on the arm of her chair, the cowrie-shell bracelet nicking the wood. Velma patted her sister's hand and settled down uneasily into the chair Reilly dragged back over the carpet then shoved in hard, locking her under the table leaf, as if to take her out of whatever action the women had decided when they left the men among the ashtrays to caucus in the hall. She felt uncomfortable, damp. There'd been nothing in the machines—no tampons, no napkins, no paper towels, no roll of tissue she could unravel and stuff her panties with. So she slid carefully into the wide bowl of the wooden chair, the wad of rally flyers scratching against her panty hose.

The women of the YWCA squeezed together on the leather couch, still chafing at the remark that as new members they should curb their "input." It was then that Daisy Moultrie's mother called the women to caucus. Daisy and her mother resumed their seats on the sofa under the window and watched Palma, then Jan, for their cue. Jan picked up her ball-point and rolled it between her hands as if still in her crafts room instructing the children in coil and slab technique. Ruby, next to her, was accepting Lonnie Hill's chair, asking facetiously, "Change of mind or just change of tactic?" for usually—and that evening had been no exception—they were at swords' points. Lonnie maintained that Ruby and Jan and Velma but especially Ruby ought to be cool, lighten up, give some slack, get back lest the group and its work get a rep as a "woman's thaang," and Ruby's retort a courteous "Nigger please." Though none of the women, seasoned veterans of that particular war, paid Lonnie too much mind. Eight years before and five years before and three years before Jan had laid back when told to get back and had watched still another organization sacrificed on the altar of male ego. "Whim," she called it, always pursing her lips just so in the retelling, "whim." As a student Ruby had been brought up on charges by the Black Student Union, charged with insensitivity, insubordination, uncooperativeness and a poor analysis of "liberation," meaning she needed to change her aggressive ways and give Black manhood a chance to assert itself. She'd been stunned speechless then but regrouped in time and lately responded to any echo of those Star Chamber proceedings with "Nigguh pul-leeze."

The old C.P. women, on the other hand, who'd gotten over in the forties with "as a Negro woman worker I feel" were willing to concede the men might have a point. The Ida B. Wells Club women had argued impatiently in the ladies' lounge that the main thing was the work. But like the sorority sisters, they preferred to splinter. They were not at their best, they said, "in mixed company" anyway.

Jay Patterson was at the lectern again, folding away the scrap of paper the agenda'd been hastily scribbled across into his inside jacket pocket and was quickly introducing the visitor, Marcus Hampden, a member of the Coalition of Black Trade Unionists, imported evidently—the women telegraphed a smirk around the room, all but Palma, who openly admired the man—to imply support of Patterson's run for the county commissioner's seat.

Once again the women took up their pens. They listened to Hampden while calculating: money to be raised, mailing lists to be culled, halls to be booked, flyers to be printed up, hours away from school, home, work, sleep to be snatched. Not that he spoke of these things.

". . . covering transportation workers, dock workers, merchant seamen, employees of public works, government . . ."

He spoke of the labor movement as the one institution where Black workers, Black people could still effect change. And while he urged them to grasp the significance of new alliances shaping up against the Carter administration, the men smoked and drummed their fingers on the tabletop and the women went on writing: so many receptions to cater, tickets to print, chickens to fry, cakes to box, posters to press, so many gifts to exhort from downtown merchants for raffles and Bingo, ads to place, billboards to commandeer, a hot-plate demo at the auto show, bands to book, a crafts-and-books booth at the school bazaar, a rummage sale, an auction of whatever first edition Old Reilly might still have on his shelves, and what home boy or home-girl-made-good-in-show-biz could be counted on for a benefit show.

". . . economy that can no longer depend on overseas markets and cheap labor, so they're moving on labor and especially on us again, in order to redivide and subdivide for their own benefit the national income before it gets grabbed up in wages, social services . . ."

Hampden had prepared a speech suitable for presentation at a more public forum, but not altogether appropriate for this gathering, a loosely strung group of colleagues, chums, frat brothers, soror sisters, business partners, co-workers, neighbors. A group that sometimes called itself a committee of this organization or a task force of that association or a support group of this cause or an auxiliary of that. A group which Jay Patterson had urged lately to formalize and structure itself for the serious work ahead—meaning his campaign. But the mention of bylaws and charters and incorporation papers fell on deaf ears, Jan had made clear, "woman's thaang" ringing in her ears and keeping her head as buried in her notes as Lonnie's was buried in Daisy Moultrie's blouse. Just a half-hour ago when Jay had made his pitch again, maintaining that somebody—looking straight at Jan and Ruby—ought to get cracking on a rough draft of the bylaws, Lonnie had leaned up in his chair and swung his gaze away from Daisy's breasts long enough to agree that yes that was certainly a first step and would've said more had he not realized, translating the looks his way, that he was setting himself up for work, so he turned to Ruby and almost gave her her cue, her lips parting and teeth opening to form "Nig" before he abruptly cut it off and agreed yes "somebody" should see about all that paper work.

Jan and Ruby sat together listening with one ear to the trade unionist and with the other proofreading the rough draft Statement of Purpose drawn up in the ladies' room. Jay Patterson was signaling with his pipe that the speech should not go on too long and to get to the good part. Hampden was now speaking of cutbacks, layoffs, shortages, breakdowns, frozen wages, soaring prices, embezzled pensions and the Social Security money looking funny. Palma was rubbing her thighs suggestively and poking Velma through the spokes of their chairs to check the speaker out. Velma was still trying to sit all the way down without sitting all the way down, settling uneasily on the sodden wad of papers between her thighs.

He was talking about the need for organizational work of the highest order and the grooming of a new leadership. Jay Patterson tapped ashes from his pipe, missing the ashtray by a good country mile. Hampden was talking about chessboards and getting the knights strategically placed, and Ruby gave a drowsy suck of the teeth for Lonnie's benefit. "Knights!" It was expected of her.

". . . the yet-untapped resources within the community that are available, available and necessary, necessary and maybe sufficient, if we'd just stop waiting for reparations from dubious benefactors, stop waiting for someone to deliver on the overdue promissory notes . . ."

There was a light ripple of applause. And Jay Patterson took the opportunity, while the speaker was making clear that he was committed, serious, ready to deal and while Palma slyly urged him to repeat his name, address and phone number cause it was always a pleasure to work with a brother ready to deal, to resume his position at the lectern and to once again take up the priority agenda item, namely his campaign and their pledge to bring it off. Hampden had barely sat down in the chair

Palma had dragged by her foot up close to her own when Patterson cleared his throat and began unfolding a wad of yellow sheets he had fished from his back pocket.

"Palma Henry," Palma was saying. "A pleasure to meet you, Marcus," her hand so far in the man's lap, he had to suck in to shake it. Velma had to smile, while Ruby took it right on out by muttering "Well, all right, sistuh," which drew enough mumblings and giggles to drown poor Patterson out.

"That's roughly the intro to my first public speech," Patterson was saying, sadly refolding the papers, since Reilly had dropped his head down and wagged it in disapproval. "And now, ladies, we'd like your input regarding—"

"We just got through telling you about this 'input' shit, Jay," Ruby said, louder than was necessary. A groan from Daisy Moultrie's mother was sufficient to stop him. He looked from the women to the men to the visitor, hoping some message about decorum might get read. He turned to Lonnie and the younger men and then to Reilly and the older men, waiting on someone to clear the air so the meeting could take its course.

"I think," Daisy Moultrie's mother began, scooting to the edge of the sofa to plant her pumps neatly on the carpet, "that we need to table the agenda and take up an item you yourself, Jay, have been trying to make us attentive to, namely, it is time we formalized this organization, elected officers, drafted a charter and put ourselves on the public scene as an official group."

"Right," Ruby interjected. "No more hastily called meetings and five-minute commitments and unilaterally drawn-up agenda items. If we're gonna deal, let's deal."

Velma felt her sister's fingernail gouging her arm. She hoisted herself up carefully and prayed the makeshift sanitary napkin would not dislodge itself.

"Now, before we proceed," Velma said, "we need to be clear, all of us, about the nature of the work. About how things have gotten done in the past and why that pattern has to change."

"Don't be so damn polite," Ruby interrupted. "It boils down to this. You jokers, and especially you," cutting her eyes at Lonnie, "never want to take any responsibility for getting down. Mr. Reilly excepted. Now, what that has meant in the past is that we women have been expected to carry the load."

"Well, I for one," Patterson said quickly, darting his eyes nervously about, fearful of the impression this was bound to make on Marcus Hampden of the Coalition of Black Trade Unionists, "have always been most appreciative of your input, most grateful for the work that you ladies have done, most—"

"Insensitive," Velma said, fairly hissed, wishing Portia Patterson were in attendance and might be bold enough to say in this gathering what she eagerly said about her husband in the privacy of her kitchen: "Not a clue, my friends, as to how the eggs, bacon and biscuits come to appear before him every morning. He makes up lists, see, of all the things he wants done and posts this list on the refrigerator door just like there were little kitchen fairies and yard elves and other magic creatures to get all these things done." Velma was thinking "abstractionist" summed him up, a perfect label for the habit, the unmindful gap between want and done, demand and get. And abstractionists make good bombardiers, good military beasts, she was thinking, wanted to say, but Palma had warned her not to get metaphorical, to just speak to the issue and to speak plain so they could adjourn and Palma could pack to get on the road.

"To put it bluntly, Jay, how could you still have the nerve to be talking about running?" Velma demanded. "We've been over this ground before. And three times we explained to you that if you refuse to relocate, to move back into the county, you simply can't run. It's hard enough trying to sell your lackluster self and nonexistent record to folks. Add to that the fact that you never do a bit of work, put up a bit of money, or ever are prepared to do or be anything but a garden-variety ambitious careerist."

"Plus, you're not even a resident," Jan inserted.

"Well, in regard to relocating," Patterson was trying to keep his face under control, "I thought I made myself quite plain."

"You are always quite plain and there's the rub, turkey."

"It's simply out of the question," he continued, ignoring Ruby. "Further, it's not necessary. There's no law that says I have to live within the county line."

"Is," Old Man Reilly murmured, his head dropped onto his chest.

"Or convention mayhap," Lonnie amended. "I'll look it up."

"Page six-seven-two, paragraph one, lines four and five," Jan was saying, tilting a fat blue book from the upright stacks on Patterson's desk and sliding it down the table, rattling ashtrays, coffee cups and Patterson.

"The issue, Jay," Velma continued, "is not simply your persistence in the teeth of law and convention"—she nodded toward Lonnie—"but the fact that it's just a definitive example of the egocentric way decisions are made in this group. And why we need to establish some policy right here and now."

"Well, well," Patterson was muttering, leaning up out of the book and taking off his glasses, "it's probably true that residence in town would . . . but ahh . . . Do you have any idea of what you're asking? To rip up my roots?"

"Roots? In the suburbs?" Ruby was laughing, slapping her thigh and rearing back in her chair. "Nigger please. That township was incorporated long after you got out of law school. You. Did. Get. Out. Of. Law school?"

The Moultrie women, perched on the edge of the sofa knocking knees, cleared their throats. Daisy's mother batted her eyelids a bit until she had everyone's attention.

"I don't think discourtesy is called for," she began, raising her brows and looking past Ruby toward the oil painting of Martin Luther King, Jr. "And I doubt that Mr. Patterson's residence is really the bone of contention, as Velma Henry has so clearly put it." This time looking past Velma to the golf trophies on the bookshelves. "The issue is, Mr. Patterson, Mr. Reilly . . ."

She was nodding to each in turn, a tactic that had once earned her much applause some ten years ago in a meeting with the city administration, for it bought enough time for Velma and Smitty to leave the room, round up community folks, call the press, and block cutbacks in city services. Daisy Moultrie's mother had been running it into the ground ever since, confused, no doubt, as to why she'd been celebrated in the first place. Velma leaned against the table. Palma sighed and counted the shells on her bracelets. Hampden, next to her, fiddled with the zipper on his cordovan boots while Velma, distracted, was remembering some absurdly shiny boots back in the days of the marching.

Jay Patterson sat down when it was clear that Daisy Moultrie's mother had no intention of relinquishing the floor. He sat down and was almost hidden by the lectern, the clock ticking away over the door, the yet-to-be-delivered speech fat and uncomfortable in his back pocket. Velma sat down too, landing on a soggy wad of paper, while the older woman picked up her pace, nodding to each of the women to join her in what turned out to be a fairly monotonous recitative.

"Who put your campaign together, Reilly, while you and Grace vacationed on Jekyll Island?"

"Who raised the money for the South Africa ad, composed it, gathered up the signatures and the money, placed it and absorbed the backlash?"

"Who muzzled the Claybourne *Inquirer*, got them to squash

the smear when your books turned up funny, Hill?"

"Who saved your ass—and never got reimbursed for toll calls, postage or gas?"

Who trudged through dust, through rain, through mud, through the corridors of the Chinese pajamas. Velma rubbed her forehead and leaned back in her chair . . .

It had been a Gulf station. Of course she remembered that, the boycott had been still in effect and she'd felt funny going in there, even if it was just to use the bathroom. Mounting a raggedy tampon fished from the bottom of her bag, paper unraveled, stuffing coming loose, and in a nasty bathroom with no stall doors, and in a Gulf station too, to add to the outrage. She'd been reeking of wasted blood and rage. They'd marched all morning, all afternoon and most of early evening to get there. Shot at, spit on, nearly run down by a cement mixer, murder mouthed, lobbed with everything from stones to eggs, they'd kept the group intact and suffered no casualties or arrests. But when they got to the park, renamed People's Park for the occasion, the host group hadn't set up yet. The banners were still drooping, missing a string in one corner, the PA system only just arriving and two cables split, the bathrooms locked and boarded up and no food, no food. Just one lone pot of field peas and chicken backs a couple from the country had hauled up there in their pickup to feed the multitudes. Velma had leaned against a tree and tried hard not to look at her feet. Two pairs of rubber thongs left on the highway, a ragged pair of sneakers abandoned by a lard can and a patch of sunflowers on some railroad crossing, her reserve pair looped around her neck, feet too swollen to torture further. The marshals dragging themselves around trying to draw people in from the trees toward the flat-truck platform. The children crying from fatigue. The students singing off-key, ragged. The elders on the ground massaging knots in their legs. And Velma clenching her thighs tight, aware that a syrupy clot was oozing down her left leg and she needed to see about herself.

Exhausted, she was squinting through the dust and grit of her lashes when the limousines pulled up, eye-stinging shiny, black, sleek. And the door opened and the cool blue of the air-conditioned interior billowed out into the yellow and rust-red of evening. Her throat was splintered wood. Then the shiny black boots stepping onto the parched grass, the knife-creased pants straightening taut, the jacket hanging straight, the blinding white shirt, the sky-blue tie. And the roar went up and the marshals gripped wrists and hoarsely, barely heard, pleaded with the crowd to move back and make way for the speaker. Flanked by the coal-black men in shiny sunglasses and silk-and-steel suits, he made toward the platform. She carried herself out of the park in search of a toilet, some water to wash up, a place to dump her bag before her arm broke or her shoulder was permanently pulled from its socket. And rounding a bend, the dulcet tones of the speaker soaring out overhead, she'd spotted the Gulf sign and knew beforehand that the rest room would be nasty, that just getting past the attendant would call for a nastiness she wasn't sure she could muster but would have to. Knew beforehand that she would squat over a reeking, smeared toilet bowl stuffed with everything that ever was and pray through clenched teeth for rain. Some leader. He looked a bit like King, had a delivery similar to Malcolm's, dressed like Stokely, had glasses like Rap, but she'd never heard him say anything useful or offensive. But what a voice. And what a good press agent. And the people had bought him. What a disaster. But what a voice. He rolled out his *r*'s like the quality yard-goods he'd once had to yank from the bolts of cloth in his father's store in Brunswick, Georgia, till the day an anthropologist walked in with tape recorder and camera, doing some work on Jekyll Island Blacks and would he be so kind as to answer a few questions about the lore and legends of the island folks, and "discovered" him and launched him into prominence.

"Leader. Sheeet."

And no soap. No towels. No tissue. No machine. Just a spurt then a trickle of rusty water in the clogged sink then no water at all. And like a cat she'd had to lick herself clean of grit, salt, blood and rage.

Palma was nudging her, the click click of the cowries reminding her even more of that time and she blew her turn, someone else taking up the "And who chartered buses for . . ."

MATRIARCHAL CURRENCY, the sign on the table had read. And she'd purchased the cowrie-shell bracelets for Palma less as a memento more as a criticism. Bought the cowrie shells to shame her, for she should've been on the march, had no right to the cool solitude of her studio painting pictures of sailboats while sisters were being beaten and raped, and workers shot and children terrorized. "Divination tools," she had winked at the peddler who'd been too eager to rap the long rap about cowries and matriarchy. Velma'd worn them that day in the park and for the duration of the march to the state capitol to set up tents. "Little pussies with stitched teeth," her aid on the PR committee had leered, touching the cowries. And it seemed as good a time as any for her to go draft the press releases.

"Velma?"

She stood up again, certain that she was leaving a red-brown smear on the chair. "Who's called in every time there's work to be done, coffee made, a program sold? Every time some miscellaneous nobody with a five-minute commitment and an opportunist's nose for a self-promoting break gets an idea, here we go. And we have yet to see any of you so much as roll up your sleeves to empty an ashtray. Everybody gets paid off but us. Do any of you have a grant for one of us? Any government contracts? Any no-work-all-pay posts at a college, those of you on boards? Is there ever any thing you all do on your own other than rent out the Italian restaurant on the Heights to discuss the Humphrey-Hawkins bill over wine?"

"And the place is bugged, of course."

"Ruby, hush."

"Drinking at the bar is all we've witnessed yet. You all say we need a conference, we book the hotel and set it all up and yawl drink at the bar. We shuttle back and forth to the airport, yawl drink at the bar. We caucus, vote, lay out the resolutions, yawl drink at the bar. We're trying to build a union, a guild, an organization. You are all welcome to continue operating as a social club, but not on our time, okay?"

"Amen."

"And from now on, when you want some 'input,' don't call us—"

"We'll call you."

"We'll notify you about the meetings. And you are welcome to join us at my sister's studio, which will be the temporary headquarters of Women for Action until we get a more permanent place." Velma felt Jan's eyes trying to get hers, felt Palma tugging at her dress. But she went on. "You all continue lollygagging at Del Giorgio's, renting limousines and pussyfooting around town profiling in your three-piece suits and imported pajamas while the people sweat it out through hard times." Palma had yanked her down in her chair as Ruby got to her feet.

"I heard that, Vee. You all hear that? We all hear that? Well, this is it, my honeys. We're at the crossroads and are gonna have to decide the shape, scope, thrust and general whatnot and so forth of this group. Let's take some time out to think it through and then we'll hear from whoever wants to speak they speak. Two-minute limit, if you please. This is it, the crossroads."

37

* * *

The roads had been washed out. The walkways between the tents were a joke. The children had found dry planks from somewhere and laid them down, but they weren't dry for long or effective. It kept raining and the walkways were mud, planks too, tents too, everybody caked with red mud. The older women paying it no mind, moving about with slop jars or buckets of fresh water or food like ancient mud mothers from the caves, hair matted and shining with henna, hands red, streaks and slashes across their faces to denote clan kinship. The tents were collapsing, the bedrolls mildewed. The portable toilets had long since not worked. The children on errands in indescribable clothes and barefoot, red mud coming up between their toes like worms, and worms too. Many down with fevers. One doctor making rounds, stumbling with sleeplessness and impotence.

Velma had gone up to the hotel, her shoes dangling around her neck, the clipboard in the ache of her left arm. She'd hitched but mostly walked, keeping her eyes strictly off her swollen feet. Gone up to the hotel to make some calls—find another doctor, locate the support group to bring food and aspirin, phone in the press notices, try to locate James' group that had gone to meet up with King in D.C.

She was hanging on to the counter with both hands, nails splitting, hands swollen, the phone too heavy to consider handling without a deep intake of breath and resolve. She could barely stand up, much less focus on the clipboard and flip pages. And behind her the easy laughter, that familiar voice. Oh those dulcet tones. And she looked into the mirror. The speaker and his cronies and the women, those women, coming down the corridor.

* * *

"I don't want to belabor the point," Velma said,clearing her throat, not sure where they were on the agenda,"and I certainly don't want to antagonize or polarize —"

"Let the chips fall where they may, Vee."

"Ruby, hush."

"—but a review of the history is important if we're to map out with some intelligence and fairness the agenda of the organization. As Ruby said, we're at the crossroads, and what we decide tonight will be . . . decisive. It's not just a matter of who's taken responsibility in the past for carrying out the work, for getting out the press releases, the mailings, for doing the canvassing, for organizing a base among campus forces, street forces, prison forces, workers, gathering the money, arranging for transportation . . ."

She was hanging by her nails on the slippery material of the hotel counter, her legs trembling with fatigue, her nose stopped up, her skin caked with mud, her face, her hair dusted with insect wings and pollen. Hanging by her nails, her backbone on fire, her bowels boiling. The switchboard cables a fabulous Indian rope trick she'd have to deal with to make the calls. The clipboard a confounding puzzle of glyphs and ciphers. And slanting across the mirror over the key rack the men without their sunglasses, hair glistening fresh from under stocking caps and fro cloths, the men carrying silver ice buckets and laughing with the women, the women clean and lean and shining, prancing like rodeo ponies—roans, palominos tossing their manes and whinnying down the corridor. And the man who would be leader.

Trying not to see them, but seeing them anyway, her eyes swimming in the mirror, slipping and sliding over a field of red silk. No bib overalls. No slop jars here. Just red silk lounging pajamas and silver ice buckets and those women. Losing her grip, the phone too heavy to hold against her ear, her eyes floating in the mirror, skidding over the raised threads that worked out a dragon of white and gold with blazing fangs and fire. Any minute she'd be a heap on the floor, a puddle of red mud in the carpet but for two hands that were holding her up up under her armpits. James? Had he come for her at last? Come to merge the ranks? Someone had broken away, had come crashing through the mirror to lift her, to drag her away, hustle her out of the door. An ice bucket banging her in the knees, the cold stabbing her in the thighs. The shoelaces strangling. Her head snapped back in the rush and shove and all she could see, the landscape of her world, was a blond hair between green threads on a field of red.

"Be cool." Palma was patting her, one of the bracelets sliding off into Velma's lap. "Don't get overheated, Vee girl." Palma was winking, being their grandmother. "Be still, girlie."

Velma ghosted a smile and leaned back, her stocking feet clutching at tufts of the carpet that softened the debate in Patterson's office.

"Be still, Velma. Just relax now," Ruby was bending with the basin, trying not to bump against the tent, damp with rain. "One monkey don't stop no show. Not one, not six. The struggle continues. Haste not, waste not. Not to mention a stitch in time. Et cetera and so forth. Just get your feet to cooperate and everything'll be just fine."

Ruby was trying to put her feet in the basin. Daisy Moultrie was brushing her hair. Velma had no control over her feet. No control over her head either. It seemed to bang around on her shoulders one minute, loll and bob the next. She feared the cronie had broken her neck shoving her out of the hotel. But the water was cool, it calmed her. The stroking of her legs was soothing too. The washcloth soft and fragrant with something Ruby always wore. But Daisy Moultrie was brushing too briskly. And the sparks that flew threatened to ignite her all over again, catch the tent on fire, burn up the stack of fliers waiting on a camp stool for her to distribute. She could hear the crackling wheeze of red silk ablaze.

"Sistuh mine, it's a hard row to hoe, but ain't nothing to go out about," Ruby was saying, flinging the water out back, the flap of the tent lifted and moonlight spilling in, the arc of water frozen for an instant, just long enough for her to believe she'd been washed clean of it all.

"How ya feel? Velma?"

And she wanted to answer Ruby, wanted to say something intelligible and calm and hip and funny so the work could take precedence again. But the words got caught in the grind of her back teeth as she shred silk and canvas and paper and hair. The rip and shriek of silk prying her teeth apart. And it all came out a growling.

"Velma!" He was out of the booth again, leaning over the table toward her, his jacket hem in her coffee cup. "Aw, baby, don't get angry about things over and done with. Come on. Let's go home."

"Growl all you want, sweetheart. I haven't heard a growl like that since Venus moved between the sun and the earth, mmm, not since the coming of the Lord of the Flames. Yes, sweetheart, I haven't heard a good ole deep kneebend from-the-source growl such as that in some nineteen million years. Growl on. You gonna be all right . . . after while. It's all a matter of time. The law of time. And soon, sweetheart, this will all be yours. You just hold that thought, ya hear?"

two

"Quit wrasslin, sweetheart, or you may go under. I'm throwing you the life line. Don't be too proud to live."

"Speakin of wrasslin with pride, Min—"

"What you say?" Minnie Ransom hadn't been aware of her spirit guide's presence, or of her own drift elsewhere.

"Say she can't hear you, Min. Don't even see you. Henry gal off somewhere tracking herself."

"Mmm. Hanging on to her's like trying to maneuver a basket of snakes on a pole. Spasms in every nerve center. And me, I feel like I've been in the middle of a hornet's nest for days. No time to recharge and replenish myself. But talking to Doc's like talking to sidewalk. He will have his little shows. What's ailing the Henry gal so, Old Wife? Not that I'm sure I can match her frequency anyway. She's draining me."

"Maybe you've met your match, Min."

"What you say?"

"Say she sure is fidgetin like she got the betsy bugs."

"She one of Oshun's witches, I suspect. What's Oshun's two cents worth on the matter? Maybe she'd like to handle this Henry gal herself."

"I don't know about the two cents cause I strictly do not mess with haints, Min. I've always been a good Christian."

"When you gonna stop calling the loa out of their names? They are the laws alive. Seems to me you need to slough off a lot more of the nonsense from this plane if you're going to be any help to me. Some spirit guide."

"Leastways I know that Oshun ain't studyin this problem, Min, cause I hear Oshun and Oye prettyin up to hop a bus to New Orleans. Carnival in this town ain't fancy enough for them. Town gettin too small for some other proud spirits I could name too."

"Bus? What are you talking about—the loa on some bus?"

"I'm talkin about them haints that're always up to some trickified business. They ride buses just the same's they ride brooms, peoples, carnival floats, whatever. All the same to them. What they care about scarin people with they ghostly selves?"

"Then you tell me, Old Wife, teller of tales nobody much wants to hear anymore except this humble servant of a swamp-hag, where's the Henry gal gone off to? I don't feel much turbulence in her now."

"Swamphag?" leaning over to flounce Minnie's dress and jangle her gold bangles, chuckling. "She's off dancing, Min."

"In the mud?' "

"Mud seems to belong to her ways, Min."

"Dancing in mud with cowries. Mmm. Twisting and grunting for the reward-applause of a bloody head on a tray. Lord, have mercy. What is wrong with the women? If they ain't sticking their head in ovens and opening up their veins like this gal, or jumping off roofs, drinking charcoal lighter, pumping rat poisons in their arms, and ramming cars into walls, they looking for some man to tear his head off. What is wrong, Old Wife? What is happening to the daughters of the yam? Seem like they just don't know how to draw up the powers from the deep like before. Not full sunned and sweet anymore. Tell me, how do I welcome this daughter home to the world, when they all getting to acting more and more like—"

"I'sh potatoes?"

"Exactly. One in here yesterday whooping and hollering about some hole in a bucket. Took me a good five minutes to recall that song, remember—'There's a hole in the bucket, dear Liza, dear Liza. Well, fix it, dear Henry'? Like that was a message to go after her husband with a hammer. I'm telling you, when we started letting these silly children arrange their own marriages without teaching them about compatible energies, about the powers, we made a serious mistake. More mixmatch mating going on, enough to make you crazy. Buckets. Full-grown women talking about a song told her to hit her husband in the head. Like she don't have options. Hmph. You know what I mean?"

"I know, excusing the part about the bucket. But course I member the woman."

"Course you do, bless your heart, and thank you. A dormant nerve in the clitoris. No wonder she restless and jumpy with back pains and her legs aching. And no wonder, no mating fuel there at all. But like I say, she got options. Just like the Liza in the song. She can just go ahead and fix the fool bucket herself and quit getting so antsy about it. Or she can go find a man that can. Always got options."

"Say which?"

"Options. Affirmation and denial. Ole no-count Henry ain't the only reality. Or she might try affirming his ability to wield a hammer or tote her some water and see what that'll do. How

44

come you squinching up like I'm talking foreign? Ain't you studying at all, Old Wife?"

"Well you know, Min, I never was too quick at learning."

"Were too. Wisest woman in these parts, bless your heart. Look how you had it all together this morning when that grieving child commenced to sit on my lap and I was about to keel over."

"You was about to dump her on the floor as I recollect."

"True, true. But little did I know till you gave me the message that there was more to the wailing than grief."

"Message?"

"You mean you don't remember? You said to check in the floor of the third ventricle. So I did and zapped a little energy up there near the pineal, good ole pineal, and those lavender beams commenced to glow, and she was right as rain."

"I said which?"

"You said 'Malignant ependyma attempting to take up residence in the base of the brain, Min.' Old Wife, don't you take notes on these sessions? Ain't you getting it all down?"

"I got all there is to be got, Min, excusin a tablet and pencil."

"You the beatingest guide I ever heard of. Did you leastways get the drift yesterday when the little honey started singing the Henry/Liza/bucket song? Well, anyhow, I don't understand these women sometime. Baby a man and then get all in a stiff cause he don't know how to fix the hole in the bucket. Sometime original mother is too much the mother, if you know what I mean."

"I don't be catching your drift at all much, Min. You all wound up today. What's troubling you? It ain't like you to be talking bout 'Are you sure you wanna be well?' What kinda way is that?"

"It's these children, Old Wife. I can handle the dry-bone

45

folks all right. And them generations of rust around still don't wear me any. But these new people? And the children on the way in this last quarter? They gonna really be a blip. But the ones pouring into the Infirmary are blip enough. Soon's they old enough to start smelling theyselves, they commence to looking for blood amongst the blood. Cutting and stabbing and facing off and daring and dividing up and suiciding. You know as well as I, Old Wife, that we have not been scuffling in this waste-howling wilderness for the right to be stupid. All this waste. Everybody all up in each other's face with a whole lotta who struck John—you ain't correct, well you ain't cute, and he ain't right and they ain't scientific and yo mama don't wear no drawers and get off my suedes, and he hit me, and she quit me, and this one's dirty, and that one don't have a degree, and on and on."

"Min?"

"Don't they know we on the rise? That our time is now? Here we are in the last quarter and how we gonna pull it all together and claim the new age in our name? How we gonna rescue this planet from them radioactive mutants? No wonder Noah tried to bar them from the ark. Hmph. Shove over some, Old Wife, it don't seem polite to poke my hand through you. I need to find some music to get it said. All this madness bout to rock me off this stool, Old Wife."

"Not madness throwing rocks at you, Min. Best see about yo sef."

"Well, I'm bearing up at least. But, Old Wife, we gonna have to get a mighty large group trained to pull us through the times ahead. Them four horses galloping already, the seven trumpets blasting. And looks like we clean forgot what we come to do, what we been learning through all them trials and tribulations to do and it's now. Come in here after abusing themselves and want to be well and don't even know what they want to be healthy for. Lord, the children."

"The chirren are our glory, Min."

"Amen on that. Wish I had some music to get it out there. These crazy folks need some saying-it music."

"In our extremity is God's opportunity."

"I'll hold that thought, Old Wife, but get your big buns out the way so I can shuffle through these tapes. Can't seem to find . . ."

"What you lookin for is in the chapel, Min, if you ain't too proud to come and join me there."

If anyone had asked her—not that The Master's Mind thought to query, or the old-timers would have interrupted, or the visitors dared, or the youth from the Teen Clinic would, or the staff had ever thought of it, or her guide or the loa who leaned against the window witnesses who of course knew, needed to—Minnie Ransom would have had to admit that she was stalling, stalling and failing, her hands resting on Velma Henry's shoulders silent and her fingertips still.

Over the years it had become routine: She simply placed her left hand on the patient's spine and her right on the navel, then clearing the channels, putting herself aside, she became available to a healing force no one had yet, to her satisfaction, captured in a name. Her eyelids closed locking out the bounce and bang of light and sound and heat, sealing in the throbbing glow that spread from the corona of light at the crown of the head that moved forward between her brows then fanned out into a petaled rainbow, fanning, pulsing, then contracting again into a single white flame. Just like the corona of the high-tension cables in the old streetcar sheds near the Bible college where day after day, drawn to like a craving, she stared at, strained toward, till one misty night many years later and in another place altogether, a powerhouse in the north, she could finally see it. One misty winter night when Venus beamed down on the corrugated roof at home and Pleiades clustered in the New York sky like the illustration of the double helix taking up so much space in the magazines and papers, she could see it. The light pulsing, the light breaking up and bouncing, swimming together in a rainbow of color, fanning out, and then the pinpoint flame.

And she learned to read the auras of trees and stones and plants and neighbors, far more colorful, far more complex. And studied the sun's corona, the jagged petals of magnetic colors and then the threads that shimmered between wooden tables and flowers and children and candles and birds.

On the stool or in the chair with this patient or that, Minnie could dance their dance and match their beat and echo their pitch and know their frequency as if her own. Eyes closed and the mind dropping down to the heart, bubbling in the blood then beating, fanning out, flooded and shinning, she knew each way of being in the world and could welcome them home again, open to wholeness. Eyes wide open to the swing from expand to contract, dissolve congeal, release restrict, foot tapping, throat throbbing in song to the ebb and flow of renewal, she would welcome them healed into her arms.

"Why couldn't it be something usual like arthritis, bursitis or glaucoma?"

"Deal with what you're dealt, Min."

"Mmm."

Calcium or lymph or blood uncharged, congealed and blocked the flow, stopped the dance, notes running into each other in a pileup, the body out of tune, the melody jumped the track, discordant and strident. And she would lean her ear to the chest or place her hand at the base of the spine till her foot tapped and their heads bobbed, till it was melodious once more. And often she did not touch flesh on flesh but touched mind on mind from across the room or from cross town or the map linked by telephone cables that could carry the clue spoken—a dream message, an item of diet, a hurt unforgiven and festering, a guilt unreleased—and the charged response reaching ear then inner ear, then shooting to the blockade and freeing up the flow. Or by letter, the biometric reading of worried eyes and hands in writing, the body transported through the mails, body/mind/spirit out of nexus, out of tune, out of line, off beat, off color, in a spin off its axis, affairs aslant, wisdom at a tangent and she'd receive her instructions. And turbulence would end.

"What ought I do about the Henry gal, Old Wife?"

"Don't you know?"

"Don't you? Ain't you omniscient yet, Old Wife? Don't frown up. All knowing. Ain't you all knowing? What's the point of being in all-when and all-where if you not going to take advantage of the situation and become all knowing? And all the wisdom of the ages is available to you, isn't that so?"

"Is? I guess I have all I'm supposed to, Min, excusin your ear, beggin your pardon. I been tryin to get you to come to chapel for some time, Min, and now look like you want to traipse off after the Henry girl and go dancing in the mud. Her pull mighty strong. You best grab hold of that stool you're on and come on to chapel."

"I'm coming," stretching up to pull down the branch where she'll find the exact leaf that will dip just so, releasing onto her finger the droplet of dew she will roll between thumb and ring finger like a drop of mercury. "Seems to me you are not making the most of your situation, Old Wife. You studying?"

"You? You making the most of your situation, Min?"

"Ya know, Old Wife, here lately you getting to be downright Jewish."

"Is that right?"

"Just a little around the edges. I ask you a question, you answer with a question."

"For a fact?"

"Quit funning," wagging her head and turning toward the break in the trees. The rainbow—lemon, lime, melon and sherbert-pink arching. "We got a problem here. I can't quite reach this chile and you keep acting like you dumb as me stead of telling me what to do. Now, suppose you just dig on down into that reticule bag of yours and fish me out a bat bone or some magic root," chuckling.

"You know I don't traffic in such, Minnie Ransom."

"You do too. Fess up, what you hauling round in that gris gris sack?"

"A few personals."

"Personals. What you need with personals anymore? Don't they orient you none around here? Didn't they tell you anything?"

"Why I need some 'they' to tell me somp'n when I got you, Min?"

"Okay. I'm gonna hush now and we gonna concentrate on this growler scowler Henry gal that's blocking my sun. She's good material, ya know. We need to get her back into circulation."

"I know this. Trouble is, Min, she got piss-poor guardians."

"Well, don't look at me. I ain't fixin to die yet just to be her guardian . . . am I?"

"Am you which?"

"I'm hushing up as of now, cause I see you are determined to be raffish," stepping high over the lemon grass toward the fountain, the cooling spray against her cheek.

"Your dress misbehavin, Min."

"Wind."

"Beggin your pardon, but wind my foot. You fixin to mess with that young doctor man behind yo corporal body. I seen you casting a voluptuous eye in that doctor man's direction. You fixin to get into somp'n, Min."

"Ahhh, so you are omniscient or clairvoyant one," leaning against the fountain for a full appraisal of this woman friend who'd been with her for most of her life, one way and then another. Nothing much had changed since she passed. Old Wife's complexion was still like mutton suet and brown gravy congealed on a plate. She was still slack jawed. The harelip was as deep a gouge as ever. Nothing much to recommend her, or to signal she was special. "You'd think they'da fixed that lip," Minnie muttering to herself, sitting down on the ledge she'd built during her apprenticeship. A fountain made from ceramic pipes she'd thought much too lovely to be laid underground conducting sewerage. A pause to view the water, to watch the fishes glinting shots of shine around the pool, the aromas from the right wafting past like a brushstroke in a cartoon. Gardenias, lily of the valley, lavender, cosmos, fuchsia, woolly apple mint, spearmint and foxglove lush on either side of the chapel's circle doors, bumblebees drunk and swollen staggering from petal to pistil.

"Come."

The journey, though familiar, was not the journey usual. Was like the old times before the gift unfolded. The days when everyone but her daddy was worried crazy about her, running off from Bible college to New York to get sick and be sent home on the train lying down. They called her batty, fixed, possessed, crossed, in deep trouble. Said they'd heard of people drawn to starch or chalk or bits of plaster. But the sight of full-grown, educated, well-groomed, well-raised Minnie Ransom down on her knees eating dirt, craving pebbles and gravel, all asprawl in the road with her clothes every which way—it was too much to bear. And so jumpy, like something devilish had got hold of her, leaping up from the porch, from the table, from morning prayers and racing off to the woods, the women calling at her back, her daddy dropping his harness and shading

51

his eyes, which slid off her back like slippery saddle soap. The woods to the path to the sweet ground beyond, then the hill, the eating hill, the special dirt behind the wash house. The days when stomping along the path, her shoes in her jumper pocket, stomping to alert the snakes that someone was coming through, she'd encounter Old Karen, the Old One, Wilder's woman, Old Wife, the teller of tales no one would sit still to hear anymore, not when the new tellers could prophesy with such mathematical certainty who would be ill and who well, who fertile and who sterile, who crazy and who all right, who deserved to live and who was bound to die and in precisely what manner.

And Minnie would slow down just as she was told. And the older woman would hold her there on the path like a mama cat with gripping teeth. A full-grown Minnie blocked, it seemed, to the women who hurled warnings at her back, by front-pew every-Sunday-spreading-no-gettin-around-them Karen Wilder hips. Not blocked but stopped by the thoughts, by the telling, watching the cracked lips slide away as though the teeth had been greased for some finicky photographer. Waiting for Old Wife to speak, Minnie'd be stomping in place, for while it was customarily polite to pause on the path and pass the time of day with neighbor or friend who'd chosen this route over the paved walks or the bus line or the highway, it was customarily safe to keep stomping because the snakes had to be warned people were afoot. So she did as she was told, not even thinking on the snakes people said were not in the woods but kept clear of the woods as much as possible and when they didn't, stomped with the best of them.

Minnie'd be stock still finally, while Old Wife's eyes stared at a spot just above her head where her hair had once puffed up before the New York trip, and stared at the sides of her as though remembering her filled out, young and plump, being sent off to Bible college in Beaufort. Held her there and the greasy teeth finally parting and "Not long, now, Minnie, and take care," coming out, jaws unhinged, looking like a vaudeville dummy. And Minnie'd stumbled off bewildered and spooked cause Karen Wilder after all was a teller of strange tales, and who could know then that the message wasn't about death coming to sting her but about a gift unfolding? Minnie eased away sleepwalking till a slither along the side or a rustle overhead reminded her to pick them seven's up and plant them down like she had good sense. Sleepwalk stomping to the mound, the hill, the special place, the rich dark earth, the eating dirt that smelled of paprika and curry, smelled of spice and sweet and bitter and sweat from the days when the Gypsies had planted their Sara, their Black Madonna, at the crest of that hill and the community of Sicilians on an adjacent hill, turned their Black Maria aside, giving Sara her back. And Minnie, climbing the hill like the Matterhorn or Jacob's Ladder one, her eyes right on Sara's wooden orbs, not daring to look back behind her toward Old Wife, felt the old cat eyes a pinpoint of light at the crown of her head.

And there, squatting in the dirt at the top of the bluff, still listening, Minnie was told to clear the path that led up to the cliffs, set the trees, fix the rainbow, erect a fountain and build the chapel in The Mind. And going there—the cooling dark, the candles, the altar—she saw the gift and knew, for at least that instant, where the telling came from.

And would go back again and again, live there nearly all the time, in the days when she had not trusted the gift, when instructions had come, it seemed, from her back teeth as she leaned against the starchy crochets of her parlor chair and let her jaws give into gravity, her tongue resting on the cusp, her lids locking out the banging dance. But what fine radio receivers dental fillings are, she learned, screening out the waves from mundane sources—police car messages, helicopter traffic signals, then all the CB foolishness—to be available to the waves from the Source.

"Remember the time you first showed up at a session?"

"I'd been there all along, Min, I keep telling you."

"It amused you some? The animal doctor and all?"

"Amuses me still," grinning with the same greasy teeth after all this time.

A vet in Bangor, Maine, had been relaying instructions to a ham operator in Orlando, Florida, who'd sent out an S.O.S. on behalf of his wounded hamster. And Minnie had been well into step three of brewing the remedy tea for her patient until "apply poultice warm to hind legs and paws" stopped her in her tracks between the stove and the pantry wall.

"Spun you right up into two jars of ginger peaches."

"But I learned to listen and to screen."

"You learned to pray some, Min. You never be listening too much. Just a little around the edges," grinning. "But you learned to pray some."

"Learning still, Old Wife, learning still."

"But ain't learned to quit casting a voluptuous eye on the young mens, I notice," chirping her teeth.

"When you gonna learn, you ole stick in the mud, that 'good' ain't got nothing to do with it? They packed me off to seminary thinking helping and healing and nosing around was about being good. It was only that I was . . . available."

"Hmph, I say, Min. Beggin your pardon."

"You a blip, Old Wife."

"Well, it takes one to know one."

"But mostly you a stick-in-the-mud," turning to watch the young doctor, Dr. Meadows, stroll over toward the stereo where the loa were setting up—drums, tambourines, flutes, chekere, gourds— walking right through them.

"I swear by Apollo the physician"—members of The Master's Mind glancing up at this odd chanting—"by Aesculapius, Hygeia and Panacea"—Cora Rider muttering—"and I take to witness all the gods, all the goddesses"—the loa nudging each other, puffing on cigars and rearing back on their heels—"to keep according to my ability and my judgment the following oath . . ."

"Quiet." Mr. Daniels dropped hands to wheel around from the prayer circle to jab Dr. Meadows in the chest.

"That's no proper kind of prayer," Cora Rider muttered hoarsely, making it clear to all within ear and eyeshot that nothing a redbone said or did could be in any wise proper.

"Shush."

"Shush, nothin. Coming in here with all that superstitious hocus-pocus like the good woman Ransom is some Count damn Dracula he got to protect his mariny self from."

"Cora, if you please."

Minnie sliding her palms down her thighs and winking at her companion. "No, good ain't got a blessed thing to do with it, Old Wife."

"Which it?"

"Any of it. Now here I am and there I am and all I am, free to be anywhere at all in the universe. And where I choose to be in just a little while is on my front porch having a nice tête-à-tête over tea with that Dr. Meadows, who would, I'm sure, be most interested in learning about the ancient wisdoms, the real, the actual, the sho-nuff original folk stuff behind them Greek imposters he's calling up and they're already there. Right there in the treatment room, if he'd only see."

"Beggin your pardon, Min, but you color struck."

"Anywhere at all in the universe, but I choose to be here with this growler scowler. And good ain't the key. It's just that

I'm available to any and every adventure of the human breath."

"You always were one for capers, Min."

"But just look at the chile's face. And I bet she had parents that told her, grandparents I'm sure, that God don't like ugly."

"God like it all, Min."

"Just a frowning and contorting up her face. A divine creation, the human face. And just look at her. One rough customer, that one."

"Just like you for the world, Min."

"I ain't studying you, Old Wife," hunkering down among the flowers by the chapel doors. "But I'll tell you this. The face is a wondrous thing. You can go anywhere, anywhere at all with a human face, journey straight into the Fifth Kingdom of Souls if that's your pleasure."

"Say which?"

"You heard me, the Fifth. Seems to me, Old Wife, that by now you should so well know all these things, you'd have things to tell me. You been dead long enough?"

"There is no age nor death in spirit, Min. Besides, I do tell you things soon's they come to me."

"Where from? I've been asking you that for years. You don't explain things clearly, Old Wife."

"You don't listen good, Min. Or maybe it's me. I never was too bright."

"When I was a young girl I thought you were the wisest."

"You thought I was crazy as a loon."

"Well, what with never combing your hair and coming to church in men's overshoes and talking to snakes and things— you were crazy as could be. But I used to watch you, slip up alongside you in the tobacco sheds and listen to you hum and talk, cause I knew you were special."

"You said I smelled, Min."

"Well, you did smell. Of dirt and gumbo and wintergreen

and nasty salves and pitch. Girl, you smelled of everything. But so wise. You had a way of teaching us kids things."

"Yawl called me a witch."

"True. But for goodness sake, we were just foolish little creatures, no more'n eleven or twelve then. Later on I wasn't too much the fool I didn't learn to listen to you."

"Didn't."

"Did too, so quit pouting. Remember how me and Sophie and Serge and Cleotus would hang around your candy stand?"

"Messing with my papers and trying to steal the pennies."

"Naw now. We used to like to hear you and Wilder talking over the old days and things like that. I know you know that or you wouldn't've been telling us kids things to do and think about and read and check out and reach for. We couldn't've grown up without you, Old Wife. None of us."

"We going in the chapel, or you plan to talk these here flowers to death?"

It seemed to Dr. Julius Meadows, leaning against the desk chagrined, playing with the buttons of the stereo, that the right hand of the healer woman was on its own, that she had gone off somewhere and left it absent-mindedly behind on the patient's shoulder. And it seemed that the patient was elsewhere as well. So like the catatonics he'd observed in psychiatric. The essential self gone off, the shell left behind. Dr. Meadows ran a hand through his hair and it crackled as though there were a storm brewing outside the window. He gazed out wondering where catatonia was, if it might be in the woods behind the Infirmary. Wondered if the two women had arranged a secret rendezvous in the hills and if going there he would find them both transformed, the older woman in full lotus under a blanket like the weathered photos his roommate had brought back from India. The younger a laurel bush, as in some legend, blooming in pieces somewhere in storybook memory.

He wanted to leave, but how to go without telling himself he was on a fool's errand, how to find some rational reason for leaving that would answer any question he might pose to himself? Need some air, he thought, rubbing the starchy jacket. Need a smoke, he thought, patting his pocket. Inching toward the exit door, he noticed that no one was paying him the slightest attention. But then that was usually the way. His presence or absence mattered to no one, not even to his patients he worried over through the nights. The knob was cold, chilled him through and through. The new paint job, finished in time for this round of visitors he was sure, was blinding.

Buster, walking himself and Nadeen closer, his right palm warm, alert to any movement on that side of her stomach, was certain that something was finally happening. He walked them still closer to see what. Mrs. Henry, his neighbor till she left bed and board, as his parents said sadly, twitched her face, cracked and crazed like the soup tureen in his aunt's china cabinet, then it was emptied out suddenly of anything he could give a name to. It was just as though Aunt Sudie had gotten up from an unsatisfactory dinner and removed the ladle from the chipped bowl, muttering, then walked to the back door, inched her foot in the crack, then swung it wide with her hip, holding the door back flat with her behind while she dumped the contents into the yard. And for a second there, he'd have been willing to swear that he saw two faces at once on Mrs. Henry. Like in an artsy photograph or like when he took his glasses off too fast. Or like he felt sometimes waking with a bump, his night face sinking down behind the day one and him touching himself to be sure he was there.

He patted the mother of his child while he searched for a "like" that would pin it down so he could be done with it and leave. He would have to be on his toes for the interviews with Dr. Serge and Mr. Cleotus. They had no patience with students who weren't wide awake and all there. Like. Mrs. Henry's double-exposure face was like. He bit his lip and sucked at the mustache coming in. Like at the airport at Christmas when his father, home from the Islands, turned at the glass and waved. And his father's sun tan, like a carnival mask with loose stringing, slipped a bit to the side of his face and Buster thought it might be time to check his prescription. That wasn't exactly the like. But to hell with like. It always got him in trouble. "Never mind what it's like," his father told him and Nadeen told him too. "Deal with what is, Buster, with what is."

He tucked in his top lip and scraped his teeth against the growth he was sure was a manly mustache and pondered the next question. How to be in two places at once? He needed to write up the interviews and hand them in next day, then he'd be done with his course work until finals. But how to be there in Dr. Serge's office and be there in the treatment room too when Mrs. Henry came round? He glanced at Nadeen, so intent yet self-preoccupied. She wasn't the most observant or lively reporter. She would no doubt shrug and say nothing much happened. "Mrs. Henry just got well that's all and then everybody left." He wondered if he really meant to go through with it, marry this girl who was barely his kid sister's age. He grazed his lips and mustache against her temples and hugged her. "Gotta go," he whispered. She never looked up his way.

Old Wife was pulling at Minnie's sleeve. "You're losing your audience, Min. Folks walking out."

"I'm gonna lose the patient too if you don't give me some directions. She's lost a lot of blood and her system's still full of gas. I just can't seem to generate the energy to bring her back and restore her."

"It'll be all right, Min. Is all right right now. Then you can go home and see about yo sef."

"Mmm," thinking about home, her slippers, the cushy couch, the throw rugs that would be bright and clean of cat fur and nut shells. The widow lady and her lodger had been at it all morning and she'd be overwhelmed at the door with lemon oil and ammonia. Or if the lodger had been allowed a free hand, the floors would be slick with van van polish and the whole house reeking of Peaceful House Incense #9. They did their best, but all she really wanted was for someone to drive the porch nails down so she could go barefoot. And for someone to move the cord of wood from the yard to the window within reach of the couch. And for someone to fix her kitchen window, propped up since Christmas with a stick of firewood. It didn't seem too much to ask. It didn't seem too much to get done for a woman who could get patients up off the surgeon's table, for a woman who could get patients to throw off their stitches, for a woman who could drive snakes out of folks' heads. But she wanted someone to do it without her leading them.

She thought of Dr. Meadows, wandering about in front of the Infirmary, studying the glyphs the old masons had chiseled into its face, reading the memorial plaques and glancing about toward the bus terminal, toward the park, as if not sure which way to ramble. And she saw herself on the porch with her silver tea set, legs crossed, swinging her new beige T-strap suedes, brushing the crease in his gray slacks. The doctor leaning in the rocker telling her all about himself.

"Free to go anywhere at all in the universe," Minnie muttered. "So why do I choose to be bothered with this gal?" But knowing that at the first sign of a shift on the stool, or a signal from Old Wife or a word from within, she would tear past the flower beds, race back along the path, sunk up to her hem in hot sand, and tilting would race down the cliffs to Velma Henry's side to take up the yoke and pull toward life.

"Love, Min. Love won't let you let her go. I'm not the leastways worried. Cause it's got everything to do with good."

"Love. Good. God. She don't want that. Getting so none of them want that. The children are spoiling, Old Wife. Want their loving done with sweet-tooth cupcakes and shiny cars and credit cards and grins from white folks."

"You believe that or just carryin on like your patients?"

"Oh, you've seen'm. Out there in deep waters showing off, forgetting everything they ever knew about sharks and the undertow."

"Why then you rip them fancy clothes off, Min, and thrash out into them waters, churn up all them bones we dropped from the old ships, churn up all that brine from the salty deep where our tears sank, and you grab them chirren by the neck and bop'm a good one and drag'm on back to shore and fling'm down and jump to it, pumping and cussing, fussing and cracking they ribs if ya have to to let'm live, Min. Cause love won't let you let'm go."

"But they want to go, that's the hurting part."

"Like you tole the lap sitter this morning, Min, when you hurt, hurt. But when you see the chirren calling down thunder and going up in flames, Min. Why then you snatch you a blanket—"

"A scabby, foul-smelling blanket off one of them mules we nary saw hide nor hair of, nor acres neither."

"Whatchu know about a mule blanket, Minnie Ransom? What on earth would you do with a mule and some acres? You was raised on eiderdowns and girls on wages fixing your breakfast on a tray. You sittin up here with your special-made clothes on and lingerie with letters on'm talking about you'd know how to get next to a mule long enough to get they blanket."

61

"And I'd throw that blanket over them chirren's head like a kidnap snatching sack and throw'm on the ground and roll'm in the dirt and jump all over them to smother out the flames till fire turn'm loose and they can live. Like you say, ole gal, the chirren are our glory."

"See, I told you, Min, you'd be feeling better once we got to chapel."

"We can't stay long now. The loa are setting up to make music for Velma to dance by. We got to free her up from fire and water so she don't drown in air like some backass fish."

"Min—"

"Then we got to summon one of the loa to see after the Henry gal's recuperation fore some God-slight notion lurking around near her master brain turn her water wrong."

"Min—"

"Check the moon, Old Wife, something's up in a fiercesome way between the men and the women and I don't want to get caught short of teas and things. Sophie gonna have to recruit some of these youngsters and train'm at gathering."

"I'ma get my walking shoes soon, Min, cause them haints fixing to beat on them drums with them cat bones and raise a ruckus. So you just leave me here and I'll talk to you after while. I can't stand all that commotion them haints calling music."

"Old Wife, what are you but a haint?"

"I'm a servant of the Lord, beggin your pardon."

"I know that. But you a haint. You dead ain't you?"

"There is no death in spirit, Min, I keep telling you. Why you so hard head? You and that gal on the stool cut from the same cloth. And a rough bolt of dry goods it is too."

"Yes, well, I'll hold that thought. But meanwhile let's get on with the business at hand. I want to go home, set my hair and brew some tea. Expecting company tonight," winking.

"Minnie Ransom, I'm gonna be right there on the porch with you. So you best be prepared to put aside any hussy notions about messing with that doctor man, you heifer."

"Lord, I hope you are recording this all. I hope you are beaming down on this scene I never auditioned for, Lord. Hope you see how your humble servant got her hands overfull with both the quick, not so quick and the dead. So when I petition you, Lord, with feeble praise and bold requests, don't turn me down now, gotta help me and answer my prayers."

"So little faith? Your prayers are always answered, Min."

"This I know. But sometimes the answer is no, Old Wife. Look who I got for a spirit guide, an old stick-in-the-mud who don't even remember from one session to the next the diagnoses and the treatment. Sweet Jesus."

"Be careful, Min Ransom, you heading for a fall. I'm not even sure you deserve your gift."

"Old Wife, good and bad and deserve and the rest of that stuff have got nothing, I'm telling you, nothing to do with it. Now you hold that thought while I get on back there and put on some music for the folks."

three

"What's with Palma?" Cecile had been looking out the bus window.

"Had a vexing dream about Velma. I guess that's why we're on our way to the Claybourne Festival."

"What's her sign—Palma's?"

"Kiss me neck. You, the staunch Marxist-Maoist-dialectical-historical-materialist who is always plenty short mouthed about the buzhwahh elements in the improvisations? You, the hard-nosed scientific bullshit detector? You, Inez, want to know Palma's sign? Backside!"

"But I'm not a materialist. I'm Chicana. No, hear me out."

Mai leaned forward. "Who's got the color film for the Bell and Howell?"

"Pass the thermos," one of the members of the troupe said.

"Cecile, you got your screwdriver handy, or a nail file?"

"Because the material without the spiritual and psychic does not a dialectic make."

"Gotcha."

"What's this vile and loathsome brew, Chezia?"

"Yerba mate, nectar of the gods."

"Her gods, Inez, are not our gods, O sister of the corn."

"Obviously. Your gods still alive, Chezia?"

"The screwdriver's married to the hammer, Nilda. You must take the whole sack and return it in one lump, if you please."

"Ask the driver if we can open the windows. The air conditioning is off, I think."

The driver was listening to the young woman just behind him. The front of her T-shirt read: Seven Sisters.

"Lonnie, my ole comrade at the barricades, sitting on a mat with a shaved head, nibbling on a communion wafer and sipping distilled water through a glass straw, Tibetan wind-chime music on the box, no Coltrane in sight, and no conversation except an occasional *Om*. It trips me out. The changes. And meanwhile Bakke and Carter and the KKK and the Nazis and COINTELPRO not skipping a beat."

"Any chance of our doing a mural for the Academy of the 7 Arts?" Mai was trying to get Palma's attention. "We've got a suitcaseful of paints under the bus."

"We're staying on after carnival or whatever it is, yes?"

"Palma, when exactly does the Claybourne Festival start?"

The bus driver, halting at the railroad crossing, eavesdropped on the conversations around him. In the seats to the side and behind were the colored women who'd gotten on in Barnwell with satchels and bags and knapsacks. All in bossy T-shirts—*No Nukes, Stop the Esmeralda, Get the U.S. Out Of* . . . It would have meant staring at unbridled bosoms to read it all. He guessed he was old-fashioned, like his son said, only that wasn't the term his son had used.

The clang clang and winking lights, left right, left right, were doing something to him. He searched through his crossword puzzle repertoire for the word, any word, a word to worry over the spelling of to distract him from the lights. He might have found one, but it was too damn hot to think and it was overheating underfoot too, scorched metal fumes in his face scraping his throat, burning his eyes. He slid the window open and hung his cap on the hook. He'd have to do something about his hair. The office was leaning on all the gray hairs. For years they hadn't hired colored guys. Now, just when he was getting some seniority, they were talking about early retirement.

"Before we sit down to work out the program with the brothers from the Academy, we need to go through these folders. These are the skits and poems and some of the posters from International Women's Day."

He hung on to the talk around him lest he overheat too. He felt light and feverish, as though he might float away in delirium any minute, leaving thirty-one passengers stranded. Which might not be a bad idea, he was thinking, his teeth bared in a grin or a sneer, he wasn't sure which. Too hot to care. And it had been one crummy lunch. And he was late. And he couldn't afford to blow the extra job, the chartered bus of doctors visiting the Infirmary. And the train was taking its own sweet, mile-long time.

"Mai, change seats with Nilda and help me with this. A piece on John Henry and Kwan Cheong. The Spirit of Iron . . . something like that. We never did work it through."

"The Central and Union Pacific race for profit."

"We could do it as a mime and narrative musical for Sister of the Rice and Sister of the Yam."

"Anything to do with metals should be done by the brothers, I think."

"Unfortunately they're all Black at the Academy, aren't they? And for the Kwan character—"

"Would you care to expound a bit on that 'unfortunately'

before Sister Palma of the Yam and Sister Cecile of the Plantain whip out their switchblade and machete, respectively?"

"You think Velma might join us? Do the music? Palma?"

"John Henry and Kwan Cheong. I'll take the notes. Keep talking."

Some notes, the driver, Fred Holt, thought. He mopped his face with a handkerchief. He'd like a gander at those notes. For three hours the women in the T-shirts had been fumbling with cameras, tape recorders, weird machines, clipboards, note pads, babbling about corn and rice and plutonium bombs and South Africa and Brer Rabbit and palm oil and the CIA and woodcuts. Now John Henry. If he knew a good psychiatrist to recommend to them, he would. If he could keep the sweat out of his eyes long enough, he'd like to look over those notes himself. Women.

"Look."

He stole a glance around. The tall Indian woman who wore a man's hat with an oily black feather stuck in the band was mashed up against the windowpane pointing up. He followed her finger, scooting down in his seat to see. A flock of birds in a low swoop over the train was sharply changing direction and heading back over the roadway as if pulled by an invisible hook.

He thought of what his buddy Porter had said the night they watched the moon walk and the shots of the earth, going through three six-packs without batting an eye. Porter talking about going to where the ice ends and the Antarctic meets the dark southern oceans of the great whales. And he had listened in a blurry way as Porter had droned on and on about dying before he ever got to see all of the earth from that view. "Only the albatross," he'd said, like he was reciting a poem, "the albatross and the swift and the shearwater see it all at once." And he wondered if Porter wanted to be an astronaut or a bird or what. Poor, poor bastard.

"Arrows in the sky," the woman in the hat said, licking two fingers and smoothing the feather from its fat to its taper.

"The arrow of Ra," someone else muttered, the one who hadn't had too much to say since boarding in Barnwell.

He didn't hear what the other women said, abandoning for a moment the machines they took apart, cleaned, oiled, fondled lewdly was the way he felt it, jerking them off, cranking handles, blow job on the lenses, he chuckled. They leaned into the windows and were talking all at once. What was there to say about this perfectly ordinary sight? A bunch of birds doing what birds do. Porter, though, might've pointed out what there was to see, what was escaping his eye. Would have made a poem out of how they ride the currents, ride sheer sunlight. Porter would have had something hip to say.

Fred Holt wiped his face again, wiped his shades, dangling them by one stem, then stuffed the damp handkerchief back into his pocket. The train was roaring in and he was alert now, not drifting, so no more need of the women, their words, their presence to anchor him. Besides, half the time they were talking Spanish or West Indian or some other language. The only one who spoke good English was the Jap, or maybe she was a Chink. Though even in regular English they rambled, interrupting each other, finishing off each other's sentences—baffling. He hadn't heard a word from the two fat ladies behind them in a while, rattling tin foil and juggling paper plates on their laps, determined it seemed to eat their way across country. They'd been talking at him a blue streak from the minute they got on until the colored women got on in Barnwell. So that was a blessing. He didn't have to answer a bunch of dumb questions about how he liked being a bus driver, about the route, about where one could get a good hot meal in this or that town. They were content now to talk to each other and leave him alone.

"Ya figure epidemics then, Gracie? Have another, baked them myself."

"My son-in-law says Legionnaires' disease is just the beginning. He says those doctors do not know what they're doing playing around with viruses and germs and things. Will kill us all, my son-in-law says. He works in a hospital, my son-in-law does. A matter of reap what you sow, I guess."

"But innocent people, Gracie."

"Chickens coming home to roost."

"But what about the people who haven't done anything, Gracie?"

"Date nut bread with orange peel. You must give me this recipe."

"I don't want to die, Gracie. I think the government should stop those doctors. Take away their licenses."

"Tie them up with their own stethoscopes. Did I tell you what that doctor who took out my you-know-what had the nerve to say to me when I told him about all the . . . gas I was letting out? Most embarrassing."

The train was thundering by, jiggling Fred Holt in his seat. Wood, coal, racks of jeeps, sealed cars with stenciled lettering revealing nothing at all about the contents. He'd heard they shipped trash from nuclear plants in cars like that. Flat cars bearing the weight of freight cars he usually saw traveling under their own steam when he did the run from St. Louis to Memphis. Dirty yellow, smudged orange, rust, gun-metal gray going by. Hear that long lonesome whistle . . . riding the blinds . . . Please please mistuh brakeman, let a po' boy ride yo' train . . . O the Rock Island Line is a mighty good . . . How long, how long has the evening train been gone . . . I'm Alabamee bound. Then a clear view. A clear view of EAT GAS ROOMS DON'T LITTER POST NO BILLS NO TRESPASSING JESUS LOVES YOU.

On his left up ahead a salvage yard, bathtubs and kitchen

sinks. Old men in tatters huddled around a burning trash can. One carefully spreading newspaper across another one lying down by an upturned tub. It could be the Depression again, he was thinking. The old bum on the ground could be dead, starved to death. He thought of the Depression years, of how the neighbors at night used to trade flour and beans and salt pork in the shadows of the tool sheds on the q.t., lest word get out food was around and they get hit in the head. How his father and mother would send him the back way to deliver sacks of sweet potatoes or meal to the poorer families. How the women would accept the food, say thanks and move off. How the men would drop their eyes and scuff their boots in the dirt and mumble and keep him standing there. How his own family ate with the lights off and the shades pulled down. How they wouldn't eat at all till his father's older brother got in from the trains, food from the dining cars wrapped in napkins and stuffed in shoe boxes. How they ate again when his father reopened the store, the platters near full, his father standing over them all with a stick and they better not grab.

A fat man with three different-colored sweaters on rushed out of a shack and chased the old bums away. Yes, it could be the Depression all over again. It is, he thought, lips drawn back. But he couldn't afford to think too long of that, the pension-fund scandal still front-page news and all the talk about oil rationing and food shortages and his years slipping by and prices being what they are. Inflation, inflation, why you want to be so mean? I got the high-price blues and I . . . and I . . .

Porter said that pretty soon the only work the likes of them would be able to get was in those nuclear plants. "The rate those places are falling apart," Porter had said, showing him some of the articles he was always tearing out of the papers, "they'll only hire the old." And Fred had had to dampen his fingers to spread the newsprint flat and to read quickly about the plants constructed right after the War, their War; how they were rapidly coming apart now. "That way," Porter said, putting another clipping down to read, smoothing out the crease and tearing it some, "we old workers are dead and gone before anybody can do a study about the effects of radiation on workers." And Fred had nodded, then muttered "cold-blooded," quickly reading over the second item about a suit against a chemical plant by workers who'd left years ago and were dying of cancer.

"That's all the good we old timers'll be," Porter had said, folding the articles neatly into his billfold. "Now, you watch," pointing his bread knife in the direction of the Infirmary, "those big shots over at Transchemical'll level that place before long. Too many agitator types over there, the educated kind, too, and they're collecting information about conditions at the plant, its effect on our lungs, I bet. Probably making tests." And Fred had stared out the diner window toward the building he'd been meaning to go by for the longest time for a checkup. But not if agitators hung round there. He'd had enough trouble in life.

Fred Holt fingered the bumps and grooves of the steering wheel and tried not to be sick. Tried not to think about the lunch, or about Porter. He hunched over the wheel, staring out, and dared himself to go get a checkup at the Infirmary.

Passing on his right was a huge plain of mud, red, like the deep-red mud near the river mouth behind the old house when he was in short pants, then knickers. A plain of fresh destruction, he composed, as if to report this sight to Porter. Not there when last he had this route. Stores gutted, car shells over-turned, a playground of rust and twisted steel. Mounds of broken green bottle glass, rusted bedsprings, bald tires, doors off their hinges leaning in the wind, flower-pot shards and new-looking brick and lumber strewn about but not haphazardly, as if a crew had brushed them off with profit in mind. Panes of glass up against a half-wall for pickup later, looked like. A project not long ago put up was now this pile of rubble. And in the middle of it all a crater. He specially did not want to look at that. Not in all this heat. Not with his stomach churning up the lousy lunch. No time for another rest stop. Late as hell. No way to make it by 3:10 P.M. And them bastards just looking for the chance to dump him before pension time.

Same old number, he thought, rumbling over the tracks. Redevelopment. Progress. The master plan. Cut back in services, declare blight, run back from the suburbs and take over.- There'd be no Hoover towns sprouting up here. There'd be high rises and boutiques next time through. Blondes with dogs on leashes and teenage kids on bikes in parking lots and station wagons and new street lights and. He sucked his teeth. Niggers. Compliant, movable niggers forever going for the oakie doke. He dropped his eyes into his lap and the light and the blue shadows there fed his mind's adventures. A raid on the lumberyards. Taking over construction companies. The revolving drum of the cement mixer. Him riding shotgun on a derrick and crane. New housing going up and him going up in a glass elevator with a hard hat on. Schools, playgrounds, stores, clinics. And they, the older men the young ones were quick to call over the hill and through, would defend it all with guns.

"What's the delay?" A voice from the middle of the bus.

Exactly. There'd been too much delay. And he meant to do his part before they wiped him out. Maybe he hadn't done all he could to help his boy through school. Maybe he'd been too much the worried father, too much the angry father, too much the put-aside father, in those days when the boy suddenly a man and making decisions he couldn't go with was going to jail every time he turned around. But he was nobody's Tom, nobody's good nigger, nobody's sit-around-on-the-porch fool. He was still fumbling with the gear stick as he slowly passed what had once been a lot of people's homes. Home one minute, a crater the next. Flower boxes, stoops, lawns slipping into the maw of the mechanical monster. The bite of the hydraulic bit breaking up potsy courts and basketball courts. Over and over in fuck-you repetition. How long, how long? A gaping hole, a grave, a pit. Nothing to even pass by in a car with the grand-children on a Sunday drive and point to and say . . . nothing. Nothing.

Like the home he'd known for too short a time, but a sweet time for a while. Pruitt-Igo raised up a monument one minute, blown up a volcano the next. And near the crater that had been their home was the pit that had been the elevator shaft down which he'd dropped Sen-Sen wrappers and matchbooks with phone numbers on them lest Wanda jump salty with him. And down at the bottom of the shaft the other dumpage. Eleven dead bodies. The rotted remains of bill collectors, drug dealers, wives, husbands, raped and missing girls of East St. Louis.

"What's happenin, my man?" The musician with the horn case in his lap was getting impatient.

Exactly. What? Everything ruined and wrecked, made old and garbage before its time. He picked his way carefully through memories to keep from tripping over one that might cost him too much. Like his lunch, the chili he should've known better but ordered anyhow. On his last run to Mem-phis, he'd gone to look at his young man haunts. The bakery shut down, the hardware store that sold everything and was perfect for hanging out in to get the news boarded up, the Palace a ghost place, shreds of bills featuring Bukka White, Willy Dixon, Muddy, Bilbo hanging near-unreadable from the falling walls. Church's Park deserted, no tents, no more music, as if Bobby Bland and B.B. had been done gone and he had no past and no future.

"Hey, my man, we're trying to make a gig."

He wrenched the stick into gear and tried to ignore the grinding and the hacking cough erupting from up under the bus. Grateful one minute, seething the next, he turned onto the highway, searching in the mirror for the bastard rushing him, reminding him of how little it would take to lose his damn job and blow his retirement.

One of the musicians, it was, who'd boarded at the old post office, not a regular stop anymore but what the hell. There they were beside a broke-down van, so what could he do? They'd stopped, it seemed, to get sandwiches and use the phone, mail some letters, stretch their legs, and the battery had got pinched and some instruments too. Or maybe the tires, or the motor. Something like that. He might have gotten it straight, might have sympathized, given advice. Might've eased into the old whatcha-know-bro he'd prided himself on in the beginning before the job turned sour. But not anymore. Damn fools, full-grown men, you'd think they'd know enough not to go off all together. Musicians. No sir, he didn't have a mumbling word to say. Drive the bus and mind your own damn business was his policy now. So many guys laid off behind some simple shit like a passenger complaining that the driver had gotten too familiar. Shit.

It was the big fella with the alligator horn case, he figured. Seemed to be the leader. Had a loused-up mouth. Looked like some prison dentist had got hold of him. Fred knew about that. A half-ass examination with what felt like a pickax in the mouth, then the grabbing up of pliers. Not even a glance at the mixing plates, not a thought to the tubes of filling stuff. Just cold pliers coming at you to let you know your teeth like you are beyond salvation. He wondered if the big fella's ruined smile ruined the lip too and approaching the horn again was like coming back to a woman you hadn't held in four long years. Wondered if you had to court the horn, shy and clumsy all over again, fearing that what was missing was more than teeth, was something so deep down and necessary there'd be no getting back to how things had been in the sweet time. He wondered if the big fella with the bad mouth had had better luck with his comeback than he had had with Wanda. Least he had a gig. But what did he, Fred Holt, hard worker for nearly forty years, have? But he didn't want to think about that or feel any kind of anything for the big fella. He had a gig, fine, and that was that.

It was hot and the gears were slipping. Maybe the cotter pin was getting chewed up in the axle. Some new young jerk in the yard had changed the wheel, no telling what he was on, goofy and full of noise. The wheel could come off. Fine. Behind schedule stopping for them musicians and trying to find change. Then stopping again to try to quiet down them damn-fool white folks getting a head start on their convention blast or whatever it was they were going to Claybourne for. And the drunken couple he'd threatened twice, actually pulling over to the shoulders, to put off the bus. Though he'd welcomed a chance to stop, get out, splash his face with the remains of his ice tea. But he'd never make it to the terminal by three. It was nearly ten of as it was. And any minute the bus might do who-knew-what. So he'd probably have to toss a coin, a nap or some dinner, cause there was that charter run to make with the doctors at that infirmary place and he sure needed the dough.

They were pitching beer cans out the windows, the loud-mouths in the stupid hats. But damn if he was going to point to the sign overhead, read the regulations, recite the law. If he got flagged down, he'd just tell the cop to take them in, haul them all in for his money. Getting so people didn't know how to act anymore. They talked in the movies like they were at home with the TV where any ole off-the-wall shit was okay. But at least the beer drinkers had gotten the hymn singers to shut up, so that was something in their favor. Though when the Jesus types had gotten on at the Farmer's Market in their rummage-sale clothes, with their battered suitcases and juice-less faces, carrying their Bibles and their hymn books, he had hoped their presence would put a halt to the risqué jokes and the foul-mouth gab of the conventioneers. That was the least they could do, bringing all that gloom onto the bus. That was what white folks like that were supposed to do, he figured, check other white folks in their madness stead of leaving it to black folks, who had enough to do given all the crazy niggers and white folks too they had to deal with day in and day out. But looked like their off-key singing and no-spunk praying or just plain being there only egged the characters in the hats on, slinging naked-lady magazines around the bus and standing up in the seats to make underarm farts. White folks. But at least things were pretty quiet now, like the two camps of whiteys were holding each other down. Stabilized. There was a good puzzle word. He formed the letters, blocked them neatly in the boxes, then gave himself over to the black-and-white patterns in his mind.

"J.D.?"

"I'm listening."

"What say we lay over in this hick town awhile—the one we going to—and get somebody to drive the car up. We ain't booked nowhere else yet."

"Suits me."

"Say, J.D.?"

"I'm listening."

"What name were you born with, all kidding aside?"

"Ask yo mama."

Fred Holt glanced at the big fella in the mirror. He was grinning, and a messed-up grin it was. Whatever that gig paid, he oughta use it to get his mouth fixed up, Fred was thinking.

The grin was sure private and just as well, enough to scare little children. Whatever his name was, it was clear that he thought it made him a friend to his horn. He was hugging the case with one arm, drumming a little paradiddle with his other hand.

He'd heard the old musicians talking when he was a kid and used to sit there in the hall of Miss Hazel's boardinghouse, hugging his knees, that naming was no miscellaneous matter. You took a name and gave your ax a name that made you both amiable to the music. They made it sound like this music was a person who could be called over and made to work for you. He'd wanted to be a musician, cept he never got around to learning anything worthwhile. What he could do on a harmonica didn't amount to a hill of beans. And too, he'd really wanted to be some kind of outdoor worker, a builder, thick leathery gloves with the fingers cut out, a hard hat, tough work boots. Old Jimmy Lyons, who used to tear up the Hammond organ over at Stompit had told him he was a four, and fours were builders, but lots of fours never got around to doing what they were put on the earth to do cause they was so busy feeling boxed in by them four sides of their nature that they didn't have sense to look up and appreciate all that space they could build into. And Jimmy Lyons had told him another thing, that the Negro people were fours and so long as they paid more attention to folks trying to pen them in, hem them in, box them in on all four sides thinking they had them in prison than to the work at hand, why then they would never get a spare moment to look up at the sun and build. That Jimmy Lyons was one philosophizing fool. Porter would have liked him. They would have taken to each other right off. But then they would've been so delighted with each other's company, Fred wouldn't've been able to get a word in edgeways.

Something made him look toward the back of the bus. Something strong and not to be denied pulled him from the past to make him straighten up and check out the boy with the wire basket in the center of the back seat. Of course, snakes. He'd had an inkling it was something weird when the strange-looking youth had got on. Goddamn snakes. On his bus. Who would believe that? Who, in fact, could he even tell it to anymore?

"Snakes! Can you manage that?" he might've said to Porter.

And Porter would've said right back, "Can you live? Can a nigger live?"

But Porter was dead. Porter was dead and he was driving an unsafe bus with drunken white folks, severe, righteous whiteys looking just like the ones in the lynch mob pictures, a pack of strange talking women with troublemaking shirts, and a retarded looking farm kid with a basket of snakes. Beat me Jesus, he muttered, beat me all in my chest. Snakes. Can you manage that?

There'd be no one to pick up the cue anymore. A pair of knitting needles had seen to that. Two goddamn needles stuck in Porter's neck at the Pit Stop. Some in-a-hurry passenger taking exception to Porter's second slice of pie, or to his neat look and fresh smell of bay rum and talc, or to the way he hadn't answered—who knew why? Not a single Claybourne paper could piece together a story from the witnesses. And not a single witness could offer a description of the woman. "It was a woman," the counter girl had told him when Fred'd asked, hiccuping so hard through the telling he couldn't make sense of any of it. So no one could say whether she was Black, white, blond, fat or a bear in a wig or a moose in a dress. For all he knew she could be on this run. The drunken woman with hair like granite, blubbering chatter, trying to talk to one of the colored guys. Or one of them T-shirts. Knitting needles, snakes, can you manage that? Life was a danger and every minute.

Wasn't that Porter's theme song? You're minding your business, staying off the streets, paying your bills and trying to make a go of your marriage. And some asshole expert releases radioactive fumes in the air and wipes you out in your chair reading the funnies. "As we sit here," Porter used to say, grabbing the edge of the counter, "we are dying from overexposure to some kind of wasting shit—the radioactive crap, asbestos particles, noise, smog, lies." And Fred would nod and push his plate away.

"Palma, were you able to reach anyone at home?" Mai was leaning across the aisle.

"No answer."

"You all right?"

Who was there to say, "Fred, you all right?" Or, "Pass the thermos to Fred. He looks a bit overheated"? Porter, the only other colored guy on the shift, used to hail him—"Hey, Fred, how's your hammer hanging?" And he'd mount the stool and holler back, "It ain't ruined my crease none." And the Pit Stop would become an okay place despite the gluey pie and the "specials" that tasted just like the regular fried newspaper meals. It beat going home.

His home was beginning to feel more like a trailer every day than a house, the kind of trailer he imagined they made dirty movies in, the kind of dirty movies he always watched holding his breath, expecting Margie to turn up in them, for there was always someone who looked like her—big sloppy tits, rough skin, never quite clean—doing something low down near the end of the movie. Margie. With her streaked and stringy hair and flat ass acting like she was some kind of movie star, prancing about the house in her drawers. Giving him her back at night like he was supposed to be grateful for whatever she offered. But he couldn't talk about that with Porter. Porter was a race man. So for all the time of their friendship, he'd never once invited him home for supper or talked about any wife but Wanda. But Wanda had left years ago. Now Porter was dead.

Porter. Had to bribe a doctor to get his papers through and get the job with the bus company. Some kind of wasting disease was eating him up. Yucca Flats, 1955, atomic test blasts—his theme song. That might be something to chat about with the T-shirts if the bus broke down. Hospitalized, discharged, no compensation, no records, not service-connected they said, goodbye, get lost buddy, drop dead. She stabbed him, they said, in the side of his neck as he leaned into his cup, lips pursed, hot coffee. He fell, they said, like cattle fall in the stockyards. Yucca Flats, Pit Stop. It was enough to make a grown man weep. Enough to make you mean. Make you want to wrench the wheel and drive the bus right through the rails and into the marsh. So easy to do, the crunchable rails rolling past, dull gray, bent and rusted here and there. So easy, the embankment sloping down a bit toward the swamp punk. So easy. He'd often dreamt of it, and the dreams hadn't scared him at all. He'd been intrigued with the notion of sinking and of being on the embankment watching. Being in the grasses hearing the thick gurgling as the waters sucked the bus under. He often thought of it, of what it would be like. Lying there at night, resting on his arm and projecting pictures on the ceiling, he wouldn't have to look at Margie's blue flannel back.

Speeding past the marshes, Fred Holt was brimming over with rage and pain and loss. He watched the upcoming rush of rails with such intensity, could see the bus crashing through the metal and thundering through the bushes down to the depths with such searing clarity, it etched an imprint on the surroundings. An imprint that became magnetized, drawing substance to it, sucking plasma from the underbrush creatures, draining colors from the trees and shrubs, snatching sound from birds, crickets and from Fred Holt's lungs, pulling life to it for manifestation in a tangible form. A complete happening it would become for any daydreamy hitch-hiker who might walk that way, for any of the bus passengers who might look that way, off-guard, susceptible.

Porter. So neat, so well read, so unfull of shit. One of the few guys around who could talk about something other than pussy, poker, pool and TV. Had wanted to be a newspaper reporter, go all over the world, go to Africa and see what that was like. They used to sit on them stools in the Pit Stop like truck drivers with their knees out and talk about Africa, piecing together whatever they knew and trusted to counter the hooey handed them in newsmagazines. They'd sit there with their knees out while the whores, half of them with jaws like Joe Palooka, five o'clock shadows and all, sat sidesaddle at either end of the counter eying them like they'd ever be that hard up. And they'd talk about family, Fred's in New York, Porter's wife and kids in Canada. And the kids spinning around on the stools would interrupt, begging a quarter for the jukebox. They argued the merits of growing up in Memphis or in Harlem. Porter talked about Speaker's Corner, calling it "holy ground." Fred would talk about the tenements behind Beale Street they used to call "The Arks." They'd laugh together at their fathers' old-time courting tales, when they'd jam a tomato stake with their name chalked on it in the girl's yard and hope like hell her father wouldn't come yank it out and fling it back over the fence. Or about their own courting days, Fred sitting up in the Palace with his hat in Wanda's lap, Porter sitting up in the Apollo with his arm around Irene, his thumb grazing her breast.

And hunched over the liver and onions with no smell to it, they'd talk about the characters in Claybourne: the slick-time gangster who called himself Doc Serge and ran the Infirmary that never paid its bills but managed to stay open somehow; Portland Edgers, who like Porter had been a race man but wasn't quite the same after that time he'd had to beat the woman who was taking in all the civil rights workers; Jay Patterson with his shit-eating grin, who never remembered your name but always wanted to shake your hand, would shake your hand two and three times a day and try to pin a button on you; and James Lee Henry, who ran the Academy of 7 Arts, where it was rumored the stash of guns and ammunition stolen from the armory was hidden; the old geezer they called The Hermit cause he lived behind high hedges in a dark house and only once in a blue moon came out, like at carnival when he'd make a speech in the park and then slip away. Of course, toward the end, Porter had made it impossible to speak any other way but reverently of The Hermit.

But whatever they talked about, Porter always managed to bring it round to Yucca Flats, 1955, atomic blasts, no compensation. The man was haunted. And now he was gone. Spun around on a stool by some crazy bitch with no better place to put her knitting needles but in a good man's life. What would he do now with his fitful nights but rehearse bus accidents on the ceiling or glare at Margie's back and get dangerous?

He saw it dart out from the marshes, scoot under the shrubs at the railing. Saw it run out onto the highway and stop, its eyes like road reflectors. A dark and furry thing offering itself up. So he took it. Eyes right on it, foot to the floor, he killed it, felt it go lumpy then smooshy in the wheel. And he dropped his hands away one at a time to wipe them on his pants. Barreling down the highway away from it, he kept his eyes strictly off the rear-view mirror. He felt hot and swarmy, felt the chili turning on him. If he could just make it to the terminal before it caught up with him. But already it was rushing him and he was helpless to keep ahead of it, could smell it jamming up his nostrils, jamming up his lungs. Fire.

The fire that time and him leaning against the house throwing up his insides. Trees like blazing giants with their hair aflame, crashing down in the fields turning corn, grass, the earth black. Birds falling down out of the sky burnt and sooty like bedraggled crows. The furniture blistering, crackling, like hog skins crackled on Grandaddy's birthday. His mother dragging the mattress out sparking and smoldering, beating it with her slipper and the matting jumping like popcorn all over the front yard. And her screaming, screaming at him as if she knew. And she probably did. His pop's store coming away from the house, leaning over and crashing down. The store a hole in the ground and just the apples stored in its cellar recognizable. Him standing in the piece of doorway swaying, char and ash sucking at the soles of his feet threatening to take him under the few floorboards left down past the apples and straight to hell for what he'd done.

Swaying in the doorway not a doorway, tar gas filling up his mouth and lungs, and all the sun that ever was crowding in behind him to make him look down where Pop had been, where a lone tin can was now, its label scorched away, a scorched patch of label here, a shine there. And whatever it held about to explode. Beans, soup, tomatoes, okra about to explode in his face. Knocked off the shelf maybe in the first cave-in, pushed to the side by a falling beam, it had gotten smacked to the side by the hoses drowning the place and gotten finally stopped by his father's head before the men gripped him by his stocking feet and dragged him out, taking their time. Speed no longer mattered for Pop. And then he was alone with the tin can parked at his feet, accusingly, growing fatter and fatter and ready to explode.

He felt like he was sitting on burrs. He couldn't afford to stop again, not with the hot-metal smell and the lateness. He just might make it. But one more holler from the grand wizard or whatever the joker in the spangled hat was, one more cranking of a camera, one more anything and he'd snatch free the pistol taped underseat and blow their fucking heads off. All of them. The pains in the ass and the ones who hadn't yet given him any trouble. Not yet. But they all did eventually. Loyal, loving, there one minute, gone the next. Troubling. But he'd gotten over Wanda and had rewarded himself with blond hair. Soft, caring one minute, pain in the ass the next, face to the wall, in a stew, in a freeze, giving him back talk or worse, just her back and no talk at all.

And of course when he got home tonight, he could count on her to ask him the same dumb thing: "Have a nice trip, Freddie?" No sleep, brains cooked, lousy meals, the worse shift, Porter dead, uniform a mess, so she had it coming. "I ran over a coon. As in raccoon. Not to be confused with the coons your daddy used to lynch." And she'd cry. Not for him, not for his chafed neck and his jounced nuts, his loss, his threatened pension. But for herself and some dead animal.

There'd be no washcloth in the freezer for his face, no tub run, no jug of tea with chipped ice and sliced lemon to drink, sloshing in the sudsy water. There'd be no decent meal to get down to make up for the chili that had his bowels in a knot. And no intelligent conversation. Just the hot still air of the dirty movie-trailer house smelling like spoiled chops burning in an unclean oven. And her blubbering on about the dead coon on the highway till she was too swollen and bleary and ugly to do anything but hit. But he might not even get the chance. The tin can of a bus stuffed and overheated any minute might explode. Snakes popping in the air like the frogs he slung from the mound back of the house, watching them pop and his mother damning his murdering soul to hell, hymnals fluttering out of them beatup suitcases, music cases snapping open and guitar strings popping, cartridge tapes spiraling across the highway a tangle. And the cameras catching it all somehow in time for the six o'clock news. Rage, sorrow, sour kidney beans and rice rose up in his throat with shredded cow spilling its terror of the slaughterhouse hammer into his mouth. He dug out the damp handkerchief, hands like claws, and vomited.

"Driver, you okay?"

"I wanna tell you people that my husband here beats up on me—"

"Give us a break and drop dead, lady, willya?"

"Nilda, pass up the napkins."

"What's the trouble up there? Hey, you're supposed to stand behind the white line for crissake."

"Don't never lose your mind on holidays or have big trouble, cause all them hospital beds are full up and the doctors are on vacation."

"Have a drink, lady, and forget it."

"What's going on up there? A summit goddamn conference for crissake?"

"Driver, pull over and let these rummies off. They're stinking up the bus. Hey! Driver! You! Boy!"

"Watch that shit."

"I wasn't talking to you."

"I'm talking to you. Watch that 'boy' shit."

"Another napkin, somebody. He'll be okay."

"Who the hell are you?"

"The 'boy' who might get around to arranging your bridgework, honky."

"Let's all be peaceful."

"Awww stuffit."

"Claybourne in five minutes. Last stop." Fred was finally able to speak.

All conversation stopped. Mouths agape, gestures frozen,

eyes locked on the driver's cap, or back, or Adam's apple, arrested, as if the announcement were extraordinary, of great import. They might have been in the playground playing "red light, green light, one, two, three." Or in a mime studio mastering "statues." Or in white jackets at a healing session watching the sutures on a woman's wrists turn from black to maroon to pink to flesh, and staring at the healer, forced to acknowledge something more powerful than skepticism, and be stunned still. They might have been leaning against a stack of bedsheets while Doc Serge, holding forth in the linen closet, explained the symbols on a dollar bill, translating carefully Novus Ordo Seclorum to them and the boy Buster standing mute and immobile. They might've been in the corner poolroom instead of whizzing past it, bars, a church, a funeral parlor at fifty-five miles an hour in a thirty-five-mile zone. Might've been in Shorty's pool hall in the exact moment when Shorty rushed to the back, skidded into the corner of the gambling table and warned through clenched teeth "the man" and had been caught in the frozen tableau till some magical bit of stage business registered in the brain as the thing to be doing to render the self invisible to the law.

They might have been sitting on a white stool as the patient or on a wooden bench in a locker room as the patient's husband, or in the driver's seat clamping down hard, throat and stomach hot and moist and like a rock, holding still the rage and regret threatening to be thrown up from the depths of the self all covered with slime.

They might've been twenty-seven miles back in the moment of another time when Fred Holt did ram the bus through the railing and rode it into the marshes, stirring bacteria and blue-green algae to remember they were the earliest forms of life and new life was beginning again. In the sinking bus trying to understand what had happened, was happening, would happen and stock still but for the straining for high thoughts to buoy them all up. But sinking into the marshes thick with debris and intrusion. Faces frozen at the glass seeing with two eyes merely the onlookers on the embankment holding their breath, or seeing closer by with two eyes the bullfrogs holding theirs in the shallows, the dragonflies suspended over the deeps and the wind waiting, the waters still and waveless till the shock of the plunge registered and the marshes sucked things under.

Silence on the bus as at a momentous event. But an event more massive and gripping than the spoken word or an accident. A sonic boom, a gross tampering of the weights, a shift off the axis, triggered perhaps by the diabolics at the controls, or by asteroids powerfully colliding. Earth spun off its pin, the quadrants slipping the leash, the rock plates sliding, the magnetic fields altered, and all, previously pinned to the crosses of the zodiac and lashed to the earth by the fixing laws, released. A change in the charge of the field so extreme that all things stop and are silent until the shift's complete and new radiations open the third eye:

J.D., his fingers splayed out on the horn case, trying to connect with the music. A tune had caught him and held him in a moment when speech, movement, thought were not possible. Something in an idiom that had to be attended to from the total interior, captured, defended. The humming sonorous from his center now was making him eager to get to the Regal Theatre in Claybourne to echo it all after six long years of dumbness behind the walls.

Mai, Sister of the Rice, coming unstuck from the web of time and place, was in the fish canneries of Alaska, the sugar plants of Hawaii, farm valley California, Manilatown, Chinatown, Japantown, all over at once calling together in a single moment the Sisters of the Rice to caucus.

Iris, Sister of the Plantain, loosening, was back in Barnwell handing out no-nuke flyers and turning in time to have an angry woman with a baby slung over her back rush up to her and spit "Sun lover!" in her face, an echo of what others like her, misrecognizing who and what she was, had spat out years ago—"Nigger lover!"

Fred and Wanda in the bedroom, oblivious to the noise of the elevator on the other side of the wall. The two of them smack up against each other like two halves of ancient fruit succulent and sweet and no cleaving on the horizon.

Nilda was in the hills readying for the medicine dance. Having dreamed the dream that could release her anytime from the earth's bands, she was waking again to the thundering of white buffalo and the call of coyote to join the peyote gatherers to dance the dance not danced in thirty years.

Palma was walking into the Infirmary's treatment room as Buster and Nadeen were walking closer, then passing right through their bodies of rushing atoms and currents. The dark aureoles of Nadeen's breasts spreading her nipples wider, the dream of wings inside the girl her own swelling, the squeeze of his hands on the girl's belly pushing her closer to her destination. Then leaning over Velma, she was saying, "She carries their baby in his hands and they carry our future in their guts," before knocking her sister off the stool.

It might've been a fingernail scraping across the window, was Chezia's thought, remembering her first encounter with panes not made of the waxed paper or the greased sheep membranes of home. Or a goat screaming, was Cecile's, her ears at home on the island where her appetite readied her for rooti and ginger beer. It might have been the shriek of mandragora root uprooted from a bruja's garden, Inez was thinking, wondering if the old hag of her village still lived. But the sound that released them from the moment of freeze was the screech from the birds returning. And after the sudden change in pitch came a change in light that could mean rain. And then a change in texture, the air granular with grit that turned the blues to pink-silver and drew eyes toward the windows for signs of a storm.

No one remarked on any of this or on any of the other remarkable things each sensed but had no habit of language for, though felt often and deeply, privately. That moment of correspondence—phenomena, noumena—when the glimpse of the life script is called dream, déjà vu, clairvoyance, intuition, hysteria, hunger, or called nothing at all. Released now, lungs sucked air and feet scraped against the grit of the bus floor. But before the passengers could get back to what they'd been doing, they found themselves leaning toward the windshield as the tall woman with the feather pointing up at the ceiling lifted from her seat and shouted "Look" as though it were a bubble-top bus.

Tendon, feather, bone and flesh were riding against a backdrop of eight-minute-ago blue, of fifty-years-ago blue, rode the curvature to the seam, flying through to what the sages of old had known about gravity and the outer edge, gazing up. Birds riding the air, riding the sun's beams and back, gliding in light in and out, hollow-boned and tiny-brained but sufficient when living in the law.

"Birds," shrugged the driver.

"Birds," said the farm boy in the rear, twisting round in his seat to check the sky, his eyebrows up, his shoulders too and the wire basket aslant in his lap. The other passengers shrugging back in answer, satisfied it was just birds, and that they flew their own way, but baffled by the outburst of the woman standing up. Fred eyed her in the mirror, his stomach settled for a moment. Nilda, still lifting from her seat, continued to stare at the ceiling agape as though it were a membrane, a veil to look through at the fabulous apparition flying back from the concealed world in the far side of the mind.

four

Obie dumped his clothes in the locker and dropped down on the bench by his daybook. It was starting up again, the factions, the intrigue. A replay of all the old ideological splits: the street youth as vanguard, the workers as vanguard; self-determination in the Black Belt, Black rule of U.S.A.; strategic coalitions, independent political action. Camps were forming threatening to tear the Academy apart. He held his gym shoe open but had no mind to lift his foot. He should make the rounds. Somewhere in the building, an on-the-sly gathering was afoot, no doubt. And tomorrow the polarities would have sharpened, the splits widened. He sat staring at the cement floor as if for cracks. He wanted wholeness in his life again.

Several hotheads, angry they had been asleep in the Sixties, or too young to participate, had been galvanized by the arrival in their midst of the legless vet who used to career around Claybourne fast and loose on a hot garage dolly. The tutorial staff were urging the group to pull up the welcome mat, close the doors and concentrate on building up the bookstore and tape library. The office staff were charging the executive committee with elitism. The study group leaders said the new crop of recruits were apathetic or stupid. The masseuse, karate master, the language teachers and the resident reggae band feeling more than estranged were asking, Whatever happened to Third World solidarity?

And too, there was the group who came by the house late at night to argue that the Academy, too visible and above ground, had performed its function, pulling folks together for a moment. And now that key people had been identified, it should be abandoned and a select group move off to the back district and organize a self-sufficient community. Velma had rejected it as too aloof a way to make a contribution.

After several tries, they modified the plan: a select few should nab some devalued real estate near the woods and move off for a year and start a brain-trust farm. And finally do what the folks in the nineteenth century had talked about at the Colored People's Conventions, finally do what the African Brotherhood had formed to do in the twenties, finally do what had been a priority item in the early sixties, then got pushed aside when the movement was redefined from the outside, but was tried anyway by the Lowndes County Freedom Party, by folks within the Peace and Freedom Party, later by the All African People's Party, what had been discussed in Philly, Little Rock, Gary, and Dayton, Ohio, but yet to be done—to blueprint a sure-fire strategy for mobilizing the people to form and support an independent Black political party before it was too late. There was the Puerto Rican Nationalist Party to hook up with, the La Raza Unida groups still functioning to connect with, the American Indian Movement to ally, and a loose, informal network of medicine people throughout the communities of color to be lifted up and formalized. That had captured his and Velma's attention. But when was there a moment, much less the material resources, to move off for a year? And so the Spring Festival had been designed as a holding action, way to reconcile the camps, to encourage everyone to work together until the plan could be put to them. But then the hotheads had brought the guns into the place and the splits widened and Obie had not moved quickly enough, been forceful enough, was overcome with ambivalence. Obie felt the image of himself coming apart in Ahiro's hands.

"Have to be whole to see whole," Mrs. Heywood had counseled them. He'd tried to stay on top on all diverse plans and keep the groups with the Academy. A deep rift had been developing for centuries, the woman taught, beginning with the move toward the material world and away from nature. Now there was a Babel of paths, of plans. "There is a world to be redeemed," she warned. "And it'll take the cooperation of all righteous folks."

Obie dropped his shoe and rubbed his chest. He was probably exaggerating, but things had seemed more pulled together when Velma had been there, in the house and at the Academy. Not that her talents ran in the peace-making vein. But there'd been fewer opportunities for splinterings with her around, popping up anywhere at any time to raise a question, audit a class, monitor a meeting, confront or cooperate. It was all of a piece with Velma around.

He'd thought he was relieving her of distraction, suggesting she pare her schedule down. But most often she was either huddled in the Chesterfield, her head dropped to her chest, preoccupied, or out of town keeping company with consoles and terminals with cutesy names like Big Blue. And the two major camps, the ones she'd held together, urging each to teach the other its language, had sprung apart. The one argued relentlessly now for the Academy to change its name from

7 Arts to Spirithood Arts and to revamp the program, strip it of material and mundane concerns like race, class and struggle. The other wanted "the flowing ones" thrown out and more posters of Lenin, Malcom, Bessie Smith and Coltrane put up.

Obie bent down and worked his foot into the shoe. He felt the strain in his midriff and wondered if he shouldn't once again invite Women for Action to join them, to move from his sister in law's studio to the Academy. There was more resistance to this idea within the Academy than he'd anticipated. It made no sense. The work was the same: to develop, to de-mystify, to build, to consolidate and escalate. And they shared key people: Jan, who ran the ceramics and sculpture division; Ruby, who coordinated the newsletter staff; Bertha, who ran the nutrition program. Velma had run the office, done the books, handled payroll, supervised the office staff and saw to it that they were not overlooked as resource people for seminars, conferences and trips, wrote the major proposals and did most of the fund raising. It took him, Jan, Marcus (when he was in town), Daisy Moultrie and her mother (when they could afford to pay them), the treasurer of the board, and two student interns to replace Velma at the Academy.

Obie lingered over the laces, the pull in his midsection masking the pain in his chest. Maybe she had come home, cut the job short, quit. She would have come home to an empty house. He should have left a note—"We're staying a few days with Cleotus," or "The Hermit," as Velma had tagged him. But he hadn't. She rarely did anymore either. She just hopped a plane to Wisconsin or wherever the computer job was. Or took off to Palma's saying nothing. Although no one over there had summoned her or was sick. Obie was pulling the laces too tight and wagging his head. What simple-ass shit was that, not leaving her a note because she hadn't left him a note. "Fuck a note anyhow."

93

He swung up, stretched and then slumped, a sack of stones swaying in his chest. And what did he call himself doing now? Hiding out. Stalling. His whole johnson was getting raggedy—his home, his work. And he was sitting on a bench in a basement talking to a locker. The fissures at home had yawned wide and something fine had dropped through. He was not taking care of business. And the one thing in the world he had always been about was taking care of business, he turned to explain to the staircase, a more organic, therefore more reasonable listener, he figured, measuring quickly wood versus metal. And then he saw the envelope sticking out of his appointment book. He did not want to read the letter again, or check over his schedule for the day again, or go into the gym either. But he'd held out the reward of the sauna and a massage to get him through it all. He couldn't just sit there. Things coming apart and he was sitting it out on the bench. The major parade to begin at midnight and he was having difficulty getting his shoes on. He didn't recognize himself.

He didn't recognize her either. Restless, lips swollen, circles under her eyes, spellbound. And didn't recognize the versions of her whispered in the halls by people who'd worked with her, knew her—"crackpot." Ever since he'd demanded more of a home life, she'd been in a stew, threatening to boil over and crack the pot all right. Or maybe the cracking had begun years earlier when the womb had bled, when the walls had dropped away and the baby was flushed out. How long would it take to know the woman, his woman? Two years living with her before he learned to identify the particular spasm as her coming? He would enter her throbbing, and she would close around him. And somewhere, as their hips swung, the bottoms of her feet stroking the fat of his calves, her thunderous buns rocking in the seat of his palms, a muscle would clutch at him, and he'd feel the tremor begin at the tip of his joint. Two years it took to distinguish her tremor from his pleasure, her orgasm from the vibration in his hands, in his calves, the quivering in his tightened balls. Two years before her calling out his name in that way would not catch him by surprise. How much longer would it take to learn all of Velma?

Someone was on the landing calling him. He straightened up but did not get up. He had no reason not to answer but he didn't. It felt right to sit there, his palms now cupping his kneecaps, his feet flat on the floor, one shoe off and one shoe on, his eyes skimming over the envelope toward the stairs. And it drew him together to hear his name called like that, the caller throwing it off the walls, tossing it in the upper hall. It focused him. The calling and then the going absolutely still, listening for an answer, the whole body and mind absorbed in it even as Obie sat there stopping his stomach and chest in midbreath. The caller sighing now, muttering, scraping his shoes against the threshold, then jiggling the doorknob. The way Velma did of late, checking and rechecking the knob, the latch, the catch, not trusting the mechanism to mesh on its own with whatever ratchet caused it to function and keep her exits possible. The house was no longer a comfortable place for her. She veered sharply to avoid things he did not see. Would slap her hand over her mouth and press her whole face shut as if to stifle a scream. And the night the bedroom knob came off in his hands, she'd backed down the hall and left the house without a coat.

Whoever it was calling him left the door ajar and Obie followed the footfalls overhead going toward the kiln. Any minute he expected other steps to sound, the caller to be joined, voices, some confirmation of a clandestine meeting. And when the time came for the procession, he'd discover a palace coup had been effected while he'd sat in the basement with one shoe on.

The caller was back at the basement end of the hall, alone, opening doors, and the sudden blast of an electric guitar made Obie start. He found himself clutching the daybook, the envelope crushed in his grip. He bent and put his other shoe on before he recognized the soloist overhead. He could see young Bobby, his blue embroidered strap across his chest like a banderillo; young Bobby taking his Jimi stance, his hands flying across the strings releasing the music, holding music in his mouth, holding the next few lines he'd play in his mouth in that pretty way that never resembled an upchuck, no matter how much Velma teased. His brother Bobby flooding the halls, the basement, playing the feedback, his main man on the amp fiddling with the dials, and letting the audience know just when something extra hip was coming up. And then the door was closed, before he could hear what he always heard from his younger brother's music: Come join me here; come join me here.

Obie moved the book and envelope away from him and breathed deeply. *They got me up here in Rikers, man.* He planted a foot on the bench and rolled his sock down, remembering that Rikers, like so many joints where the family is caged, had been built on top of a garbage dump. They had his brother Roland in prison for rape this time, and Obie knew it was no bum rap. He let his foot fall to the floor.

They got me up here mopping floors, bro. She'd been mopping up her own blood with the mop Roland had threatened her with, taken from her, and hit her with, surprising her from the garage window. Mopping up her own blood when the police arrived. A Black woman, forty-six years old, four children, her husband in the reserves for nine days. Roland climbing in the window, stepping over bikes, skateboards, stacks of comics, a burnt-out TV. She'd been in the kitchen mopping the floor. Roland had sent him the newspaper clippings.

Awwwww shit, man, ain't like she was a virgin. Obie had flown up for the trial. *Shit, she was probably on the pill.* And he had studied them both. Roland, hard mouth and surly, his head dropped to the side bobbing like the hydrophobic patient he'd helped Doc Serge get to the hospital three summers before. *Don't cry, bitch, or I'll really hurt you.* The woman huddled on the stand, pinched, nasal, but determined to get justice. *Be good to me, ain't nobody been good to me.* She might have been their Aunt Frances, an older sister. She was. *Be sweet now and I'll be gone fore your children get back.*

They got me in a box, man. When you going to get me out? Obie'd gone to see him in the Tombs, hand grabbing at his clothes, mildew rotting the shirt off his back. "This is fucked up, Roland," he had started to say, but Roland was talking about the money, the debt. "We're richer than the land, Roland." But he didn't get a chance to say what he meant, Roland cutting through with a sneer and talking not about the land their father had tried to give them, after nearly fifteen years of absence, but about the fact that Obie had rejected his share too and the portion of their dead mother's rights. And maybe that had been a big mistake, he wanted to say, but Roland was calling him Big Man, Revolutionary Man, Straight Up and Down Got It All Together Man and there was no room for talking.

Be good to me, bitch, cause no one else has so you take the weight. The cramped and scribbly writing though was saying other things, about the lame lawyer, the racist judge, the kangeroo court, the vengeful bitch, the rough-off artists in the joint, the lead-pipe shakedowns, the lousy food, the lousy break. No cigarettes, no money, no visitors, no luck, no pussy. He'd actually written that he was so horny he'd fuck a rat if it stood still. *Don't scream, bitch. Clench those muscles down there and be good to me.* The woman had held herself together on the stand, to get it all said, trembling for justice.

I need to get out of here. Are you going to come through for me, brother man?

Obie bent to roll his other sock down. He was feeling dizzy, nauseous, but not like those mornings in the beginning when they thought the baby was on the way. Sour now. Sweet then, until they learned they had lost their child. They were running a bookstore then, rolling the paperback racks to the wall to make room for the Che Lumumba Club on Monday nights and the local Panthers on Tuesday nights and the Young Lords on Wednesday nights, and Sophie Heywood's Study Group on Thursday nights. Everyone seemed to be pulling in the same direction then. But that of course was selective memory, a chump way to excuse the self from the chaos of the moment, longing for a past or for a future as if there were no continuum, and no real thread that energized and carried one, as if time-pieces ticked away in separate lockers he could open, close, lock up, climb into or fall out of. *I'm your brother, man, come through for me. You do it for everybody else, I'm blood.* Obie tossed the daybook into the locker and kicked it closed.

The gym smelled funky. When Velma and the sisters had been taking karate, the maintenance crew had made a point of cleaning regularly. Now it was necessary to keep the windows open to give the place an airing. Obie stood at the window stretching, stretching out to the wind to feel its purpose. Arms wide, legs apart, in an open body position, he was sure there was a plan, a pattern that would reveal itself if he'd but stay available to it. He sensed a plan of growth for himself, for him and Velma, for the Academy, for the national community, for the planet, felt it too strongly, too often, too thoroughly to despair. And so he stretched and breathed deeply, trying to pay attention to what he saw and heard and felt around him and inside.

Outside in the yard that doubled as parking lot and general hangout, the motorcycle club was gathering. Leather pants, jackets, silver studs spelling out names and threats, crushed hats or helmets, gloves, men straddling bikes or standing around profiling, the women seated waiting. Obie eyed the women sitting with their backs to the window, their asses splayed out on the black leather seats or leopard-skin seat covers, or held from spreading by thick denim or tight leather; their backs arched as they held on to fenders behind them; their backs bent as they leaned forward grabbing at the ape-hangers. Women. Women talking in bits and pieces, mostly waiting, mostly impatient waiting, waiting for the men to straddle the machines and turn on the power and take them somewhere.

In the beginning, Velma had asked about the women, did he still see any of them, were they at least friends? And he had shrugged, what was there to say? He'd thought himself deeply in love each time. And they'd loved him, at least they'd each said they did. But they kept killing his babies. Junk food addicts, toxemic pregnancies, miscarriages. Excited mothers-to-be, suddenly sullen and unreachable, terror-stricken, abortions. Pills and foams and curses and shouts and long harangues about you must be kidding you think I'm some fool you sweet talking no dealing or double dealing jive ass drop your seed any ole where and keep stepping and what am I supposed to do kiss my ass and later for all the fucked-up nigger man shit. The pattern is clear. And the new pattern of growth unfolded itself the minute Velma had winced and held him round, "What kind ot poor, abused sistuh would want to kill your baby, James?"

The plan had unfolded, the plan of work and development. Partially at least. But now he was stumped. Where to take the Academy? And where was his partnership going? What was he to do about Roland, about Velma, about anybody? He was halfway out of the window, his chest swelled, his arms out as if measuring his wing span, his nostrils burning from too big an intake of air, his lungs stuttering as he tried to expell it all before he burst. The men and women in leather were saluting him, yelling hello up at him, waving at him, shine glinting off black goggles and dark shades and something in him lifting an arm to wave back. And then two women bent, leaned their heads in together, tipped the bikes to whisper. He could see their lips in the side mirror that angled away from the handlebars. Whispering and looking back at him.

Crackpot. Someone a few days ago had actually called Velma a crackpot. How fitting, though, when he thought about it. Something was definitely percolating with a fury, bubbling up and running over the sides. She eyed him these days from within a crusty depression; huddled in the Chesterfield, picking at herself as at a sore. She might catch fire any minute, break the vessel, and all he knew of her drain off, become ignited, burn away. Obie held on to the window jamb and tried to exhale his chest and stomach flat.

five

Nadeen saw it happen, saw something drop away from Mrs. Henry's face. Nadeen had not wanted to move closer, but was glad Buster had moved her off the spot. Cause if she'd gone on standing there, she would've run screaming into the halls. And if she'd gone on standing there, she would've found some way to get on top of a table and clog away in them shoes Mrs. Heywood had gotten on her about. If she'd gone on standing there, she would've had to make some kind of move and some kind of noise. She still wanted to make some noise, wanted something loud going on, something louder than just the scratchy sound of Buster's mustache against her face, louder than the new whispery way he'd been talking lately in her ear, louder than the swish of his corduroy pants as he left her.

She could never go down into the cellar without noise, without grabbing the old muffin tin off the hook and scraping it along the wall, scraping her knuckles sometimes but she didn't care, cause the main thing was to not hear the mice or the rats or the squirrels or whoever they were scurrying around down there when she went for the maternity clothes in her aunt's trunk. Or home alone or babysitting by herself, she'd have the radio, the stereo and the TV all going full blast and calling anybody, Cynthia even, to talk and laugh with to get the spooky dark to stop in the hall and no fair creeping past the line of the door, she'd pray, when she turned for a second to bite the sides of her thumbs.

She didn't know what she saw fall or what she saw once, whatever it was, that fell, fell away from Mrs. Henry. But the whole thing was scary, at least at first it was, and she kept trying to put the brakes on, but Buster kept on inching them closer. And then it wasn't scary at all. Felt okay. She felt a straightening. What she caught a bit of at the falling away did something to her spine, made her stretch up like they were always telling her to do at the clinic, only not a real reaching like into high cupboards or the top shelf of the linen closet. Just to think up and stretch the spine. So she'd made up a game in the past three weeks of hanging pecan pies up in the air, of hanging up cans of root beer and sometimes bundles of dollar bills that she could have only if the top of her hair knocked them down from the make-believe strings and she could catch them.

Minnie, too, was feeling up, was clucking her tongue against the roof of her mouth and humming. Velma's frequency was lowering as she danced away from the humming toward music of an earlier moment, the radio by the bed. Velma's growling a groan now swirling round the concentric circles in the roof of her mouth in search of a seam, a break in the curvature, a way to get out and away from the sour-sweet taste of sex coating her tongue, Obie whispering hoarsely in her ear about the moist coils of her tunnel drawing him in deeper. And she wanting to deny him herself, to hold back, to deny herself, to withdraw into the sheets tangled under her knees. Her groaning spiraling up to break through the roof of her mouth and thunder up to her brain. Velma's frequency sharper as she drifted back toward Minnie's humming. And they met somewhere in the air near the window, Minnie and Velma, pulling against each other and then together, then holding each other up out of the fall, holding each other stable on stools.

"You'll have to choose, sweetheart. Choose your own cure."

"Choose?" Sleepriding and sleeptalking, not sure where she was, Velma felt herself sinking.

The passengers in the bus incident were not so sure where they were either, or why they should be sinking into the marshes, their spirits yawning upward, their eyes throwing up images on the walls of the mind. The bus rocking, slipping down for a tour of the caverns. Nilda Wyandot looking at Cecile's straw hat, the goldweights from the motherland hanging from the brim, the whittled figures and palmetto charms from home dangling from the inside of the wide brim. Cecile Satterfield looking at Nilda's hat, a black felt Andes affair with a straight-as-the-crow-flies feather stuck in the band as was customary for a traveler away from home. Seeing each other as in a dream only just now recalled. Recognizing each other as sister-friend for life, they fly up out of the roof of that bus and are back on the road in another.

Fred Holt at the bottom of the marshes with the steering wheel off and in his hands, trying to comprehend the new situation by apprehending it like an amoeba, swarming around it, surrounding it, absorbing it. Then Porter appearing in hip boots like he'd been fishing on a Sunday morning, hailing him, "How you faring, brotherman?" And him saying right back, "Fair to muddling. Fair to muddling. And you?" And Porter looking up through the green and grinning, "The toss was boss, but the pitch was a bitch. A sunken bus! Can a nigger live?"

103

The two of them talking rapidly, adjusting fast to underwater muscles, not sure what else they might be called upon to adjust to in the next few minutes, so talking fast about firsts, since firsts are appropriate at new beginnings—the first big fight, Porter dreaming of the Golden Gloves, remembering the climb into the ring all right, but the next memory the sting of smelling salts in the nostrils; the first car, Fred's 1937 green Pontiac and the best damn chariot ever made; the first woman, or at least the first time they got their pants creamed and their hands sticky.

And when Nadeen got over being scared and finished with stretching her spine, she felt still another thing about seeing Mrs. Henry's face lift off and a prettier woman appear. She felt special, felt smart like she'd never felt at home or at school. Something important was happening and she was part of it. Something bigger than the two-plus-two way everybody else lived from day to day was going on and she was right there and part of it. Whatever it was that had fallen away was showing her another way to be in the world.

"There's nothing that stands between you and perfect health, sweetheart. Can you hold that thought?"

"Nothing can hold me from my good," Velma drawled, reciting a remembered Sunday school lesson, "neither famine, nor evil, nor . . ."

A barrier falling away between adulthood and child. Like the barrier that dropped away for the passengers on the highway silent and still in the hum of the wheels over asphalt, silent and still in the sonic boom echoing back from a blasting event to occur several years hence, and to occur with so powerful an impact, its aftereffect ripples backward and spreads over their moment now, giving them a glimpse of their scripts which they can acknowledge and use, or ignore and have to reexperience as new. Always the choice. But with attention able to change directions as sharply and as matter-of-factly as the birds winging toward Claybourne.

And then a fourth thing. Nadeen felt a kinship with the woman she did not even know, had never met, had only heard about from Buster who lived on her block or from Mrs. Heywood who considered both her and the woman her goddaughters. She'd seen the covers fall, knew the feeling, the nakedness of it. Graduating from the shelter of closed-in desks wide enough to hide behind with fingernail polish and love notes and a stick of gum thrumbled up small and tight for popping right into the mouth behind the desk lid—then suddenly the wide open, one-armed chairs of high school and everything out, the drooping socks, the ashy legs, the banged-up knees, the too-short hand-me-down clothes stretched over her swelling belly.

But Mrs. Henry didn't grab herself up small and tight on the stool or try to duck her head down and hide or anything. She wasn't even trying to fix herself up in front of all the people. Didn't even check to see if the hospital gown was open, which it was, and if her behind was out, which it wasn't cause she had on panties, but still. So Nadeen didn't feel like clenching her thighs tight anymore or putting the brakes on with her shoes anymore. She moved closer all on her own, Buster not even there. Because it was all right now. And this was the real thing. And she was about to know or maybe already knew something her smart-ass friend Cynthia, for all her knowing, would probably never know. Nadeen knew she was not the stupid girl her teachers thought she was, or the silly child the nurses thought she was. "Babies having babies," her neighbors had sighed.

She could argue now with folks at the clinic. How come she was old enough to sign the papers giving consent for the baby

105

to be taken care of when it came, but wasn't old enough to sign for herself, had to have her aunt and the social worker give consent? It was always the same—too old to do this, too young to do that. No more. Nadeen moved closer and would have moved right up to the two stools to join hands with the healer and the woman, if the prayer group weren't there around the two like a gate. She was a woman. Or at least, she wrinkled her nose to herself at too big a jump, she was womanish.

"Can you afford to be whole?" Minnie was singsonging it, the words, the notes ricocheting around the room. Mr. Daniels picked out one note and matched it, then dug under it, then climbed over it. His brother from the opposite side of the circle glided into harmony with him while the rest of the group continued working to pry Velma Henry loose from the gripping power of the disease and free her totally into Minnie Ransom's hand, certain of total cure there.

"Can you afford it, is what I'm asking you, sweetheart," Minnie persisted, ignoring the sighs of impatience that issued from the visiting doctors, nurses and technicians.

Several checked their watches, amazed that only five minutes of silence had ensued. It had seemed so much longer, that quiet moment broken by one of their members reciting the Hippocratic oath then exiting. Five minutes or not, there was still the lecture to be worked in before they reassembled in the lounge to pick up their conference kits and jackets and compare notes. The slide show and talk the administrator, Dr. Serge, would present that would answer all the questions put on hold at the morning session about the history of the Infirmary, about the fusion of Western medicine and the traditional arts, about the drug rehab acupuncture clinic, about this healing business, and about the controversial liaison with agencies such as the Academy of the 7 Arts—that was bound to take

106

more than an hour. And it was no short stretch of leg to the corner where the driver Fred Holt would be waiting, but not too long he had made clear, for departure. Several shifted their weight from one leg to the other, trying to get the group's attention, trying to get a consensus about leaving.

Many of the strollers-in, Lily cups in hand, passes or prescription slips flapping and rustling, were as eager for Doc Serge's talk as the visitors, particularly the part about how the workers of old held steadfast against the so-called setting of standards, the licensure laws, the qualifying exams, the charges of quackery or charlatanism or backwardness, the attempt to take over the medical arts by the spiritual and material capitalists. Things always got right lively then. And it was almost as pleasurable hearing Doc Serge knock down all of the visitors' arguments as it was to hear about the courage and resourcefulness of the old bonesetters, the old medicine show people, the grannies and midwives, the root men, the conjure women, the obeah folks, and the medicine people of the Yamassee and Yamacrow who'd helped the Southwest Community Infirmary defend itself and build itself through the years.

The rest of the old-timers, though, remained in deep concentration, matching the prayer group in silence and patience. For sometimes a person held on to sickness with a fiercesomeness that took twenty hard-praying folk to loosen. So used to being unwhole and unwell, one forgot what it was to walk upright and see clearly, breathe easily, think better than was taught, be better than one was programmed to believe—so concentration was necessary to help a neighbor experience the best of herself or himself. For people sometimes believed that it was safer to live with complaints, was necessary to cooperate with grief, was all right to become an accomplice in self-ambush.

They were proud, frequently, the patients that came to Mrs.

Ransom. They wore their crippleness or blindness like a badge of honor, as though it meant they'd been singled out for some special punishment, were special. Or as though it meant they'd paid some heavy dues and knew, then, what there was to know, and therefore had a right to certain privileges, or were exempt from certain charges, or ought to be listened to at meetings. But way down under knowing "special" was a lie, knowing better all along and feeling the cost of the lie, of the self-betrayal in the joints, in the lungs, in the eyes. Knew, felt the cost, but were too proud and too scared to get downright familiar with the conniption fit getting downright familiar with their bodies, minds, spirits to just sing, "Blues, how do you do? Sit down, let's work it out." Took heart to flat out decide to be well and stride into the future sane and whole. And it took time. So the old-timers and the circle concentrated on their work, for of course patients argued, fought, resisted. Just as Mrs. Velma Henry was fighting still what was her birthright.

"Sweetheart?" Minnie was crooning, taking up both hands of the patient and clutching them in her lap.

While the others watched, not quite sure what to make of what was apparently happening to the patient, Cora Rider was jutting out her bony chest, certain it was she who had routed the noisy doctor, sent him out of the room with his blasphemous prayer. "Apollo!" she snorted to herself. No telling who a redbone will call on when faced with the black truth, she chuckled to herself. Bad as them workers down at the chemical plant—she fussed under her breath, not sure yet why the two seemed connected in her head—forming a committee to whine complaints to the very uglies who were making life so miserable in the first place. Calling on the big shots, hat in hand and bent at the knees and all, as if the big shots cared a hoot about safety gloves and ventilation and special ways to deal with asbestos and all them poisons down there. When who them workers should've been calling on were the crazy characters that had broken into the armory and stolen a lot of guns. "Men!"

"Lawd, Lawd, Cora."

Cora rolled her eyes at her sighing friend, Anna Banks. Forever calling on the Lord for something she ought to be able to handle herself. And the first to get high-handed with her about playing numbers when no commandment said a thing about gambling, but sure had a thing or two to say about taking the Lord's name in vain. When they played cards on Friday nights, Anna Banks called on Jesus. Like Jesus ain't got nothing better to do than be her Whist partner. And when Cora and her partner ran a Boston and reminded Anna the game was rise and fly, why then she'd call on her mama. Poor dead woman roaming around on the other side trying to get her bearings and her fool daughter yelling at her to stack the deck on the next go-round to teach Cora and Bertha a lesson. It was enough to make you bust a girdle, Cora roared inside, assuming you was dumb enough to wear one in the first place. But that doctor beat all. Probably the first time he'd ever had a chance to learn something useful about curing and caring, and he right away calling out people from fairy tales. Might just as well try to get Goldilocks on the telephone for all the good Apollo could do. "Damn fool."

"Cora, please. Lawd."

Just like the patient that morning, stumbling in calling on guns, calling on a joy pill, calling on her dead mama, instead of putting herself in the hands of the very one God had groomed for just such occasions, the good woman Ransom. "I feel so bad," she had wailed, setting Cora's teeth on edge, "I want to blow my brains out, give me something." And Cora had wanted to pull at her own hair the way the woman kept doing as if guns and pills grew there in all that henna for the picking. "I don't want to feel this way," she kept shouting. And the louder she got and the more she banged herself all in the face, the more the room tipped for Cora till she felt knocked right out of her shoes. And the good woman urging the wailer to let her mama go, to go ahead and hurt and holler, but to let the woman go. "Hold my hand, daughter," she had coaxed the wailing woman. "Let me share your pain. And your joy. I hurt with you and rejoice with you, for your mama's finished with this and gone on to come again another way." But then the woman just climbed into Miz Ransom's lap and like to knock the chair right over. And still yelling about give her some magic pill. Wanted to swallow her mother and grief with the pill, drink down sorrow and keep her inside, as though a daughter could give birth to her own mother. It was enough to scare the pants off of you, great big overgrown woman wanting to be Miz Ransom's baby and her mama's mama all at the same time and sliding off Miz Ransom's lap, the whole room on the slide, it had seemed to Cora. But Cora held up, did not faint or embarrass herself.

Miz Ransom rocking that woman like the mothers of all times hold and rock however large the load, never asking whose baby or how old or is it deserving, only that it's a baby and not a stone. But all that was changing. And that was the part that was really knocking Cora off her center these days. Cause she'd been there and she'd seen the little children brought into the place burned, beaten, stabbed, stomped, starved, dropped, flung, dumped in boiling water. It was a sign of the times. Too much to bear, but she held on and never fainted and never lost her faith. Invalid mother-in-law cranky and smelly, rifled mailbox and neighbor kids in her yard with no manners, beauticians lying that they didn't get a chance to put in her number, smart-aleck youngsters telling her she was killing people in

Africa by giving crime men her gambling money, church folks igging her cause she didn't dress fancy. But Cora Rider held on, didn't traffic in gossip, wished no one ill, kept the faith. Cause her dreams assured her of one thing if nothing else, that she would be rewarded when things turned right side round again. What goes around, comes around. So Cora continued with good works and a life of harmlessness. And she stuck out her bony chest and rubbed her eyes dry against the fluff of her sweater.

"Answer me now," Minnie insisted, leaning into Velma Henry.

"Afford . . . Choose . . ." Velma groaned, sore and sodden, coming in from the muddy planks, stumbling, her feet entangled in sheets, reeling toward the sound of tambourines and joy, reeling and rocking on the stool, the mud going white linoleum underfoot, the tent canvas, the bedroom walls yellow latex paint, and the sting of disinfectant overpowering, making her squint. "But I thought   "

"You think I mean money? Mmm."

Nadeen's eyes were riveted on Mrs. Henry's wrists now, thick brown wrists no longer banded by narrow red and black bracelets of flaking flesh. Healed. Nadeen felt a movement at the base of her stomach. Something leaped in her, like the baby Jesus leapt when Elizabeth, big with John, saluted Mary. She stretched her ears toward the woman. Would she ever finish answering whatever it was the healer was asking? Or would she just reel and rock on the stool until all the scars were healed? Nadeen breathed shallowly in light pants, as they often did in practice class. She was oblivious to the sharp intake of breath, the gasps, the stirrings around her as others began to take notice. This was the real thing.

She had never seen a real healing. Her aunt had taken her

to the summer tents, promising circus. But that didn't count, wasn't the real thing. A turkey-neck preacher throwing some poor cripple down on the platform and shouting heal, heal, heal. Like being saved that time, the preacher plunging her under. And for nights and nights the drowning dreams, the claws of seaweed dragging her down and her crawling on the water's floor, eyes and ears sealed in mud. Then waking with crumbling teeth and frozen jaws not knowing where on earth she was, and Aunt Myrtle by the bed on her knees ready to turn the nightmare into a vision of Jesus, a visit from God. "God don't lead you to deep waters to drown you, Nadeen," she would whisper, "merely to cleanse you," and would then want to hear her confession and the message from God, and would insist they go to the tents for a confirmation.

Revival healing was just not it. The rolling in sawdust, the talking in tongues, the horns blaring and people crying, folks tearing off their clothes, the little kids whimpering. Grown people, grown-up adults who pinched you in church for squirming, who passed you on the block and told you to pull up your socks and be tidy, who got after you about your schoolwork or about wearing your hair to the side or with a streak, who told you to keep your pants up and your dress down, who stood up at meetings and said the younger generation had no self-control and no sense—rolling all over the ground, their clothes all messed up and underwear on show, talking out of their heads, totally off their nut. That was not the real thing.

And them spooky sessions in the woods her younger cousin used to dare her to, sneaking off in the night with two pair of kitchen curtains to tuck and pin around their hips like skirts. She hoped and prayed they weren't the real thing. The bloody chickens, the stuck pigs, the dancing men with their red glow cigars, and women too puffing like chimneys on a train. Everybody jerking and shaking like they were having a bad time. And couples dancing, doing the nasty, sweat pouring off them and their clothes like rainy windowpanes. She didn't want that to be the real thing, no. And though her younger cousin would climb over the fence and throw herself into it, Nadeen preferred to watch through the fence and then run on home. Cause, no, that was not the real thing. That was some kind of crazy business. And dangerous too. Knives and swords and burning sticks and garden tools twirling and the dancers with their eyes closed, crowded as it was. No. This was the real thing.

This was what it was supposed to be. A clean, freshly painted, quiet music room with lots of sunlight. People standing about wishing Mrs. Henry well and knowing Miss Ransom would do what she said she would do. Miss Ransom known to calm fretful babies with a smile or a pinch of the thigh, known to cool out nervous wives who bled all the time and couldn't stand still, known to dissolve hard lumps in the body that the doctors at the county hospital called cancers. This was the real thing. Miss Ransom in her flouncy dress and hip shoes with flowers peeking out of her turban and smelling like coconut Afro spray. Even Cousin Dorcas, who had gone to specialists as far away as Boston, said this was the real place and Miss Ransom was the real thing.

And even Buster, who never gave anybody a play, even Buster, who had to be begged to come to the Infirmary, had to be threatened by Uncle Thurston to take the father classes, even Buster had said Miss Ransom was for real, and Buster didn't even say that about his own mother. But he had told Nadeen that if she was really pregnant and not just trying to fuck with his mind, and if the sucker did manage to grow to anything, well then he guessed it would be cool for the old lady to be in the delivery room when the time came.

Nadeen folded her arms over the swell of her baby and

wished the two women would get on with whatever was left to do. It was getting kind of spooky again, the two of them rocking and clutching with their eyes closed and Miss Ransom's hand trembling and all. She'd heard these sessions were usually quick, that sometimes she simply hugged you and then you jumped right up and bump de bumped all the way home. It was a little after three; she hoped it wouldn't be much longer. She had a bone to pick with the bossy nurse at the Teen Clinic. And she had a fitting at four o'clock. She was not going to the Carnival Ball in anything but a fine gown, not with her belly out the way it was. She could just see Cynthia looking at her sideways saying, "Girl, what's your malfunction? You look like a penguin."

"Afford?" Velma was still muttering like she'd never heard the word before.

"Oh, I don't mean money, sweetheart. You know that."

Velma guessed she did. Nearly everyone in Claybourne knew that much. It was chisled over the archway of the Infirmary: HEALTH IS YOUR RIGHT. Translated by popular practice: Pay what you can when you can if at all. Yes, she knew that, if she didn't know anything else on that stool, head numb, eyes crossed, circuits blown, working hard to get herself together to at least pay attention to the lift and stretch of the old woman's arm reaching toward the stereo dials. Music? Music. She had thought she'd heard some music. Well, what was this anyway, a healing or a jam session?

Velma was spinning in the music. A teenager at the rink in a fluffy white angora and a black and white checked skating skirt. Spinning in some corny my gal sal merry-go-round organ grinder music. Just the thing, the skaters joked, to keep Black folks off-balance. Spinning. The photo-lined walls, the concession stand, the rows of lockers, the entranceway, the organ stall —all flying around, merging. Photos on the lockers, the mayor shaking hands with a keyboard, the organist playing the cash register in the entranceway to the ladies' room, racks of hot dogs suspended from the lobby light, spinning. The mud mothers on the ice building a fire, fanning the babies.

Trying to scream, or maybe it was the weight in her left-hand pocket that was tipping her to the side, a rock a white kid had thrown at them from the bus, a bracelet Palma's best friend had stolen from the 5&10, her keys. The weight pulling her to the side, the left blade not planted quite right on the ice. But Velma afraid to think on it, correct it, lest her ankles bump and she fall, or worse, she spin and twist like the Turkish taffy figures in cartoons.

Spinning and something very much the matter. Radios going and slide shows and movies and the records of special effects—waterfalls, and buffalo stampedes, and guns and high-pitched wailing, and chanting. Spinning, and then the women by the turnstile covered with leaves, covered with mud. And it's too cold for them babies, young Velma wants to shout out. But the words bubble like foam in the chapped cracks round her mouth then whip around her cheek, the back of her neck, her ear, and seal her mouth closed.

"I can feel it when something ain't right," Lorraine was saying to Jan that time, her foot out of her mules and on the kick wheel, her thigh bunching through the shiny skirt she'd kept from the old days. The pottery wheel spinning.

And Velma was like the lump of clay, two hands holding her on the wheel, one hand pushing her hard up against the other in an effort to get her centered. And she was turning and lifting at last, the ridges of her sides smoothing out, rising moist and

115

spreading, opening up, flaring out. But a lump in the beat, the rhythm wobbly. The healer's hands steadying her, coaxing her up all of a piece.

"Like being in bed with a Black trick who's been sleeping white a long time, ya know?" Lorraine hiding her eyes, certain she'd gotten the attention of the girls. "The beat's just off." She paused while they howl. "Way off."

"A loss of rhythm," Jan said slowly, mulling it over. The ceramics group too intrigued with what Lorraine is wearing and saying and promising for the afternoon to pay much attention to Jan's efforts to bring them back round to the clay. Jan leaning, holding her hands over Lorraine's jug as if it might spring off any minute.

"A lump somewhere," muttering it, not wanting to interrupt the dialogue between the girls and Lorraine, or miss the points of correspondence in what's beginning to look like an interesting parallel. Velma holding up one of the plaster bases, chipping a piece off. The girls can watch Jan and Velma and listen to Lorraine and get several lessons in one.

"Sleep white and your rhythm goes right off. Hmph, hmph, hmph."

A piece of plaster from the base is buried in the clay, throwing the jug off its axis. They all can hear the offbeat.

"That Reilly boy's on the offbeat track. You watch and see," Lorraine said to Jan and Velma. And the whole group watched the jug wobble up sideways as if it were Teddy Reilly himself.

"Let's concentrate on the clay now," Jan finally said, clearing her throat with a theatrical flourish, just as the sliver of plaster came tearing through the terra cotta walls.

꧁ ꧂

Velma tapped Ruby and then tucked her feet under her on the couch, and tried not to give Robert a target. She didn't blame him for being warm. Jan had picked a not-so-cool time to do what she was doing. She was tracking him across the carpet, throwing her hands about, trying to explain how difficult it is to pull up straight if you're a girl and no women are getting their wagons around you, or if you're a boy and no men are getting their wagons in a circle.

Robert was lining his golf club up with the edge of an old bugle bell. There was a bridge made of wooden hangers tied together with the pants rod removed, several "psych" jars of water, and some pebbles from the fish tank strewn about the carpet for effect.

"Look, that's his business. Or his father's," Robert said. And Jan waiting for him at the bugle bell was pressing the soft V at the base of her throat as if to dislodge a fish bone.

"You could talk to him, Robert."

They all watched the golf ball roll under the chair and then drag another inch forward on the shag.

"And just what am I supposed to say to him? 'The sisters don't like you humping white girls?' 'Keep off the Heights fore they lynch ya, boy!'?"

"Oh, Robert."

And Ruby muttering that what somebody needs to do is get a wad of lamb's wool and a can of chloroform and bring the brother home. Robert's look makes the roots of Velma's hair tighten. He's swung his club over his shoulder like a back scratcher and is all for abandoning the ball in favor of the cards, which is what the two invited them over for. But Jan is still trying to coax him out of the sandtrap.

"It's not about sisters being uptight, Robert. Or white folks being uptight. It's about the boy himself. Old Man Reilly is so old. And that boy's been to all those white schools, white camps."

Robert is considering a bank shot off the legs of the chair.

Ruby reviews her freshman math. But Robert buries the club head in the carpet, folds his hands, and gives Jan his attention.

"I always took you for your word, Robert. Nation building?" Jan's whispering, realizing finally that she might have done this in private. But Velma appreciating finally why she didn't. 'And don't forget to build the inner nation, Robert."

"The nation," Robert says, checks his watch and takes his shot.

"I don't believe this," Ruby snorts and Velma pushes a pillow in her face.

"It's like trying to build a bowl when you haven't got the clay properly centered," Jan was saying after Robert left the house, confident they all agreed on a common reference for 'it.' "It'll rise, it'll flare, it'll look good for a minute. But it'll wobble and tear. It won't stand up."

"Who you telling?" Ruby was on her feet wrassling a chunk of air onto a wheel of similar substance. "Yeh, like trying to get this bowl done without doing a scientific analysis of the objective conditions and primary issues."

"Ruby. Quit."

"Or taking a serious position on the woman question, the national question, the gay question, the so-forth-and-so-on questions."

"Just stop, Ruby."

"It's a case of Little Red Henism most of the time. Notice how fewer and fewer people are ready to build. Hence my bowl here is jeopardized."

Velma and Jan laughing and holding each other while Ruby wrassles the bowl in the air, her head wagging no, no, miming with each spin the tear that was growing more critical, the lump that was curling the lip of the bowl over in a sneer.

"Your performance just does not make me feel good, Ruby."

"She's perverse, Velma."

She was on the piano stool with the baby in her lap. They were turning, getting taller, her feet farther and farther away from the pedals, the baby riding, his legs round her waist. And James was at the desk editing the Academy manual. And Mama Mae was sitting in the horsehair Chesterfield, chanting in that way of hers, "Dahlin, when M'Dear told me the news, I fell on my knees and cried, 'Glory!' It's a beautiful thing." She was misting up, and the fact that she'd passed up the opportunity to emphasize that she'd had to get the news from M'Dear about the adoption made Velma misty too. "Lawd, all them babies; all them babies inside all them places waiting on us to bring'm on home." And Velma was turning slowly on the stool, smiling at Mama Mae, smiling at the baby there was no name for yet, big as he was. Then James standing, turned toward the window, arms wide to the sun, then turned toward her and the baby. "I orient myself," he smiled. "I de-occident myself," she answered. A private joke whose origins they'd forgotten and Mama Mae frowned, leaning over to take her grandson from its funny-talking mama.

"Health is my right," Velma finally said with some clarity, no longer reeling and rocking on the stool. Her eyes were opening and the healer's hands were patting her. "My right," she said again.

Just what so many patients maintained indignantly when the bill came. The original statement had been more than done in bas-relief over the Infirmary archway more than a hundred years ago by carpenters, smiths and other artisans celebrated throughout the district in song, story and recipe and immortalized finally in eight-foot-high figures of eye-stinging colors on the east wall of the Academy of the 7 Arts. Those black men

119

of old who had flat out refused to haul them stones anutha futha no matter what the surveyors and other standing-about-with-pipes experts had to say on the subject of gradients and silt and faults and soil mold. Cause the stars said and the energy belts led and the cards read and the cowries spread and the wise ones reared back in their rockers, spat a juicy brown glob into a can, shaded their eyes and took a reading of the sun and then pointed—that spot and none other.

So the Southwest Community Infirmary, Established 1871 by the Free Coloreds of Claybourne, went up on its spot and none other at the base of Gaylord Hill directly facing the Mason's Lodge, later the Fellowship Hall where the elders of the district arbitrated affairs and now the Academy where the performing arts, the martial arts, the medical arts, the scientific arts, and the arts and humanities were taught without credit and drew from the ranks of workers, dropouts, students, house-wives, ex-cons, vets, church folk, professionals, an alarming number of change agents, as they insisted on calling them-selves. The Infirmary at the base of the hill; its north windows looking out toward the post office that had gone up on the first bluff where cars, buses and trucks shifted gear for the second pull up. And the Infirmary's sun deck overlooking the Regal Theatre marquee which jutted out so close to the curb, bold children on the school buses would lean out on a dare and snatch bulbs or remove letters from the racks leaving baffling announcements, while the driver shifted gears for the final pull up to Gaylord Heights where a fountain ought to have been, or a plaza for couples to promenade about on Sunday after-noons, or a public garden with a pond and some of the statuary on exhibit in the halls of the Academy should have been. But where stood like a sentinel, the gaslight in front of the wrought-iron gate of the Russell estate, eager to annex unto itself the whole of Gaylord Hill, the prime real estate of Black turf that ended somewhere between the lane—where the bus turned carrying away the chemical plant workers and Heights' domestics and the schoolchildren—and the mailbox some six hundred feet below the gaslight. The flame in a nervous flicker always. Fire going out. Animals closing in. The tongue of the flame darting, striking at the globe. Each year a new globe to replace the one shattered not by the fanglike flame but by the bus riders just before turning into the lane. Each year a globe more ornate and preposterous than the last, as if the Russells were convinced it was their manifest burden to bear the torch, to bring light to the natives of Gaylord Hill.

It was said though in the stories, songs, jokes and riddles of the district that the lamp was not gas but electric and drew upon the power line that fed the Regal and the rest of the establishments of the Hill, that, of course, had to foot the bill, and wasn't that just the way? And more than one community sage would look toward the Heights on viewing the dimming halo of the Regal's marquee on foggy nights or upon hearing the groan as the Infirmary switched to its own generators, power from the main line dwindling, would nudge a kid and point toward the top of the hill and explain, "Their world-wide program, their destiny, youngblood, is to drain the juices and to put out the lights. And don't you forget it."

When the scaffolding went up in the spring of 1871, the stone masons mounted the face of the Infirmary to chip free from the chosen stones all manner of messages responsibles might read to their charges. Some messages written out to be read by anybody who'd mastered the alphabet. Others, more finely carved and worked over, to be read by initiates of the order only, those selfsame secrets of alchemy attempted in the carvings of Notre Dame miles away from the seat of knowing, those selfsame instructions of the arcana burned, buried, smothered in the cradle but persistent, those selfsame knowledges and mnemonics sacked, plundered, perverted. But over the Infirmary arch all of it pure, insistent. And when new, had urged the originals to transverse the globe to share the wisdoms with the peoples of the Solomons, the Philippines, the China Seas, the Indian Ocean, Mexico, Europe, Arabia, Mesopotamia—the neighbors who'd been set adrift at the splitting of Pangea.

All of it gazing down in stony insistence on Dr. Julius Meadows standing on the steps, looking over his shoulder at the paint job in the halls of the Infirmary. White, white with a flush of pink, like an udder left too long without milking. That's my country self talking, Dr. Meadows frowned, coming down the steps. And it was his country self admiring the tabby wall that wrapped around the back of the Infirmary holding the woods off. And it was his country self wanting to set foot on the crushed-oyster-shell walkways that led to the sheds where the generator hummed. Looking up, he saw merely sandstone faces, wheels, five-sided puzzles, basalt, grape clusters, bricks and coils that could be snakes to the fanciful of mind. Figures, glyphs, warnings, bricks, carvings, arches—it was all the same to him, a building. He looked toward the curtains of the treatment room, then turned his back, blushing, for the idea of actually making a journey through the woods in search of two catatonic women branded him a fool in his city mind.

Dr. Meadows moved quickly toward the avenue as if with purpose, trying to make some sense of his behavior earlier, his actions now. Reviewing the Hippocratic oath after all this time, it was peculiar, a compulsion. He had wanted to call them out, dialogue with those beings behind the names, know the gods he'd given allegiance to. To converse with one's principles seemed both the height of sophistication and the height of ridiculousness at the same time. Seemed primitive. Seemed

. . . He lost his point and then lost himself among the children out of school, adults out of work, shoppers, workers from the chemical plant's second shift smudged and smelly and in search of a quick bite to eat.

There seemed to be a contest going on between the record shop and the neighboring bar, an ear-splitting electronic version of an old Wild Bill Doggett piece he had once danced to hitting him at his back, and a spastic rock piece he'd never heard assaulted him head-on. "Band of Thieves" he tagged the first group, and it was getting so he had to look hard at the musicians on the bandstand when he went into a club these days, the white boys had it down. "Chinese band," he labeled the latter, as his father had called the group he'd planned to hook up with. "A bunch of opium heads." So Meadows had gone to medical school.

"We need to bring scientific thinking to the masses," a kid in a Levi suit was haranguing his buddies, the youths marching along four abreast. Meadows had to step into the street and walk around a parking meter to avoid getting hit by their book satchels. "The masses are still reacting out of infantile emotionalism."

"Mostly it's diet," maintained the one who had almost broken Meadows' kneecap. "Diet and stress."

"Izat right?" an indignant drunk, snatching at the passing satchel, was challenging the four young men to a talk-off. But they continued on and left the man reeling, so once again Meadows moved toward the curb. This time he was stopped by a group of skinny old men in shirt-sleeves leaning up against a Coup de Ville, eying three young girls dancing in the middle of the street, swinging a red plastic tape recorder back and forth as in a relay race.

"I feel so sanc-anc-tee-fie-eyed."

"Before you can get sanctified, girlie, you gotta be saved."

"Save your breath, Shakey Bee, can't tell these young girls a thing."

The third man was squinting like he was in need of an aspirin. It was Meadows' guess that he simply wanted his cronies to shut up so he could watch the girls in peace.

"How you get saved?" one of the girls asked in mock seriousness, arms out like the radio was a kid sister she was swinging. The quiet man with the headache appealed to Meadows. Couldn't he make everybody be quiet and just enjoy the floor show? The girl asking the question had superb tits, Meadows noticed. "How you get saved?" she asked again, her head to the side as if she didn't know she had magnificent tits, as if that was not why she wore her crushed leather belt like a tourniquet. "I seriously want to know."

"Surrender."

"Surrender?" She rolled her eyes and did a snaky move with her hips the headache man fully enjoyed. "What kind of surrender?" She was looking straight at Meadows. Meadows thought it wise to cross the street.

"Surrender? Counterrevolutionary batshit," said the skinnier of the three girls, imitating someone who evidently wore a cap with a bill, for she mimed the yanking down of a cap as she spoke. "Surrender is antistruggle," she announced in this other person's voice, making the third girl giggle, but Meadows doubted she knew why.

"Is that what they're teaching you at school these days?" The man was shrugging off the headache man's hand plucking at his sleeve. "To curse your elders?"

"Aww, man, it's spring and it don't cost us anything to enjoy all the pretty flowers. Why you want to get overheated?" Headache pleaded.

"Wait up now. I ain't through talking to you."

"We through listening, less you got some money," Tits said.

"I got some money," Headache spoke right up, both hands digging in his pockets.

"What you got?" The other two had shot past him, but the brazen one was once again looking Meadows square in his mouth. "Gloria, check this out. Ever seen a nigger blushing?"

"He a nigger?"

Meadows crossed back over to the other side, wondering why he was putting himself through all these changes. But it had been so long since he had simply walked in a Black neighborhood, been among so many Black people. He wished he knew someone in Claybourne he could call up and invite for a drink, or call up and be invited for dinner.

"Supper. Suppah." He mouthed the word, relished it. There was an elderly man at the bus stop greeting the passers-by. He looked like Meadows imagined his grandfather had looked. He laughed and showed his bridgework. He looked like a man who might be interesting to have suppah with. Meadows was tempted to take the bus, strike up a conversation and . . . But then there was a sidewalk café coming up where two good-looking women were eating salad out of one plate with their fingers and talking, enjoying themselves. A nice place with chinaware and amber-colored glasses and silverware that shone. Not at all what he'd have expected to find in this neighborhood. He thought about sitting down and having a glass of white wine. But in front of the entranceway was a group of young men and women so intent upon what a tall man with a bow tie bobbing at his throat had to say, that they wouldn't make room for him.

"I'm not here to boogie, but to jolt you back into your original right minds."

"You a dreamer, mistuh." A woman coming out of the café, stuffing an apron into her handbag, broke through the group and backed Meadows up against the white ironwork fencing.

She looked like she knew a thing or two, it seemed to him, at least about how to make an opening for herself. "Dreamer," she sighed, looking straight at Meadows as though they'd spoken of just this topic at breakfast and she would now take his arm and they would go home together. She was looking at him and then she wasn't, had moved on. And Meadows changed his mind about the wine.

He continued toward the corner, hearing the voice of the tall man in bow tie clear over the heads of the crowd—"History is calling us to rule again and you lost dead souls are standing around doing the freakie dickie"—and adjusting his pace to each beat in the traffic, people scurrying or dawdling or bumping into each other, dreaming along the pavement—"never recognizing the teachers come among you to prepare you for the transformation, never recognizing the synthesizers come to forge the new alliances, or the guides who throw open the new footpaths, or the messengers come to end all excuses. Dreamer? The dream is real, my friends. The failure to make it work is the unreality." Meadows was out of earshot, but the words still resonated. His city and his country mind drew together to ponder it all.

"As Dr. Arias is wont to say, Butch, 'The most confounding labyrinth of all is a straight line.' " Doc Serge was holding forth.

"Buster," the boy muttered, glancing around him, embarrassed by his surroundings.

"Take money. If you want it, getting it is the easiest thing in the world. One need understand just a few simple principles that govern supply and demand. Understand? The problem is not to get it, but to stop getting into a funk about wanting it, going all around Robin's barn dodging and feinting trying to justify the appetite. Simple laws is all. Laws as inexorable as gravity. But they don't teach basic principles in the schools. So people have no discipline about living. They have no religion. You hear me talking to you?"

"Yessir."

"And what is religion, you might ask. It's a technology of living. And what do I mean by technology? The study and application of the laws that govern events in our lives. Just that. Now, take one of the first principles, supply and demand . . ."

Buster knew he wouldn't get what he came for. He might just as well have stayed in the healing room. All he wanted to know for his paper was what pageant the Brotherhood planned to do for the Spring Festival. The rumor was they were going to reenact an old slave insurrection. The writing workshop at the Academy had been working on a script, he knew, about the rebellion that had taken place on the Russell and Alcorn plantations just days before Harpers Ferry. And one of his classmates, who'd offered to work with him on the term project and then changed her mind, had already interviewed Sophie Heywood, who was said to be the great, great something of the boardinghouse keeper who had bankrolled the uprising and, together with another boardinghouse keeper from the Coast called Pleasants, was prepared to bankroll the original plan for Harpers Ferry, which was to arm the slaves. But then John Brown had "broken discipline," as the brothers at the Academy would say. And Harriet Tubman and Fred Douglass stepped back, "You got it, white boy, run it," and the boardinghouse women had taken their money and booked.

Sitting there on the stepladder, trying to keep towels from falling on his head and trying to keep his hands off the stacks of soap he wouldn't mind pocketing, it occurred to him that there was no reason why Dr. Serge should tell him what had always been kept secret until the very last minute. Only the

Brotherhood—the sons, grandsons and nephews of what years ago had been the Mardi Gras Society before gangs then drugs busted up the network—knew what route the parade would take to the park and knew what skit would be performed as the main event of the festival. The most anybody else could find out was the general look of the costumes or at least the colors of the various "families" or "tribes," or "gangs" or "clubs."

He'd tried asking around the Academy, but brothers his own age said right to his face that his paper was dumb and that he should be working with one of the committees if he wanted to get into something hip. He'd tried to approach Obie, figuring as a neighbor and all he might help. He'd listened, but then he'd pretty much said the same thing, that the committees were hurting for workers. There was a research team working up a paper to take to the UN a petition as was Malcom's directive. And there was a fund-raising team pledged to contribute so much toward the formation of a Black Commission of Inquiry to dig further into COINTELPRO. And there was a group that had shown him a petition calling for a safe earth. He supposed all of that was important, but he was just trying to get his paper together and do the student thaang. His instructor wanted the first draft in the morning.

"You've got good skills and you've got drive," one of the brothers from the karate studio had told him. But just when Buster had thought he had an ally, the brother had added, "But skills and drive without consciousness and purpose make you dangerous, man, dangerous to the community." And he'd turned his back on Buster to shadowbox in the mirror. Then Obie and another dude Nadeen's uncle had sent them to talk to, a marriage counselor no less, started piling papers on him: Amnesty International, UN Charter on Human Rights, COINTELPRO, the Freedom of Information Act, Panthers, RAM, IRS, AIM, Attica, the Wilmington Ten, the Charlotte

Three, the FBI, the CIA. But not a scrap of anything about what he'd come for.

The most he could get out of his cousin Ruby, who never stopped feeding papers into the copier and moving back and forth between phones and tables and baskets and clipboards saying she had no time to talk, had to go open her shop, was that thinking seriously on insurrection might just set the future in motion. He'd written it down, not sure if she was putting him on or not. One never knew with Ruby. And he'd filed through the material they loaded him down with. Maybe when he got to editorial writing the stuff might come in handy.

Buster changed positions on the stepladder and glanced at the doodles and scribbles on his note pad as if considering how to take down what Doc was lecturing about. He'd never become a good journalist. He never got what he went after. Maybe he'd just make up something. His instructor wouldn't know the difference. Probably couldn't care less.

Which was exactly the decision an equally demoralized young man who was using the name Donaldson had come to sipping flat beer at the sidewalk café less than a block away. There'd been no word on the street about the armory heist. No lead anywhere on who might be sitting on the cache of rifles. And trying to infiltrate the Academy was not that simple, he'd tried to explain. Those guys were close blood relatives, had grown up together, had ties from way back. And the women were not a type he'd run across before. Played everything close to the chest, didn't open up. The times were different. A few years ago, picking up info, picking brains was the easiest thing in the world. Everybody was running off at the mouth at the drop of the hat, eager for a "press conference" at any time of day or night. Things were different now.

With his record it was not likely he'd be invited to go to school, get trained, become a regular. The special police task force and the FBI recruited openly now on the Black campuses, set up booths even during career week. What did they need with him? He laughed in his beer. And here he was—ready, willing and able. But how was he going to get onto a campus with his record? So how could he get anywhere unless he came up with a solid tip, a big one?

Five days and nights Donaldson had been on the street, smoked out every breezy mouth in town, laid his super-deluxe rap on three foxes up at the Academy, spread what little bread he had around hoping to spring something loose. Nothing. Less than nothing, trouble. He'd almost blown it, so anxious to pull from the joker in the Pit Stop diner who had seemed to know a lot about the vets who ran the Academy's sports programs for the kids, and the vets being prime suspects, Donaldson had aroused suspicion. It had taken quite a bit of fast thinking on his feet to cover himself when the joker started asking him where'd he grown up, what kind of work he did in Claybourne, who'd he know, where'd he hang out. And some fancy footwork to cover his tracks when the man turned up on page one face down on the diner floor. But what to report? What did he have to turn in? He could make something up. He'd done that before. Hell, it was done all the time. Even the pros did it when sources dried up. They'd already made their minds up anyway. He knew who they were after. And the bloods up at the Academy were probably the ones anyway. So what the hell. He'd wing it.Decided. Done.

Buster had not as yet made his decision. Doc had turned suddenly, interrupting his train of thought, and leaned out the door of the linen closet.

"Bantu Bootehhh! heh heh." Doc had hooked one arm around the shelf divider and was leaning his body against the doorknob, flirting with the nurses in the hall.

"We're going to report you, Doc."

"Who to? I'm the man in the shoes around here, heh, heh, heh."

Doc seemed to have forgotten all about him, looked ready to stroll out after the women. Buster was not prepared to sit there and wait. It was all kind of stupid anyway, trying to get an interview in a linen closet. And there wasn't time for much delay. Doc was due in the auditorium soon as Old Lady Ransom did her thaang. He examined his notes. All Doc had talked about was money.

"Now, you take that little one with the test-tube rack," Doc Serge was saying, gesturing for Buster to come to the door or at least lean forward. "A pathologist. More to the point, a hummingbird. Looks fragile. But those dainty wings can carry her on some long-distance flights on some long-distance nights, heh heh. All she needs is good management."

"Sir?" Buster had stood up then sat back down.

Doc Serge turned and resumed his position, one elbow on the shelf with the pillowcases, one elbow opposite against a pile of blankets, one crane leg crooked in front of the other. All he needed was a straw hat and cane. Some doctor. But then he wasn't a real doctor, Buster reminded himself. He ran the Infirmary, kept it going, and they called him "Doc" just as years ago when he ran a gambling joint, his father had told him about, they called him "Faro." What his father had not told him but Buster had found out after some snooping was that he'd had a few other names in his day like "Candy Man" and "Sweet Bear."

"I don't care who you are or what your aspiration—doctor, poet, elevator operator, milkman, barber, reporter—it pays to study The Law. And I don't mean the man's law—course that pays too, heh, heh—I mean The Law. The problem with the man is that he always gets half the story and then bungles it. Dates right back to the Greeks. They go to all that trouble to

131

ransack Alexandria and then blow it, fumble the ball, miss the message. 'Equal before the law.' Fine. Bet you think you know what that means."

Buster shrugged while the man unbuttoned his jacket, jerked his wrists free of his cuffs, took up a cake of soap in one hand and presented it to his audience, took up a blanket roll in the other with a flourish. "See these? One black, one white?"

"Yessir."

Doc held his gaze for an uncomfortably long time. Buster met it, but it was a strain to keep still and not shift his eyes. It was a pity Doc didn't have a bigger audience. He was too much for one. He let go and the roll and the soap hit the floor.

"Notice."

Buster noticed that the soap shattered and the floor was a mess. He noted that the blanket roll had come undone. He wasn't sure what else he was supposed to be observing.

"Landed at the same time. That's equality in the law, in the law. Nature's Law. Gravity, Butch."

"Buster."

"Now, take supply and demand. You probably think you know that one, studied it in high school economics class, right?" And I bet you think it has something to do with capitalist economics, right?" He wasn't waiting for answers or any other kind of response. "Has very, very little to do with capitalist economics. More to do with the ministry, with marriage, with—"

"Pimping?" Buster was feeling brave. He doubted that anyone had ever dared to get that familiar with Doc Serge about his past. But the man had gotten into *his* business, hadn't he? Come right to his house and sat him down with his father and launched into a long rap about Nadeen and the baby. "Does it occur to you that that baby you are considering aborting might be the very one who will deliver us?" That had worked fine with his father but had cut no ice with Buster and his mother. Buster still maintained the baby wasn't his. "What difference does that make?" Doc had argued. "Law of averages says you take care of this one, some other young man will wind up taking care of yours and so forth." His mother had called that sheer illogic and left the house. Buster had to admit he'd been grateful for the visit, though, because shortly after that Nadeen's uncle had come by with a pistol. And while Thurston had a rep for being a very reasonable and peaceful type, the type that usually could be depended on to cool out the hot-heads on LaSalle Street, still there was no telling what he might have done, given that Nadeen was not only his niece but more a daughter.

"Yeh, like pimping," Doc said, not skipping a beat. "A woman in the hands of an undisciplined player is very nearly as dangerous a situation to all concerned as atomic energy in the hands of capitalists, as any kind of power in the hands of the psychically immature, spiritually impoverished and intellectually undisciplined."

He was warming to his subject, had unbuttoned his vest and changed the position of his legs.

"Yeh, pimping too. If you're going to be a player and not just some mooching miscreant and misuser of women and women's knowledges, you've got to study the principles that govern the game."

It might have been a paper he was delivering at a national conference on physics. Buster was beginning to enjoy the performance. Doc held out his hand, or rather held it up out of the pillowcases and wagged one finger at a time.

"Principles such as the law of reciprocity, the principle of attraction and repulsion, good ole supply and demand again . . ." His watch was now in view and Buster sensed this could go on for hours.

"Sir? What I wanted to know—and I realize your time is short and all—what I'm doing my report about—"

"I'm getting to that. Okay. If you are not curious about the difference between a prime player and a mere pussy peddler, then let me come at this another way, Butch. Because it is important to understand the basis for the Brotherhood and its activities. No sense half-knowing a thing. Cause half-knowing is not sufficient. Look at the mess the half-knowers have got this country in—got this world in. Now check this out"—fishing a dollar bill out of his watch pocket—"know Latin, Butch?"

"Bus . . . no sir."

"The man thought the new age and the new order began with his arrival on these shores. Hah! They convinced us they knew about this country's manifest destiny. Clearly they were totally ignorant about its latent destiny, its occult destiny. Understand? Now, its latent destiny is a Neptunian thing, a Black thing, an us thing. Following?" He waved the dollar until Buster leaned forward and took it, examined it. "And the new age has only just begun to be ushered in. So to understand the depth of the question you so nonchalantly ask about the Brotherhood, you need to understand many things about the times. Do you know what time it is?"

Buster was not about to go for the chump bait and look at his watch and then have the man yell Duuumeee at him in a linen closet.

"It's the third year of the last quarter of the twentieth century, Buddy. A very crucial moment in human history. Six years, six short years away from 1984—and I don't mean Orwell. The last quarter . . ." He was examining his manicure it seemed, and deciding, evidently, to change manicurists. "You play basketball, so you know a lot can happen in the last quarter. All sorts of surprises, upsets, right?"

"Yessir."

"Well, all right." Now he was lifting his pocket watch up like a yo-yo. Maybe it wasn't as late as Buster had thought. Maybe the wrist watch was just a piece of jewelry, something he wore to complete his ensemble and the vest pocket time-piece the functional piece. Though what would complete the picture, Buster was thinking, studying the three-piece suit, the vest, tie, pocket hanky, was a gun holster. Administrator or no, Doc Serge always dressed like a first-class gangster in a foreign movie. There was probably a slouch-down white hat that went with this suit.

"It's late. I'm due in the auditorium in less than five min-utes, if I read Miss Ransom right. Now, Buddy, if you're half the young man I take you for, you'll track down Dr. Arias, who is one shrewd cookie. And then, if you're smart and very, very lucky, you'll try to see The Hermit." He was fastening his vest and jacket now and shaking down his sleeves. "You did say you wanted to talk with Cleotus Brown?"

"Yessir."

"Well, dismissed."

Doc Serge sucked in so the student could squeeze past. And it was just as he'd said, the kid was half the man he took him for. He left without asking where Dr. Arias might be found or how to get to see The Hermit. Doc watched him go down the hall and brushed his ring against his chin. And it was just as Cleotus had said, there was no charge, no tension, no stuff in these young people's passage. They walked by you and there was no breeze of merit, no vibes. Open them up and you might find a skate key, or a peach pit, or a Mary Jane wrapper, or a slinky, but that would be about all. Or maybe you'd find some-thing totally unidentifiable. Might just as well be aliens from

135

another planet. Definitely directed by energies from elsewhere.

Doc felt momentarily deficient. He knew a lot of things, but he was nonplused by the new people. New, unattached, unobliged. They were either adrift or freed up, it was difficult to figure. And the new women were even more confounding than the men. He couldn't do a thing with them. He no longer trusted his knowledge of their language of gesture and rhythm. When he walked up to groups of young women at the Academy talking with each other, he felt an intruder, felt he was missing their timing somewhere. But this was not his province. Sophie and Cleotus had the gift in that area. His gift was managing the Infirmary.

Doc patted down his bush, raked among the silver hairs around his ears and strolled out of the linen closet as if stepping from the barbershop fresh and fragrant. He needed to look in on Minnie and tell her to shake a leg. It wasn't like her to run overtime like this. He would do the abridged version of his lecture for the visiting medical folk, for this was the night he did his rounds on LaSalle Street like Doc John among the lepers.

Doc listened to the smart click click of his Spanish boots on the tiles. He nodded toward the maintenance crew in such a way as to signal he didn't much appreciate their lollygagging around the juice bar. He bowed deeply whenever he met one of the women workers he thought needed his special brand of attentiveness. He headed in the general direction of the treatment room, feeling that familiar wave of energy surge through him. In another minute, he sensed, he would generate enough energy to found a dynasty, lift a truck, start a war, light up the whole of Clayborne for a week.

"I am one beautiful and powerful son of a bitch," he told himself. "Smart as a whip, respected, prosperous, beloved and valuable. I have the right to be healthy, happy and rich, for I am the baddest player in this arena or any other. I love myself more than I love money and pretty women and fine clothes. I love myself more than I love neat gardens and healthy babies and a good gospel choir. I love myself as I love The Law. I love myself in error and in correctness, waking or sleeping, sneezing, tipsy, or fabulously brilliant. I love myself doing the books or sitting down to a good game of poker. I love myself making love expertly, or tenderly and shyly, or clumsily and inept. I love myself as I love The Master's Mind," he continued his litany, having long ago stumbled upon the prime principle as a player —that self-love produces the gods and the gods are genius. It took genius to run the Southwest Community Infirmary. So he made the rounds of his hospital the way he used to make the rounds of his houses to keep the tops spinning, reciting declarations of self-love.

six

Holding on to the rail to get off the bus, Palma didn't have time to see him, to prepare herself, to throw open her arms, or to wonder how he'd gotten there ahead of her. There was no time to get her mind working: Had Marcus received her wire or happened to be in Claybourne for a different reason and was at the bus terminal to meet someone else? When she stepped down to the bottom step in rocky terror, gazing down at the pegged jeans, the green-lacquered toenails, the Carmen Miranda shoes, looking down in disbelief—could this be her in this getup?—she was being lifted. And all the step-by-step to-do-the-minute-I-hit-town went right out of her head. She never quite touched the curbstone. And she didn't quite get a look at him before she smelled him and felt him, the faint vanilla fragrance warm and custardy, his soap, under the bite of citrus, the shaving cologne she'd never liked, the aggrey beads on chewed leather around his neck imprinting themselves on her sternum. Then his chin so sharp in her neck, his

138

beard scraping her cheek raw. He was hurting her.

Or maybe she was crying because she was that glad to be home and to find him there. Or maybe the crying was fear, his presence confirming what she'd been dreading about Velma, that something terrible had happened to her sister.

The morning before, Palma had run across a photo of her sister among the sheet music and been stunned, scared. A photo she'd never seen. Velma in shorts and halter squinting into the camera, her arms turned out so that the unsunned and exposed insides showed childlike and vulnerable, as if waiting for the shock of the alcoholed cotton and the sting of the needle. And such tension in the hunched shoulders, the neck, the torso, Palma had dropped it, and the photo had curled up tight on the floor like a white pencil. It had taken effort to flatten it out again to examine closely. Velma's face a blur but the eyeballs black and sharp as though someone had stabbed her there with a black felt pen. Rigid, fearful, Velma had looked insane, her bush spiked out like the bromeliad behind her, the knife-like red buds the plant shot out like flames, like a jagged halo.

It was an old photo, taken the summer before at the beginning of Velma's comings and goings, of her complaints that Obie and Lil James were driving her nuts. Talking in an odd way but never quite explaining what the matter was, complaining about sexual harassment on the job but not offering an example in that stand-up comic way she had—no anecdotes, just her reaction. And not saying why all this should be getting to her at this late date. There was nothing new about Obie's ambivalence—should he and Velma hire help to do the "mother act" or should Velma and maybe both of them cut back on community work?—or the boy's vacillation: one minute a responsible teenager, the next a crybaby, the next a rebellious kid. And there was certainly nothing new about supervisors trying to do the shakedown samba. And since summer, Velma was getting more and more tense, leaving her house with larger and larger suitcases, popping into Palma's at odd hours, coming to the breakfast table wrapped in pieced-together bedclothes—sweat shirt, rain poncho, most anything —and walking like a board, mumbling about a migraine or a nightmare or some ill-defined bad feeling she could not shake. She'd pace the kitchen unable to bend and sit down it seemed, until Palma got the kids off to school and could run a tub for her to soak.

The morning the troupe were due in Barnwell for the No Nukes rally, Velma had come to the table stiff-necked and silent and bitten right through her juice glass.

The photo—the stiffness, the blood-red flowers—had triggered in Palma the dream of the night before: Velma spitting splattered teeth into a rusty can whose ragged lid cut her lips. And Palma had rushed to the phone. Had Velma remembered to rinse her mouth out with warm salt water? Remembered to see a doctor? Palma, hanging on the phone, reliving the panic, the tedium of removing bits of glass from tongue and gums with her tweezers. Reliving the rush with a dishtowel full of cracked ice and ignoring the looks of her children.

Palma, one hand holding the phone, the other stretching out the scrolled photo, surrendered up to the flood of dream fragments, premonitions, replays of conversations: "Do you think, Palma, that suicides reincarnate more quickly than say—" She was crowded off her chair. And then her period stopped abruptly.

"Hey." He dug her chin out of the folds of his sweater and kissed it. "It's only me, baby. Marcus. Everything'll be all right." He handed her his hankerchief. He was laughing, she felt it ripple against her stomach. But she felt worry in his chest, felt a drop in the heat of his breath. She shivered.

140

She didn't have time to ask him any of the questions forming in her mouth: Had he seen Velma? Heard anything? Was Obie in town? Had Marcus gone by her house, were her children all right? Had there been a burglary or a fire in the apartment? Had Velma moved back to her own house and simply forgotten to have her calls transferred from Palma's place? Had she changed jobs again without notifying personnel? Was everything really all right? No time. Cecile and Mai were off the bus now, crowding her, waiting to be introduced, kissing her goodbye, trying to make room for the other passengers waiting to pull their luggage out of the storage compartment.

"We'll meet up later at your place, yes? The program begins in the park at midnight?"

"But first we eat, Mai," Cecile was insisting.

Palma tried to handle the introductions, stumbling over their names, her voice catching, the look of Nilda and Cecile so altered she could not quite get her bearings. Chezia and Inez pulling the women on in the direction of the Avocado Pit.

"Health food?" Cecile appealed over her shoulder to Palma. "Don't let them serve me no sick-girl lunch, please. I want pig. I want conch. Fungi. Ackee."

"Good food," Nilda and Chezia were saying, hustling Cecile on to give the lovers space.

"I don't favor plant-life sandwiches with cobwebs. Palma, direct us to the place of the serioso chefs."

Marcus quickly pointed out Alex's Bar B Q and then his hand returned to the shivery place on Palma's shoulder. He held on to her until she gave him his handkerchief back.

"Marcus, my period stopped." She watched him hear it, watched him wait, mull it over and wait. That was not the way to say it. But how to explain the moony womb and the shedding of skin on schedule? How to explain the pull of Velma, the tug of her clock compelling? How to relay the alarm?

Last Monday she awoke suddenly, wondering whether she could get the posters, the flyers and the T-shirts into the duffel bag. But when she opened her closet door, there was Velma in an old leotard of hers and a kitchen curtain draped like a sarong and rummaging among sheets, pillowcases, fabric, shoe boxes in search of a tampon or a sanitary pad. Then later, the morning and afternoon spent packing, checking the slides, marking the poster rolls, Palma's period arrived eight days early. Not surprising. It always happened that way. When the children complained that Aunt Velma's sudden appearances on the sofa or in the bathroom or in the family budget were jarring, that her visits completely wrecked the order of the house and everybody's timetable, Palma had smiled but yes.

"Monday and then Wednesday, Marcus. Just one and a half days," she tried again and felt him waiting, worried, his hands pressing her shoulders toward him. How to explain the dread on Wednesday in Barnwell when the flow had stopped abruptly, no sign, no stains, no bloated feeling, nothing? And then not being able to reach Velma at the apartment, the house, the job?

"The kids haven't seen her since Monday night, Marcus." But that didn't explain much either. Velma often contracted with out-of-town computer jobbers, or worked odd hours on terminals all over the city. And the kids had their own peculiar schedules. He was pulling her slightly to him if she wanted to come. But she didn't, not yet.

"Velma?" He was studying her face and she was straining to push to its surface the terror she hadn't been able to articulate.

"Marcus, something has happened to Velma."

He didn't say that something was always happening to Velma, that her dogmatism or her naïveté set her up for constant happenings of a melodramatic sort. He didn't say that

Velma had a husband, a therapist, an orgone-box partner, a godmother, a lover, a health-club masseuse and a crew of friends to bail her out of whatever she had fallen into. He didn't say Velma was a grown woman, a wife, a mother, and not Palma's baby sister anymore. And he didn't press her into his chest to try to cajole her out of her anxiety. He did not embrace her closely and whisper any of the men-comforting things guaranteed to set her teeth on edge, remembering Sonny, her ex-husband: "Don't worry about it" or "You're overreacting, woman" or "Let's talk about this calmly, baby." Marcus didn't say anything. He left her on the sidewalk and stepped into the street, snatching off his cap, and hailed a cab.

Palma was swaying on her platform shoes, staring at the velveteen-shirted back of Nilda up the street and just at that moment noticing that Nilda and Cecile were wearing each other's hats. She inhaled deeply and felt worse. The women were in front of the rib joint talking to a brother on the roof. Flames were shooting out of the chimney, but what that meant did not register. The women had stopped and were carrying on a comic conversation with the man on the roof throwing ladles of soup from a steam-table bucket toward the fire, beans and onions sliding down the blackened brick of the chimney when he could get close.

"Save the soup, brudder. You've got a built-in hose, you know."

"Much bad booze as he drink," a passer-by remarked. "Be like pissing pure gasoline on the flames."

Smoke billowed out of the doorway; customers sooty and choking stumbled out and leaned on cars, the bus-stop post, the mailbox, coughing. Palma could make nothing of it. It was all as in a dream. Then turning on the wooden shoes to watch Marcus playing matador in traffic, the ridge in his bush from the press of his cap like a strangling band around his head, she wanted to reach out and touch him, lean out and fluff up his hair, rake her fingers in his bush the way he often raked in his mustache when it was time for him to leave, to catch a plane, to go home to a situation he said little about. In the bedroom door with his fingers making scratchy noises, covering his mouth, and searching for soft words to slug her with, but what could he do? And what could she do on the sidewalk in her crazy shoes, her hand out, her body leaning, but he so far away?

"Some serious cooks on Auburn Street," Cecile was saying loudly. "Or is the establishment under siege?"

"Ultimate pig," Chezia announced. "This is where you get the ultimate bar b q, Cecile."

Palma was leaning forward, longing to bury her hands in Marcus' hair. The sidewalk was moving under her as though she were on the beach, the sand sucking away underfoot. She heard the pounding of shoes toward her as if the routed customers had heard about a fish sammich giveaway down the block. Either the women had decided to eat somewhere else or they were headed for her. It was not a dream, she realized. And she was falling, coming up out of her shoes, leaning toward the clouds of too-purple smoke from the chemical plants' stacks. And then he was there, helping her into a cab and Cecile shouting something at her as she stumbled, cracking on her shoes. And then, settled in the back seat of the cab, Palma was centered again and angry, felt mean, sensed suddenly that Velma was all right just thoughtless, selfish. Velma was always all right, it was the people around her that were kept in a spin. Palma had been vacillating between anger, dread, calm, alarm and rage the whole day. Now she settled into anger.

"She ought to leave a message with someone when she takes off like this."

Marcus put his arm around her and nudged her bag. "We go to your place and make some calls. Do you know this Jamahl joker she's been seeing? Got his address or something?" He was urging her to fish around for her address book.

"That'd be just like her. Her son doesn't even know where she is these days." Palma was itching to know the place, to walk in, walk through walls, through that Jamahl turkey and knock Velma right off the sofa.

"Plan to strangle her this time for real? Or just threaten? Or just grumble?" He hugged her.

"I dunno." She handed him the spiral address book; she couldn't concentrate. She looked out of the window and tried to breathe easy. They passed Cecile and the others heading for the sidewalk café, but she didn't see them in time to wave. The cab passed the Infirmary and Palma scratched her head. "We'd better check the hospitals," she muttered. "She rarely remembers to take her pocketbook when she goes out these days. That Velma. She could be anywhere. And no I.D."

The cab was turning the bend at the back of the Infirmary where the woods began. They passed the Old Tree where Minnie Ransom daily placed the pots of food and jugs of water for the loa that resided there. Old Tree the free coloreds of Claybourne planted in the spring of 1871. The elders in coarse white robes gathered round the hole with digging sticks, the sun in their eyes; planted the young sapling as a gift to the generations to come, as a marker, in case the Infirmary could not be defended. Its roots fed by the mulch and compost and hope the children gathered from the districts' farms, nurtured further by the loa called up in exacting ceremonies till they buzzed in the bark, permanent residents. The sapling shooting upward past the wire and string armature those first few springs till the roots took hold and anchored, and the spinal column straightened on its own to tower upward from earth to sky, from soil to rain clouds even when the building had been raided and burnt to the ground. The branches, reaching away from

145

the winter of destruction toward the spring of renewal, the body letting go of its sap as the new halls and rooms were whitewashed, the branches stretching out and up over the first story as the collective mind grew. The leaves, like facts, like truths, unfolding slowly after much coaxing season in and season out, sporting dew in crystal-flashing splendor, shiny green atop, pale green beneath, the veins faint but sinewy awating further fertilization. The flowers, knotty black hard then berry brown, then lavender and luminous, promising the perfect fruit of communal actions. The old roots surfacing for a look around, tough, earth-hugging networks of fingers and limbs around the base of the tree that marked the beginning of the right-hand path that swerved past the generator sheds to join up with the left-hand path leading right under the buildings' windows and out toward the woods, trod yearly by the loa who danced and stomped unseen by those pretending not to know of spirit kinship, attended each generation by a certain few drawn to the tree, or drawn to the building, called to their vocation and their roots—messenger, teacher, healer, clairvoyant, clairaudient, clairfeelant, clairdoent—waiting for the moment of eye to eye encounter and embrace, weary and impatient with amnesia, neglect and a bad press. Called upon so seldom, they were beginning to believe their calling in life was to keep a lover from straying, make a neighbor's hair fall out in fistfuls, swat horses into a run just so and guarantee the number for the day. They were weary with so little to perform.

Weariness leaned on Sophie's Heywood's spine. She was leaning over the wastepaper basket in Doc Serge's office wondering how long she'd been sitting that way praying for her goddaughter. It had been a wave of nausea that moved her from the desk to the basket, the whole of the suede and leather seat tipping forward smoothly on its swivel base as if to dump her, her hat sliding forward revealing the bald spots and bunched scar tissue at the back of her head that never seemed to heal. But something about the swing and rock of the chair, the glide of it across a bit of purple carpet on ball-feet, had distracted her from the buzzing throb in her temples and the lift and drop in her stomach.

Had anyone come into the office, had anyone been able to get past the shield Doc Serge had thrown up to insure his childhood friend her privacy, they would have thought something extraordinary in the balls of paper, cellophane strips, cigar bands and pencil shavings had transfixed the woman. Perhaps a fire, the way she held her hands cupped over the wastebasket as if for warmth.

You never really know a person until you've eaten salt together, she told herself. But she'd gone through many a bitter experience with Velma, and still she was baffled. What had gone wrong? What did it mean?

She had been listening for years to the starchy explanations from the quacks who called themselves guidance counselors, social workers, analysts, therapists, whose views had more to do with their own habits of illusion than anything rooted in the natural, the real. Mama Mae might have faith in fools whose faith resided in a science that only filled people's lives with useless structures, senseless clutter, but she knew better. They needed some way, she knew, to be in the world, to move about, to explain things, to make up things to go on living blind. In time. And in time Velma would find her way back to the roots of life. And in doing so, be a model. For she'd found a home amongst the community workers who called themselves "political." And she'd found a home amongst the workers who called themselves "psychically adept." But somehow she'd fallen into the chasm that divided the two camps. Maybe that was the lesson. Maybe the act of trying to sever a vein or climbing into the oven was like going to the caves, a beginning . . .

Sophie opened her eyes. The walls were alive. So many possibilities. But not now. Relax, she instructed herself, resuming her former position. In time.

And now she was not even wondering anymore about time or motion, was simply staring into space. A no longer middle-aged widow woman on a sumptuous chair on a purple rug on a parquet floor on a cement stage fixed in red clay, on a bed of black dirt and then the wood and bones of an old buried-over cemetery.

On sand, silt, ash, on rock, tar pits, the earth's crust, its pin. And at the very core of the earthworks her stomach dropped down to and at the center of the universe her temples throbbed toward and somewhere in between where her heart beat, the divinely healthy whole Velma waited to be called out of its chamber, embraced and directed down the hall to claim her life from the split imposter. But called out from the mouth of the heart, coaxed out silently by baby-catching hands. For not even for her, not even for this would Sophie break discipline, break her silence. She almost had after a mere sixteen hours of the new moon. Once to cry out when Serge's assistant had called her on the phone. But the news of the spitting, biting, bleeding, thrashing Velma, "actively hallucinating," the man said—it had so taken her breath away, she could get nothing in her throat to work. And once again she'd almost spoken to settle Cora Rider's hash, but her eyes had accomplished what her mouth would not. But the hardest test of all, wanting so to speak her speak to her godchild.

And did you think your life is yours alone to do with as you please? That I, your folks, your family, and all who care for you have no say-so in the matter? Whop!

Sophie leaned back in the chair. And the chiffon roses on her hat were finally still, were finally through with bobbing and fluttering. She sat still though the chair dumped her, sat still though her legs climbed through circles on the same longitude where Mighty Titans poised underground like dragon's teeth snapping at the life of radishes, yams, grasses and grains, altering the natural cycle, heating up the earth. Climbed on through several circles, through turbulent waters in search of a saline solution, through earthquake landscapes, and landslides, and grumblings where the grinding of the earth's plates gnashed disturbed. She sat still while motion raced through the office seeking its lack, searching her out, attempting to lure her from stillness, sucking at the petals on her head, slapping at her earrings, tugging at her belt buckle, beating against her wedding band to no purpose, like hammering cold iron.She was still.

It could've been a 4×4 cell she sat in, a metal ledge of a cot and not hot leather severing her legs from her thighs, a concrete floor with bloodstains her feet pressed against, a stinking toilet with no lid she stared into. Her neighbor Edgers, not fatigue, bending her head down.

Forehead icy, downpour from her nose, Sophie was swimming in a broth. And once again she almost broke the spell, a threat of an old gospel or line of scripture quivering under her tongue. Silence. Stillness. To give her soul a chance to attend its own affairs at its own level. She breathed quickly, lightly, dispelling pictures, thoughts, sounds. But Velma's Swahili wailing-whistle filling up her head. Velma throwing her shadow across the screen door that day she came back to marry James Henry and not Smitty.

"M'Dear?"

"Ho."

"I'm back."

"I can see that, Vee."

Working hard to dump the bread-pudding face into the

wastebasket and clear her head. Those lumpy freckles so like raisin moles on her Mama Mae's face and shoulders, but on Mae's daughter like eruptions, the ooze of Velma's lava threatening any minute to engulf everything.

"How you and everybody doing?"

"Everybody doing" would be Smitty in the wheelchair straining, Smitty between the parallel bars groaning, Smitty on the gym mat fighting his way back from the floor and the Academy master pulling no punches. Smitty with a towel around his neck smiling for life, winning for life. Velma's letters to Smitty abruptly stopping. Velma home to marry James Henry. Velma flinging her life into an oven. How to explain that to Mama Mae when she returned from church retreat?

Behind Velma by the pole beans was Edgers in his overalls, a light dusting of sawdust saying he'd been to the mill and her porch would be fixed. Edgers standing there with his sheriff-ruined hands hugging each other behind the bib of his overalls, the purple nails, the bunioned growths, the gnarled joints. Hands that could manage an ax or a hoe, but nothing so dainty as a wooden match.

And Sophie going to the screen door to let Velma in, one hand on the latch, the other in her apron pocket fingering the fragile blue matchbox Edgers had handed her one day, the day they could finally look at each other and finally speak without holding their breath. To light a pipe was easy enough. She'd been lighting Daddy Dolphys' for years. And the other men's who turned up in her yard to trim the bushes or turned up on her porch to bung the cider crocks or secure her mailbox. All the men of the district who had no wives finding their way to her house to pay off the debts they said they'd been owing her husband for years, they said. "Give me a light," they each said in so many ways, having none of their own. Edgers at least supplied his own fire, his own light, his own sweat, his own energy. And gave light. Always found the space to let the sun in. Never ever cornering her to say she was a settled woman and ought to quit her activities and settle on a man, a sewing machine, a stove. Never once frowning on her work, her traveling, saying only, "I'll mind the place" or "Do you want my truck?"

Edgers was standing by the pole beans scraping his work boots against the edge of her brick walk, and she held her breath as his words floated toward her. "Get used to me please, Sophie" was all it was. Then turning to attend to things: mending the fence, liming the trees, sharpening her ax for her, turning over the earth, dumping out sacks of bonemeal, chicken droppings, a compost of his own making that would promote new growth, new life. And no sense telling him he needn't, cause he needed, and she knew it each time she combed her hair, and she needed. "Get used to me please, Sophie," he had said after all this time. She thought she had.

"Got his nerve," Velma had said, wiping her feet on the mat as if to kick up dust and jute in Edgers' face. "How could he look you in the eye after what he's done?"

"And what's he done, Vee?" moving aside to let her in.

"What's he done!" Velma searching her face for signs of amnesia or senility, Velma clearly under the spell of the "rumor" version of her beating in the jail. "That bastard ought to cut off both his hands." Then closing her eyes as if the mere thought of Sophie's terror was too much to bear even in memory, even secondhand. And Sophie wanting to grab her by the shoulders and shake her, shake her for Smitty, shake her for Edgers, herself, shake her till her head flopped. Edgers had had a pistol in his neck but had refused to go on beating her and been beaten himself.

Sophie exhaled it all out and tried to go blank, tried to switch off memory's pictures and supplant them with peaceful scenes. To go gathering, the feel of the basket handle on her arm. To talk with the lemon grass, enlist the cooperation of eucalyptus. They didn't mind her, did not resist her. Always came up easily in her grip. Eyebright in the underbrush calling. Bladderwort singing. Calamus around the salt marshes. One of the few places the spirits had not withdrawn from in disgust—neglected, betrayed. Cool breeze. Walking barefoot. Quiet lapping of thick waters against the embankment. The gathering of fresh things, natural things, fish herbs, salad greens. Natural growth, no forced foods to weaken the will to live. No old, dead food for the folk of her boardinghouse. Food in tin cans on shelves for months and months and aged meat developing in people's system an affinity for killed and old and dead things.

Wasn't that what happened to Lot's Wife? A loyalty to old things, a fear of the new, a fear to change, to look ahead? Sophie's favorite lesson at the Academy: Lot's wife and the changing order. She'd been ossified. To go gathering, Sophie sighed. And let her soul get on with its gathering and return with greater force to its usual place. But so hard to do.

What the hell, Vee, did you think you were doing, cutting on yourself and trying to die in an oven? And with so few seasoned workers left. Whop!

And how would Mama Mae find her daughter in the spring? Sophie eased back into the chair and let it lift and swirl her, imagining Serge spinning so, while the Infirmary workers tended their duties and he in his wonderful chair contemplating new ways to implement the pleasure-box principle. She smiled for him. How simple life was for people like Serge who maintained that all knowledge, all energy, all problem-solving techniques resided in the groin, the loins, the pelvis. She smiled. But she longed for contact with her drifting soul, longed for illumination and realization, for conscious contact.

So many things she needed to learn yet, to understand, to share. But she would not break her discipline to comfort herself in a shallow way. Would no more break discipline with her Self than she would her convenant with God.

Fred Holt took the shortcut through the Infirmary yard. He nodded to the boys and young men roosting on the tabby wall, passing joints back and forth, passing pint bottles back and forth, or just sitting and talking. Some were waiting for the girls, scarce women, who waddled to and from the clinic each day between three and four. The men reminded him of the wives who used to congregate outside of the Palace or the Regal, waiting on their musician husbands, waiting to take them home. Some of the other roosters were waiting no doubt for the swayback girls from Safe Harbour, the shelter the Academy and the church ran for runaways. There was a big stink about that in the papers lately, since most of the kids had run not from their own homes but from those other "homes" and were under court order. Those Academy folks were in for it unless the ministers could work something out with the authorities. Between the trees and the cars and vans of the parking lot behind the Regal, he could make out the Wall of Respect of the Academy.

He almost stepped on it, a small bird calling to the air. A tiny bird that had fallen from its nest evidently, had fallen into a plate some not-so-hungry picnicker had left behind. Fred glanced at the plates, pots and jugs and wondered what kind of weird picnic it could've been, so much food left. He tilted his cap back and stared at the bird and wondered what he was supposed to do about it. It had been a day for birds, he chuckled to himself, glad to be out of the driver's seat and on foot. Leaning against the tree on the other side was a couple murmuring into each other's face, oblivious of the bird, the plates, and him, and not seeming to know about the caterpillars that were known to drop from this particular tree from late winter and straight through spring. They were leaning against each other, her hands under the front of his shirt, his hand cupping her neck. Fred took off his hat and rubbed his outstretched arm against his sweaty forehead. Tie your apron high, Miz Lucy, he whistled to himself moving on, wondering at what point a hairy green worm might break up the idyll.

Coming out of the rear parking lot, he got sandwiched in by two winos hunkered down in the old stage-entrance doorway of the Regal and a boy with a bike. A mud puddle was in his path, the pigeons circling, fluttering, crowding each other for a drink. He didn't like what the sight of the nasty pigeons or the puddle was doing to his chili-ruined stomach. The bums weren't any better, snot-nosed and filthy. He waited on the kid to move. He was taking his time down on one knee tying a sneaker that looked like a planter or a magazine rack or one of them satchels he'd seen in shop windows designed like a basketball sneaker. Fred was glad he didn't have to feed this kid. Fred was glad he didn't have a kid anymore. He didn't seem to have a son anymore either when it got right down to it.

"Hiya doin?"

"Hey."

Fred waited. But that was all he was going to get. One of them self-contained types. His bike basket crammed with folded newspapers he'd be slinging around all over town. Fred could just see the kid at the doors collecting for the week. Nobody'd give this kid any song and dance about no change, or come back next week, or I paid you already. Not with them feet. A mere twelve or thirteen, he had feet that could put the garbage compactor companies out of business.

"Scuse me."

The kid had finally looked up and was rushing now sort of,

folding down his thick white socks he probably washed every night himself on one of those old-fashioned washboards, if they still sold them, folding the socks down neatly over the top of the incredible red and white shoes. A good kid. Not the type to give his parents any grief, unless they were the sort that had groomed him to be a brat or a momma's boy. Fred searched himself for something to say to him, something appreciative and friendly and encouraging. But the boy on his feet now, those incredible feet, was hiking up the kickstand and preparing to move out, pausing only to look at the winos and then at Fred. Fred straightened and tried to do in posture at least what the mud puddle and the pigeons wouldn't permit, to create distance between himself and those bums. The boy might be measuring his own possibilities, studying them as a preview of things to come. Fred wanted to stand for something opposite, for something hopeful and good. He stood there trying to look like what he'd hoped he could be for his son. But the pigeons were splashing his pants, his shoes. And his concentration was broken each time he looked at those "bindle stiffs," and longed to blockprint the word neatly on newsprint with a freshly sharpened No. 2 pencil.

"Take care, son."

"See ya."

And the moment had passed and Fred felt corny. He looked at the drinkers and looked at the pigeons and philosophized: So used to dipping your beaks in muddy water and turpentine, wouldn't know what to do at a fresh lake spring if you got a paid vacation.

"My people, my people," he sighed aloud, eying the two gents who were eying him, hunkered down in the glass-splattered doorway passing the bottle back and forth, picking around in a pile of butts they'd evidently gathered for just this moment. He tried his hand at caring.

The uglier of the two was lighting a match and cupping it very . . . Fred decided to just go ahead and say "tenderly" just for the fun that was in it. The bum got the butt lit but had to suck like crazy to keep the stubby, bent thing going, blocking the draft kicked up by the pigeons with his knees like maybe his ancestors did at the mouth of the cave. The other was very ceremoniously skinning back the brown paper bag and rubbing the bottle with his dirty sleeve. They toasted each other, drank, toasted Fred, drank. In another few years, who knew, he was thinking, his mouth drooping matching the drool of their lips. And then he was walking on their side of the puddle, making them draw in their feet. Red wine oozing down their scraggly jaws and darkening greasy collars. They toasted each other again, grinning, as if to seal a bargain: no head hunting in each other's caves. They toasted Fred's back as he muttered shit, their arms high, another victory over cannibalism, it would seem.

"Happy carnival," one of them drawled, and Fred lifted his arm in a half wave, half brush-off.

"Bindle stiffs," he sneered, blocking the letters neatly.

Folks on the Hill were readying up for the festival or whatever it was. Kids racing by with streamers and balloons. Masks and noisemakers in store windows, flower carts on the sidewalks, the incense peddlers in granny-square caps of holiday colors. Years ago when he'd first settled in Claybourne, things didn't officially start till the first Saturday after spring. In some parts of town, the Catholics kicked things off on the Tuesday before Lent. The Greeks had a parade on the first Saturday after Easter. But in the community Hoo Doo Man broke out of the projects with a horned helmet on some particular day near the first of spring and led the procession through the district to the Mother Earth floats by the old railroad yard. It always caught Fred off-guard. He could never keep track of the day from one year to the next. The talk on the Hill, he was overhearing, was that things would get started at midnight tonight in the park.

"Got your lists ready, pardnuh?"

"You know it," Fred hollered toward the old man at the bus stop who was loosening his false teeth and wrapping them in a not-so-clean hanky. What lists these might be was a mystery to Fred. He vaguely recalled though, pausing in front of the Regal to read the concert posters, that there'd been a bonfire years ago and Margie had insisted on going. But it seemed to have been winter, New Year's Eve as he recalled. People were supposed to write down all the things they wanted out of their lives—bad habits, bad debts, bad dreams—and throw them on the fire. Margie would never tell him what she'd written, but it couldn't've been much, just a strip from the flap of an envelope, didn't take but a second to scribble whatever it was. Fred ran his hand over the posters. This was great, live music again at the Regal after all these years. The place probably smelled like mothballs, mothballs or mildew. Had been a church for a while, then a place for rummage sales. For a while a community radio station had been housed there. For a season musicals from Broadway had played the Regal. But for a long time it had been dark.

"I'm wishing for the moon," the toothless man crooned behind him, anxious for Fred to hurry up and turn away from the posters and join him. That would be the other list. One was supposed to draw up a list of dreams and pin it on the Mother Earth float, or stick it in the horn of plenty, or shove it up her skirts or something. He'd seen envelopes and dollar bills tacked to the side of the float, scraps of paper pinned to the billowing skirts of the woman who rode the rickety thing through the district to the old church. He never could see getting in a funk about it all, it was all foolishness. Stead of writing Santa Claus notes, people ought to get armed and get with it. He turned from the box office and gazed across the street, wondering if there was anything in the story of guns hidden there in the Academy.

"Our finest monument," the man was saying, pointing a shaky finger toward the Wall of Respect.

"Yer right there." He stared with the faith of x-ray eyes. He'd like a chance to prowl around invisible in there one time. Be invisible and free to search.

That was what Porter had been beating his gums about those last days, being invisible. He'd thought at first Porter had lost his marbles. But seems he didn't mean invisible invisible like the old Claude Rains movie. Something stranger it turned out. Porter had been out early walking around the salina, as he called the marshes. And whom should he run into but the town character, The Hermit they called him. And for three solid days, when it wasn't Yucca Flats '55 and dying, it was The Hermit's views on this and The Hermit's views on that, and being invisible. For a hermit the guy was sure gabby, the way Porter kept going on and on about all he'd said.

"Invisible is being not visible, Fred, not looking like the something or someone a cop is after or a trickster is expecting."

"Looking different from what's expected."

"That and more, Fred. Like when you're looking for a four-hole, thick blue button to sew on your jacket, the tape measure and needle pads and all that other stuff you just don't see. You barely notice the two-hole brown buttons."

What did Fred know about a sewing basket. But he'd sat there in the Pit Stop chewing on the spongy bread while Porter had gone on about being invisible.

"They call the Black man The Invisible Man. And that becomes a double joke and then a double cross then a triple funny all around. Our natures are unknowable, unseeable to them. They haven't got the eyes for us. Course, when we look at us with their eyes, we disappear, ya know?" He ordered another cup of tea and made the waitress pull out everything in the back hunting for some honey she'd been silly enough to say she'd once seen back there when he asked. Since when did Porter drink tea and honey? Even had his own sack of loose tea. Fred had thought it was marijuana for a moment. And thought again old Porter had really lost his marbles pulling it out that way.

"So it's not just looking different, Fred, but being different. Your true nature invisible because you're in some incongruous getup or in some incongruous place or the looker's got incongruous eyes. Ya know? He's one shrewd cookie, The Hermit. His name's Cleotus. Fine old dude. I'm going to study with him soon's I get on the night shift again."

And that had hurt Fred, hearing Porter wanted to go on nights. They'd raised sand about being put on nights all the time, cause they were colored was the reason. And almost as hurting, not being able to crack on The Hermit anymore. He'd changed status overnight from nut to wise man. But the hurtingest part was the voice, something in Porter's voice like Wanda's when she found "the way," joined up with them Muslim people, talked off the wall in a voice that shut him out. All the time she was saying he should come with her to temple, should come hear this or that speaker, but something in her voice was locking him out.

"How long you think it'll take?" Not sure what he was asking Porter but trying to stay in.

"Like he tells me, 'Ain't no graduates from the university I study at.'"

"How long?" Maybe he could wait it out. Maybe it was a sometime thing. He had hoped for that before and lost. "How long does it take to learn to be invisible?"

159

"Don't know."

And those were the last words he'd heard out of Porter. And he still didn't know whether it meant nobody knows, or the wise man wouldn't say, or he, Fred, could never know, or that Porter didn't need to know cause the question was totally beside the point, ignorant.

"You ever been over there? Big place, lotsa doins at the Academy."

Fred shook his head no then yeah then bobbed his head any ole way as the old-timer nattered on and on. Well, maybe he'd go see The Hermit. Maybe the man had some answers. Fred was pretty sure he had some questions. But at the moment what he had were needs: to shower, shave, get into some fresh clothes, do the last run, get those doctors out of his hair, maybe go out on the town, catch the show at the Regal. He was smelling something bad and wasn't sure whether it was the old man or himself. He inhaled carefully. There was throbbing in his stomach, trembling in his throat, and he didn't have a fresh hanky. He nodded to the old man and headed back toward the Infirmary.

seven

Obie tried bouncing from the waist, then chinning on the bar in the doorway of the massage room. He felt a catch in his side. Tight muscles and joints, he instructed himself, contain suppressed feelings, memories, energies. He tried thinking that through, tried recalling recent entries in his journal. He was blank. He'd been using a confounding code, worried that Velma might snoop. That would never have occurred to him before.

"The Obo!" The masseur was grabbing his face in his hands and Obie embraced him, patting his back with both hands. It never failed to trip him out, this effusive Korean from Arkansas. He owned every album his homeboy, Pharaoh Saunders, ever cut.

"When are you going to come to my class?" He was helping Obie onto the table, wasting no time, arranging the sheet. "I want to teach you about release points. You already know about pressure points and that's tough enough for combat. But for health—stress points, release points. Your back's one big rock quarry, Obo."

"Your hands are like hammers."

"Hey, I'm a gentle man." He had taken his hands away in mock offense, but wasting no gestures, rolled the kimono sleeves onto his shoulders. "Like the song says, 'Massage is my meditation and my dance.'"

"You just make that up?"

For an answer, Obie was flattened out on the table. He felt drowsy. Chin greasy from Ahiro's hands, his head was slipping off the table, eyes level finally with the band of pane between the window shade and the window ledge. Through the hedges, he could make out the Regal across the street, and past the parking lot, the tabby wall where the brothers sat shooting the breeze.

"I'm not trying to slide your wedding band off, just trying to get out the knots. Relax, breathe deep."

But *she* couldn't relax. Not Velma. Walking jags, talking jags, grabbing his arm suddenly and swirling her eyes around the room, or collapsing in the big chair, her head bent over. He'd grown afraid for her. She talked on the surface, holding him off, shutting herself off from herself too, it seemed. And at night, holding her, he felt as though he were holding on to the earth in a quake, the ground opening up, the trees toppling, the mountains crumbling, burying him. Then he'd grown afraid of her.

"Pressure points of the human body . . . pressure points of the system . . . the U.S. . . . pressure. Yeh." He heard himself drowsy, distracted. His conversations of late seemed no less than Velma's diversions. "Points of the body . . . apply pressure to the system . . . parallel . . . interesting."

"Your enthusiasm, Obo, whelms me over. Don't talk. Relax, listen. You remember them Euro-Americans over at the Hurdy

Farm, just two hours out of the city, that new-age community, they call it? Heavy. they say Claybourne's a major energy center, one of the chakras of this country. How you like them apples? Talk about some parallels? They're trying to recruit Third World people. Check'm out sometime. But for now, relax. Just give me your leg, Obo. Your calf feels like a brick."

She was like a brick, a stone, a boulder that would not be moved. He didn't know how to lift her; he didn't know how to satisfy her anymore. "Give me your tongue." And she might flick it dry, totally preoccupied, over his bottom lip, and he would suck at the tip while the blood engorged his joint. He would rub against her, trying to get her attention, and she would mumble something. But only that he get up, turn the lights on, and take the robe flung over the closet door down and shake it out. Night after night being sent to the closet or the chair to assure her there was nothing there and no one there that should not be there. And coming back toward the bed looking at her twisting in the covers or climbing on the pillows, he would stare at her opening glistening and wet, inviting, misleading. He would gather her up again, but inside she was dry and her muscles clenched before he could enter deep, clench and shut him out. "Let go, Velma," groaning into her neck. "Don't let go, Obie," trembling in his arms.

"The whole town's waiting to see the parade, Obo. The smart money says you militants are planning to shoot up the town."

"Haven't heard that word in a while— militant."

"Was that a side step?"

Ahiro's hands waited for about eight beats, then bore down on Obie's shoulders, flattening him out again. An old blue Packard in the back lot of the Regal had moved and now he could see the double windows of Doc Serge's office. Maybe Doc could help. Velma had never much cared for the man, but he'd explore that. There was the woman with the gift on staff there too. Maybe. And maybe he could spring Roland and bring him home.

"I hope you don't have any more appointments today." Ahiro was helping him turn over, patting his back as though apologizing for having not solved the rock quarry problem. "You need some steam, the whirlpool. And if you want, I can get you back on the table around four-thirty. Your chest is like a granite slab." His voice was sorrowful. "Obo, you know what you really need?"

Something in the way his voice dropped and trailed off made Obie hold his breath then lift his head, one eye open. Was Ahiro about to offer him a joint or was he about to hit on him? Obie squinted.

"What?"

"A good cry, man. Good for the eyes, the sinuses, the heart. The body needs to throw off its excess salt for balance. Too little salt and wounds can't heal. Remember Napoleon's army? Those frogs were dropping dead from scratches because their bodies were deprived of salt. But *too* much—"

Obie opened his eyes in time to see Ahiro's hands finishing the statement, one hand flowing along a current of air, stopped by the other clenched, fisted and gnarled. And then his hands were on him again and Obie closed his eyes. Ahiro was making flat circles in Obie's stomach with the heels of his hands, pressing then releasing. Obie felt his stomach flutter the way it had the day he'd followed Velma and lost her in the supermarket. He hadn't known what he'd expected—a rendezvous, a visit to a fortuneteller, streaking through the streets. She'd simply gone shopping for groceries. He'd been almost disappointed. He'd hoped the new prayer partner, swami, shrink or whoever the Blood called Jamahl was, would turn out to be "it." He would have liked something concrete to fix on.

"You're not listening. A good cry, man. Nobody here but you and me. Your masseur is like your doctor, priest. You know what I mean?"

"Hey." Obie gave him a brotherly punch on the arm. "I hear you."

"Well, okay then. Too much stiff upper lip is not good for the soul. You British?"

"Naw, man."

"Too much face it not so good either. Next thing you know, you're forced to fall on your sword. You from Japan?"

"I heard you, Ahiro."

"Well then, are you from Macho, whatever country that is?"

"Do your meditation and your dance, Ahiro. I'm too tired to laugh."

"Never be too tired to laugh, Obo." He was working on the balls of his feet and Obie was sliding up the table, his head dropping off. Looking out the window from that angle, he could see the dome of the Regal Theatre, tarnished and spattered, but shining. He could see the underside of the Infirmary's sun deck, the weathered planks, a nest in the crook of one of the braces.

"Or too grown to cry, Obo."

Obie lifted his head. "Hey, Ahiro."

"What?"

"You Black?"

"I look Black?"

"You sound just like my mama."

For a split second there when Ahiro came around the table with his arms outstretched Obie thought he was going to follow through on the mother act and gather him up in his arms. But he leaned over him, his sleeves falling in Obie's face, and opened the window.

"Breathe deep, really deep, and I'll have you weeping in no

time. Breathe deep. Too bad the air's so bad in this town. But at least there's the music."

The raga reggae bumpidity bing zing was pouring out all over Fred Holt from the open windows up over the Regal where elderly women freed up from girdles and strict church upbringing bumped, glided and rolled to the variation of cheft telli that the four musicians on drum, oud, finger cymbals, chekere and the pan fashioned.

"Stomach flutters, ladies. Pant, pant, pant." The dance teacher explained straight-faced—heel glide, pose, softened knee, stomach flutter, then dancing across the floor in veiled gathered pants and a coin bra—that orgasm exorcised demons and that these warm-up exercises were designed to strengthen the "central enthusiastic" muscles. The women tittered, hooted, blushed, or said "right on" with teeth gripping the lower lip in, depending on their hearing and their rearing and her delivery. Many much preferred the serious talks before the going across the floor part of the session, the part about temple dancing and sacred thighs and women worship and such like. They could deal with that. It was like the daydreaming of girlhood, the dreaming that drew them to the romance paperbacks, the soaps. But Miss Geula Khufu, formerly Tina Mason the seamstress' daughter, saw to it that they dealt with it all: temples, cabarets, bedrooms.

"Don't cheat the body, don't cheat the spirit, ladies. Do the whole movement," she was saying, singling out the three Black women and whispering, "Remember?" and then weaving her way through the group to say to the Lebanese and Greek women, "Remember?" and then confronting the one professional dancer in the group, a Pakistani— "Remember?" Her veil sliding off the shoulders of the other women as if to say she was not ignoring them; their roots in the sacred, their roots in the pelvic movements were different that's all. She touched a hip here, a knee there, correcting, coaxing, not that she expected much from most of them, they were not ancient women after all. And the one little Chinese woman who was, welllll there'd been no strong African presence in China, just a visit long ago in a golden boat with giraffes and gold and spices, a quick hello. When she was sure that no one was chafing for being ignored, she returned to the Black women, the other ancient women, arched her brows sharply, triple-timed with the brass zils, her hands, fingers snaking over her head, and mouthed the word again. "Remember?" It was all right with everyone else. The woman was a mental case. But the classes were fun and Geula was a welcomed madness.

"Follow me, ladies, and breathe like you mean it," leading the serpentine procession past the windows front, side and back, kicking them open more widely with a flexed foot. "Shake it like you mean it, shake a wicked ass, ladies. Shake them moneymakers, ladies." "Ladies" was always delivered with a tincture of iodine. She'd started out with "bitches," then "witches," which was just too much, too much. Some-times to puff them up on rainy days she'd say "goddesses" or "queens." That always sent the drummer right off. The women had finally sat Miss Geula down and exercised their democratic rights. There were eight votes for "ladies" and six for "god-desses." Five held out for "sisters" and were lobbying all the time.

The pan man in dreadlocks and knitted cap aimed his mal-lets straight for the Academy windows, his contribution to the new community germinating there. He'd been known to use the word "postule" when referring to the way the teachers there were steady realigning cultural and political loyalties, breeding new people. But the ladies, some of them, blanched at the word and drifted away to chew on their carrot sticks and wait for the break to end. Then he started using "seed," which disturbed some, but excited others he noticed. Nowadays he said "enzyme" and grew to like it. It was scientific sounding, slightly mysterious, was, finally, exactly the term he'd been after to explain the work of the Academy in this moment in time in human history. Pan Man squinted, trying to make out the shapes, movements, faces even of the forms in the window across the street. It was the best place he'd found in all the seven years he'd spent in the States trying to educate people about the meaning of the pan, the wisdom of the pan. He bent low over his oil drum and played like a man possessed.

The music drifted out over the trees toward the Infirmary, maqaam now blending with the bebop of Minnie Ransom's tapes. Minnie's hand was before her face miming "talk, talk" graceful arcs from the wrist as though she were spinning silk straight from her mouth. The music pressing against the shawl draped round Velma, pressing through it against her skin, and Velma trying to break free of her skin to flow with it, trying to lift, to sing with it. And she did lift and was up under a sloping roof eavesdropping on herself and Jamahl in the orgone box under a pyramid and not believing a word of it, not going for one bullshit line of it, but listening to the instructions that would ease the knots. "Submit. Don't be so damned stubborn, Velma," groaning under the needle in her mind. And not resisting it, only him. She was not a fool. A jive nigger in a loincloth and a swami turban was a jive nigger whatever the case. Up in her perch so like the talking room of childhood, peering through the floorboards and eavesdropping on the people below. Up in the air under the roof, later, watching herself and James locked in a struggle that depleted and strangely renewed at the same time. And she leaned down to lift the needle, to yank the arm away, to pull apart the machinery in favor of her own voice. She would sing. Minnie would spin and she would sing and it would be silk. But when she opened her mouth out came fire. And she was a dragon hovering over the room, flicking her golden smoking tail against the attic walls, the outstretched wings scaly and iridescent, the crimson eyes, the open jaws of blue smoke and orange flame, clawing at the planks of the floor, plunging through loose fill and plaster and wood and air and carpet and wood and loose fill and cement and clay and dirt and down down into a drum.

She had gone to the marshes once. It hadn't been a decision or even a thought. In retrospect, hugging herself inside the shawl, it hadn't even been an act. One minute she was arguing with her prayer partner, Jamahl, whose so-called solutions to the so-called problem always lay in somebody else's culture: Tai Chi, TM, Reichian therapy, yoga. She argued that the truth was in one's own people and the key was to be centered in the best of one's own traditions. She could have gone on all night. But then she felt it again, surrounded, flashes of pictures, scatterings of sounds. As though she had the stereo headset on ears and eyes and was thoroughly into the whatever it was. The next minute she was at the marshes.

There'd been a man there at first in gum boots with a basket, she assumed, of frogs. He'd touched his cap and moved off as though he'd known she wouldn't get her mouth working in time. And there'd been a dog with a nasty gash on the back of its neck. That had stopped her, fixed her on the spot. That was the moment she formed the words: "I've come to the marshes. I've just seen a man in gum boots. I'm looking at a wounded dog who is looking back at me." As if it had waited for her to catch up, to find the place in the script, the dog paused and then dropped down of a sudden and wallowed in the mud close to the shallows. And she'd been humbled watching it. A nondescript dog, wounded, come to the place to heal itself in the earth.

There was a fallen tree by the patch of swamp punk. It

seemed to be there for sitting. She sat. She knew she was waiting because she was no longer watching. She was aware of the dog's being there nearby, its paws in the air, its torso twisting. But she wasn't watching, she was waiting. She wasn't sure for what, for her clothes to feel like moss, for a tuning of strings, for a wind in the reeds, for her breathing to synch with the pulse of sap around her, for the trunk to sink, splinter, rot and become humus for new growth? Since confrontation was her style, she formed the words to establish some order: "I am waiting to confront it."

She waited. And it was no different from the waiting most people she knew did, waiting for a word from within, from above, from world events, from a shift in the power configurations of the globe, waiting for a new pattern to assemble and reveal itself, or a new word to be uttered from the rally podium, from a pamphlet picked up at the neighborhood bookstore. A breakthrough, a sign. Waiting. Ready. She waited as though for battle. Or for a lover. Or for some steamy creature to arise dripping and unbelievable from the marshes. She waited for panic.

Panic. Pan. Pan-Africanism. All of us. Every. God. Pan. All nature. Pan. Everywhere. She was grinning, as she always grinned when she was able to dig below the barriers organized religion erected in its push toward a bogus civilization. "I'd welcome panic," she said aloud, certain of it. That said, that done, and nothing forthcoming, she was waiting no longer. She was drifting, her gaze skimming the grasses, sliding to the far side of the marshes, its borders outlined by the salt froth on the inside, the crusty short grass and salt-stiff calamus on the out-side. Traveling past was a cluster of gnats dancing in the air lit at intervals by fireflies. Then up toward the hills on the far side of the spindly woods she used to play in as a child. The upcoast was showing her its bones in a straight selvage of blue-black rock. The river not visible at all from where she sat, sunk deep between the far woods and the dark rock hills, having long ago carved out its path, then turned, turned away its waters toward the Savannah, its preference the merging of the waters. But it let slip a minor current that would not make the turn, that went underground through the salt beds then surfaced, miles later, in front of her, a marsh.

It was the perfect place for it to happen, whatever there was to happen. On the site of metamorphosis. River, rain, underground spring, marsh. She felt ready. Not tired and fed up, not beaten down and resigned, but ready. But maybe it didn't happen like that. Still, if it was going to happen, this was the place. The first place she had run to as a child fleeing the house.

Things were active around her. What she'd thought was lichen coating the tree trunk with mottled green and white, or what she thought were fungus ledges that grew straight out from the bark in beige shelves were colonies of bugs moving very fast. And for a moment, she thought she felt the head phone clamped on, sounds surround her and a pulling down. It occurred to her that if they slowed down, they would look, at a glance, like what they were—bugs. And if they speeded up, they'd be not visible bugs looking like lichen, but the idea of bugs resonating in her brain. Time. Time not speeding up but opening up to take her inside.

It seemed quite reasonable and friendly and useable sitting there with things occurring to her rather than tracking her, haunting her, terrorizing her, catching her up, taking her over till she thought she was losing her mind. Which was nothing compared to the thought that she might become a permanent cripple, of no serviceable use to any one anymore. So, to maintain order she tried forming some other words gleaned from this visit, this calm. Something she could tell herself when the crowding began. When the pictures began. When the mud mothers called out to her. Something she could remember to be wide open with so she wouldn't have to invest all of herself staying intensely occupied, eyes, ears, mind riveted on the task at hand, the work ahead, lest she be taken over.

She found no words. Nor a brief passage of music. Nothing stayed fixed and available for later.

Tightening the shawl about her, vaguely listening to the music, feeling the healer's hands on her arms, she remembered that that marsh visit had failed to inform her days and her nights, it had failed to inform her mind, the minute she got up from the tree. Whatever had occurred, stayed behind. And home again, the terrors crouched behind chairs and bookcases. Velma shuddered and sank deeply into the music.

The dumm tete tete tak tat diir tik piercing the wall between the dance studio and the one skinny roominghouse left on the Hill, jammed between the Regal and the Patterson Professional Building. Campbell roused himself from the chair, his arms asleep, his nose clogged, prickles in his legs, needles in his feet, hot and dusty under the rag rug he'd thrown over himself for a quick nap, shorts soupy and shirt salt-stiff after a jog through the Heights pumping up neuro-adrenaline, the only antidepressant he trusted now. He stretched and jumped free of the chair as if taking off a lead coat.

Duummmm dah dah dum tete tete dii irrr. He checked his watch, springing into the shower. Three hours at the café, the writers' workshop at the Academy, the late class with the widow woman Heywood. He tried a scissor kick in the shower and the rubber mat did not fail him.

"Give me an S, spiral breath," rubbing himself briskly with the towel.

"Give me an O, rolling in dough," climbing into his pants.

"Give me a good Ph, for health, sis boom mama."

"Give me an—" he took the bannister down to the first landing.

"Mr. Campbell." His landlady was in her doorway tut-tutting and stuffing clumps of gray up under a bright white wig advertised no doubt as platinum. He smiled and buttoned his shirt. He recognized a hopeful from Central Casting when he saw one. "About the rent . . ."

The classic script. He could've written it himself, except he abhorred the cliché. "Not only do I have the rent," he said, pulling his pockets inside out and flinging gold coins, drachmas, pesos, yen all over the hallway, money she chose to ignore in favor of the usual check backed by equally imaginary currency, "but I'm going to mention you in my very next article, a feature piece on the Spring Festival. Covering it exclusive for the dailies and the weekly. None of them have sense enough to send out one of their own reporters. It's the big time, Mrs. Terry."

The landlady backed into her doorway, tut-tutting while the crazy man Gene Kelly-ed down the front steps, racing behind the paper boy, doing throaty sounds like the sports car she'd just bought for her nephew. She did not close her door though. She waited till he was well on his way before she tiptoed out and looked up the stairwell. She wanted another peek into that telescope he had up there. Though what could possibly be going on over at the Academy that could be so interesting, she hadn't a clue.

The bike waffled for a minute till Lil James, called Jabari now, stood up on the pedals, found a graded curb and could get away from the jerk growling at him. Campbell stood, arms akimbo, watching the kid strain up the hill, the cords standing out in his neck, shoulders, his arms bulging. He tipped his hat he wasn't wearing to acknowledge effort like that. It looked as though any minute the boy's jeans would tear, his shirt rip, his clothes pop off and fly up like the kites the kids were writing notes to God on and releasing on the day before festival.

eight

Meadows would have preferred a walk in the woods. Stumbling about aimlessly amidst trees and squirrels on the hunt for the essential selves of the patient and the healer would not have been nearly so alarming as fumbling along the pavement, crossing streets for no reason, attracting attention to his foreignness, attracting danger. To walk in the woods, one needed a gun, just a prop to guise the meandering. In these unknown streets, who knew what was needed? All he had was the blue notebook from the orientation packet. And it wouldn't stay put. He was sure he had worn his pocket lining thin sliding his fist in and out to readjust his grip. It occurred to him to roll the thing and jam it into his belt. He even considered carrying it in his mouth like a bone. Passing an old lard can rolling around on the curb, he toyed with the idea of pitching his notebook in it and catching a plane back home. But he'd taken such careful notes. And he felt . . . drawn was the word, to the place.

"Supper. Suppah." He mouthed it as the old man with the

gold tooth at the bus stop might. He pictured himself safely tucked under a hefty table leaf, a threadbare but clean tablecloth covering his lap, chipped bowls overladen with food hemming him in, and friendly boarders passing platters, easy with each other, easy with him. He found himself daydreaming on a family he'd never had: a mother who ran a boardinghouse and who treated the roomers as kin, a father who told the women hands off and taught the boy how to handle a hammer, a gun, a carving knife at Thanksgiving time. So he walked the streets at loose ends making up things to keep himself company. "Suppah." It sounded so homey, frugal but homey.

"Triflin. Man, you so triflin." He said it the way he imagined the woman from the café might. Not contemptuous, but affectionately surly.

He smiled and turned a corner without a clue as to what to do with himself now. It had been years since he'd had more than two unscheduled hours on his hands. His dawns to dusks to dawns for so long crammed full with the hospital, the Guild, pacemaker executives and their barbiturized wives and traumatized offspring, meetings, seminars, insurance agents, pharmaceutical salesmen, burglar-alarm specialists, head nurses vying with him for jurisdiction over patients, his partners dumping troublesome cases on his desk and keeping the Medicaid and Medicare gold mines for themselves.

He'd been walking the streets for what seemed like hours, sweaty and hungry one minute, exhilarated and greedy to see more the next. Some blocks back he'd passed a park where kids, youths, adult men and women, elders, all in bright T-shirts with "7 Arts" stenciled across the back had been setting up as if for a fair. Tables, tents, awnings, rides, fortunetellers, candy booths, gymnasts with mats, nets, trampolines, oil drums from the islands, congos from who knew where, flat trucks, platforms, pushcarts and stalls of leather crafts, carved cooking spoons, jewelry and the like. He had meant to stop and pick up their literature but it would have meant crossing a boulevard with no traffic lights or pedestrian markings. Now he couldn't remember how to double back.

Where he walked was quiet and vacant. Lots, closed stores with fly-speckled windows, a bank where a man looking like that Doc Serge should be standing, a watch chain across his vest. But there was no one and nothing much to look at.

He felt in Claybourne like a late arrival to one of those obligatory cocktail parties, hanging by the bookcase or leaning against the baby grand trying to catch the party's beat. Always exhausting his repertoire after two encounters he finally became the three-toed sloth he's always known himself to be, counting the blacks and whites of the party and then of the keyboard, tracing the pattern in the rug with one spit-shined loafer, oblivious that the other was planted mercilessly on his hostess' crepe de Chine slipper.

"Putty-colored three-toed sloth," he said aloud in the empty street, and having run out of sidewalk, crossed over to turn still another corner.

"Putty-colored three-toed sloth," his stepfather's idea of a nickname, was usually his signal to go home, to finger another soggy sandwich, drain his cup or glass if he had one and leave. But he wasn't going home now. He was going to stay. There was something drawing him, tugging at him to be recalled. Greensboro, Montgomery, Port Gibson, Little Rock, Hattiesburg, Lowndes County, Cairo, Illinois, Claybourne. He'd sent a check. He knew that much. He could recall the check, the broad strokes he'd made with a flat-point pen, the yellow check with his old phone number on it. But the rest of it would not come clear.

"Happy Mardi Gras!"

Like a shot ringing out. The quiet of the woods disturbed.

177

An explosion by his ear and birds breaking from cover. Dressed in women's evening wear, the exaggerated shoulders and opulent sheen from Hollywood's white-telephone period, three young Black men came prancing toward him, streamers curling down floppy from their wigs, balloons bulging through the clothes. One held a toy trumpet to his lips and puffed and blew, though the mouthpiece never came in contact with the sloppily applied lipstick. His décolletage was bumpily hairy.

"We're thstarting in early," the blond wig said. "Come thoin usth."

Meadows stood frozen on the spot.

"Wait a minute. Can't go anywhere looking like that." The third one with green balloon bosom and a pillow for buttocks had plopped his tote bag down on Meadows' toes and was fussily pulling out a pink satin gown, yards and yards of it like a magician's length of scarfs.

"Don't worry." He did not alter his voice as the others did, nor was he wearing heels. Just the wig, his own mustache, a striped taffeta jacket pulled in at the waist over Jean Harlow lounging pajamas, mix-match socks and tennis shoes.

"Just put it on and the role will play itself."

He stared at the gown. Were they serious? They didn't seem like queers for all their carrying on. He looked them over thoroughly, since they made it clear it was expected of him. They were more his age than not. Maybe post office clerks or bus drivers. The man at his feet wore a wedding band and what looked like a marine ring. Blondie had a gash across his left brow, the bunched-up scar tissue giving him a querulous look. The bloodshot eyes said alcoholic, though he didn't seem to be tipsy, just confusing for Meadows. The trumpeteer carried a beaded evening bag that looked antique. He might be somebody's father. Meadows had never been to a Mardi Gras, maybe this was how one dressed for it. The mannish mix-matched socks, though, relieved him. Surely this was a joke.

"Carnival's getting so stuffy around here."

"And tacky."

"But yeth, Trixthy my love, tack ack ee." Blondie was helping to spread the pink gown out. "We thought we'd get a head
start and thet a whole new tone, give carnival thum classth.
Know what I mean, thweetie?"

"Are you all transvestites or what?"

He could not believe his ears. Could not believe what he was
hearing had come out of his mouth. He stared at the most
reasonable-looking one, noticing for the first time that in addition to the ballons he was fleshy around the breasts and lumpy
all on his own around the hips. And the mustache was clearly
crepe he realized now. A hermaphrodite perhaps. Then this
scenario had more to do with . . . Black men didn't mince about
in the streets for a joke. Still.

"You're a sca-reeeeeam, thweetie. Say thomthin elseth. You
talk so cute."

"Speak. Speak."

"You want this lovely number or not?"

Meadows found himself bending to help stuff the satin and
lace back into the bag. They were cracking up at him one
minute, then dancing by him single file the next, Blondie
sassily flipping Meadows' tie up at the last minute. The chorus
line looked more like a chain gang shuffling into meals, Meadows was thinking. Or prisoners filing past him for a squirt of
pesticide from the spray gun. He'd never have to do that kind
of work again, he was telling himself, glad to have something
to tell himself as they whipped around the corner shouting,
"Have a carnal carnival, dearie!"

A moment later it was like none of it had ever happened.
The street was quiet, empty. No dogs even, no moving cars.
Just a piece of purple streamer on his shoe.

179

"What was that all about?"

He headed for what looked like a shopping center up ahead. Carnival did strange things to people evidently. No Black man he had ever known goofed on himself like that. He shrugged.

Just a year before he'd been asked to participate in a Bicentennial pageant, a benefit given by the Guild for a school for deaf children. That was the closest he'd gotten to a carnival. Crispus Attucks, a good part he'd thought. He had been flattered, had gotten a number of history books and acting primers out of the library, was ready to do it till he overhead at a Guild meeting that the role was to be played in blackface.

On folding chairs directly in front of him it was being discussed. Two of the so-called radical contingent who were forever disrupting the meetings calling for a caucus though they never did attract more than one or two Taiwanese or Pakistanis, who invariably left them to join either the main group or the Third World caucus Meadows hadn't yet talked himself into joining.

"You're kidding. Burnt cork in 1976. How droll."

"Seems the spade they asked to reenact the dying for liberty"—and here the teller slumped over the chair in a mock swan dive, his hands wagging Al Jolson–style over his head. And it would not have been an effort at all, no effort at all, he could feel his foot rising, no effort at all to slip a loafer into the seat and shove the cocksucker onto his head—"is too light to convey the message across the footlights."

"Blackface? Far fucking out. The Third World group'll slaughter him."

"Lynch him."

"Tar and feather him first. How gross."

They'd giggled and he'd left. And for three nights running he'd rehearsed his speech, the arch of the eyebrow, the curl of the lip, the sneer gilding his well-modulated voice. But no one ever contacted him further about it to give him the chance to decline.

In his fantasies, snatched moments between racing from the emergency room to psychiatric to the subway to the deli to the office he shared as junior member with three ex–Park Avenue GMP's, he saw himself in burnt cork, Crispus Attucks returns, ignoring the tomato sauce on the chest, turning his musket on them all, mowing down the red coats, the white coats, the rest of the sons of bitches. And that had been his sole encounter with anything resembling a Mardi Gras.

Just in front of him, sauntering out of a package store and throwing back over her shoulder at him a smile, a challenge, was exactly the kind of woman his father used to yell "Hey, Big Stockings" at. She had her elbow planted in the flesh of one hip, a wine jug held out in the crook of her finger. But before he could work out his strategy, a flashy young dude stepped between them and took the jug in both his hands like it was a bowling ball. They leaned their heads in, looked back at him and laughed. He reddened and slowed his pace, expecting to have to jump any minute the wine jug rumbling down the alley toward him. He cut down a side street. And then that encounter too drifted, gave way as though it hadn't happened, gave way to the stark reality of the street.

This was evidently where the poorer people lived. There were broken-down stoops that looked like city and leaning porches that looked like country. Houses with falling-away shutters and brick walkways that wouldn't make up their minds. Claybourne hadn't settled on its identity yet, he decided. Its history put it neither on this nor that side of the Mason Dixon. And its present seemed to be a cross between a little Atlanta, a big Mount Bayou and Trenton, New Jersey, in winter.

Dented garbage cans, car shells, old venetian blinds that

hung askew. Across the way a half-dressed woman in the open window, her breasts resting on pillows laid on the window sill. The block so like his first a hundred lives ago when Army recruiters would set up booths in the empty storefronts and slap a poster up, the sudden bright colors eclipsing tattered liquor signs and old billboards urging the people to vote for Miss Ballantine. In spiffy uniforms, with scrubbed faces, the white and Black recruiters would be joking with the young men, passing out mess-hall menus and glossy photos of soldiers in warm winter uniforms. How he'd wanted to get on line and have his hand shaken and be told he could learn a trade with Uncle Sam, be sent to school, be somebody. Did they still recruit like that?

Meadows shuddered. Meadows jumped. A snarling dog was heaving himself against a fence whose rattle said it might not hold. Stiff-legged and all teeth, the dog growled and snapped at the wire mesh, his body trembling.

"Don't pay'm no mind, mister." A woman in housecoat and slippers grabbed the beast by his collar, dragging him back from the gate, mashing his head down between her knees. "Shush, Roger, shush." She was holding a bag of garbage. She would be opening the gate to get to the garbage can on the curb. Should he reach over the fence and take the bag for her? Would Roger find his way out of her knees and attack him? Meadows hurried down the street.

A dark-skinned man with a cap yanked low over an unruly bush sat on the bottom step of one of the stoops up ahead. A wool plaid jacket that belonged on a boat or on a hunt. Elbows wedged between his knees, stock still and waiting for a duck or a deer or a woman. Only the rifle was missing. Welfare man, Meadows typed him. The small-change half-men who lived off of mothers and children on welfare.

He had seen them, made a study of them, knew the look,

the posture. In parks, on roofs, in bars, on stoops, but especially in supermarkets running their whining line while the women reached round them for a can of whatever was on sale. The boymen grabbing at their pocketbooks or their arms and the women saying "Naw, man, gotta feed my kids." Then the whine heard all over the market and the women mashing the can against the shelf for a two cents off for dents. "But mama, look here" or "Say Baby I gotta" and then the "Naaaw man." But never a name, never names. A ritual. Market theater with anonymous personae.

He'd seen them back the women into the frozen food tank, bending their bodies back as if over a sofa arm, over a bedstand, pressing and pleading for a dollar walk-around money, or sixty-nine cents for a pint to share with Shorty on the roof, or fifty for a game of pool with Bumpy, or thirty-five cents to put them into contending with the teenage basketball stars, or a dime or a nickel or a penny for the gumball machine. And by the time they got to the line and the welfare mamas were fishing out the coupons, worn out with all the haggling, the boymen would lean in for the kill, mashing their joints into the women, mashing the women into the shopping carts, the mesh outlined on ass or hips, the purses clutched so hard the vinyl tore. "A dime, woman, a damn dime." And the women, defeated, would dip into the coins and give it up, then look over the items moving along on the belt for the one thing the children might possibly do without.

Meadows approached the man on the stoop, his eyes on the two shoes jutting out that would have to be walked around. He studied the posture, the clothes, the nappy hair sticking out from under the cap. He had him pegged. He didn't have to look into the face. He never looked into the faces anyway. The nameless players were faceless too. To look was not part of it. He couldn't look. He always turned his face away. They scared the shit out of him. Not in the bars so much, even when they were nasty drunk. Not on the streets so much, even when they stalked him and anybody else they thought they could put the bite on. They just angered him then. But in the supermarkets the boymen were frightening. Frightening because the women were there, there and losing. And because he was there, there and helpless.

Never a basket, never *with* the women, the boymen raced in *after* the women in a rush of need and gotta and right now. And never a name—mama, baby, woman—but never a name. And he would turn away, but stand there hearing it. Crushing the lettuce and looking for glass to smash, that mysterious directive from childhood In Case of Emergency Smash Glass, like ticker tape spreading across the produce. He wanted to turn and beat them. Bend the boymen into the stacks of frozen food and beat them with a rock cornish hen or a ten-pound carton of solid hard chitterlings.

And all the while moving up on line, he'd grip the cart handles till his knuckles went white and he'd turn his face away, bury his eyes in the *TV Guide* or the *Jet* but hear it anyway. "Well, a dime then. Damn woman, just a dime." And he'd hear the weary sigh from the woman. Hear the pocketbook open and he'd turn and watch the woman, they all did it the same way like they'd all studied under the same drama coach. They'd peer into the cavernous bags, wanting no doubt to fall in, jump in and close themselves up in there and be unavailable forever. And why did they never do it? What was it that kept them from diving in head first? What in that five-flight walk-up drudge of a life with babies and babies and pee-stained mattresses and welfare investigators poking in closets and cutting them off and cutting them down and these half-men whining and pleading and bending their wash-bent bodies into the cold tank—why not? But always the hand came out of the bag with little clutch purses, and the purses were snatched at greedily by childish unmannish hands. "Wait now. Just you wait one damn minute, man."

One day he would snap. One day he would mount the counter shouting, "Use names for crissake! Haven't you niggers got any names?" He would run amuck in the supermarket.

Meadows was laughing out loud. Trampling the man's feet and laughing out loud.

"Watchit, honky!"

"Honky! You muthafuckin dumb bastard, don't you know a Blood when you see one?"

"Get the fuck off my feet, whatever the fuck you are."

Two more men were coming out of the doorway. Then a woman with half her hair pressed and the other half raw came onto the porch, children swarming all around her hips.

"You on the wrong side of town, buddy."

Meadows moved on fast. The warning from the tall dude by the door was not lost on him. Fat chance of trying to explain his feet's behavior in terms of supermarket memories. Or trying to share the joke of the ubiquitous red box from subways, public buildings, movie houses that offered the magic instruction In Case of Emergency. And there he'd be in the supermarket flying over the baskets to get at the boymen, landing in a clutter of cans and boxes and not a bit of glass to be had. No one remembering to buy a jar of pickled beets to supply him with the talisman. And there he'd be getting pummeled by an army of these boymen who had read his intentions and put his name out on the wire. And him yelling, "Quick, somebody hand me a blunt instrument and quick, quick somebody smash some glass. This is an absolute emergency."

"Hey you."

Coming up behind him were the stepped-on man and the tall dude from the doorway.

"Wait up."

It was pointless to run. There were no alleys or driveways. And who knew what lay beyond the three-bar fence that read DEAD END? With his luck, a sheer drop to a four-lane highway.

"Hey, buddy, we ain't gonna bother you." The door man held his hands palms up, the ancient sign, no spear, no knife, no hand grenade.

"You lost? . . . In some kind of trouble?"

They were studying him. By now they'd know he was not a honky. He felt himself coming into focus for them, like the movie stars on the lids of Dixie Cups he'd licked long ago into being. Coming into view for them now, his red-gold hair of no less than five grades—curly in front, stringy in back, wavy round the ears, slick on top, and downright nappy at the center. The barbers always went at the nigger hair with clippers ablaze but couldn't bear to clip the curls or shorten the back no matter how he instructed. Haircuts were a freak show. He licked his lips and tried to be patient. Now the grain of his skin would be coming into view, like a 35mm blowup. He was never more clear to himself than when Black people examined him this way, suspicious. He felt his nostrils flatten. For all his mother's pinching, his nose splayed out into his cheekbones now as if for the first time, as though willed. And now they were checking out his clothes, the cat in the cap eying his watch. They were satisfied he was one of them, he sensed. Though he wasn't fool enough to think being a nigger saved him. He felt his feet poised for flight, his arms flexed for a rumble. His adrenaline was up. The coagulants working doubletime in case of wound, in case a gush had to be staunched.

"Whatcha doin round here?"

He tried to see under the bill of the cap. The face was a layer of shadows. The voice sounded suspicious but not dangerous yet.

"I . . . I'm visiting the Infirmary."

"Oh." They exchanged glances. "You one of the new medics?"

"Yeh."

He was calm enough now to see them, feel them loosen up. The tall one, in a well-ironed denim suit, fished out a pack of cigarettes by the tail of gold cellophane and studied the picture of the camel as if for his next line. The shorter one in the cap kept his eyes on Meadows' watch.

"We've been having some trouble around here . . ." The pack was being offered to him. He waved it aside with what he hoped was a cool air of nonchalance. "Transchemical's been sending goons . . . spies . . . bad times . . ." The man seemed to be making a question of it. What would he know about labor problems at the chemical plant if he were on a visit to the Infirmary? Meadows waited.

"What's your name and who you work for?"

"Hold on, now." The taller one was pulling Stepped-On back by the arm though he hadn't moved; his words, though, had shot forward and Meadows had backed up. "Where's your sense of hospitality? Your manners?" The tall one extended a hand. "I'm Thurston. This here's Hull. They call him M1. Meanest nigger in de worrld and you gotta come along and step on his foot."

"Feet, man. The fool stepped on my feet. Both of them."

"Hey, I'm sorry . . . I've had a rough . . . I'm really sorry, broth—"

"You got a name, bra thuh?" The nasty one jutted his chin up at him and now he could see the whole face, the eyes. If this is what the welfare boymen looked like up close, so close, he'd keep on keeping his face turned away hereafter.

"Meadows. I work for Doc Serge," he lied, inspired.

"Doc?" They exchanged looks again, visibly impressed. "Hmm."

"He tell you to come round here and step on my feet?"

"Daydreaming. Just . . . man, I am really sorry . . ."

"You lucky, Meadows. If he'd been drunk, you'd be dead. Did Doc send you round with a message?" He paused for just a beat, then lowered his voice. "He's still coming tonight?"

Meadows curled up the notebook against his fly, wondering if his subconscious was trying to signal him. But then he was sorry; the gesture had drawn their attention. They were looking down at his joint. He dropped the pad and discovered he was too afraid to retrieve it. "They've got a healing going on," he finally figured was something hip to be saying.

"Oh yeah?" The dude called Thurston, which had come across to Meadows as Thirsty, seemed genuinely interested. The other one was still doing his x-ray act. "Who?"

"A Velma Henry."

The two men exchanged glances again. "Obie's woman," one of them said. Meadows didn't see which; he chose that moment to bend for his notebook.

"What's the matter with her? He finally bury his foot up her ass?"

"Dunno." Meadows addressed the notebook.

"Something happen to her over at the plant?" Thirsty had lowered his voice again and was massaging his chin. Meadows shrugged. It didn't seem appropriate or discreet to say he thought it had been an attempted suicide. It hadn't looked like a serious attempt anyway, not compared to cases he'd seen in emergency. In addition, whatever he might say would only provide further questions he knew he could not answer. So he shrugged again and hoped they'd be interested enough to go make a call and leave him alone.

"Doc'll know." Thirsty was checking his watch, then waving them in the direction of the house. "Come on." Thirsty straightened his jacket and was moving back down the street as though it was understood Meadows and the friend would follow. The man called Emwahn was obviously waiting for Meadows to move, so he did. They fell in around him, flanked him. Meadows was on guard again.

"Where you staying?"

He rolled the notebook up and jammed it into his pocket. "Nadir's."

"Who?" They both stopped, and he was now far enough ahead to consider making a run for it. But he hadn't got past their stoop yet and there was a man sitting there breaking open a six-pack. And who knew, maybe the raging dog up ahead would jump the fence and come at him.

"You mean M'Dear? As in Maa Deeear, everybody's good ole boardinghouse grandma?"

He felt himself redden and they had caught up enough to see it. So they laughed at that too. He was sure the woman in the floral hat, the woman who ran a boardinghouse, had been introduced by Doc Serge as "Nadir." He'd thought it country-classic.

"You somp'n." The one in the suit slung an arm around his shoulder and was wagging his head. "Callin people out of their name. Didn't yo mama teach you nuthin? I won't embarrass you by asking you our names. My name's Thurston, as in need for a beer. This is Hull as in Walnut, called M1 as in rifle. Come on, my man, let's have a beer. Wish we could extend an invitation to grit, but the cupboard's Mother Hubbard's."

"The larder is lean."

"The refrig renigged."

"The bones are picked clean."

"And the breadbox is the private preserve of the roaches."

They slapped five in front of him and he smacked their hands recklessly. And they laughed again. And Meadows wondered if he would get off LaSalle street alive. He was a yaller nigger in costly cothes with an Omega watch. An out-of-town cornball who'd stepped on somebody named Ml and called him in earshot of kith and kin a motherfucking dumb bastard. Friends had been killed for less. He'd seen a man impaled on a cue stick for questioning the rack up. He'd seen a woman drowned in a bucket of Kool-Aid for broiling the steak medium well instead of medium rare. On Saturday nights he'd seen life-long friends dragging each other in all cut up, seen shot-up buddies who'd picked up the tip laid down for the barmaid or had said Richard Pryor wasn't funny, or had dropped a deck of cards on the table with the seal split. He'd seen men who'd survived Korea or Vietnam together hauling each other into emergency apologizing to each other, a boot the only thing holding the foot and leg together, a starched collar holding a lopsided head on. Meadows exhaled and poked a fist right through his pocket. What the hell, he thought, squatting on the steps between them, a beer's a beer. Whatever happened, he wasn't stumbling aimlessly around the streets anymore, at loose ends, alone.

nine

"What's the good word, Short Cakes?"

"Pussy. And another good one is—"

"Never mind." Ruby walked her elbows across the tiny café table. "That kid's mouth's getting to be an ecological disaster area," she moaned, dropping her head down into the crook of Jan's elbow.

The rest of the kids, tottering on skateboards or leaning their bikes against the railing, went right on talking to Jan while Short Cakes, balancing his skateboard to a standstill, took the opportunity to pinch from Ruby's plate what he took to be a crab apple.

"Yawl going to the park tonight?"

"Wouldn't miss it for anything in the world," Jan answered, searching the table for something suitable to offer the kids.

"Then you won't be firing the ashtrays tonight?"

"Tomorrow."

191

"Do what?" Ruby looked up in time to see the kid bite into the hot cherry tomato.

"Fire. Bake. Harden. Cure."

"Oh, clay."

The women clamped their mouths shut, waiting for the hot pepper to register. The kids in on the joke hunched the others.

"Mighty powerful pickling to get past all that foul sewerage." Ruby laughed as the kid reached over the café railing to take a swipe at her, his face contorted. Speeding away, he meant to fling the hot tomato back over the railing but his aim was off. The kids ducked and it landed splat on the arm of the tall man in the bow tie, leaning against the railing by the entrance step, talking with the crowd of young people who wanted to know how come Muslims weren't around like before. The paper boy leaned over and took the napkin from Jan and in passing it, got drawn in by Bow Tie, who was very interested in his paper route. The skateboard kids took off down the street on the ninth wave. The bikers, front tires high like a circus act, sailed into the street on the back tires only, slapping the metallic behinds of their thoroughbreds.

"That's Velma's boy. The one with the papers."

"You mean the one with the feet. I know. And ain't that Tommy Jeeter's boy?" Ruby was waving a tattered napkin at the back of the speed demon with his mouth on fire.

"Gail says yes. Jeeter says no."

"Jeeter must be crazy. Could've spit that kid right out of his mouth. Looks more like Jeeter than Jeeter. He better claim that boy. This is a small town and Jeeter got lots of daughters growing up all over Claybourne. But what he care, what a man care about—"

"I hear where this conversation is headed, Ruby. And I do not want to hear no niggerman shit this afternoon. Can it."

"That kiln big enough for Short Cakes *and* his daddy?"

192

Ruby mumbled it, dropping her head down on her arms.

"What's the matter with you here lately, Ruby?"

"Nate's on the road," she muttered into her arms, trying to pull herself up. "Or maybe it's something in the air. Maybe it's Velma. She's a for real drag lately. I think we need to ask her to step down, she's wearing everybody to a frazzle and taking on more work than she or anyone else can handle. Driven. Compulsive. Or maybe . . ." She flopped back in the chair and stared out at the gray, purple clouds. "I dunno. Malcolm gone, King gone, Fanni Lou gone, Angela quiet, the movement splintered, enclaves unconnected. Everybody off into the Maharaji This and the Right Reverend That. If it isn't some far-off religious nuttery, it's some otherworldly stuff. And check that out."

Jan turned, trying to follow Ruby's gaze. Past the microwave oven and the espresso machine was the makeshift stage where the musicians were climbing down for a break. The one brother in the band was wearing a Blues Brothers T-shirt.

"And Nate and the guys can't find a gig in town. It's enough to make you scream, ain't it? Next thing you know, some white boy in top hat and tails, or maybe a dreads wig, will come along and pied pipe all the folks to the lobotomy wards."

"Don't start, Ruby. You always wind up getting things all mixed up and maudlin too." Jan picked among the remains of the salad they'd shared for one last shred of red cabbage. Ruby had asked her a serious question a moment ago but then their favorite waitress had stopped by their table to say goodbye, stuffing her apron in her bag, and Jan hadn't answered. Who, Ruby wanted to know, who could effectively pull together the folks—the campus forces, the street forces, the prison forces, workers, women, the aged, the gay. And Jan had thought Doc Serge but didn't get to say it, even after the waitress left. The thundering of ball bearings had interrupted them. And just as well, for she'd been idly shuffling the Tarot deck, forgetting how scathing Ruby could get about "that stuff," and The Magician had slipped from the pack. Lately each time the team had sat down—Daisy Moultrie on the Ouida board, Mrs. Heywood's protégé on the energy maps, Bertha with the cowries, La Vita with the charts—The Magician had fallen from the deck. She wished to discuss her misgivings about Doc but in her own terms, wanted to discuss how a people turned around might not read the difference between the figure straight up and the figure reversed. Ruby was looking at her sideways and Jan wanted a peaceful lunch. She plopped the deck in the top of her bag, the cards immediately spilling between her eyeglass case and her cosmetic sack. She snapped her bag shut.

The two women leaned back while the waiter cleared away the salad plate, noted their clean forks and missing napkins, and offered each a corner of his apron to wipe their hands.

"Those your kids?"

"Some of them used to be in my class." Jan looked up. "Some take classes with me at the—"

"Academy," Campbell said. He couldn't help it. Had been meaning to make some contact with the woman for weeks. She was always on the run and rarely ate on his shift. "I'll get you a damp towel."

"Ya know," Ruby leaned forward. "I don't want to press anything on you, but getting back to this leadership question. You and Serge are the only—"

"Ruby?"

"Okay, Jan, but the truth is, I'm glad you got fired. I mean it. Murder-mouthed in the yard, jumped on the stairs, ripped open at recess and still you wanted to go right on trying to teach hardened crap shooters the beauty of train A leaving the station two hours before train B, traveling at X minus miles per foot."

"Ruby?"

"And I know, Jan, things are great for you at the Academy, but it's a waste of your talent. The Academy's nonfunctional in the broad sense, too inbred. You can't leave the heavy business of running this city to the fools like Jay Patterson and the like. Now, you know I don't believe in all this 'fate' stuff you characters be into up there in your little study group, but doesn't it occur to you that you were relieved of duty, so to speak, so that you'd be freed up to take on some serious work?"

"Ruby, do me a favor?"

"I know, I know. I'm being a drag."

"Is anyone on the grill? I don't trust that microwave."

Campbell had quickly slid a plate of steamed washcloths onto the table and now glanced around toward the service-counter window to the kitchen. She would want toasted banana nut bread, he knew that. First break in traffic and he would do it himself. He nodded. She smiled. She was a serious sister and good-looking too in an offbeat sort of way—a pointy Dick Tracy face, plucked eyebrows, braids piled high and held in place by a tie-dye scarf, always a tie dye of brilliant colors, so that it looked like she carried a basket of snakes on her head. Did the books at the Academy and taught sculpture at night and ceramics in the afternoon. Odd combination. He hoped she'd be around when he got off. Maybe he could ply her with toasted cake for the next two hours.

"Leave it to me," he said, just in case she hadn't read him. "Banana nut bread, toasted." He set down the cups, a larger pot of Red Zinger tea than they'd ordered, two plates of spinach quiche, and a plastic bear with a yellow hat where the honey came out of. The women looked at the bear, looked at each other, looked at him. "I just work here, yawl," he shrugged.

A reeling drunk was doing the rope-a-dope number against

the railing for the benefit of Bow Tie and the youth, but they were engrossed in a discussion of the Honorable Elijah's heir: Wallace, Farrakhan, a yet-to-be-known? Campbell stepped away from the table to urge the drunk on his way.

"I wanna talk to teacher lady. Hey." He was hailing Jan, who did not recognize him. "Ain't you the schoolteacher from up the way?" His finger pointed toward a VW station wagon parked at the curb, toward the chemical-plant smokestacks in the distance, toward the sidewalk he stood on as he fell along the railing again. He approached their table as if he too were on a skateboard. "I support education," he announced to diners looking away from him or through him. He pulled a pint bottle from one of his uniform's many pockets and examined it carefully for damage. "I pay my taxes. See." It was show-and-tell time, the seal ragged and dirty. "See how much taxes I pay each hour on the hour to educate the children? Such dedication deserves applause, don't it?" Six men at the round table under the awning toasted him and he bowed and drank. Bow Tie bowed too and continued talking about messengers.

"Who are you?" She stared at him as at a long-forgotten object of historical importance, heard about, finally encountered. An ancient piece of pottery. The Rosetta Stone. A scroll from a pharaoh's tomb. She held her breath. He seemed to be holding his too, pulling himself up out of the fumes to stand before her steady, revealed at last. She tried to memorize the lines, the planes, the puffiness here, the broken capillaries there, as though instructed she'd have but one chance to bone up for the exam, one chance in a lifetime to know it. He was somebody. That was as far as she could get. She might get Bertha to throw the cowries on it; she might spread the Tarot on it. He was no Fool, and not the Joker—a Fool who's been around—either. But he was somebody in her kin and she would know it. "What's your name?" She asked it quietly, the way you would a child suddenly appearing out of nowhere on your front stoop in the middle of the night half dressed and scared, or an alley cat who insists its presence on you and will not drop its stare and gets you hypnotized into believing it's come straight from Egypt with the word.

"They call me one thing or another." He had grabbed hold of the railing just below Ruby's elbow and was teetering back and forth. "Good luck, teacher lady," bowing deeply from the waist. "Take care." He strolled off.

"What was that about?" Ruby shivered.

"I dunno. Eerie. I get the feeling . . ." But she hadn't isolated any of the feelings well enough to put a name to. She shrugged, troubled.

Ruby tipped her chair back to get a good look at the drunk crossing now between a mail truck and a milk truck. He seemed to be heading toward the lot that swings down toward the park. "He's made a remarkable recovery, seems to me. Not so much reeling and rocking as bopping and strutting. Isn't he one of Doc Serge's cut buddies?" Her chair was dangerously tipping now and but for a disturbed diner at the next table, she would have fallen backward. "A regular Scarlet Pimpernel, he's disappeared. Change that to the Green Hornet. Was that a hospital orderly outfit or garage attendant uniform or green beret or what? I get my greens mixed."

Green. Jan strained to recall a conversation half heard. She'd been loading the kiln with the masks Obie had asked for for the Parade and trying to meet Ruby on time. Behind the utility rack, on the other side of the wall, a meeting was going on. The Brotherhood most likely. Several had come into the hall, stood behind her door, almost closed it locking her in, and then appeared to be suspicious at finding her there. Something about a man in green giving the signal for things to start.

"Velma coming? Or can I gobble up everything?"

"I dunno. We were supposed to meet this morning. She didn't show."

"No telling where she is," Ruby was saying, attacking the quiche. "She blew the second executive committee meeting in a row last night. Probably another one of those out-of-town jobs. How she ever got clearance to do government work with her background is past my brain. Big-time computer jobs for civil service and so forth."

"I thought she was working at the plant."

"Transchemical? Velma? How'd she manage to juggle that contradiction, working for De Enamee? Either she's lifting info or sabotaging the works. Ahh! I've hit on something?"

Jan sat still, feeling Ruby waiting, waiting and not chewing, knowing she'd stumbled onto something.

"Well, Jan, if it's such a big secret, then pass me that squeezable bear. I need to squeeze me something. Ohh ohh ohh for a stationary man. Stay shun nary maa ah an. You know that Nathan Hardge has been on the road more days this month than he's been at home?"

"He coming home for the festival?"

"I'm so sick of all this festival crap. Couldn't get any business done at all at the meeting last night, everybody talking about the festival. But check this. Me and Bertha did get this done. And this is what I was getting ready to talk about when you thought I was going off about Jeeter and man shit. A Manhood conference. Velma worked on it a bit last week." Ruby was diving under the table, wrassling with her ubiquitous tote bag. "Cause let's face it," she said from under the table, "Women for Action is taking on entirely too much: drugs, prisons, alcohol, the schools, rape, battered women, abused children. And now Velma's talked the group into tackling the nuclear power issue. And the Brotherhood ain't doing shit about organizing."

"Oh I dunno. The Brotherhood has—"

"Bullshit. They've gotten so insulated and inbred up there in the cozy corner of the Academy's east wing having their id ego illogical debates, no one even sees them anymore. And you know it. So quit the understanding, standing-by-the-men, good-supportive-sister crap. Cause you the one that started it. Yeh you. Weren't you telling Velma just last week that half the shit that goes down between men and women is leftover nonsense between brothers and brothers?"

"What?" Couples and business gatherings at the various tables were turning their way, watching Ruby drag the bag up into her lap to wrassle with its contents. The Academy. Jan was tired of hearing the Academy applauded or lambasted whether because of the Brotherhood or the programs or the kids or now this rumor of guns. It was like Mrs. Heywood said: Keep the focus on the action not the institution; don't confuse the vehicle with the objective; all cocoons are temporary and disappear.

"Ruby, What's that song Sun Ra does about this planet being a cocoon or a railway station or some kind of temporary . . . a spaceship?"

"Because men jive around with each other instead of dealing for real and later for all the beating-on-the-chest raw gorilla shit, all the unresolved stuff slops over into man/woman relationships."

"Give me an example, Ruby. Or better yet, shut up."

"Sistuh, please. Give yourself an example. You were brilliantly expounding on the subject just last Tuesday. I got my own troubles," yanking at a spiral notebook that was caught in the straps of the bag. "We designed a questionnaire. A thing that could be sent out to get ideas for workshops, panels, speakers, films and stuff like that. Mostly"—flopping the notebook on the table and shoving the teacups out of the way—

"the questionnaire is designed to provoke some thought about paternity and rape and misogyny and what have you." Ruby flipped furiously, yanked out a bunch of papers and handed them across the table. "See what you think. Here, take a pencil and edit away."

"In other words, Ruby, you want my 'input.'"

"Don't be difficult. We worked round the clock on this thing. Besides, we need you. I'm a ball-busting bitchy so-and-so. Velma's a dogmatic hard-liner thus and such. And Daisy's big and fat and still lives with her parents. You, on the other hand, are above reproach. So sign on. I want to hand it to Velma to pass on to Obie, assuming they're speaking these days. He's the only one up there likely to get them brothers off their big fat rusty dusters and—"

"Ruby?"

"Okay, okay. I will be cool."

It sounded like thunder in the distance at first and people paused, forks poised, glasses halted, heads turned this way or that as people sniffed the air, studied the sky or otherwise attempted to discover whether a storm was coming. Drums, only drums. From somewhere near the corner of Gaylord and Tenth came the pittitt tibaka bata of small drums, echoed by the rada rada booming from the park. Then the jukebox from inside the café drowned it all out with the strains of a recent release of Dexter Gordon's "Tower of Power." The tinkle of glasses and metal against plates resumed and the hubbub of the outdoor diners rose.

Ruby twisted round in her chair, frowning at the musicians streaming by the dessert cart to a special table in the corner. She hoisted herself up two inches, pressing down on the fragile wire arms of the chair to do it, and cleared her throat.

"When the Europeans stopped killing Christians and became Christians, that was the end of Christianity and the beginning of Christendom and Christidolatry. And when the white boy quit lynching niggers and became a nigger, that was the beginning of the Wild Bill Dogget revival and the beginning of Bloods wearing Blues Brothers emblems. When O when will confusion end, my sistuh. Tell us, O Janus-faced Janice, what's the deal?"

"They're drummers in the park, Ruby. Why don't we go now? Dancers and incense and fresh fruit. Don't you have a booth?"

"Too much confusion down there. No, I don't have a booth. I'm sick of all this pagan spring celebration shit. And everybody handing out flyers about this rally and that meeting. Scattered, fragmented, uncoordinated mess. I'm so sick of leaflets and T-shirts and moufy causes and nothing changing. All I want is a good blowtorch and some paying customers for a change. And if one more rat-tooth muthafucker strolls into my shop asking to trade some cockeyed painting looking like a portable toilet for one of my masterpiece bracelets I'm gonna run amuck in the streets, I swear. Let's go have a drink somewhere. Or are we waiting for Velma?"

Jan put the wad of papers under her elbow. She was in no mood for the cagey questions and printed confrontations.

"I'm not sure Velma's coming. We were supposed to meet at the lawyer's."

"Oh? Tell it."

"Well . . . She's probably sick. And no wonder. The plant is not a healthy place to work, even in the office wing. Do you know that all the workers have to report for a medical once a month to the company infirmary, plus they can't see their own records?"

"Never mind that." Ruby had reached across the table and tapped Jan's arm. "Tell it."

Jan exhaled noisily and frowned. "It seems somebody at the plant wiped out the entire records."

"How does 'somebody' do that?"

"By moving low values to first byte and then propagating it through the entire data base."

Ruby patted Jan's arm and let the cigarette dangle for a minute before she puffed, letting it out through half-opened mouth and nostrils. "You wanna break that down, teacher, to some basic Ronald McDonald–type English."

"This 'somebody' fouled up the entire computer bank. Erased all the records. All gone. Total blank. Empty."

"Beautiful. And they think it was our very own Friday Foster? But you said 'lawyer'?"

"She was called in and questioned."

"Let's say 'interrogated' when we tell the tale."

"Ruby, let's not say anything, okay?"

"Aww shucks." Ruby placed her cigarette in the ashtray and pulled her chair in closer. She set the teacups on the blowing napkins and then jammed her hat on tighter. "Velma do it?"

Jan stirred her tea, stalling. She was not sure why she hesitated to speak of it since she'd gone this far, was not even sure how she'd developed the theory. "My hunch," she said slowly, "is that Jamahl did it using a touch telephone. You remember Jamahl."

"The guy that always smells like incense, yeh. But touch tone? You're losing me." Ruby hunched forward on her elbows, hugging the pot, cup, honey and saucer to her so that Jan too could lean forward at least as far as Ruby's wide-brim hat would allow. They looked and felt like conspirators. The waiters, several passers-by, a few people from nearby tables glanced their way. At a table in the corner by the service-counter window, the informer calling himself Donaldson looked up from his note pad, leaned away from the table he'd been studiously eavesdropping on to lean toward the table by the railing where the two women sat huddled, oblivious of the napkins, candy wrappers, matchbooks blowing up against the table legs.

". . . had robbed a bank out in California, Sacramento I think, by using a touch-tone telephone to speak directly to the computer to make withdrawals, by-passing the recording apparatus . . ."

Donaldson could make little of the whispering. He settled back in his chair. The three men to his right were far more to his liking anyway. At that table were three out-of-work writers, exploring the possibility of a script to present at the Academy writing workshop that night. They were waiting on Campbell to take a break and be a sounding board. They had three ideas. One, the kidnapping of the two men who possessed the Coca-Cola formula; the ransom to be broadcast world-wide a month before the 1980 Olympics—Russia, France, China and the U.S. must each divest itself of all nuclear arms and space hardware or there'd be no more Coca-Cola produced. They rather liked that one. The taller of the two had clipped articles about Coca-Cola franchises in the Soviet Union and the People's Republic to the one-page treatment and placed it on the edge of the table, vaguely aware that some nosy joker at the next table was ruining his eyes trying to read it. The second treatment called for a less-expensive budget. The two men paid to guard the Titans, instructed to shoot the other in case of bizarre behavior, have each come to the conclusion that the other is a security risk and stalk each other through the bunker. The third was similar. In a plane circling the strategic warhead site in Phoenix were the two men with the keys to destruction. On orders given over the hot line from the Pentagon, they're to insert the two keys simultaneously to activate the missile. At the moment, the plane has hit some bumpy weather and flown above the turbulence. They've had to use oxygen for a bit and are now totally bananas and scheming to insert the keys without the order. They're that bored, nuts, frustrated. The three Bloods slapped five and toasted themselves with Perrier and lime.

"Campbell will want to check the fact sheet. He's a bug about documentation."

"I know. I've typed that up on the blue sheets." The older brother took the opportunity to lift his brows and dart his eyes in the direction of the informer.

"Yeh, I checked him out the minute we sat down. I recognized him from before. Calls himself incognito. We ought to work him into the script somehow. Blow his cover."

"That'd be stupid. At least we know him now."

"True."

The three huddle together in imitation, it would seem, of the two women by the railing.

". . . and Jamahl used to pick Velma up for lunch at the office and ask a lot of questions about the system, she was saying . . ."

Campbell gave his writing buddies a five-minute sign, then worked his way around the round table under the awning, gathering up glasses and emptying ashtrays, one eye on his work, the other on Jan and Ruby, curious about what secrets they might be sharing. With one hand, he anchored the tray on the edge of the table so as not to interrupt the men at their game. With the other hand, he flapped the bill against his teeth and watched and waited.

They always spun to see who'd pay for each round of drinks. There were six of them, five white Americans and one Japanese who kept his own liquor supply in one of the bar's lockers— plum wine, sake and a Mason jar that looked like corn liquor to Campbell. They always sat under the awning and usually at one of the two large round tables on his station. They always tipped well and always drank a lot. Their repertoire of games was extensive and peculiar to their profession. In a day or so, Campbell planned to introduce to them a new game, a board game, as soon as his papers were filed at the copyright and patent office. For now, he watched and waited.

They were spinning a cigarette lighter. Sometimes it was the salt shaker. Usually it was the instrument with the knobs and the centigrade markings he'd at first associated with quality control at a textile mill but knew now gauged water levels. The lighter head pointed to The Whiner, who groaned immediately and mopped his bald head with a napkin.

Campbell had names for all of them: Sudsy Sam, who always ordered a pitcher of beer and a frosted stein; Rising Sun, who never wore white shirts and ties like the rest but bronze-colored shirts with kimono collars; Piltdown Pete, who seemed too dumb to be a nuclear engineer, was no doubt some sort of lower-echelon technician they allowed into their august company because, perhaps, he was so totally out of their league he usually wound up paying the checks; Krupp's Kreep, in Orlon shirts and hats that were too small, forever lecturing about the necessity of beating out the Ruskys; The Grim Reaper, a name they themselves came up with, for he was constantly spoiling the fun by calling attention to the latest studies that threatened the expansion of nuclear power plant production; and The Whiner, who had kids with braces, an overwhelming mortgage, problem-prone in-laws and a frigid wife, all of which he managed to bring into the discussions whatever the topic.

"Ahhh, let's see," The Whiner stammered, glancing around the table but catching no one's eyes. Rising Sun was working a cigarette into an ivory holder and reaching for the lighter. The rest had eyes riveted to their wrist watches. "You guys have managed to cover all the good methods. Let's see." He was swinging his thighs, banging his knees under the table, reminiscent of one of Campbell's early tormentors in grade school. The Whiner was tapping his nails against the tabletop, rapping louder and louder, his legs swinging more and more furiously. "Suppose I were to pull an insulation sheath over the water gauge and then insert a piece of stiff plastic—"

"Jam the water gauge with a credit card or an I.D. badge? Hell no. Stafford's already done that one. Pay the check."

"Wait a sec. Hear me out. I didn't say anything about the coolant system or the water pumps."

"Time's up. Pay the waiter."

"That's not fair. You guys are really not being fair. I've got two minutes."

"Two minutes start to finish. You haven't even identified which section of the fail-safe system you're tampering with. Waiter, another round of drinks. Another pitcher of beer, and make sure the stein is good and frosted. Pay up, Nickelberry."

"You guys are really not fair. This is a stupid game anyway. Unpatriotic to say the least. We could be court-martialed for this."

"We're not military, Nickelberry. Just pay the man."

Campbell scooped up The Whiner's credit card and whisked the tray away. If he was fast and the relief waitress had come in on time, he could get back to Jan in minutes. Maybe sit down with the two women for his break. He'd see his writing buddies soon enough at the workshop.

". . . had this dream. I told Velma about it and she just looked. You know how she looks when . . . anyway. In the dream Jamahl was sitting on a black leather barstool with a red touch-tone telephone on the table. He had a yellow scrap of paper on his lap and he was . . ."

"Is there a warrant out for her or what? How serious is it?"

"They're calling it a routine inquiry. Naturally they're trying to keep the whole thing quiet. Not only because of all the records—payroll, orders, invoices—hell, I don't have a clue as to what they had computerized, but"—Jan scraped her chair closer to Ruby, tipping the brim of her hat back—"there's another reason. They've been shipping flatcars of slag, they call it, some kind of contaminated sludge, right through town to some burial grounds for radioactive waste that a plant in Alabama uses."

"And Velma pulled the info and passed it on to some investigative journalist, right? I've been following the Jack Anderson articles."

"No, I don't think so."

"Passing it on to some environmentalist group, then?"

"I really don't know, Ruby. She called me to ask me to put her in touch with some lawyers. As for lifting, remember last time she leaked some material?"

"How well I remember. And the turkey got up in court and named his source. Funny how a subpoena can scare the shit out of you. What's the rest?"

"I don't know, Ruby. That's why I was hoping she'd come this afternoon for lunch. She blew the appointment this morning for the lawyer. A friend of mine, and he was some pissed."

"No wonder she's been acting so crazy." Ruby slumped back in her chair and let her arms dangle behind her. "Pressure. I'm such a crummy friend. Here she's been under all this pressure lately, and I've been so insensitive."

"No wonder. She really needs to get out of the plant. Everybody does."

Ruby took her hat off and placed the brim under the legs of her chair. It was hot and muggy and the gusty wind was no relief. She leaned back again, swinging her arms and looking up at the smeary clouds. "If the fumes are anything to go by," she said, looking toward the smokestacks, "Dante didn't tell the half of it."

More practical than the game Fission, and a bit less cynical than the game Fail-Safe Phooey, was the board game Campbell'd developed and hoped to market through Parker Brothers —Disposal. Each player received at the start a sum of money, some property—nuclear reactors, uranium mines, etc., 5,000 pounds of uranium tailings and a load of contaminated items to dispose of. Campbell went over it, congratulating himself on his brilliance. It was one thing to be a child prodigy. It was quite another to demonstrate a persistent genius. He turned the grill on and carefully sliced three hunks of banana nut cake from the loaf.

The boxes on the board where one stopped, given the number thrown on the player's dice, were marked "trench"—but one had to move within the next throw before the food chain was affected, "storage plant"—but there was a card announcing build-up which obliged the player to move off the spot, "carbon steel container"—but one had to pay the bank fifteen years' salaries for three guards, and there were cards marked "going critical" and "carbon steel corrosion" which necessitated a move. It was an exasperating game, guaranteed to either drive you nuts or urge you to join the international antinuclear movement, or at least send a check to Mobilization for Survival.

Campbell chuckled, standing guard over the grill with the spatula. It was bound to make him a fortune, or at least free him to pursue with sleuthlike tenacity the many tips of big stories he could never get a paper or magazine to underwrite. Disposal had appeal for the armchair philosophers, the alarmists, the pragmatists, as well as the reality-denying types. It incorporated the ferociously acquisitive features of Monopoly with just the right touch of self-righteousness. Best of all, it frustrated and provoked. In short, it was American. He'd managed to incorporate, too, the brilliant contribution Rising

Sun had made to the round table's games—Fix, a game of doublethink and doublespeak the men usually played when they were fairly sober. In case of plant failure, breakdown, accident, corrosion, some situation requiring repair or shutdown—all of which were initiated by boxes on the Disposal board marked "pick a card," the stack of cards containing announcements of repairs needed at plants owned by the players—the players could elect to pay the cost of dismantling the plant and disposing of contaminated parts, assume the cost of shutting down and doing repairs, or they could elect to put in a Fix—that is, hire a team of experts to conduct a study proving that the defective parts were neither vital nor even necessary to plant operations. Fix cards could be purchased or traded.

Campbell was none too nimble turning the slices of cake over to brown, but no matter. Disposal was a winner. An educational board game for sophisticates of the nuclear age, he'd described it. And while he enjoyed the part-time work at the café and the occasional lurid tales he hacked for *Bronze Thrills* and *Tan Confessions,* he well knew what he'd been groomed for and what each postponement of the big story, pursuing instead the lesser news assigned by the new editor, cost him.

He'd begun a better-than-credible series on nuclear energy while he was still in school. The old editor had had high stock with the publisher then. But it was a small-town paper after all, too small to garner the kind of attention that could lead to a Pulitzer. But he continued with the articles even though the paper repeatedly rejected them. He'd managed to have the first in the series reprinted often, however, his coverage of the Coral Gables high-energy conference. Outmaneuvered the major dailies that time, and could still outthink the big-time reporters sent to the various conferences from New York, L.A., Chicago, D.C. They never paid him any attention, just a baby-face spook from a hick-town weekly. They'd peer at his press badge, ask patronizing questions about the Claybourne *Call* and smile that smile.

But at Coral Gables, he'd been the only reporter who'd understood the allusion to Mulla Nasrudin, the hero of his first tutor Mustafa the Magnificent, who insisted he came from Armenia and not Lebanon. Mulla, Anancy, Shine, Greek mythology, Scandinavian lore, the Chinese classics, the Koran, the Book of Tobit, the works of the Essene, the Sufi—Mustafa had him master them all and usually taught all subjects through the Mulla tales. So when the physicists at Coral Gables had to resort to metaphor, allegory, proverbs, folk tales to illustrate principles too confounding in scientific argot, his old acquaintance Mulla had been called out to rescue the tongue-tied panelist and muddled conferees and given Campbell the edge. The edge and the clue as to what the big story of his career was to be.

What came to Campbell, leaning over the typewriter stand in the pressroom then just as he leaned over the grill deep in thought now, was a flash in the brain pan, and he knew he'd struck gold. Knew in a glowing moment that all the systems were the same at base—voodoo, thermodynamics, I Ching, astrology, numerology, alchemy, metaphysics, everybody's ancient myths—they were interchangeable, not at all separate much less conflicting. They were the same, to the extent that their origins survived detractors and perverters. How simple universal knowledge is after all, he grinned.

The editor then was simply intrigued by Campbell's ability to discuss fission in terms of billiards, to couch principles of thermonuclear dynamics in the language of down-home Bible-quoting folks. So he'd been sent, though with a stingy expense account, to cover the UN's Stockholm Conference on the Environment, where he managed to work the goddess Khali and the loa Shango together with Thor and Neptune into his reports of the weather workshops.

"Camp, you through here?"

He nodded, distracted, as the relief waitress nudged him to the side with her hip and worked up an omelet.

He was not through. There was a story, a big one for Claybourne anyway, shaping up at that moment, one big enough to move him from the local school-board hearings assignments to what he'd been waiting for, preparing for. Rumor had it the Academy cohorts planned to reenact an old slave insurrection. This at a time when the National Guard had been put on alert because of the labor-management crisis at Transchemical. And a vigilante group was rumored to be ready for the march, should it turn into some kind of action. The Special Task Force too, it was hinted at the precinct, was coming in to assist in the investigation of the armory break-in. Rates of unemployment, nonemployment, homicide, drug traffic were so high, the city administration had asked the editor to soft-pedal it. And the power plant was under attack for having got caught hiking their rates before putting the fix in. He'd helped at least in that, uncovering the fact that corporations had huge bills year after year and the suburban counties had run up quite a tab, but local residents had had their water, gas, lights shut off when they protested the padded-looking bills. There was a big enough story if, in the next forty-eight hours, he could stay on top of it.

"Table seven's filling up, Camp. Want me to clear?"

"I'd appreciate it."

Campbell glanced through the service window at a group of women who had just entered the café and were stashing media equipment on the two empty chairs at the big table. He read their No Nukes T-shirts and smiled. Life is a gas, he told the dessert plate.

211

Campbell approached table two in mock-sheepishness, sliding his offering in front of Jan, who took the moment of diversion to remove the wad of papers she'd kept from blowing away with her elbows. She rolled Ruby's questionnaire into the loops of her handbag straps, then gave the waiter and the dessert plate her attention.

"Got zapped by the microwave?" she asked, suspicious.

Ruby swiveled the plate a bit, reared back and screwed up her face. "Is it organic?" She poked the cake with the tip of her fork. "Or carcinogenic or what?" She turned to Jan, sitting tall in her seat. "You will note that I have mastered the crucial buzz words of my era."

"Plutonium's both organic and carcinogenic," Campbell said. "That is to say it comes from nature, albeit remote regions of Africa. Not only natural but mutagenic."

"You're not suggesting—no, of course he's not suggesting, is he, Jan, that this is toasted pluto buns, just correcting my faulty mutually exclusive formula." Ruby was using her supercilious voice, Jan noticed and sighed. "Well, you've got the floor, Bro, and I've used up my buzz words. Run it."

"Banana nut cake. I toasted it on the grill. Gas flames." He was speaking strictly to Jan, smiling his laziest, easy man smile, and totally ignoring the other woman and what sounded like a royal command. Close-cropped bush, weighty jewelry, wiry body, flowing clothes like royal robes. It was her eyes that clinched it, never on him, not deigning to take him in. She simply waved her hand in his general direction as though it were a foregone conclusion her order would be carried out, and he would stand there dutifully holding forth on the subject of plutonium.

Campbell continued to ignore her even as she smirked, " 'Albeit,' a literate waiter, as I live and breathe."

"You have a class tonight? Or other business up at the Academy? I'm going that way later."

"No, we're going over to the park in a while. Maybe catch the concert at the Regal if there're still tickets. The festival begins tonight," Jan said.

"Perhaps I'll see you then," he said, taking a long lingering time to release his grip on the clean fork he handed her.

Campbell moved off to pass out menus to the media women. He glanced toward the round table. Krupp's Kreep was lining up cufflinks, rings, and the tops of the salt and pepper shakers. They were evidently preparing for round one of Fission, having gotten bored with Fail-Safe Phooey.

". . . triterium and deterium. And for a catalyst, let's try something inexpensive, something available to your average high school chem lab."

There were times when they played the game of putting together various fissionable elements, fuels, propellants, outlining processes, conditions, possible containers, that Campbell could actually see the unbonded atoms on the table, so many colored balls on the green tablecloth like after the opening break, various colored balls settling into position waiting for the cue, waiting for the next shot to overcome inertia and go banging, bouncing, colliding all over the table. They were an unstable group of men, Campbell concluded. And to think the Rosenbergs could be executed while six blabbermouth engineers breached security practically every day.

"Of the three pestilences that plague our community— agents, hustlers and fools—I do believe that hand-pumping turkey is the worst. So I repeat, Jan, you need to seriously consider running for office."

Jan missed seeing Jay Patterson making the rounds of the café tables, pinning buttons on where he could, where he dared in some cases. She missed seeing too the young dude, making dangerous entries in his daily log, withhold his hand and make his jacket lapel unavailable to Patterson. She had turned the other way; she thought she smelled smoke. Then she thought she recognized the sisters in the T-shirts.

"Ruby, aren't those the sisters that turned the conference out last year, remember? The Black United Fund conference? Or was it the International Women's Day thing? No, it was the testimonial to Sophie Heywood. Remember?" She turned back around in her chair, but Ruby, holding on to the railing, had tipped her chair way back to watch Jay Patterson attempt to horn in on the gathering near the entrance step.

"That man's pitiful. And who's the joker in the Rudy Vallee get-up, bow tie and all? Those young folks haven't budged a muscle since we've been here. The Stepford students," Ruby was saying, turning to face Jan. The woman she leaned her chair against was the only one who heard the remark and was amused, curious, but nonetheless annoyed by the burden on her back.

But Jan didn't hear her, she had turned round again. Daughters of the Crops. Sisters of the Fruit. Jan pursed her lips, on the half-chance that the memory cells in her mouth had better storage and retrieval faculties than her brain. Palma's friends. The Asian sister had done a song about the pig-iron furnaces of China. There was a long piece they'd ended with, a colored sister solidarity piece, operatic almost, a fuguelike interweaving of the voices, the histories, the lore of Caribbean, African, Native American—"Seven Sisters! Remember?" But Ruby was still not facing her way and Jan felt a bit silly, exclaiming aloud. She turned back toward the large table hoping to catch one of the sisters' eyes, but they were buried in their menus, and the dark-skinned sister in the black felt hat was talking very rapidly, as if reciting the words of a song they all had to put to memory right away. It was clear she wanted to eat and that what enthusiasm had gotten her started was waning now. Jan smiled their way anyway, remembering that Velma had played piano for the group and had gone touring with them the summer before.

"In all the years I've known Velma, it wasn't till then that I realized what a serious musician she was. Ruby, you listening?"

"Velma?" All four legs of Ruby's chair thudded down against the tile. "I think she's lost her marbles. Know what she asked me the other night? Suicide. When is it appropriate to commit suicide. Appropriate, I remember that was how she put it. And did suicides reincarnate right away or have to wait around till full term. Full term, I'm practically quoting verbatim. Stone crazy. Those fumes at the plant have eaten up the sister's brain, I'm telling you."

"Suicide?"

"And what do I know about suiciding, reincarnating and what have you? I know from amber and trade beads, from brass and soldering and so forth. Scared me to death. Totally out there."

"What did you tell her?"

"About when it's appropriate to do yourself in? Hell, what do I know? I guess if you're a duty-bound officer of the crown and you've been hounding Jean Valjean through the woods, across the borders, through the sewers of Paris, making his life holy hell and then the kindhearted sap turns around and saves your ass from drowning, why then I suppose it's appropriate to fall on your sword or fling yourself into the Seine."

"Ruby, never mind all that. What do you think? Was she serious? You know, serious, serious?"

"She crazy."

"But you say that about everybody."

"Am I wrong? Hell, Claybourne getting to resemble the back wards of the asylum more everday."

"Velma, Ruby, Velma. Do you think she was trying to tell you something?"

"I can't get too worked up over Velma's crises anymore, Jan. There've been too many. She'll be fine. Sometimes she takes everything so . . . seriously, gets disappointed, even when she knows better." Ruby was drifting, was a student again cutting classes, and going off to war. She was in the drenched tents bathing Velma's muddy, swollen, bruised feet. "She's so . . . what's the word? And works so hard to be guarded, defended."

"The drive for invulnerability usually leaves one totally vulnerable," Jan mumbled. "Take U.S. policy on nuclear armament for a case in point." Jan waved the idea away. It was not where her mind was. "Why didn't we think to ask the kid? Velma's boy? He might've known something."

Ruby shrugged. "I thought we did, no? Were we trying to avoid being worried? I'm tired of worrying about Velma," Ruby said, trying to sound annoyed and to be done with the wet tents and bloody feet. It was tiresome being anywhere but in the now moment.

ten

Sophie Heywood rocked and glided in Doc Serge's chair, its orbit a four-by-six oval patch of purple pile. But in the next moment the chair was a swing lifting out as in an amusement park ride. The desk, floor, wastebasket, Mama Mae driving home in the deacon's car, Velma inching along a drainpipe like a worm and Palma in pursuit, Minnie on the stool hugging Velma, the grille and faces sifting stories through it to her— all seen in a whirling blur from above as Sophie rode the circumference in search, her thoughts of Velma cleansed now of distaste, charged now with blessing and a dim regret as when single friends realize when one marries that they move about in separate solar systems ever after.

The place was dry and barren, red dust, red rocks, and the swing chair buoyant now, the neck of a parachute catching and the billowing out of the silk raising swirls of red dust around her feet. Not a touchdown, Sophie was suspended while she watched her godchild cutting up on the stairs of the Patterson

Professional Building, leaping from the landing in her maypole dress of crinoline petticoats and dotted-swiss pinafore, the dress billowing out and the child suspended over the staircase for an incredible cool moment, the twitch of vestigial wings a reminder of that earlier flight from the red place of rocks Sophie journeyed through now, the breeze of the silk stirring up clouds of red dust. And then the drop and then another, bouncing down, sailing down now toward a pinpoint of heat and light below, dropping through layers of soundlessness and then birds and wind and then the tree-green-sweet against her teeth, and then the change in heat, the sun-held earth releasing its greeting and stretching up to meet her. And somewhere there she found Velma in a nightgown roaming about with a nub of a candle stuck to a jelly-jar lid.

"I had this dream the night before the gas, M'Dear," the voice traveling through the grille. "There was a war going on. Delegates from the People's Army were invited to come and negotiate the peace. Obie was there and Smitty and Clara Shields, who was my desk mate in elementary school, and Maazda, the original Sister of the Yam, and I don't remember the others. The treaty signed, they were asked to pose for the historic photograph. They took their positions in front of the bandstand at Douglass Park. The photographer was dressed in high collar and sleeve garters and it was like we were more in a movie than in war. Over the camera was a sheet not a black cloth. But when the sheet was pulled off the camera, it was a machine gun, M'Dear."

"What else?"

"They dragged one of our people out into the courtyard. Emaciated, M'Dear, like the cadavers in the medieval wood-cuts. They took him to the wall, propped him up. It was the yard of the old waterworks."

"Where the power plant is now. Next to Transchemical."

"Yes. I think it was Smitty. It looked like Lil James, but I seemed to understand in the dream that it was your son, looking like my son." And she had rushed them, nothing but kitchen shears between her and the rifles and Smitty and the wall and the hill looming up behind gold and mammoth. "A shot rang out." She felt the crack against bone and stumbled, gray slime running down the side of her face. Red but gray. Her mind running like mud. "The end was so . . . nonchalant, M'Dear."

"And?"

"I made up my mind."

"The dream is one piece, the correct picturing of impressions another. Then interpretation, then action. You always were too hasty, Vee. What is the photo scene?"

"Posturing? Naïveté?"

"The waterworks?"

"Emotion?"

"Not all wars have casualties, Vee. Some struggles between old and new ideas, some battles between ways of seeing have only victors. Not all dying is the physical self."

"Death of habit, idea, a time?" Velma sits down on a log and ponders. "Seeing. Dying."

"To announce a new beginning." Sophie tugs on the lines and the silk ripples. "And was the wound near your eye, Vee?"

Velma traces the line from the wound to her eyebrow to a spot between her eyes. Sophie leans out of the chair and places a shell there, then stretches her ear toward her godchild's forehead and listens . . .

Velma smelled Minnie Ransom near, coconut cream sachet or body oil or hair grease.

"Bless you," Minnie said, her hands holding Velma's head, which had begun to wag uncontrollably, her right palm flat against the forehead, the left at the back as if fingering an egg.

"Choose your cure, sweetheart. Decide what you want to do with wholeness."

Velma was peering through a triangle of space between Minnie's elbow and her waist, to get to the window. And then she was peering through an opening in a jade bush to get to the tree. She overshot it, or rather went through it and banged into the tabby wall, the crushed oyster shells scraping her eyes. She pulled back to get on the near side of the tree. A small bird there, fallen over on its collapsed wing, the other flopped out and quivering at the tip, its head tucked in as if to hide but only for a moment to catch its breath. Then the tiny head out and up, the beak opening and shutting, calling to the air, calling to the air.

"The source of health is never outside, sweetheart. What will you do when you are well?"

Velma once again focused on the woman's arm as it swung away from the crown of her head toward the stereo. But she still could not concentrate on the music. She was skating the rim of the bush tub, the empty shells gaping. Skating the rim of the tub in imitation of M'Dear's circling overhead until the circles were in synch, drawing her to the center.

eleven

Mai stared at the blank top page on her clipboard. It was eluding her. Her great-aunt's story, the one she'd hoped to get down the minute she was seated, if she could remember it right. If she could get a pinch of it, she was thinking, she could pull out the whole of it intact from the past. Something Cecile had been saying about the woman-charged culture of Dahomey had sparked it, thrown a light in a dark corner. The mamba priestesses of the voudon, the amazons. Perhaps the contrast of Mai's story and Cecile's, the two family stories rubbing against each other in Mai's mind. But even before Cecile shared the story of the mothers in her family, something had flashed a light around in the jumble of those old told-to's. The smoke perhaps, the bar b q shop ablaze. Mai worked on it. It was like reaching in the back of the drawer for the emergency twenty-dollar bill fallen down between the drawer and the back of the desk. The nails of two fingers barely getting a grip, the tips of the fingers reading the difference between wood and paper, then slowly a slip of it is between the flesh of the fingertips so it can be pulled forward. She knew it would come. The main thing was to relax and maintain a light concentration.

"Are you aware that you are being stared at?" Iris said.

Mai looked across at the Japanese gentleman to her right. He was rearranging the daisies and jonquils in the slender apothecary jug in the center of the table he shared with several flushed men. Mai reached toward the center of their own table and ran a fingernail up a stem and across a petal. And it came sailing across her eyes. The flower boats. The floating bordellos on the bay. The saffron sails. The hanging lanterns. The young girls gathering up their silken robes to dive into the bay. Her great-aunt rescued from the burning flower boats at thirteen and taken to California. There chased in the streets, fingers pulling at her hair. Run down in the muddy streets, raped and scalped. The boats had at least been aromatic. Life had not been honorable, but one could buy oneself in time from the boats. Maybe marry. Maybe . . . an old story passed down on Mai's maternal side huddled together in the internment camps of '42, keeping themselves alive with the stories. But keeping separate even then, even there, the threads of the Japanese, Chinese, Filipino elders. Stories keeping the people in the camps alive while the bill in Congress to sterilize the women of the camps got voted down by one vote, one vote. And then the silence. A whole generation silent about the camps. Then the hand reaching back, the pen dipped, the stories alive again to keep the people going.

A crisp snap as if of boat sails or robe sleeves, and Mai looked up. It was the café's white and yellow awning flapping, the scalloped edges turning up sharply at the corner to show their oilskin innards. But there was more than the wind. There was a rumbling somewhere. Mai glanced around as she shook down

222

the ink in her pen. Others at the tables strewn about the patio were looking up as if waiting for a flash of lightning.

"Thunder? Rain?" Cecile paused long enough in her express delivery on the fire rites of macumba, condomble, obeah, shango, lucumi, santaria, winti, voodoo—none of which, she hastened to make plain, she held any belief in; she was simply answering Chezia's question—to anchor down the napkins with the ashtrays.

It sounded like a rumbling of the earth, like a procession, like marching, bare feet stomping along a dirty path, the jangling of canteens against machetes worn at the belt, forty or more marchers maybe, carrying rattling impedimenta, moving up from some hidden place below to appear any minute in view of the café. Some people by the rail glanced over at the vacant lot, but the drums from the park below were distinctly different. Others, seated near the corner where the tile design and levels changed, looked down the side street. Several tabled on the side-street patio leaned out of their chairs or simply went ahead and stood up in order to get a fix on the what and where that sounded to them like neither thunder nor marching.

Chezia gripped her pendant, moving the tips of her fingers across the figure of Kashisk, god of wind and rain, her thumb fingering the thirteen constellations engraved on the back, the center figure raised, the rattlesnake Palma insisted on calling Uraeus but which she'd been taught at school to call Pleiades. She was pulling on it so that the leather thong, the original strap her godmothers had looped around her neck that last night, rubbed the hairs on the back of her neck. She'd originally planned to give it to Gimma, the original Sister of the Plantain from Trinidad. But Gimma had gotten a job at the workers' college in Barbados and had left the troupe suddenly. Recently she'd thought to present it to Inez, the original Sister of the Corn, but right after the blazing bar b q Inez had caught the plane to Albuquerque to organize another troupe. Chezia looked at Mai now; she too planned to organize a Sister of the Rice contingent and another Seven Sister troupe. Chezia unknotted the thong, remembering what Great Mother had counseled that last night at home. Kashisk was the last of the gifts she hadn't yet released to travel through the world beyond the village.

Chezia smiled. Iris had leaned over to brush her hair up and adjust her collar, thinking that was why she had dropped her head down and was screwing it about. Cecile had stretched across the table with her palmetto fan and given her a blast of air, thinking she was hot and uncomfortable. Now, as she lifted the necklace over her head, even Nilda, who had been sitting quietly with her arms folded in her lap and her eyes closed as if asleep, moved to help her. Mai, little Sister of the Rice, was absorbed in her scripting. Quick, black, sleek figures dancing across a floor of white as her felt pen beat out the music. Chezia draped the necklace over Mai's head, Kashisk clanking against the metal clamp of the writing board.

"I want you to have it, Mai."

Mai tucked her chin in to examine what had been familiar for nearly a year, but was now somehow a brand-new thing. She pulled Chezia to her and kissed her on the forehead just as the mothers had that last night, weaving flowers and glowworms into Chezia's hair, dropping garlands upon garlands around her neck and then kissing each youth between the brows before sending them down the mountain to go off to school.

"Raining in Barnwell, I suspect," Iris said quietly. And they were all quiet, contemplating the distance traveled—rain. Years ago rain meant splashing in puddles, mud pies, rain barrels, watering the stock, the crops, rain water for shampoos. At the very worst, rain had meant colds. And then the lens widened to incorporate mud slides and floods. Now that contaminated soil that had provoked the local folk of Barnwell to join with hundreds of safe-earth activists was uppermost in their minds, each rain meant contamination leaching inches ever closer to the water table, spelling the ruin of the Savannah River and all who lived in it, on it, by it, from it.

Velma was under the quilts with eucalyptus, Tiger balm, honey and lemon, apple cider vinegar and hot salt. Her mother was hugging her. Palma and Smitty, perched at the foot of the bed were playing with her toes through the covers. Her father in the doorway, the stuffed kangaroo under his arm for the asking. And she'd never been more cared for.

Her wet clothes were on a hanger by the heater. The pink taffeta dress with the white dotted-swiss pinafore, the crinolines with three layers of ruffles, the hair ribbon, the white stockings; the Mary Janes were on M'Dear's cedar chest, stuffed with newspaper. On the nightstand was the program, the yellow tassel dangling over the edge of the table. And M'Dear came in with white gloves running up and down an imaginary keyboard in the air then on her chest, tickling her. No one fussed about her running off after her recital. No one asked her where she'd gone and why she'd stayed out in the rain. M'Dear was being Mickey Mouse in *Fantasia* and Mama Mae was hugging her. And she'd never been more cared for. And she'd never been closer to whatever it was she'd been hunting for in drainpipes and closets and mirrors and in the woods, listening for through floorboards and doors and heat ducts.

Her legs were moving under the covers as if she'd been riding a bike all day and rode still. She was discovering that peddling the bass notes can do that to your legs too, the bass vibrating through the feet, up the legs, settling in the thighs, the behind, the legs riding the keyboard down under all

225

through the night. She had been surrounded, the giant pipes curved round the choir stall and she at center. And they had kissed her then and let her go off, and they kissed her now and she scooted down under the quilt and promised not to catch the pee-new-monia and die and never play organ again and make them proud. And she had never been more cared for and talked at and fussed over but not fussed at about ruining her hair when Mama Mae'd stood up all morning with the curling irons.

She was ice-skating now, her legs moving under the quilts, snow flat against the window like kindergarten paper lace. And the music rumbled in her hands, her feet, against her behind on the bench, all around her. She was surrounded by music and had never been more at home in the world than through the organ. Not at the merry-go-round cause those tunes were old-timey, not at the roller rink cause they played the same songs as the baseball games on TV on boring, got-to-be-quiet Sunday afternoons, and not at the skating rink cause that organist was so corny the music was enough to make your blades tuck in and lose you your balance. In her skating rink under the quilts in the dark the music was her own. And she was on the ice now cutting the figure eight on its side with ease.

Someone was talking to her but the organ music was drowning it out. Someone was saying something to her, giving her instructions to guard against colds. Confusion in the head causes colds, something like that. But murmuring so low. And she reached for it, reached down into the music for it but dipped too deep. Like waking with a thought you want to get around, want to scoot down past to catch the dream by the tail before it sinks, not knowing the thought was the tail right there at the surface, the thought the key to the elusive dream. And it swings overhead where you're not awake yet and flies away and leaves before you surface, is gone and leaves you bobbing on the surface without a clue. But throughout the day, a shift of the leg on the bus and the leg remembers a bit of the story as it lay tangled in the sheets. A color in a dress passing by and the eye releases what it stored the night before; an aroma, an overheard and by midafternoon the dream's reassembled itself and the message washes clear again: "She's talking behind your back and is not your friend. It was Sylvia who wrote those nasty things about you on the wall of the handball court." Or later, "That one is an agent, a plant, a provocateur. Watch your mouth." Or, "See about that tooth. Abscess, poisoning your system." Or, "It's a faulty analysis that's causing paralysis and not fear of monsters." And lately: "When you go in the office, sit in the light and make them squint to see you. Choose a chair of an innocent color. Act as though it is understood you are above suspicion and are being interviewed not interrogated, being considered as a possible member of the investigating team to solve the mystery of the emptied storage centers, blank terminals."

But she'd had that dream long before she'd even taken the job at the plant, before the headhunter called her to set up appointments, before she'd put her résumé together. It had begun the night of the recital, that long ago, and continued for years as a recurring motif. She'd awaken rubbing her knees that had pressed against a walnut and chrome desk rather like the one in Jay Patterson's office, definitely the one in the vice-manager's office of Transchemical. Eighteen years ago she was on her knees in the spare room that had been Smitty's play-room before he'd left for boarding school, twisting from the waist to take in the handiwork that marked the room as M'Dear's own—the quilts, the stripped rocker, the open-work dresser runners, the curtains with the glyphs and veves de-signed by a woman friend called Minnie. She was leaning out the window of the old place, where M'Dear had taken her five years before that the first time, rescuing her from an angry peach switch. The old place on the water where the walls sweat and the floor looked wavy and green when you looked across it from the pillow, but blue and bulgy when you sat on your knees by the window.

M'Dear Sophie and Daddy Dolphy in twin red and white polo shirts tied at the bottom, midriff out, in twin white sailor pants, a thousand buttons on one side of the belly button, a thousand buttons on the other, rolled to the knees. You could see they'd been at it awhile, the salt line on their shins like a hem Mama Mae might puff with chalk, jerking you round and round by the arm while she squeezed the red rubber ball on the yardstick and fussed if you fidgeted.

They had been dragging the bush tubs along, doing it together, dropping the handles with a clank every now and then when a favorite record dropped down. They'd tango across the sand and gravel, cheek to cheek, cracking up. Then bending again to scoop up the oysters with their hands, the shovel abandoned by the old boat hull where the Victrola was. The shovel lying on its side, a salt line across its broad middle. They bent and scooped and dumped, filling the tubs, singing along with Nat King Cole doing "Nature Boy." And when they couldn't stand it, leaving the tubs to dance again, then putting the record back on the pile cause it was a favorite.

Velma leaning out the window and learning how it was supposed to be when it would be for her and wondering why Smitty would want to go away when he had such wonderful parents. M'Dear and Daddy Dolphy filling up the tubs. There'd be a crowd over later to dance and eat and play pinochle and coon can. Laughing couples who kidded each other in front of friends about dopey things caught out at, couples having arguments but for show only, for fun. And there'd be kids for her to play with, reasons to not come to the phone when her daddy called her to find out when to pick her up and take her home. And it was good to be a godchild learning all these things.

And when "Nature Boy" dropped down again, Daddy Dolphy wiped his hands on his pants and led M'Dear to the dance floor, the flat packed sand area just beyond the pit dug for cooking and the corn piled like firewood. And no chance of them backing into the hole by mistake, they danced close up, thigh to thigh, dancing on a dime like the teenagers at the Douglass Center when the grownups would leave and whoever had had the job of getting the bulb now screwed in the twenty-five-watt blue bulb, dancing on a dime. And when the song ended, Daddy Dolphy sang it again, " 'The greatest thing you'll ever learn' "—them holding on to each other, parting slightly to look into each other's face, and then hugging again, maybe patting the other gently on the shoulder, back, behind —" 'is just to love and be loo-oved in re-turrrn.' " The early morning cold wisps curling from their mouths like messages in the love comics her mama strictly forbid. And then he would drag both tubs along and M'Dear would bend just like the gym teacher teaching how to shoot from the foul line, only Miss Watson did it like an outhouse squat, M'Dear like a wonderful demi-plié.

Tomorrow it would be her job to gather up the empty shells in two tubs. One for crushing into the front walkway. The other to put back into the oyster beds, cause the babies needed something to snuggle up to, attach themselves to. Seemed sad. Empty shells. A mean trick even. But M'Dear Sophie and Daddy Dolphy said to do it, always give back, always take care. So it had to be all right.

"The house's an empty place, baby."
They were not dancing, they were not working together.

They were barely walking together, Obie on the outside turning every now and then to make sure Lil James wasn't goofing off with friends along the way, Velma walking briskly, her elbows crushing the pocketbook to the ribs on one side, the *New York Times* on the other. It was getting to be like a play, this walk from church. Neither took what was being played out as any kind of real truth but knew that in order to get the quality of even stage realism, one had to believe a bit to be considered believable.

"What would it take to be true to one another, Obie?" To be true. To be trued to. To come true for herself. She felt betrayed. She slowed down because he did and he did because the boy did, leaning into a car parked at the curb. School friends. She looked over the items in Hall's Variety Shop wondering where all the window stuff of recent years had gone— the Africa-shaped earrings, pick combs, fist tikis, posters, maps, dashikis, geles. Everything happened so quickly, too quickly.

"What brought all this on?" he was asking, coming up to the window as she was pulling out again, picking up her pace. "All I said was you're giving the best of yourself away and come home so drained."

"You said 'throwing away' the best of myself, as if the community—"

"I work hard too, Vee," pressing his hands against his chest. "I respect your commitment, your work. I love the folks. But I care about you and the boy too. And now you've taken this job."

"What brought this on actually is that I said—all I said was Lil James is sure getting independent, growing up fast. Got a paper route, buying his own clothes, thinking about renaming himself." She looked back over her shoulder at their son in his three-piece suit.

"But the way you said it, resentful, as if trying to talk yourself out of pain, the pain of loss. But you haven't lost him, Vee. You push him away and then act betrayed, but you haven't lost him."

"Are we talking about the boy or about us?"

"All right. Let's talk about us. Of all the times to be taking on out-of-town jobs."

"You're sleeping around," she said, stopping abruptly to say it, to watch how it caught him at the back of the neck, the back of the knees, feeling how it caught her at the pit of the stomach. "That's what this conversation is about," she said when he turned and took a few steps back toward her. "And you're using the boy as an alibi or a rehearsal or dry run or subtext or something not straight. It's not like you, Obie, to be . . . deceptive."

"Velma." He'd thrown his hands up and she'd thought it meant surrender, then realized he was just asking for time out. Lil James walked around them on the curb side, then cut back in between them to relieve her of the newspaper and to take from his father the hat he refused to wear anytime and anywhere but on the way to church. Lil James was openly smiling a sad smile. He felt sorry for his parents. He gave them privacy, walking on ahead.

"We've known each other too long, Obie, been through too much, been too much to each other. Why lie about such simple shit. And you been lying for months now, complaining about *my* aloofness, *my* fatigue, *my* job, willing to totally mess with my sense of what's real in order to throw up this smoke screen. You are sleeping around, Obie, and not very discreetly. And it sets one lousy example for your brother Bobby and all the little brothers. You are," she said stonily when he opened his mouth to answer. "And that's all there is to that." She followed her son's lead now, glad to not have to figure out what route to take to M'Dear's for breakfast.

231

"And you don't care?"

"Testing my tolerance before you come clean?"

They walked in silence to the corner and Velma noted how different things looked and felt now that it had been said. A subtle rearrangement of the world. For a while she had begun to doubt her perception of everything. There were trying enough shifts in her perceptions as it was. She needed all the clarity she could get. And she would have it.

"I've always taken you at your word, Obie." And now there was no trust. Not like before. Things would never be the same. She marveled at how profoundly disturbing "simple shit" can be, an accumulation of fissures in the fabric of what was her sense of things, how things were, what statements meant, how they stood.

"And I've always taken you at your word," he said quietly, reaching for her hand. "Why didn't you tell me, tell us, about the new job? You just sprang it on us."

"Can we settle on one theme for this dialogue before the variations get too cumbersome?"

"We're talking about trust, the loss of trust, breakdowns on the afrophone, misleadings and misreadings. Baby. I'm sorry."

He kissed her before the light changed but it didn't help any. It was too late for anything but war. And then retreat. And then a stupid affair with a man she wasn't certain she even liked, certainly didn't trust. She called it "interesting for the moment," and avoided the word "revenge." That tampered too much with the image she held of herself.

"Train," someone said. The word was being passed around the café the way news of food, fuel, medical supplies might be relayed in the days of change-over ahead. Diners on the side street facing the avenue could peer between the pots of Swedish ivy, peer between the cars and trucks, between the post office and the motel and see the gray, rust, orange, smudged and sooty cars of the train rumbling by.

"I thought it was thunder for sure that time," Piltdown Pete said, and several of his colleagues nodded or murmured in agreement. Rising Sun ran a finger back and forth from the base of his throat to his chin and smiled knowingly.

"A lie," he said quite distinctly. Piltdown Pete did not ask the Asian for an explanation; he was staring across at the vacant lot where he still half expected an army of savages with their thumping drums to come swarming up over the mounds of bottles and cans to engulf the whole street. Grim Reaper was quietly measuring the pace, intensity and color of the smoke streams that poured from the Transchemical stacks in the distance and simply did not hear the remark, the challenge. Krupp's Kreep had snapped his plastic stirrer in half and, satisfied the rumble was not a sneak attack, looked directly at Rising Sun as if about to challenge him, his memory of '41 so evident on his face, it drew a smile from the man in the bronze shirt. But only momentarily. For Krupp's face now registered Hiroshima, and, Rising Sun put out his cigarette and swung his gaze again across the aisle at the woman—Eurasian, Cambodian, Nisei, Sansei?

Now that the "thunder" had been identified as the train it sounded like nothing else but. Locals at the café laughed at themselves, that they had failed to recognize so familiar, so ordinary a sound. And yet, several locals did use the rest rooms as an excuse to check the side street and be sure. It had sounded so loud, so ominous.

"This place so ramjam with people, how can I work out without an elbow in my neighbor's ribs?" Cecile was studying the menu, wondering whether the oysters could be trusted.

"Speaking of trains," Iris said, eager to assist Cecile in breaking the mood, "is the John Henry–Kwan Cheong piece pulled together?"

Nilda was waiting for someone to answer; no one did. She was caught up in the animated pictures in her mind. Jackrabbits. A speaker at the Barnwell rally had explained that the rabbits, having built their warrens in the contaminated soil, were spreading danger. Luminescent jackrabbits lighting up the night. Railroad trains traveling across the prairie, tourists shooting glowing rabbits from the window. The carcasses piled high at the trading posts. Pelts shipped east for coats, rugs, handbags. Phosphorescent corruption. Nilda changed position, dug her hands in the pockets of her denim skirt, dissatisfied with the pictures. She had been aiming for something else, something to reconnect her to that moment on the bus. She reached toward her feather and found her hands instead on straw and remembered she was wearing Cecile's hat. She dug in her hair for the thunderbird barrette and held it tight.

"What do you think, Nilda?" Iris was asking her something.

The buffalo treaties should be part of the railroad piece, no doubt. But it was peaceful with her eyes closed, her hand in her hair clutching the turquoise, the tiny figurines of Cecile's hat creating little breezes, tinkling tunes, helping her to reconnect.

Down the street, noisy but harmonious, strolled three of Jan's former students, the one in the middle in a lime-green suit, the two flanking him in blue jeans and 7 Arts satin jackets. The one singing bass was bent over, popping his fingers as he snapped his knees in a modified cakewalk, laying down the baroomph dit dit diir bottom. The tenor, his head thrown back, was stabbing the air in front of him with a crooked finger as though testing the resiliency of cellophane. The baritone was in the middle, one minute his arms wide so that the lining of his lime jacket revealed itself as cut from the same bolt as

234

his tie, the next squinching his whole body together to cup the invisible mike to his mouth. It was clear to all who turned their way that the trio was doing one of his originals; he was the only one who knew the lyrics. They were drowning out the musicians onstage inside the café who had just started up again.

"And when my baby says, it's too late, sorree . . ." In unison they crossed their arms over their chests and dropped their heads sorrowfully. "It just backs me up and turns me rrrrround." They crossed their legs over and turned with a back leg hop-slide that drew a trickle of applause from some of the audience, who didn't know the best was yet to come. "But I keep on coming, just keep on coming on strong." The three, in precisioned timing, spun as if on ball bearings, then, hands at waist like Baptist preachers, they shuffled one-leg, hopped, then strode boldly to the railing, gliding on the last beat. "Cause that's the kind of man I am."

Ruby was enjoying the serenade. But as she looked from the 7 Arts stencil to Jan, thinking about the rumor and Jan's close connection with the cowboy fringe at the Academy, she buried her mouth in her hands and frowned. She could actually picture her friend passing out rifles like so many report cards. "Be sure to get these signed, boys, and bring them back as clean as you got them."

Jan, smiling, a little embarrassed by the attention, was looking from the brothers to Ruby, thinking about the rumor and Ruby's association with the more militaristic hotheads. She imagined them lined up at her shop—and Ruby outfitting the youths in chest plates and shields—"And the rat-teeth muthafucka that dulls the shine on my masterpieces better not come back here without his own chamois cloth."

The whole café on that side broke into enthusiastic applause, Rising Sun banging his ivory holder against the side of his wine glass, capturing Iris' attention if not Mai's. The boys stepped back in unison, spun, snapped out a bow from the waist, and continued on down the street, slapping five.

The two women avoided each other's eyes for a moment until the singing dimmed and the trio crossed over toward Gaylord, heading for the Academy. Jan and Ruby watched, bobbing their heads and smiling rather than trusting themselves to comment on the talent, the youth, anything. Both fished amongst the objects on the table, hunting for the thread of the conversation that had been interrupted.

"Velma's predisposed to strife and conflict and crises. It's how she learns, by struggling through. One of the things about her chart—"

"Janice, please. None of that dharma, karma, brahma stuff. I'm up to here. Getting so I can't get a decent conversation nowhere in this city. Don't anybody talk political anymore, talk Black anymore? If it ain't degree degree, it's job job, boogie boogie, or some esoteric off-the-wall sun/moon shit. Look, the main thing I wish you'd get serious about is the next election. You really must."

"You know, Ruby, you ought to settle down and have babies. Can't leave it to the kids and fools, ya know," Jan said, browsing through the wine list.

"You're not funny, but I'll get off your case." There was still the rest of the night to get done what the group'd assigned her; it really was a serious matter. And Janice was such an excellent worker. Ruby reared back in her chair and gazed about. "Speaking of kids and fools, there goes my cousin Buster up the way. Developing into a first-class ass. Was bugging everybody at the Academy this morning trying to find out what the Brotherhood's up to for the procession. It's embarrassing, cool as I am, having a jerk for a relative."

"And what is the Brotherhood up to?"

236

"You know better than me." Ruby shrugged and once again their eyes bounced away.

"Your cousin looks pregnant, Ruby."

"You're sharp. He is. His body's taken on the weight his mind still refuses to accept. Very young the girl. Fifteen or something and none too swift. There ought to be a workshop at the Manhood Conference on pregnant fathers, a much-neglected topic. When's the last time you heard a decent discussion of pregnant men and male menopause and male moon cycles and the like?"

"Last time us sisters got together."

"I mean in an official way?"

"Ain't sisters' rapping official enough for you?"

"Jot some notes on the subject on the back of that questionnaire."

"I wish I could say I was too busy enjoying the music to be bothered."

The musicians in the café were attempting Latin. The speakers were hung over the espresso machine and music wafted out of doors on the aroma of espresso. Iris dropped out of the conversation long enough to calculate the months since she'd strolled up Broadway in the afternoon, checking the prices of avocados, mangoes, sugar cane along the way to her favorite China y Latina near the Olympia movie house. And how long it would be before she'd hear again Yorican spoken unself-consciously as opposed to the way she composed her pieces. How long it would be before she would have rice and squid again at El Mundial with loudmouths who knew how to eat, or something fancy at Victor's with Paco, go to the mercado under the viaduct and shop for the old woman who ran the *botánica* on the first floor of her apartment building, dance with Popi in the street while his cronies kept time bongoing on the checkerboard or beer-can timbale-ing or slamming down dominoes singing with their eyes closed and always *corazón, corazón* and love ever *siempre* and passion *caliente,* and a high-note *esperanza* lifting the old men from the chairs and their pants baggy but the singing magnificent.

Easier to feel the distance from New York—pain, than from home—vague. The old streetcar sheds of Piedras, the casino on the hill behind the firehouse in Ponce, the resort Paco had taken her to in Rincón for their honeymoon. It was dim, a lot less vibrant than the New York memories. She could barely remember anything about home, for home had really begun with the Mobilization for Youth theatre project, the St. Mark's poetry group, the committees of defense for Carlos Feliciano, the Puerto Rican Student Union at City College, and then the Young Lords. She'd written faithfully to compañeros of CAFU, a feminist action group that had sent expressions of solidarity to the Young Lords in the early seventies when she'd been correspondence secretary. She'd kept up communications over the years with most of the Independentistas, FUPI, JIU, MPI, who had direct and immediate links with groups in New York. But she'd gotten cut off in a way traveling with the troupe: transplants all, Inez from farm valley country, Chezia from the Tupercuin hills, Nilda from the contested Black Hills, Mai from the hills of San Francisco they liked to joke, or the paddy fields of Berkeley, Cecile from a maroon community in the hills of Jamaica. Only Palma was at home, and not even, she said it herself. Home was with them or in the studio or with her main man. But "eventually we all come to the hills," like in the poem. And they had to evoke it with music, dance and *encantados.*

Iris had ordered a fruit salad, a bowl of plantain chips, a sweet roll or bun if they had, and coffee, explaining carefully to the waiter that she wanted the coffee in a bowl and wanted

the milk scalded. She was trying to stay awake till it got there.
She had toyed with the idea of taking a leave and making a
quick run to New York, but the group had dwindled so fast.
And she'd promised. There was a Black Women's Conference
in New Orleans to start with. A major reading sponsored by the
Before Columbus Book Project to end with, just days before
she was due in Mayagüez for the start of summer session, not
even enough time to lock herself up with the Berlitz long
players. The kind of Spanish demanded at U. of Mayagüez she
wasn't putting down at all, *nada nada.* But in between New
Orleans and the Bay area were several campus appearances, a
benefit for the farm workers' union, some kind of Black and
Indian thing that was jumping off right after the Tuskegee air
show, and two visits to the joint. Iris got weary just thinking
about it all. But that was always the way. The minute they got
to setting up, though, it was all beautiful again, things popped,
and she cooked.

"I think they're friends of Palma and Velma's, yes?" Mai
was jabbing her pen in the direction of two women by the
railing clinking glasses of white wine. "Maybe they know where
Velma is. We should ask?"

Iris nodded yeh maybe, noticing how dragged out they all
were. It seemed an effort for Chezia to turn her head. Cecile
was bent over her plate, shrugging. Nilda had opened her eyes
long enough to notice only half her order had come and now
seemed fast asleep. Iris said nothing further, just smiled as Mai
smiled when the two women looked their way. She was content
to sit there and listen to the music. She listened for all of eight
bars, hunting up under the trumpet for the congas. She had
seen the musicians go by and knew not to expect much. Ersatz
salsa. She thought of the last time she'd caught Ray Baretta.
It had been too long. La Lupe. She could cry, it had been that
long. La Lupe, La Lupe, La Lupe. The thought of recruiting

La Lupe as the next Sister of the Plantain woke her up. It was wild. It was perfect. La Lupe, her replacement.

"Taste, Iris. It's billed as a piña colada. Tell me I'm not crazy."

Iris waved Cecile's glass away. She was saving herself for the black-bean coffee, drowsing in her chair thinking of how Paco made it with the nasty sock thing and wondering if he'd started packing yet, sent out any feelers, found a lead on a job yet. They were both going to try to get through law school together. It was loco, but.

"This is the kind of rum we use back home for cooking." Cecile was pouting, flirting with Campbell. "You don't drink it, brudder, you light it up." He took her glass away, very noticeably not flirting back. Cecile and Iris exchanged eyebrow lifts and slumped in their seats a bit, trying to second-guess where the wind would spring up next, under Cecile's hat which was Nilda's, under the tablecloth edge, under Mai's dress.

"I hope it doesn't rain," Cecile said, motioning toward Nilda, who sat beyond the shadow of the awning. "How would we get her to move?"

"Self-centered? But that's a good thing, Ruby. Velma's never been the center of her own life before, not really."

"You mean that Obie and the kid is the sun the dear sister revolves around or what-have-you?"

"No." Jan sucked at her sticky fingers. "Neither of them, but especially Velma," she emphasized, "ever set things up so they could opt for a purely personal solution."

"Quotes around 'personal,' if you please."

"I hear you. It's like what you were saying earlier about wanting to retreat from confusion to your shop, just you and the jewelry making. Confined space, everything under your sure control. Not that you mean it. But that's what I mean by 'personal.' Velma has worked hard not to hollow out a safe corner—yeh, quotes around the safe—of home, family, marriage and then be less responsive, less engaged. Dodgy business trying to maintain the right balance there, the personal and the public, the club/heart cluster versus spades/diamonds, and a sun *and* Venus in Aquarius . . . Ahh, I knew I'd get a rise out of you, Ruby. But it's good she has put herself at center at last. If that's what you meant by 'self-centered.' "

"Jan, I'm sick of the subject."

Ruby sighed and clasped her hands behind the chair and cracked her elbows. "I think my ass is falling asleep and my legs too. I also think this has been the first conversation we have ever had out of doors that didn't get interrupted thoroughly by some joker sidling up with the 'hey mama' or 'hey foxes' like what we could possibly be talking about is nothing compared to some off-the-wall nonsense a brother could lay down. Don't cloud up. I'm just stalling, that's all. Trying not to be an alarmist. Last time I pronounced somebody crazy, you were ready to line up the psychiatrists. Remember? You went tearing after Tina Mason's mother to get her to tackle Tina to the mat?"

"You really had me going."

"Now, that bitch is really crazy, that Tina. Do you know what her latest thing is? She's got the studio over the Regal now. And she plans to revive the ancient Earth Mother cult. Got posters, buttons, flyers, costumes, the works. And guess who she plans to cast in the role of ancient primavera, support stockings and all? The boardinghouse lady who's great-grand-somebody got Harpers Ferry rolling. What's her name? The one whose son got messed over in the antidraft rally the year we met."

"Sophie Heywood."

"Now, can you imagine that old bird traipsing down the

street with Tina's crew in their X-rated all in all, a daisy chain around her head, flinging yams and golden delicious apples to the multitudes?"

"As a matter of fact, I can. Mrs. Heywood will be riding the Parade float this festival."

"And half her mixed-bag crew of witches are doing this dance on the Heights Saturday night called Freedom in Romany for the Gypsies. That's a dance. You should see the flyer. And check this—she calls me to ask if Nate would be interested in joining her band of merrymakers—"

"And would he?"

"Nigguh pul-leeze. *Who?* That bitch crazier'n hell. But I'm not talking about that brand of lunacy. Velma . . . I wish she'd get here. I'd like to hear more about the computer caper."

"Well, I'm glad Velma wasn't here in time for dessert, Ruby. The mere mention of plutonium and she goes off with dire predictions about a police state coming to insure or at least minimize against unauthorized access to nuclear materials. She has so little faith."

"In what?"

"The people."

"All this doomsday mushroom-cloud end-of-planet numbah is past my brain. Just give me the good ole-fashioned honky-nigger shit. I think all this ecology stuff is a diversion."

"They're connected. Whose community do you think they ship radioactive waste through, or dig up waste burial grounds near? Who do you think they hire for the dangerous dirty work at those plants? What parts of the world do they test-blast in? And all them illegal uranium mines dug up on Navajo turf— the crops dying, the sheep dying, the horses, water, cancer, Ruby, cancer. And the plant on the Harlem River and—Ruby, don't get stupid on me."

"You're sounding like Velma."

"Hell, it's an emergency situation, has been for years. All those thrown-together plants they built in the forties and fifties are falling apart now. War is not the threat. It's all the 'peacetime' construction that's wiping us out. And remember that summer we met, all those TB mobile units in the neighborhoods? Giving out lollipops and donuts and the kids going back two, three, four times for an x-ray. Oh, Ruby."

"Yeh, I know there's a connection," Ruby sighed, releasing her hands and dropping forward. "Pass the carafe."

"Has the executive committee decided to take on the nuclear issue?"

"I voted it down. Wait! Hear me out. Now, we formed the group mainly to insure 'input' in local politics, right? An interim tactical something or other until the people quit fooling around and decide on united Black political action, right? There's no sense taking on everything."

"But Ruby, sistuh, heart of my heart, will you just tip your chin slightly northwest and swing your eyes in the direction of Gaylord and tell me what do you see? You think there's no connection between the power plant and Transchemical and the power configurations in this city and the quality of life in this city, region, country, world?"

"Sold. But can't I specialize just a wee bit longer in the local primitive stuff—labor with the ordinary home-grown variety crackers and your everyday macho pain in the ass from the block? Yawl take on this other thing. It's too big for me. I'm just your friendly neighborhood earring maker."

"I hope you're kidding. Here, have some more wine, the tea's cold."

"What I need is a real drink. Let's go hang out, unless you're deliberately hanging out to get something going with our literate friend, albeit a waiter?"

"What?"

"Janice, please. He's done everything but bite your neck and ravish you on the table."

"Oh, I don't think he . . . just a friendly type brother . . . I mean . . ."

"That is bullshit of a non-biodegradable sort. The man's got eyes. Deal with that at least."

"Ruby, do me a favor."

"Okay. I will shut up and drink my wine like a good girl and then I will pay the check with this bogus credit card I traded a bogus Benin gold weight for."

"You will pay cash money in the hand. It's the least you can do having saddled me with this questionnaire and a major decision to make about my life."

"Right. Fine. Now, is it my imagination or are we at a rerun of *Singin' in the Rain*?"

Several young people who'd been boogie-ing in front of the record shack and others who'd hung drape-style around the café railing had rushed into the café's table area and were broken-field running among the tables, some walking wolf-style as if puddles already threatened Romeo Ballad loafers, Yo Yos, Candies and Converse All Stars. Others were ducking in anticipation of clearing the awning that could in no way be dripping yet, but it was. A sudden downpour with no warning, the light only now shifting from metallic lemon to a purple-gray. Customers by the railing had already begun dragging their tables across the prized quarry tile, knee-bent walking and carrying their chairs on their behinds, these odd-shaped creatures colliding with equally strange bent-over runners darting in and out between waiters, the runaway dessert cart, and one or two stunned customers returning from the rest rooms caught up in a turbulent not-sure-what-something-hey-watch-it happening.

Campbell got hemmed in the corner by the service counter, his order pad pressed against his throat, his elbow in a bowl of fruit salad not picked up. And he'd been about to make a connection; he'd been clutching at an idea and it was trying to come together, congeal, get structured into something speakable. But now, with the ball-point leaking against his shirt, the stain leaching ever closer to his skin as the contaminated soil in Barnwell reached the water table—it was slipping past him. But in the months ahead he would remember—the height of divinely egocentric association—that lightning had flashed lighting up the purple, smeared sky just as it came to him. Damballah. A grumbling, growling boiling up as if from the core of the earthworks drew a groan from the crowd huddled together under the awning, in the doorway, as if to absorb the shock of it, of whatever cataclysmic event it might turn out to be, for it couldn't be simply a storm with such frightening thunder as was cracking the air as if the very world were splitting apart.

And whatever it was, it was no mere feet-thrumming intrusion of kids on ball bearings careening down the pavement, nor the drum talk of the dance studio tete tete bak a ra answered by the kabate dada rada from the park. Nor the rumbling of railroad cars. It could be the thunder of cannons. It could mean war. Or angry gods demanding someone be flung into the crater, volcanoes boiling up, vomiting up flames and lava, death running in the streets soon to overtake the café. Or an explosion at the plant.

Folks were crowding together, sharing edges of chairs with strangers, offering bits of scalloped shadow from the oilskin roofing, spreading tents of newspapers on companions' heads, holding their breath, trying not to hear the dire prophecies or damn-fool hunches of professional talkers accustomed to being asked their two cents worth and used to people listening.

Many years hence, when "rad" and "rem" would riddle everyday speech and the suffix "-curies" would radically alter

245

all assumptions on which "security" had once been built, many would mark the beginning of it all as this moment. This moment, this light, this place, these strangers. All would be fixed more indelibly on the brain and have more lasting potency than circumstances remembered of that November day in '63. This moment, heart jarred and lungs starved, would supply the answers to the latter-day version of "What were you into when they wiped Lumumba out?" Or, "Did you ever go past the Audobon Ballroom after they gunned Malcolm down?" Or, "Where were you when the news came of King? Of Ho? Of Mao? Of Che? Of Fannie Lou? Were you wearing a fro the time they were hounding Angela across country? Did you raise funds for Mozambique, Angola? Were you part of the Movement? In D.C. in '63? Did you help pull the U.S. out of Vietnam, Eritrea, South Africa? Did you wear a Fair Play for Cuba button? Did you send defense funds for Joanne Little, for Inez Garcia, for Dennis Banks, for Russell Means, for the Wilmington Ten?" One would ask and be asked, "When did it begin for you?"

One would make the journey to the café as if to market to trade news, hunches, interpretations of news, gossips, dreams, flashes picked up from official and nonofficial sources regarding what was happening in other districts, other countries, other continents. And no one would say "across the border," for that entailed tiring explanations, obliged the speaker to be precise about what border was meant— Where Legba stood at the gate? Where Isis lifted the veil? The probable realms of impossibility beyond the limits of scientific certainty? The uncharted territory beyond the danger zone of "safe" dosage? The brain-blood or placenta barrier that couldn't screen plutonium out?

"I could do without the sound track and the special effects." Ruby shivered, grabbing hold of the table and urging Jan out of a freeze. "Sounded like the set for an MGM musical. Now

I'm thinking this must be *Poseidon Two* or *Son of Inferno.*"

And Jan had lifted her end of the table, muttering into the teapot, "I hope it's not . . ."

One would venture out into the streets to the café or some other familiar place from the old days where gatherings looked trustworthy and there huddle to trade stories, sifting and sorting among the tales as if at a rummage sale, taking on those pieces still wearable to get them through the passage, rejecting those pieces too threadbare, too contaminated, too cumbersome.

One would run the back roads to the woods, not jogging in unpaid outfits, trampling shoots, not moving in with tents, dope and bombed-out playmates mouthing off about "We're into nature," not hiding out in Wordsworth or Kerouac, excusing the self from social action, but running to the woods in hopes of an audience with the spirits long withdrawn from farms and gardens all withered and wasted, bringing eagle-bone whistles or gourd rattles or plaster saints or rakes and seeds or gifts of soap or sacks of cornmeal or sticks of licorice or cones of incense, anything one had to place on a tree-stump altar or a turned-rock shrine to lure the saving spirits out to talk and be heeded finally Stumbling through the thorns and briars, following the rada rada big booming of the drums or the weh weh wedo riff of reed flutes, running toward a clearing, toward a likely sanctuary of the saints, the loa, the dinns, the devas. And found, would open up and welcome one in before the end, welcome one in in time to wrench time from its track so another script could play itself out. One would tap the brain for any knowledge of initiation rites lying dormant there, recognizing that life depended on it, that initiation was the beginning of transformation and that the ecology of the self, the tribe, the species, the earth depended on just that. In the dark of the woods, the ground shaking underfoot, the ancient covenants remembered in fragments, one would stand there, fists pummeling the temples, trying to remember the whole in time and make things whole again. And remembering too that thunderclap heard in the café years ago that was Ogun's shouting answer to the African workers who labored for life's renewal, was Thor at the anvil beating swords into spades, was Wagner's Siegfried striking a blow, was living archetypes sounding the knell of the authoritarian age, the thunderous beginning of the new humanism, the new spiritism if only attention could be riveted on the simplicity of the karmic law—cause and effect. There were choices to be noted. Decisions to be made.

It was raining a furiously relentless rain as if it meant to go on forever. Ruby abandoned her trampled hat, watched it slide away under the railing. Rain drumming on the tables, tiles, awning, answered by the sucking thud of people running by, the squish of cars and trucks and car horns getting stuck. A woman's voice, high-pitched and hysterical, called out from somewhere "Fredieeeee?" and sent chills up the collective spine. The hanging pots were swinging, overflowing, dollops of mud on the tile, some falling at last and banging, the contents oozing away in a slide.

Ruby pulled the turtleneck up that was a hood and hugged her friend closely. Both thought the same thoughts but could not speak, simply hugged each other tightly, trying to think of something funny to break the mood, break the other's hold.

Jan was flexing her hands against Ruby's back as if arthritis threatened or honey was bonding her fingers. A muscular response to some dimly heard instruction in her mind to loosen her grip now on all notions of the seemingly complete world, release her hold on notions that might lock her to the old.

There was a second flash of lightning and that gesture of the spread-open hand, that thought unfinished but intuited got fixed and would hold its shape for decades to come. "I hope it's not . . ." spoken into the teapot marking Jan's beginning.

248

Suddenly, it was quiet but for the rain. The waiters were passing out napkins like medicos with bandages at the front. And in a while joviality would ease back into the company and erase the terror. But in too short a while the very threat of rain would revive the terror, be more terrible than anything experienced by anyone in that rehearsal moment. Rain that would cancel out the possibility of any joviality and make a napkin wipe-off a ludicrous memory not to be repeated by any sane person.

Nilda, her hat blown off, her hair barely held down at the side by the barrette, barely secured in back by the leather strap, was still sitting with her eyes closed and her arms folded in her lap. Cecile had shouted when they moved to shove the table closer to the wall, cutting off the waiter's exit and possibly his circulation. Though Campbell had been stunned still with no thought of movement that might jar the idea taking shape, so simple a connection, he'd known it for years but had failed to appreciate it. Of course everything was everything. Hadn't Mustafa taught him that? And he'd written it down on the back of the pad. Damballah, he wrote, represents, he wrote, and scratched that out, Damballah is similar to, he wrote, and scratched that out, Damballah is the first law of thermodynamics and is the Biblical wisdom and is the law of time and is, Campbell wrote, everything that is now has been before and will be again in a new way, in a changed form, in a timeless time.

Neither Cecile nor any of the others called to Nilda sitting there three feet from the awning, an island unto herself. It was clear she was not asleep and was not concerned with the rain's pelting of her velvet shirt, darkening now to blue-black ink. Nilda was in the hills with the *peyotero*, listening to the tongue of the sacred cactus where Our Elder Brother, the Deer of the Sun, resides. In the hills, becoming available to the spirits summoned to regenerate the life of the world.

twelve

Dom tete teke dom diir
One side of the Hill calling to the other.
Bateke teke bembe wahh
The call and response, drums on the move, a gathering summoned.
Rada rada boom tete wahh
Echoed from the park.
Rada rede tum vida omm
Feedback and contagion.

Slashed tree pitch ooze chopped down hollowed out rum burnt tree drums green black mottled-gold thumped. Velma can feel them in the walls as she races down corridors. A corn-meal-marked trail. Pollen veves on the walls blurred as she runs through passageways in search of a particular chamber that might not be sealed off if she hurries and doesn't think too much on limitations. "I can't read drums, so how do I know

they're saying 'barrier dropping'?" She regrets the thought.
The corn meal is slippery now, no traction, off direction, the
drums pushing the walls out of shape and a draft of air in her
face and she could lose her breath once and for all. Reed flutes
blowing fuah diah in her hair, her nose, her lungs. Tripping
over notes and thoughts and falling up the attic stairs, a tonic
breeze pushing through the cracks in the floorboards, she is
face down now pressed between the slats. And breath returns.

"Sweetheart?"

She pulls up and sits like a cat, one paw resting lightly on
a Christmas bulb. She is imitating a sphinx, playing distraction:
M'Dear wants to talk of Christ; she prefers charades. She is
sphinx now and watches child and godmother pack away the
tree ornaments in tin boxes of excelsior.

"No more room in that box, M'Dear."

"In the heart? Room in the heart, Vee?"

"You mean like no room in the inn?"

"There was no room in the heart, Vee. And you?"

Understanding now, still and watching like a sphinx, poised,
centered, music coming at her through cracks in the walls,
floors, window frames. A wind in the rib cage, a tremor in the
lungs rustling the package straw in the floor of the heart.

"She's off again. Take care, Min, you don't lose her."

"Time to hit the yellow-brick road, is it? Stay close, Old
Wife."

A brass band coming, shiny sounds making the passageway
slippery. The barrier down as promised and she can skip along
now. Cymbals crashing by her ear and the leaves shuddering
as the procession passes. She waits in the branches of Philo 101,
time streaming along below her in the tree. Dogs caught in the
shower shiver, growl and bite the curbstones. Cats with their
ears laid back hiss, seeing what the marchers will not train
themselves to see.

"So what do I do now? Iz you iz or iz you ain't my spirit guide?"

"Loan her some of yo stuff, Min. And don't be stingy."

"I'm bout worn out."

A grand piñata suspended festive from the branch. The hitting stick once a stake in young Min's yard, once a stake in a robber baron's heart way before that. The children shrieking and jumping strike down bits of grace. And Velma jumps out of the tree and is on the path going asphalt, running backward now the way Nilda had once prophesied.

Hoo Doo Man looks at her with maroon eyes and leaps out of the LaSalle Street projects at her snarling, feathered bonnet tossing, beads and tiny mirrors flashing in the yards of maribou trailing and twisting behind him as he bounds, all manner of wanga clanking on his breastbone. She is caught in the crush of neighbors streaming out of doors now, the child sent out to call up the sun, having given the signal to begin. They're heading for the first watering hole of the day, the package store, with rattles, tambourines, zimbi gourds and paper cups. The rada tambours in the suede hands of the young brown boys and dark old men trotting alongside the procession chanting praise songs to their chief, who waits on the balcony overhanging the Regal marquee. Cups of wine passing overhead to keep the praises coming on smooth. And she is trying to back out, to run the other way.

"That's Velma Henry for you," one on-the-side-liner remarks. "Always going against the grain."

"Always was contrary."

She is trotting backward down Gaylord Hill with no brakes on, skidding into bus posts, colliding into flower-smothered floats where folks pin on notes, prayers and dollar bills. Musician men tie scarfs around their hips and hand her one. Red scarfs, red war, red wound, red Ogun, who can endow the gift of prophecy and cure, protector of warriors and travelers too. She ties her sash, her red hips darkening in the rain.

Rope sashes holding up croker pants and burlap tunics drenched and tightening. Metal collars on necks wet, the chain passing through loops linking row on row of elders, younguns, men and women fastened to the side panels of the truck padlocked and rain-spattered. Someone hoists her up by the wrists and there's no pain. She is jammed between bodies barely rocking as the truck, like a rag-and-bones cart, trundles along the cobblestone street.

She looks for Obie. Head shaven, tattoo burnt in left forearm, he is there. He sees her. She sees him; she sees too the guns wrapped in cloth, the bombs of two-inch pipes buried in the sawdust pile the children sit on. This is not his way. Who talked him into going along with this? She stares the question at him. There are so many between them now, there can be no privacy.

"Do what I tell you," he says. "Get away. Be safe. This once."

She shakes her head, stubborn.

"Why won't you give me this one thing?"

"If I start giving, Obie, I'll give everything," she does not say. She backs out of the truck and it thunders past.

There are chains on the doors of the Regal theatre. To lock gate-crashers out, explain the security guards. But folks break through the line to rap on the glass doors—"I gotta use the bathroom," "Emergency, lemme use the phone," "My kid's in there," "But I've already got my ticket," when a guard juts his chin toward the closed-down box office. Chains on the door and folks inside for the concert and the short-wave speaking of things getting out of control all over town. And what would the audience do if they knew the Regal had been opened without a proper fire inspection and was now locked up by a bunch of

Keystone Kops who might be able to find the key if trouble started, but then again might not?

It's raining harder now and the line disperses. Folks free now to leave. Free to run elaborately off at the mouth about their ingenious and fearless plans for getting into the Regal, for breaking kin and neighbor out of the Regal if only it hadn't gone and rained. And knowing all the while—which makes the telling all the more extravagant—that the moment to do whatever there was to do had come when they were being driven out, had come when they were being told to line up, had come when the doors were being closed in their faces, had come when the bar bolts were being thrown, had come when the chains appeared.

She's inside. The audience deliberately mistaking the thunder for a backstage drum roll. Last time a demonstration was threatened at Transchemical, all power was cut off in the district and blamed on the storm most folks remembered as a drizzle merely. So they hear drums.

She would sit still and remember not to kick at the seat in front or Mama Mae would slap her knees. And she kept her eyes off the cave in the wall. She liked looking at the giant Blackamoors against the side, bulging chests and balloon pants, looming straight past the box seats and up toward the sky, the chipped noses and scaly turbans hardly visible in the dark. Their huge fans that Mama Mae called "bald chins" waving in the navy blue heavens with the clouds and stars. She liked them, might ask to be taken to the bathroom if she could escape for a chance to run her hands over the vests that looked like gold. But the curve in the wall that her unruly eyes always tried to slide around for a glimpse of the rubied swords hanging in the cave, hanging in space like a magic trick, she would not look there. The swords had disappeared when she was seven. This disappearing act was magical enough but the pictures that started coming in the cave—the mud mothers with enormous teeth painting themselves with long hair brushes, painting pictures on the walls of the cave—that was too much. She would lean way back in the seat and stare at the phony sky and wait for the movie to end. Just as she leaned back in church in the wooden pews and waited for the sermon to end, determined not to look in the dark hollow behind the statues standing in the walls around the congregation.

In the attic they came in the mirror once. Ten or more women with mud hair, storing yams in gourds and pebbles in cracked calabash. And tucking babies in hairy hides. They came like a Polaroid. Stepping out of the mouth of the cave, they tried to climb out of the speckled glass, talk to her, tell her what must be done all over again, all over again, all over again. But she hung an old velvet drape over the mirror and smothered them. They were not going to run her off her own place. Not the attic.

Mothballs drop from sweaters, from plastic sacks hung near the window. Mothballs roll from boxes where the squirrels have been gnawing before repelled. Mothballs roll across the attic floor till inertia holds them near her feet. She leans from the eaves as from a branch and misses nothing.

The marchers, trudging alongside the truck, are soaked. Wetbacks, she smiles. Something to tell Inez if the sisters come for lunch. There is much movement in the truck. Someone unwrapping guns, distributing armloads of weapons, tearing open boxes of ammunition? What for? She can't remember. Children, unseated, scoot between legs and jump from the truck to join friends on the sidelines. Some race across the street, taking chances in the traffic that's not been closed off.

Even from her perch it is clear the chains are made of cardboard, a patina of black, greasy paint glistening in the rain, running like make-up, like mud, like mind, like time. Velma shivers and then relaxes. Something silky cool but body warm is being pressed against her.

Grownups on the sidelines are cheering artificial chains and actors, the floats, the costumes, the whole idea of festival, rushing the procession on toward the park, toward the sizzling food, the steamy pushcarts, the incense-fragrant booths, the drums and the dancing.

There's cheering in the park, then jeering, wine bottles being hurled from cars speeding by, cars not of the district. Bottles, cans, rocks, jeers like the rock-concert night, that time she talked Obie, Palma and Marcus into going, not for the music but because they needed to know so much more about Claybourne's finest, about riot-control techniques. And the lead singer spotted straights in the front row with flash cameras blinding as at the zoo and sang FUCK! in their faces. And the cops rushed the stage as the chant Pig! Pig! went up and bottles too, cans, rocks went up from the audience and came down from the trees where the troublemakers waited. And Marcus said, "Later for this." And Obie, grabbing the sisters by the hand. And no one said "I told you so" or "You and your damn research" because it had been an instructive evening.

Squad cars pull into the park, sprawl all over the grass, an officer tells the Festival Committee that the permits have been revoked and there are questions too about the licenses to sell food, especially booze in City Park. She gets there too late to understand what is happening but sees the cops seeing a rioting horde of nigger-niggers and other-type niggers racing from the park green, abandoning their litter, rushing for the hill back of the vacant lot where only gods know what weapons might be stashed, grappling up the hill, uprooting shrubs and bushes in the climb to the main street lined with boutiques, cafés and travel agencies, stampeding the tourists and racing down the block toward the Hill to the Heights for the shortcut to Transchemical. And they call in for reinforcements. The vigilante on the airwaves moving out.

The people who've already bid carne vale, following a different calendar, turn in the street and see a disciplined army or a mob, a shaming reminder of things best forgotten, or an interesting bit of theatre rained out, too bad, or thank goodness cause everybody's nerves are shot, the whole town on edge.

She is in the park around the bonfire singing. Minnie is there, M'Dear, Doc Serge and some older man she doesn't know by name, the face faintly familiar, but the green uniform throwing her off. And Obie is there, Mama Mae, Palma and Lil James called Jabari now and Marcus and. And someone or something hovering near daring her to look, to recognize. Not an old friend but someone she hasn't met but ought to know but dare not look at. A taboo glance, formidable, ancient, locking her jaws, her thighs, keeping her head down. Medusa, Lot's Wife, Eurydice, Noah, she will not look. She keeps her eyes on her feet, swollen from stomping. They are all stomping, agitating the ground, agitating an idea, calling up something or someone, and the idea clusters in the image centers and settles there. She will not look at that either. It is taking all of her to concentrate on not looking.

She would not have cut Medusa's head off, she is thinking, watching the mud come up worms between her toes. She would simply have told the sister to go and comb her hair. Or gotten a stick to drive the serpents out. Serpents or snakes? She draws a line in the dirt with her big toe.

Different remedies for snakebite and the bite of the serpent, she'd been hearing for a lifetime. Daddy Dolphy had told her too in the woods that time. M'Dear had dropped her basket and slit his shirt with her shears before Velma knew what had happened. Had pushed him on the ground and taken his knife from him and slit open his shoulder before Velma could cry out. "Quick, salt." And she'd managed to find it in the gathering basket and knew somehow it was salt and not some other odd thing to be bringing along to the woods. Daddy Dolphy had gulped some, held some in his mouth and was ripping off his sleeve when M'Dear snatched a fistful of leaves from a bush and packed a salt poultice into the wound and tied up his shoulder tightly with the sleeve tourniquet. "Helps neutralize the venom," M'Dear explained, her voice calm, as if certain the twisting of the sleeve would do the rest. "To neutralize the serpent's another matter," Daddy Dolphy had winked, taking deep breaths.

She thought she knew that. At some point in her life she was sure Douglass, Tubman, the slave narratives, the songs, the fables, Delaney, Ida Wells, Blyden, DuBois, Garvey, the singers, her parents, Malcolm, Coltrane, the poets, her comrades, her godmother, her neighbors, had taught her that. Thought she knew how to build immunity to the sting of the serpent that turned would-be cells, could-be cadres into cargo cults. Thought she knew how to build resistance, make the journey to the center of the circle, stay poised and centered in the work and not fly off, stay centered in the best of her people's traditions and not be available to madness, not become intoxicated by the heady brew of degrees and career and congratulations for nothing done, not become anesthetized by dazzling performances with somebody else's aesthetic, not go under. Thought the workers of the sixties had pulled the Family safely out of range of the serpent's fangs so the workers of the seventies could drain the poisons, repair damaged tissues, retrain the heartworks, realign the spine. Thought the vaccine offered by all the theorists and activists and clear thinkers and doers of the warrior clan would take. But amnesia had set in anyhow. Heart/brain/gut muscles atrophied anyhow. Time was running out anyhow. And the folks didn't even have a party, a consistent domestic and foreign policy much less a way to govern. Something crucial had been missing from the political/ economic / social / cultural / aesthetic / military / psychosocial / psychosexual mix. And what could it be? And what should she do? She'd been asking it aloud one morning combing her hair, and the answer had almost come tumbling out of the mirror naked and tatooed with serrated teeth and hair alive, birds and insects peeping out at her from the mud-heavy hanks of the ancient mothers' hair. And she had fled feverish and agitated from the room, flopped languid and dissolved at Jamahl's, lest she be caught up and entrapped in glass, fled lest she be ensorceled, fled finally into a sharp and piercing world, fled into the carbon cave.

And now, standing there barefoot on the ground in the park, she still could not face up, would not lift her head to look at anything but her own swollen feet. She might steal a glance sideways at the woman next to her and study the elegant shoes, the red and gold and white sequined ruffles at the hem of the extravagant gown, the hands clasped with three wedding bands shining on the ring finger—before she wrenched her eyes back to the safety of her swollen feet. There might be an answer. But she would not look up from her feet.

It was a woman all right next to her, trying to get familiar. She used the same brand of sandalwood soap too. She felt her more than anything else. A glow, as if she were beaming at her, not daring now but inviting her to look. She didn't risk it.

What was her name? M'Dear never used a name. The mailbox probably read Mr. and Mrs. Lot. Period. Surely she'd gotten the flyers, she was on the mailing list. Seen the posters, read the papers, knew what they were trying to do to effect change. Maybe the thing to do was invite the self by for coffee and a chat. Share with her how she herself had learned to believe in ordinary folks' capacity to change the self and transform society. What in hell could anybody do with a saltlick in the middle of the LaSalle projects anyway? There were no cows in Claybourne anymore. She drew another line in the dirt.

I was out of town, she would explain to the silent bride. Sorry I missed the wedding. Heard the cops turned the reception out and nabbed Bubba Orph. Now, if Leadbelly could turn a heart-of-stone judge around with a strum or two, surely there's no need for you to be laid out on a slab in the Infirmary. We can redeem Orph's guitar. Where the pawn tickets?

"Sweetheart?"

Some kind of wife, some kind of mother you turned out to be. Your children hanging in the bedroom doorway snickering at their daddy. My mother would have knocked us clean across the room. And then the lecture, her cooking spoon raised and her eyes slit warning no back talk and you better not roll your eyes or suck your teeth. "So long as you are in this house, you will respect your father, who puts food in your mouth and clothes on your back."

"Sweetheart?"

They called her Sweetpea. Her name was Barbara Watson. She'd come down from Syracuse to work with SNCC and find a husband. "Those niggers up there have no politics." Came down from D.C. a full decade later for something Velma was not sure she had to give.

"Driving to West Palm Beach to see my in-laws. Ex in-laws. Still friendly. Thought I'd drop by and see how you all are making out, pay my respects. Heard you and Smitty never did hook up. Should've grabbed him myself."

"Well . . . we're still here," intimidated by a look that said anything but respect.

"You seem the same, Velma. Crazy as ever." Looking at the tables tumbled down with leaflets and pamphlets, the boxes of rolled-up posters, the mimeo machine in the middle of the living room. "Same o same o, hunh?" touching her hair, a color Velma couldn't remember. She didn't know what the sister wanted, sitting there smoking one after another, describing her latest march down the butt- and spit-spattered aisle of City Hall, talking on and on, bits and snatches of jailhouse anecdotes and back-road remembrances, as if all that had happened a century ago and the war was over. Asking after everyone but not listening to Velma's answers. And that smile that was anything but a smile.

"We're all still here" was all Velma could think to say.

"And still into the same idealistic nonsense, I gather," sounding edgy, irritable. "You honestly think you can change anything in this country?" Her anger flaring now, bewildering.

"I try to live," Velma said, surprised at her evenness, "so it doesn't change me too much."

"You'll learn," she snapped back and seemed to be getting up to go, except she wasn't, just changing positions. And Velma was waiting for the bedroom clock to go off so she could announce she had a meeting to attend.

"You'll learn," she said again.

"I want to learn to grow, to become . . ." no longer talking to Barbara Sweetpea Watson. Her lips soft against each other, Velma was searching for a way to finish the sentence, wondering if indeed it was already complete.

"Well," she said, and this time she was dumping cigarette case, lighter, address book and pen into her bag and rising to go. "Just thought I'd come by and see how everybody's doing. Like being in a time capsule, ya know?" She was trying to exit on a big note. "Thank god I got out of here in time." She was trying to slam a swinging door. She sounded tired.

"We're still here." Velma shrugged, not at all tired. There seemed to be so much more to say. She shook out the glad-you-

261

stopped-by the way Mama Mae would, upending her bag, but no grits left.

"I wish you well, Sweetpea."

"So long."

"Shove over, Old Wife, while I put this music on. Whatcha think, something low down and nasty or something upbeat and inspiring? The Henry gal is coming through. Now which?"

"It's immaterial to me, Min."

"You hear yourself? You're a blip if there ever was one."

"Takes one to know one, Min. You gonna dismiss them haints? Seems like they plenty folks calling on em."

"They're free to go wherever and that's no lie."

"Hmph."

Strains of some sassy twenties singer crackling low and indistinct grazed Velma's ears with "Wiiiild women doan worrreeee, wild women doan have no bluuuzzzzzz." Like the hissing of the primus stove in M'Dear and Daddy Dolphy's oceanfront cottage, like the zzing of the zimbi gourds, the snakes in sister's hair, the buzzing of them spooky trees outdoors where no bees ever were no matter how hard you looked. She thought she heard some singing, something about being no angel chile. She was about to suck her teeth when the voice urged her to get real wild, was about to suck her teeth and mutter "signifyin sister," meaning the singer and the healer too. She moved to wrap Minnie's shawl more tightly around her. She could be coming apart, totally losing her self. That woman in the park, who was that but another her, a part?

But then, clear and bold, stopping her in mid-act, her arms in an arc, clear and bold as if recorded fresh that minute, as if incarnate and not a wave, not a spirit captured by an electric tongue come back to speak, blasting new and not from her long-ago little-girl days hanging out in Palma's growing-up-girl

262

days, came an alto sax loud and insistent taking over the air, jarring her out of her fear of splintering, blaring through her head. Not the hucklebuck as in do-the-hucklebuck, do-the-hucklebuck in some five watt blue bulb stomp down street alley dance hall place and she with too much make-up on getting maneuvered into a dark corner thigh on thigh and nothing romantic and nice about it. But Charlie Parker doing "Now Is the Time," coaxing from her something muscular and daring, something borrowed first from books and imaginings then later from Palma's giggly narratives in the dark sharing a pillow, borrowed till she earned it for herself on that first piano in the church and learned to listen to linears and verticals at the same time, new time, rhythm bam.

Y'Bird so bold and urgent and the Hawk doing something to the soles of her feet, she all but pushed off from the floor to fling herself out of the window, out of the window and into the dark socket of the tree knocking on the inside as if eager to be a drum or join the chorus of voices speaking to her as from a dream, into the socket and seeing the baby bird that crashed there crumpled now and calling to the air, fluttering around Minnie's govi and zin and dream for sure cause how could she know what to call the jugs and bowls but in a dream? Out of the window, stepping nimbly over the pitchers and pots and twirling in the yard, dancing round the perimeter of the tabby wall to the front of the building to count off the Infirmary's pillars like her teacher M'Dear had taught her to do: first pillar, God is; two, God is all and all is One; three, there are spirits; four, there are prophets; five, there'll be a day of Restoration; six . . . But the pillar M'Dear had saved till she came through religion and came of age was no longer there, had been struck by lightning years before and removed. But still the archway held.

Day of Restoration, Velma muttered, feeling the warm

breath of Minnie Ransom on her, lending her something to work the bellows of her lungs with. To keep on dancing like the sassy singer said. Dancing on toward the busy streets alive with winti, coyote and cunnie rabbit and turtle and caribou as if heading for the Ark in the new tidal wave, racing in the direction of resurrection as should be and she had a choice running running in the streets naming things—cunnie rabbit called impala called little deer called trickster called brother called change—naming things amidst the rush and dash of tires, feet, damp dresses swishing by, the Spirits of Blessing way outrunning disaster, outrunning jinns, shetnoi, soubaka, succubi, innocuii, incubi, nefarii, the demons midwifed, suckled and fathered by the one in ten Mama warned about who come to earth for the express purpose of making trouble for the other nine. Demons running the streets defying Earth Mother and Heavenly Father and defiling the universe in a stampede rush, rending, tearing creature ideas jumping through billboards and screw-thy-neighbor paperbacks, the modern grimoires of the passing age.

And she standing now in the wet streets as if there were a choice available now that she'd been rescued from the scissors and the oven's gas. Saynday in ancient moccasins passing by her, outrunning them all as spoken of in Nilda's poems, as woven in the wampum belts, as drawn in the sand, as beamed from the Horus eye, from the feathered-serpent's eye, as sung about when the Seven Sisters took the stage. And she'd have to travel the streets in six-eighth time cause Dizzy said righteous experience could not be rendered in three-quarter time. But this was Y'Bird not Dizzy and she was holding fast the rim of the stool lest she fall off and lose the beat altogether and be lost.

"Let her go, Min. Dancing is her way to learn now. Let her go."

"And what about my legs? My legs. We might lose her. Give her your legs, Old Wife."

She could dance right off the stool, right off the edge of the world and collide with comets scheduled for a splashdown on her fiftieth birthday and not miss a thing, dance off into space with snakes in her hair and tusks sprouting from her gums and her head thrown back and singing, cheering, celebrating all those giants she had worshiped in their terrible musicalness. Giant teachers teaching through tone and courage and inventiveness but scorned, rebuked, beleaguered, trivialized, commercialized, copied, plundered, goofed on by half-upright pianos and droopy-drawers drums and horns too long in hock and spittin up rust and blood, tormented by sleazy bookers and takers, tone-deaf amateurs and saboteurs, underpaid and overworked and sideswiped by sidesaddle-riding groupies till they didn't know, didn't trust, wouldn't move on the wonderful gift given and were mute, crazy and beat-up. But standing up in their genius anyhow ready to speak the unpronounceable. On the stand with no luggage and no maps and ready to go anywhere in the universe together on just sheer holy boldness.

Boldness and design, M'Dear would say, always said on the subject of Black anything and why hadn't she listened? Dispossessed, landless, this and that-less and free, therefore, to go anywhere and say anything and be everything if we'd only know it once and for all. Simply slip into the power, into the powerful power hanging unrecognized in the back-hall closet.

Velma felt her knees falling away at right angles, felt the curtain going up on a drama of none other than her own pantied stuff center stage. And so what? She didn't have time to care, to pull the hospital gown down cause she was in the streets and in a tunnel on her hands and knees and burrowing under the quilts in M'Dear's bed, mutton suet and sassafras oil warming her chest and cared for, cared for, and being fed tincture of something wonderful and awful from a spoon, washed down with chicken soup, while M'Dear told her that long tale of hers in a tongue not known then like Nowalemme dow ta slip Apraydelawd, not being real words till later. Speaking a special tale in a special voice and she up under the quilts sucking on a chicken bone, eager to crack the bone and crack the code, suck at the secret marrow of the thing. And M'Dear droning on: "Back in the days when the Earth was steady and the ground reliable under foot, we made our covenant with our Maker and were given our instructions . . ." And leading her on, into, down past familiar, drawing her from the known words and always ending talking about the power, the power available if we'd only look in that back-hall closet.

And damn if she didn't want to get right up from between the healer's hands, get up and quit being some "funnytime sandwich" as Mama Mae would say, and go ask her godmother about them things told at night fluffing up the pillow for her and smoothing down the sheet over the quilt to kiss her goodnight. All the talk that had begun the day Palma'd led her back by the hand from the marshes and M'Dear had said it was only proper to do one's seeking on one's knees, which shut Palma up and Mama Mae too. Get up and go seeking again, knock on all the doors in Claybourne and quick too before the procession began for real. Knock and be welcomed in and free to roam the back hall on the hunt for that particular closet with the particular hanging robe, coat, mantle, veil or whatever it was. And get into it. Sport it. Parade around the district in it so folks would remember themselves. Would hunt for their lost selves.

And hadn't Nilda and Inez told her about hunting? Hadn't Maazda explained what it was to stalk, to take over the hunted, but not with arrows or bullets but with the eye of the mind? And hadn't she observed the difference, watched the different brands of hunting? The pulling of the bow, the pulling of the truck alongside the prey and mowing it down, taking it over. The cars pulling up alongside a woman or a kid ready to sell the self for a Twinkie. Bringing down a bird or a woman or a man stalked at a dance. Taking over a life. That was not hunting as the sisters explained it, sang it, acted it out. To have dominion was not to knock out, downpress, bruise, but to understand, to love, make at home. The keeping in the sights the animal, or child, man or woman, tracking it in order to learn their way of being in the world. To be at home in the knowing. The hunt for balance and kinship was the thing. A mutual courtesy. She would run to the park and hunt for self. Would be wild. Would look.

And up under the brass of horn and cymbals was the sister still singing faintly, "Wiiiillld women doan worrreeeee." But it was hard to concentrate cause something was happening, she was about to surrender it up whatever it was. Well hell, she'd always been wild. And probably looked the perfect Halloween scare thing there on the stool with her matted hair and ashy legs and mouth crusty like something heaved up from the marshes.

"I might have died," she said aloud and shuddered. And it was totally unbelievable that she might be anywhere but there. She tried to look around, to take in the healer, the people circling her, the onlookers behind. But there were so many other things to look at closer at hand. The silvery tendrils that fluttered between her fingers, extending out like tiny webs of invisible thread. The strands that flowed from her to Minnie Ransom to faintly outlined witnesses by the windows.

Doc Serge was studying the patient, watching the draping action of the rough white gown. He could do something with goods like that if he took hold of her right. She was studying the webbing, not certain she was fully conscious. How like the women in his stable years ago this woman was, women who studied themselves for some tangible measure of their allure, their specialness, but never quite knowing what it was. Money was the tangible evidence he offered of their attractiveness and his, their power and his, till they would do anything to keep his attention and his answers. He gave Obie's wife his full attention and hugged himself. Someone would have to work with Obie now. He would work with this one. He chuckled and waited for Minnie to be done, to bring the woman through this first phase, to release her, to hand her over.

He'd have to handle it carefully and keep ole Faro well leashed and under control. It would be like grabbing for the rails and in grabbing you had to be careful. If you caught the rail wrong, you couldn't get a foothold and you might wind up with a bunch of hot cinders down your neck from the stacks. A bad grip and a small bump over the old bridge would dump you right in the drink. An abutment coming up, racing into view as the train turned the bend, the slats of the fence merely brushing your ass if you were lucky, crushing if you weren't. You could at least lose your hat.

They used to toast him back of the barbershop, were really toasting his hat. They called it the magic stetson, the kind of gray fedora Stagolee had killed Billy over. He'd been wise to get rid of it. Gone, there was nothing for his well-wishers to fasten on to in their need for legend and fable, nothing but what he hawked. "And that one cross the street?" And the men would press in the doorway. "Got jaws on her pussy that'd make a dead man come." The need for magic, for legend, for the extraordinary so big, the courage to pursue so small, they would crowd him and leave him no space to turn around in and change.

Doc released his hold on himself and ran his hands over his hair. Later for hats, he chuckled to himself. There was work to do. What was Minnie fooling around about? The woman had come through already it seemed.

Doc plunged into a tomato handed him by one of the young nurses who always packed a lunch for these sessions. He smiled at her, at Minnie, at himself, widely showing all his wisdom teeth, the only thing displayed not purchased but well earned. Smiling because probing with his tongue the juicy flesh of the fruit and watching Obie's wife come alive in a new way and ready for training, he could do nothing else.

Suddenly there was a rumbling which, though slight, captured most of the people's attention because just at that moment the door to the hall opened. They expected to see a medicine cart being rolled in, or a laundry basket on the old-fashioned coasters, or a food truck loaded down with trays, its weight amplifying the wheel's trundle. Fred Holt walked in, mouth open and one finger up, ready to ask how come the odd numbers on that side of the hall ran out at 31. But when he stepped into the room and spotted the gangster fella who was calling himself Doc Serge these days, and then, scanning the room, recognized the visitors who were looking at him in turn, checking their watches, frowning and turning away, he began to step back out. He'd expected a small office, a little desk, and a tidy nurse who would quietly direct him to Room 37 for a checkup. His eyes weren't prepared for the expanse of the room or the crowd. And then it got dark and he got worried. But it was only that he had bumped into the light panel on the wall, trying to exit. It took a minute to get it together. What with the storm-blackened world outside and the sudden loss of light, it was quite dark but for the glint of metal and the sheen of cloth. And it took another minute for him to notice that the object of everyone's attention was the pair of women near the window giving off all the light. One done up like a mummy in a shine-in-the-dark shawl, it looked like. The other a featherweight with fifty pounds of bracelets on. What the hell was going on? A séance or a jam session? What was going on? A couple of the doctors were trying to catch his eye with just that question. Prompt was one thing but this bus driver was two hours early.

He picked up his pace. It took one more minute to, one, flash the card the receptionist had given him, by way of saying he was there on his own business; two, to regret having done that, for who wants to know that the driver about to take you on the highway at fifty-five miles per hour is a sick man?; three, to figure out where he was and who was who. So this was the mojo lady he'd heard about. Kind of frisky-looking, he thought. Seemed like she should have some old-looking clothes on, beat-up slippers, and look like a frog.

He was working his way toward the front to take a good look, when Doc Serge started toward him. Fred thought he was about to be thrown out of the room, but the Doc fella was simply heading for the window to look out. Fistfuls of grit were being hurled against the panes. Schoolkids horsing around in the yard, he figured. But something about the way Doc was looking out of the window told Fred it wasn't kids fooling around, but nature herself. Okay by him. It made more sense to get his checkup, grab a bite in the cafeteria if they had one, and hang around the place, maybe meet this healing lady and kill a half-hour or so until it was time to board the bus—than to try to stick to his original plan and get caught in a downpour.

He noticed there was another door. It probably led to a hallway where he would find the rest of the odd numbers, at least Room 37. Meanwhile, it felt okay to just be there. The longer he looked at the two women, especially the classy old broad, the better he felt. He glanced around the room, recognized a few familiar faces—riders, a neighbor, the boys from the barbershop. There was no one who looked like agitators or troublemakers to him. Porter had probably gotten that all wrong. It was beginning to raise sand out there, and Fred wondered if he'd closed the windows on the charter bus. If there was anything he could do without, it was a gritty seat and leaves down among the pedals. After he saw a doctor, maybe he would stroll down that way and check things out. A brown-skin girl in a green uniform, he noticed finally, was looking over his shoulder at the card he carried, Then she pointed toward the door at the other end of the room. So, he was being thrown out after all.

She might have died. Might have been struck by lightning where she sat. But then she might have died an infant gasping, but for M'Dear Sophie's holding hands. Might have drowned in her baptism gown. Or legs wrapped round some strange man's head, too strange for repetition ever, holding on to his ears lest he make a sudden move, balancing more than weight on the pin of her spine and thinking her heart would give out any minute and not because the fucking and sucking was all that *petite mort* good, but because this weirdo she'd picked up in the library of all places kept lifting his head every other stroke, his breath reeking up at her over her trembling belly, to tell her what he was going to do to her, crazy things he was going to do with broom handle and vacuum hose, as soon as he finished doing what he was doing to her. And how to pull away and get away and not be hurt? Who could tell what mad thing he was capable of? And of all things to be taking up precious space in her head, where strategies needed to be laid out and studied, but some odd piece of lesson overheard in M'Dear's class about the master brain being in the uterus, where all ideas sprung from and were nurtured and released to the lesser brain in the head. And damned if it didn't seem to be the case.

She might have fried in that SRO hotel that terrible summer on the road when some two-timed bitter wife sloshed gasoline under the door. Not her door but the door of a woman met on a march who wouldn't hear of Velma and the kids sitting up all night in the bus station or taking a chance in the churchyard with blankets, but gave Velma a key to her room and gave her too the nightmare wife cursing through the door and flinging a book of matches in the puddle. And no phone in the room and the fire escape rickety and the kids, no matter how they yanked and shoved and screamed, moving like they were under water. And she was descending a rusty ladder that turned Lil James and Palma's girls red, wondering what sort of lesson this would turn out to be when her lungs cleared and her head cleared and the anger, smoke, rage and soot gave her space to think and feel it through?

Might have bled to death in the Coke machine area because Emergency was full up and the head nurse was making it crystal clear that coloreds weren't serviced there. Trailing blood through the ambulance yard, her bundled slip pressed against her head that'd been slam slam slammed hard against the concrete floor when a junky going nuts had been tossed in the cell with the women demonstrators while someone in front counted out the money for the fine very slowly.

But always there was a tug to come on, get up, move out nudging her back toward life. Even standing by the open drawer in the kitchen forgetting all she knew, even climbing into the oven forgetting who she was was tugged, was claimed. "Move out"—

And the assistants lifted her on the litter and carried her out of doors to the straw mat in the courtyard where well-wishers could pass by and give advice, read signs, interpret, hand her medicants fresh chopped from the bush to chew, fresh brought from the market to burn and inhale, fresh purchased from the apothecary to drink or swallow. And the ground rumbling as if a stone were being rolled away and someone reading that too. Velma, some lives ago, on the mat, on her back with feathers and bird bones and a sheet of painted bark spread over her.

Voices droning. Readings. A crab had attacked a fisherman and held on or dropped off into the sand meaning. A fig unripe had dropped from a tree and burst open, mud oozing smelling like stink fish meaning. A mushroom cap toppling like a severed head meaning. A wheel falling off its axis face down meaning. And ole Baron Sam clinking by looking for an invitation to sup. But the walkabout marabout coming sooner and sending the dancers/readers about their task, to dance, to leap about. They act the fish, then fly and are the birds, tail in the air and fingers hunched under arms they go monkey, dancing and loud, acting the medicine people who leap the healing circle and wait for what we run from troubled. They act the sun. Head, arms, hearts rich with recitation and the word. They send a child to fetch Velma from her swoon and fetch a strong rope to bind the wind, to circle the world while they swell the sea with song. She is the child they sent. She is the song.

"Be calm," Minnie Ransom crooned, her words going out over Velma's hunched shoulder and into the room like warm hands caressing, staying, thunder shaking the room. And it was Pony, Daniel's twin Poindexter, who took up the song, mouth wide open now and notes cutting through the gloom. Velma tried to hear it, couldn't hear it but felt it press against her skin, pushing her back into the cocoon of the shawl where she died again.

The gas lines, six blocks of enraged drivers lined up at the pumps and a well-wired time bomb, zombie-ized in the prison treatment center, turned into the streets running amuck. Or run down and trampled in the storming of the utility companies, or the taking of the food sheds or the Pentagon.

Dying in uniform when everyone not white, male and of wealth is drafted to fight on foreign turf but not for oil or diamonds or labor or markets, but for burial grounds. The bodies piled high near the borders of warring nations, bodies that cannot be cremated because of the smoke and the wind and the rain, and can't be buried because missiles would be heated up by the contamination and there is no room anymore underground, space taken up by equipment and uniforms. Bodies that can't be launched into space anymore because NASA has long since gotten a reply, and beings out there are sick of Howdy Doody and spinning satellites and telstars and intrusive rocket probes and have made the terms clear. And can't be shipped for burial to Antarctica because the cemeteries heating up there have already melted the icecaps and tidal waves have inundated half the earth.

Might have been killed for the prize of her gum boots, mask and bubble suit in the raid. The unrecognizable children who run the streets taking over abandoned social service agencies and subways and concert halls and armories finally taking her over too. Offspring of the children who roamed in vacant lots and city dumps years before when old smoke detectors leached americium into the dirt, their clothes, their genes. Kids who dug up for fun the contaminated uniforms and instruments, the abandoned uniforms of workers hunted by the angry mob awakened too late and misdirected in their hatred. Those kids grown up twisted and wasted giving birth to the ones shunned, turned out, driven off who found each other and ran in packs and found her on the street, beat her down and snatched her protection which would bring a high price on the open market.

Lying there on her back, smaller than she'd been in years, lighter, feeling free, shoulders no longer bowed from the weight of the suit, nostrils stinging, breathing air strongly chemical, detergent, chlorine, and something faintly remembered from the generator in chem lab when she was a student many long years ago. And the stockaded compound too far to drag herself to even though she was feeling this light. A pain in the center and she jackknifes, waiting for the convulsions to begin. She cries out but the children are moving off swiftly, the sucking sound of their spongy feet the only thing she hears. They leave gelatinous smears on the pavement and gluey smells where they'd stood beating her down onto the ground that threatens to suck her under where she lies and twists.

Her last glimpse is of something familiar, something from the old days when she was young, a slingshot in the pocket of one of the stompers. A forked stick jutting out like a willow switch that a water witch of old would use divining water, scanning the ground, dipping and nodding and finding what no geologist can find as quickly. A slingshot with which to shoot the five smooth stones against the forehead and penetrate the middle eye and pierce the veil. She is smiling, on her back staring at what used to be called sky.

She had asked a simple enough question of her teacher: Why is God called the alpha and omega? And that triggered the alphabet lesson, one symbol a week. M'Dear taught the alphabet in a way that made Mama Mae leave the room and shut the door. She couldn't remember Y, the forked glyph whose vibe was holy to seekers. All Y had meant to her was the wishbone she and Palma tussled over, which always broke to no one's satisfaction.

But lying there on her back she was upright in the wet street, a Babel of paths before her, but her choice made long ago. The fork in the road. The wishbone. The switch. The water witch wand. The slingshot. Y'Bird. It was all the same, somehow.

She did not regret the attack of the children. She regretted only as she lay on the straw mat, lay on the ground, pressed between the sacred rocks, lying on her back under the initiation knife at an age when the female element is circumcised from the boys and the male excised from the girls, regretted only as she moved the knife aside and the shiver ran from spine to crown and she bled and the elder packed cobwebs and mud that would not dam the gush and she bled on as she'd dreamt she would. Regretted, lying between the rocks and staring up at the clouds surrounding the moon, clouds so like the cauliflowers Mama Mae filled her lunch pail with, clouds like wispy cotton snatched from dentists' dispensers, regretted that she would not get promoted to the next class to learn about the nature of life on earth and the human and spiritual purpose because the planet was plunging into darkness as she was twisting around toward the last of the light, her tongue probing her mouth for signs of breath, slapping around out of control and ripping open on the serrated teeth till she was bleeding from everywhere.

"I'm getting a message." Minnie yanking frantically at Old Wife's dress and grabbing air, her guide gone off to chapel at the critical moment. Minnie moving quickly, pressing her tongue down hard away from her back molars. It was coming to her like a siren, not at all like instructions. A frequency not used before, more shrill than the signal from Saturn's rings, less timbre than the telling from the Ring of Wisdom, more static than the CB's or traffic waves. A wiry, shrill siren that spun in her head like a gyroscope. She was holding her jaws and heading toward the path, moving swiftly through the woods not cloistered now at the crest by the sheltering branches but thrown open, clear. Gliding over the lemon grass damp against her legs, her shoes squishy like never before. She pauses merely to check the rainbow. It is not there, its colors absorbed by needy people, its vibes spiritualizing, soaked up, left faint and toneless. She pulls down quickly the branch to finger the moist leaf, to drink from it and chew the leaf, trying to give herself pause to think, be calm, breathe in her surroundings. Old Wife running up.

"Pentagon."

"Say which? You mean like that thing you draw in the dirt with five points?"

"Pentagon."

"Where's it at?" Old Wife turning and casting suspicious glances.

"Lower left bicuspid. Loud and clear. Red alert."

"That right?"

"Why didn't you tell me? Is this it?"

"Whatcha mean 'it'?"

"Oh hell, why am I wasting time with you," Minnie says, turning, wondering if there is time to race back, to appeal to the loa who can short-circuit, engulf, misdirect an electric charge jumping from cloud to cloud even as she stands there looking up at what should have been the rainbow. Why hadn't she given the sacred jugs and pots a really good sweetening with some baking soda and prepared something extra special for the loa's festival? It was nothing to them to jump the clouds or swallow up the flash in a cloak for the asking.

"And what makes you think it ain't them haints messing about with the electricity?"

"Not now, fool. Not now."

"You ain't got the sense you were born with, Minnie Ransom. Everything's all right. I'm with you."

"Oh my lawd," Cora Rider moaned before Anna Banks could say it. They clutched each other and grabbed at strangers too and there was nothing soothing now about the singing. It was like *The Phantom of the Opera* and every other spooky movie she had ever seen. She wished the Daniels would quit.

"That one was enough to shift the needle on the university's seismograph," Doc said, the heh-heh smothered in his throat constricted with fear. The room was shaking, and Claybourne was nobody's California.

Nadeen held a chair and steadied herself. The baby, rushing from the front of her, had slammed into her back, turned and was now shifting around trying to distribute its weight. She closed her eyes and panted one two, one two.

"That was the kind of thunderbolt that knocked Saul off his steed and turned him into Paul," Cora said, releasing her friend to move toward the young girl and brace her. This was no time to be fainting or going into labor, not when the good woman Ransom was so close to bringing her patient around. She walked the girl to a chair carefully. But for all her caring and concern, Cora was busy checking calendar and clock, trying to calculate a three-digit number she could box for the morrow. Years hence she would remember that the beginning was not the payoff, not the beautician finally coming across with the money she had won, but was the moment Pony Daniels of the circle raised his voice and sang about the time his dungeon shook and his chains fell off.

Velma would remember it as the moment she started back toward life, the moment when the healer's hand had touched some vital spot and she was still trying to resist, still trying to think what good did wild do you, since there was always some low-life gruesome gang bang raping lawless careless pesty last straw nasty thing ready to pounce, put your total shit under arrest and crack your back—but couldn't. And years hence she would laugh remembering she'd thought *that* was an ordeal. She didn't know the half of it. Of what awaited her in years to come.

Fred Holt would remember that something happened to him, happened inside, something he knew no words for and would not attempt to describe until six years later when his son was finally able to trace him to the Resettlement Center. He would remember the first part easily—He was in the chair having his blood pressure taken for a final check and thinking about going to the concert at the Regal, was thinking about the dude with the prison mouth, was grinding his teeth cursing a certain dentist's soul, when lightning flashed and he found himself hunching down in the chair, bending to tie his laces though they didn't need it. But he noticed the nurse was right down there with him and they both laughed. And settling back in his seat, waiting to hear whether they wanted a urine sample or not, he thought he saw from the side-street window Porter strolling out of Mount Shiloh Baptist Church, nonchalant about the rain, nonchalant about the fact that he was supposed to be dead. And he tried to fling open the window and shout while at the same time explaining to the nurse returning with his folder and the appointment card that he had to go that very instant. Then racing to the door that led down the stairs to the side street. He took them two at a time and then he fell, falling in wet leaves that felt like dog shit underfoot. The picture of himself on his behind stayed in his mind for a long time. Falling and trying to get up and trying to run to the opening in the hedge to see as he'd seen from the room and to shout across the street but when he got to the sidewalk there was nothing, no one there.

The wind dumped its cargo of paper bags, candy wrappers and bus transfers gritty and limp at the edge of the bus kiosk he ran toward finally when the downpour came. He stood there not hearing the buzz and flutter of paper up against the plastic panes. Porter in his last days had acted just like that, blasé blasé, nonchalant, less and less concerned about the things so hard won—the day shift, his apartment lease, his grooming habits, his own ideas even. It was as if Porter were detaching himself from his job, his surroundings and from Fred too. As if preparing himself for a new life. Fred Holt shot his eyes around him and whispered quietly, "Porter, you there?"

A young couple in paper streamers dying red and green on their necks and arms ran into the shelter and smiled his way as they tried to dry each other off with tissues and damp hands. "Kiosk," he muttered to himself for something to fix on, fingering a pencil in his left pants pocket, humming a song lest the couple think he was talking to himself. They were paying him no mind, were glancing up and down the block and then taking a deep breath before dashing across the street to cut through the Infirmary yard, moving with a determination he would recall many years later when people raced across the borders to new frontiers.

Campbell stood flattened against the service-counter wall looking first toward the round table where several men with rain-plastered hair tried to comb the whorls into some order, then looking toward the other big table where Jan and her stubby friend sat with the media women, passing around napkins and using the tablecloth to dry each other's faces. He wondered what effect the storm would have on the Brotherhood's pageant, on the Academy's procession, on the police's program, on the vigilantes' plans, and on his future. Something more than storm was up, he figured, rejecting the idea that ordinary lightning, thunder and rain could elicit so profound a response from everyone. They were doing a good job of playacting: Just a storm. None of the conversations around him yielded anything he could use. But years ahead at blue-ribbon panels and organized seminars, he would have occasion to say that the beginning was ushered in by an unusual storm. He wondered if the portable radio in the kitchen might inform him of similar storms in other parts of the country, in other parts of the world. He occupied himself by totaling checks and testing his memory. Was a comet due to appear anytime soon? Had a colliding asteroid been predicted? Was some country test-blasting?

Dr. Julius Meadows would say that it began on the stoop listening to M1 and Thurston and their buddies talk about conditions at the plant. He would say that partway through the discussion when the first rumble of thunder had been detected, listened to, called an explosion at the plant and then discounted as weather merely, he'd taken time out to vow to give the Hippocratic oath some political meaning in his life. He would describe at length the tavern they took him to, five grown men running through the streets, splashing in puddles like schoolboys whooping and hollering, ducking into the place loud and raucous and being greeted by equally boisterous men, the rusty, ashy, scar-faced denizens of the neighborhood bar where it was certain one was wont to part another's hair with a chair on the slightest provocation. Would describe how he helped to pass out flyers about the rally. Would get up to show how the woman from the kitchen shook out the flyer he handed her as if to check for roaches, then smoothed the flyer against her breasts pressing out the damp creases and then took her time reading it as he ran the spiel as Thurston had. Would get sober and dignified explaining that at that moment he understood that, talking about the health hazards at the plant, the woman leaning away from him as if to get a better view of the hole in his head or as if to avoid contagion, understood that industrial arrogance and heedless technology was first and foremost a medical issue, a health issue, his domain.

By the fall of '83 he would have taught himself that the reason they went to the Tip In Tavern was not to pass out leaflets or to scout up tickets to the Regal concert but to set the scene for his conversion. By the winter of '83/'84, while twisting around in his dentist's chair, pushing the metal arm away from his jaw and arguing that a second x-ray was not only not called for but dangerous, Meadows would have earned a reputation among his colleagues for being a stickler about certain "regulations," "measures," "obligations" to the public. By the spring of '84, doing his taxes and checking the nuclear exemption clause in his insurance policy, he would have already queried administrator B. Talifero Serge about a position at the Southwest Infirmary and sent an angry letter to the local TV station and gone on the air to say that the TB mobile units in the Black community had screens that were longer than any others', long enough to cover the genitalia of youths coaxed into the trucks by lollipops, comic books, and free passes to the local discos. But none of it would really come together as a coherent and focused narrative until the summer of '84 when he lunched with Mrs. Sophie Heywood and Mrs. Janice Campbell and the man he'd come to call Doc and heard the younger woman hold forth on what to expect now that Pluto had moved into Scorpio for a long spell.

"A planet of immense power. Annihilation and transformation. The planet of complete and total change."

And the older woman would ask him, flipping open the Bible, whether he understood the significance of certain tamperings with the script.

"The expressions about the second coming and Armageddon, for example?" And he would shake his head no; it had been years since he'd had occasion to even look at a Bible, except to move it from the phone table in the hotels to a drawer.

"Should be translated 'presence of Christ' and 'new age,'

not . . ." And Doc would catch his eye and wink, two men humoring the women.

It was the first crack of lightning and thunder that made Palma duck into the shelter of Marcus Hampden. And he held her and held too the weight for her, her dread, annoyance, and now alarm. Standing by the flat truck watching for a minute the young Academy boys serious and efficient with the unloading of chairs and tables, they then straightened and began combing the park with their eyes. A few people were scurrying for cover under the trees, older folks snapping out their newspapers in preparation for tent hats, but most of the early arrivers to the park simply strolled about, hailing friends, groups of brothers eying the sisters, groups of sisters eying the brothers, children fussing at kites that would not get up off the ground. There were a lot of people, considering the early hour.

Young men bopping by, yards of leather strung across back and over shoulders to hold tool-worked cases so small that keys and cigarette packs peeped out. Magenta, lime, copper-colored shirts unbuttoned to the belt, thin gold chains at the throat and a buddy cracking, "Maaan, why don't you comb that nappy chest?" and folks falling out. Sisters with beaded braids swinging as they sashayed toward the bandshell where the food booths were setting up, moving over pebbles and scraggly grass on pencil-thin heels or clumpy wedgies. Vendors unpacking sacks and boxes of flashlights, candles, Darth Vadar laser sticks, maracas, eight-track tapes, film, banners, straw hats, fans. Folks walking along with trays strapped around their necks selling bags of peanuts, leaning in closely to this or that one selling bags of pot. Incense bundles in tinfoil, coke in tinfoil packets. The balloon man. A fat youth in clown white juggling baseballs. An old man with a risqué talking dummy on his knee drawing a crowd toward the benches. Portable radios, TV's, phonographs with Ashford and Simpson "Don't Cost You Nothing" vying with Peaches and Herb, Roberta and Donny, kiddie shows, news reports. Two Bloods in skinny black clothes, derbies and bright-yellow suspenders, skate dancing on a patch of cement near the bandshell, the crowd predicting how hip the Olympics'll be once Black folks take over the ice competitions and then introduce the art of roller-skate dancing to the world. Drummers in dreads and knitted caps, beards, sandals, with cowbells and chekeres, working out on the hill. Women slumming from the Heights jiggling about, twitching to take their clothes off, settling for a veronica or two of their disco skirts mistaking the parkees ducking past to clear the trees for playmates.

The wino couple from Palma's old neighborhood holding each other up, eggshell stepping with their cups and brown paper sacks, managing to make it to the flat truck to sit down, smoothing down each other's clothes, each other's stringy, grease-waved hair, the kind of hair Palma and Velma had called "good hair" until Mama Mae explained the alcohol source of the waves. Looking up and answering bleary-eyed and incoherent that no they hadn't seen Velma, and didn't have a clue as to who Palma could possibly be.

"Should we wait here?" Marcus was looking for a way for them to sit down comfortably.

It seemed a sensible enough suggestion to her. Eventually everyone came to the drums, and cars and trucks were arriving already with the master drummers and dancers from the back districts. No matter where Velma was, she'd hear the drums and come to the park. Palma had her mouth open to say "Yes" when the rumble of thunder took hold of the park, arrested everybody in their tracks, Marcus staring down at the ground as if waiting for it to crack wide open. And still the lightning had not finished, was still blinking, stuttering, as though it meant to stay on forever once it took hold. And they would have occasion soon, and then way into the future too, to decode the look that passed between them the moment Marcus lifted his eyes and his mouth fell open and Palma dropped her eyes from the sky and moaned.

Obie had been bobbing around in the whirlpool when the thunder struck, shaking the building. Bobbing around in the swirling waters, breathing along with the water's pulse, with the pumping jets that throbbed against the back of his shoulders and the soles of his feet. Trying to maintain equilibrium, trying to find a balance between the longing for clarity and the dread of finding too great a challenge of reunion. His body too far down in the hot water one minute, and slippery as he was from the massage oil, slippery as his elbows were hooked on the rim of the pool, he could go under. His torso buoying up the next minute, the front of his body out of the water, not getting the benefit of heat and the forced currents. He'd been thinking of blueprints, the blue waxy kind with scraped white lines, trying to coax his subconcious to surrender the plan, to surface, take over, and reveal something he knew he must know to pull it all together. But dodging it too.

Legs and feet floating gently to surface, his hands flat against the water's green, the plan floating up to the threshold of consciousness and the knotty problem coming loose in his muscles, his joints, his brain. Then the building shook and he opened his eyes in a daze, staring at the lumpish green and gray on his right ankle—the elastic with the locker key on it. But still not awake, not even with pandemonium breaking around him, yearning and premonition still washing through him as his pool mates hustled themselves out of the water, some heaving themselves over the sides of the pool sending waves against him. And he watched as in a dream or dozing in the movies.

Some pulling up on the hooped rails of the steps, kicking spray in his face. Others leaping clean out of the water, as flying fish, as if ejected by the waters' jets.

"Hey, Obie. Somebody wants you."

A wonderful message or not in his ears, at the back of his head, swarming through him. Velma wanted him. The folks wanted him. His brother Roland wanted him. And oh did the cops want him. Thunder rumbling up from the bottom, trembling the water, shooting through him and showers blasting full force then shut off abruptly, doors banging and brothers dripping and stumbling about in clouds of fog and steam, talking loud and flamboyant in defiance of whatever the interruption in their ablutions meant.

He didn't realize how close he was to believing it dream, to falling back to sleep in the water's heat, till he felt a hand on his arm. And he came more fully awake to the white toweled figures moving along the black rubber mat walkway in a pile-up, brothers streaming out of the sauna, the steam room, the alcove where the mirrors and hair dryers and shavers were, exchanging notes and extravagant bravado and flat facts about the dimming or flickering of lights in various parts of the spa.

"Phone call, Obo."

He was disoriented still, trying to turn in the water to take in the moon face looming over him. Ahiro down on his haunches, blue kimono sleeves dipping into the puddles beyond the rim of the pool. Obie was breathing along with the flickering lights, stuttering, stuttering. Longing and fear like the ebb and flow of the water, the intake and outtake of breath, the doo ahh dooahh of a group of singers huddled in the alcove door to sing down the thunder, the ripple of green to and fro across the forehead of the masseur, his friend, the messenger of strange tidings.

"Phone call." A smooth brown leg with bunched calves

stretching out for balance and an arm extended to pull him up. And now he was turning over and over in the pool, his elbows digging into the tiles, scraped raw and bleeding. Phone call. Was someone calling to say Roland was dead? Had escaped? Had a hostage by the throat demanding to see him?

"Said to come to the Infirmary. Sounded important." Lifting out like a weightless fish, his scales, his flesh oozing away from his bones, dropping down into the waters, releasing him. "You okay, Obo?"

He padded across the tiles tucking his towel, squeezing his hair, popping water from his ears, fighting to come awake. Velma. Ahiro trotting along beside him on the rubber mat, his zoris squishing splat-splat, so Obie breathed along with that, as good a rhythm as any.

"You okay now?"

Nodding, going through the doorway to the locker room, a shift in climate, a drop in temperature, a sudden quiet; the brothers had bypassed the clothes locker in favor of the lounge, where phones and light and vending machines and other signs of civilization assured them.

He was still damp inside his clothes, his shirt smack against his back, when he hit the stoop and met the wind and the downpour. Motorcycles were skidding down the Hill, shredding kites and flyers and brown paper bag masks. Panel trucks were pausing in the traffic while young boys climbed out of the cabs to get to the back, flinging jackets and newspapers over the drums and horns. Trees were littered with leaflets. A young girl in dazzling orange harness directing schoolchildren at the crossing. An old man caught in the middle of traffic, looking for a break to make a dash. Obie was rocking on the top step, dread welling up as the curbs overflowed. Velma. The rain's music more insistent than the drumming sounding from across the way.

"Ubi Obie! Hey, my man. What it is?"

Someone shouting from a van stuck in mid-descent from the Heights. Someone who called to him from a bullhorn of rolled-up newspaper getting limp and soggy then pulled in the window, but the arm remained and the hand gestured upward as if this were a sensible traffic signal to the taxis and bikes behind: taking a turn for the up. And Obie remembered Sonny and Graham were on security, so he looked up, searching the windows of the rooming house where surveillance had been rumored; young Bobby had sworn he'd caught the glint of binoculars on two occasions. The suspect window empty. The tops of buildings lost in the fog, the Regal's dome faintly gold in the purple-gray patches of clouds smeared across the buildings.

Several students who'd bunched up behind him on the Academy steps broke past him to jump on the back of trucks painted for carnival, smeared and running red, green, black in the streets. And he wondered what the hell he was waiting for. Someone had called from the Infirmary and there he was watching the kids scramble on board, throwing satin jackets over the drums and each other's heads, yanking yards of plastic from the cleaners out of a sack and tearing off lengths and passing them around. Rocking on the top step, vestigial wings twitching, the drums sounding from the studios unsmothered and loud, the wind heaving newspapers against his pants legs, the wind blowing plastic into one youth's face and both becoming odd beings sent to earth at the moment encased and then peeled to walk among the people as kin and bring them through the passage.

"Obie! Come on, man. Rain or no rain. It's time."

"Later!" His voice like a foghorn. His legs rubbery as he dashed into the streets, his cuffs full of water. And he would remember in the days ahead how the look of a particular Chevy grill, a Ford truck fender, an Alabama license plate, the treads of a Goodrich tire made him pause, stare, forget he was in a hurry. Pause in the middle of the double yellow lines, thinking about the face sucking in plastic, featureless, looking at the old man there in the street hugging a lumpy hankie, rain streaming down his face, featureless. Paused. But not because of the traffic or the rain or the odd notions creeping through his brain about alien beings, or the dim memory in the shoulder blades of wings and the flight long ago and the instructions. But an eye. There was an eye poised on him, an energy focused on him from somewhere, an eye clarifying him, arresting him.

"I'd run for shelter if I knew which way to run," the old man shrugged with an apologetic grin.

"The Academy's open," breaking the spell. "Coffee in the lounge." He pointed. "And hot soup." He was going to turn, halt the traffic from the Heights and escort the elder by the elbow, safe passage. But he was caught again in the beam of the eye, fixed. And again he looked toward the window young Bobby had pointed out, trying to pierce the fog, water splashing his eyes to a squint. A flock of birds were banking sharply over the rooming house to avoid the Regal's dome, the rear guard dragging away a cloud of dark purple.

You're welcome at the Academy," he mumbled, the words trailing away; the elder had already found a break in traffic and was broken-field trotting toward the curb. Released again, he made for the side lot, the shortcut to the Infirmary, no longer hunching his shoulders and crowding himself slender through the downpour. He walked stiffly, expectant. He was breathing shallowly, any minute a bullet. And then he was in the safety of the movie house's shadows, the pavement going earth underfoot, an embrace of tree smells, new leaves, and the Infirmary yard's odd mix of odors—creosote, mildew, rot, tree mold, and too the fragrance of newly turned earth, the sweet of sap, sap rising to renew, but activating the mold too as if there were no way around it.

"Brother Obeah, what's going on?"

The young brothers who normally posted themselves on the walls that kept the woods out and the yard neat were huddled in the doorway of the generator shed, several girls behind them peeking out over shoulders or between triangles arms made with pockets, peeking out at the rain, out at the oily rainbows in the puddles of dirt, others holding their noses and making beat'm-in-the-head gestures at the backs of two winos pissing against the stage door of the Regal.

"Looks like everything's going on," Obie shrugged, slowing and then moving on. Two girls shared a look and sucked their teeth, clearly disappointed by the dull response from the legendary man of the Academy.

"The doings rained out or what?" The same two, exchanging looks with lifted brows, their own group's wordsmith a turkey too.

There were nods and shrugs and dumb show as everyone looked up at the sky, the two critics leaning out over the shoulders of their boyfriends to spot the birds tearing past the Regal, taking the clouds with them and letting a little gold shine down for a moment. It was an odd silence, this silence before the blanket of gray silver needles that was the rain, its music monotonous and nothing clever being said. And Obie passed the sheds, remarking to himself that silence was not the way. These word wizards, these say-smart-sorcerers, masters of metaphorical coinage that kept the language of the district vibrant and new, mute. No memorable quotes, no nommo notes to remember later, to give shape and punctuation to the tale he would tell in the days ahead, the where-were-you-when-it-began response. And over his shoulder he followed the trail of their eyes toward the stage door, as if backstage in the Regal was the answer, the word. As a child he'd learned there in the wings how the cards were marked, where the rabbit was stashed, how the swallowed sword collapsed, of what the boldness of the jazz musicians consisted. He'd learned all that in the days when they'd tried to revive the Regal, revive vaudeville, give the local talent a play. And now the young folk stared out through the rain as if getting past the splattered glass, the wine bottles, the smelly ole men, the rusted lock on the stage door—they'd find out where the fingers go in the back of the head, the back of the eyes, to make talk come out.

"Oh God." The girls were moaning in chorus, grabbing arms and jackets and pushing their backs against the shed's door while lightning was panting somewhere on the far side of the woods.

"Holy shit, the ground's moving."

"Cut it out."

"I ain't playing. Can't you feel it?"

"Fucking earthquake."

"Quit it, Bo Peep. I mean it now."

He almost made it to the back door, slipping on the wet leaves piled high and covering the bottom step. He almost made it, slipping, reaching for the knob, his shoes soaked and sluggish, Velma? Velma? welling up in his throat, stretching toward the door and a pulling in his side, ducking to escape whatever it was thundering toward him, breathing along in gasps with the trees' roots down to darkness, branches up to light, the building holding its breath, standing against the thunder coming. Then everything went phosphorescent and he fell, stripped by lightning, gold splashing in the granite's dents before the door. One shoe lost and all the faith and courage that had been holding him up gone, and the challenge of reunion flooded away, and the dread of the moment and moments ago soaked to mush, his pants torn and his knee bleeding. Stripped by lightning, he would say in the days ahead, his flesh fallen away and nothing there on the back step but his soul with the stark impress of all the work done and yet to do, all the changes gone through and yet to come, all the longing and apprehension as he'd watch human beings becoming something else and wondering what it had been like for the ancestors watching the first wheel be rolled down the road. On the back steps fixed, the damp of mildew jamming up his nose, the damp of new earth turned and waiting trying to free his lungs, the knob just out of reach of his hand sliding down the door with the rain.

"Get on up, Brother." A command at his back and the giggle of two young girls imitated then hushed. And he couldn't. His legs shot, his ankle sprained, his knee bleeding, his elbows sore, the breath knocked out of him in the fall, couldn't get up and so he did get up. Got up as a switch was thrown and the couples jumped from the shed door then returned laughing, the hum of the generator sudden and soothing for no reason any of the wordsmiths could capture in a name. And he saluted them in a daze, the sky opening and the Regal releasing molten gold into the fog, the drums sounding in a playoff with the thunder. Saluted the future, gold splashing in his eyes.

The Lady in the Chair is rising damp but replenished like the Lady Rising from the Sea. The drums are still calling from the building across the way, answered ragged and indistinct by drums in the distance. Rain is pelting Doc's windows and the curtains blowing out then folding in damp. Sophie looks out wondering if she'd left the bedroom window at home opened, wondering if her costume hanging from the drapery rod is safe. *The rush and stampede for shelter from nature created the wind.* She watched the wind whipping curtains out of buildings, white and pink and yellow spirit arms signaling. Had Velma found herself?

Fear and dread at the unspeakable level puts thunder in the air. The zig-zag strike between the clouds crackling down. Would Velma find an old snakeskin on the stool?

The sky is lit by tomorrow's memory lamp. Slate rained clean, a blessing. At least a twenty-four-hour delay, respite. A blessing. Twenty-four more hours to try and pull more closely together the two camps of adepts still wary of the other's way. "Causes and issues. They're vibrating at the mundane level." "Spirit this and psychic that. Escapism. Irresponsible, given the objective conditions." Rain. Delay. New possibilities in formation, a new configuration to move with. A flood one moment in time could drown the earth, the next create fish farms in the deserts. The wind that lifts everything up this minute used to bury it all in the sand last time.

Children streaming past the window on skateboards, bikes, skates, on foot. Balloons spotted, kites limp, masks dangling from their cords and trailing behind like the kites won't. With masks it was the same. A plaything or a summons. Be a fool or become a god. Timing was all and everything in time.

Sophie leaned against the sill and squinted into the streets alive with so much more than she was able to see yet, but in time, she counseled. Once Minnie brought Velma through perhaps the girl at last would be ready for training. She'd waited a long time for the godchild's gift to unfold. Had had long periods of doubt that what she'd sensed that first meeting, the infant sliding easily into her hands, was actual, read correctly, and not just the product of an overworked imagination of a godmother too serious about her role, her calling. But there'd been signs and times in church, in the attic, in the woods when Velma had started, gone mute, stared, become very still that renewed the notion and Sophie'd thought maybe,

maybe. And while the girl had never shared what she was seeing, experiencing, was no doubt rejecting before it could imprint on the mind, Sophie waited, waited now, adjusting her hat and pulling the damp dress away from her legs.

She'd missed seeing what was happening to Velma the woman, had not been attentive, gotten blocked, sidetracked. But what had driven Velma into the oven, Sophie was certain now, was nothing compared to what awaited her, was to come. Once Minnie opened her up and welcomed her back anew, renewed, Velma would begin to see what she'd been blind to, what Sophie herself was blind to but knew. Of course she would fight it, Velma was a fighter. Of course she would reject what could not be explained in terms of words, notes, numbers or those other systems whose roots had been driven far underground. Sophie vowed to concentrate more fully and stay alert and be at hand, for Velma's next trial might lead to an act far more devastating than striking out at the body or swallowing gas.

It was clear the downpour was no spring shower, that she'd been given time to finish fasting and the silence. Sophie pressed her forehead against the cool of the glass and gazed out. Choices were being tossed into the street like dice, like shells, like kola nuts, like jackstones.

"Each happening for weal or woe can—"

"I don't wanna hear that. The Henry gal's coming through with more than I can handle at the moment. Now, what about that Pentagon message I got which nearly split my head?"

"Not yet you didn't."

"What you telling me, that my jaws don't ache, that my teeth ain't knocking their knees together? Speak plain, woman. This chile is creeping around hunting for pain and when she's satisfied it ain't there she's gonna start bumping into other things that are, and I ain't ready. Now, am I having a flash forward, or am I getting as batty as you?"

"Like you always say, Min, everything in time."

"Mmm. None of this ain't happened yet? Some of this is happening now? All of this is going on, but I ain't here? All of the above? None of the above? Will you at least tell me, is it raining or not?"

"I'm here to help with the patient, Min."

"Don't hand me no somesuch about division of labor at a time like this."

"Gonna be a long night, Min."

Minnie Ransom sighing. She knows it'll be a long afternoon and a longer even night. The kind of night that drives men of the Heights out of doors crazed and into the district on the prowl searching out disaster. "To jerk off like at a lynching," Doc would say. The kind of night when women of the district check and recheck the covers on the sleeping kids and hope that if the footfalls on the creaky stairs are not their men, then pray they're with some other woman safe.

"Gonna let me wrassle by myself, hunh? You always were a stubborn, weird old smelly witch, ya know it?"

"But, Min, that's how I choose to manifest myself this time."

Minnie Ransom staring. Her hands sliding off the shoulders of silk. The patient turning smoothly on the stool, head thrown back about to shout, to laugh, to sing. No need of Minnie's hands now. That is clear. Velma's glow aglow and two yards wide of clear and unstreaked white and yellow. Her eyes scanning the air surrounding Minnie, then examining her own hands, fingers stretched and radiant. No need of Minnie's hands now so the healer withdraws them, drops them in her lap just as Velma, rising on steady legs, throws off the shawl that drops down on the stool a burst cocoon.

Also available from Vintage Contemporaries

. . . .

Where I'm Calling From
by Raymond Carver

The summation of a triumphant career from "one of the great-short story writers of our time—of any time" *(Philadelphia Inquirer)*.

0-679-72231-9

Wildlife
by Richard Ford

Set in Great Falls, Montana, a powerful novel of a family tested to the breaking point.

"Ford brings the early Hemingway to mind. Not many writers can survive the comparison. Ford can. *Wildlife* has a look of permanence about it." —*Newsweek*

0-679-73447-3

Bright Lights, Big City
by Jay McInerney

Living in Manhattan as if he owned it, a young man tries to outstrip the approach of dawn with nothing but his wit, good will and controlled substances.

"A dazzling debut, smart, heartfelt, and very, very funny." —Tobias Wolff

0-394-72641-3

Mama Day
by Gloria Naylor

This magical tale of a Georgia sea island centers around a powerful and loving matriarch who can call up lightning storms and see secrets in her dreams.

"This is a wonderful novel, full of spirit and sass and wisdom." —*Washington Post*

0-679-72181-9

Anywhere But Here
by Mona Simpson

An extraordinary novel that is at once a portrait of a mother and daughter, and a brilliant exploration of the perennial urge to keep moving.

"Mona Simpson takes on—and reinvents—many of America's essential myths... stunning." —*The New York Times*

0-679-73738-3

. . . .

Available at your local bookstore,
or call toll-free to order: 1-800-793-2665
(credit cards only).

VINTAGE
CONTEMPORARIES